PRAISE FOR
MOONGLOW

...age-turning and passionate, Lori Wilde's novels are always a ...elight!"

—Jill Shalvis, *New York Times* bestselling author

"*The Moonglow Sisters* is everything I love in a book. It's emotional, funny, tender, and unforgettable. I couldn't stop reading until the last wonderful page. Lori Wilde writes characters who always speak to my heart."

—RaeAnne Thayne, *New York Times* bestselling author

"Every now and then a book comes along that touches every emotion, from heartrending tears to belly laughs. *The Moonglow Sisters* is one of those rare books. From the first line to the last sigh, it was amazing."

—Carolyn Brown, *New York Times* bestselling author

"The resilience of the bond between sisters is tested on a rocky path toward healing in this engrossing tale of secrets and betrayals. Lori Wilde's infinitely relatable characters make *The Moonglow Sisters* a must-read."

—Julia London, *New York Times* bestselling author

"Wilde reunites three estranged sisters in this powerful tale. . . . Wilde's fine characterizations and pulsating plot will please readers who enjoy family sagas."

—*Publishers Weekly*

The Wedding at Moonglow Bay

A Novel

LORI WILDE

A V O N

An Imprint of HarperCollins Publishers

THE WEDDING AT MOONGLOW BAY. Copyright © 2023 by Laurie Vanzura. All rights reserved. Printed in the United States of America. No part of this book may be used or reproduced in any manner whatsoever without written permission except in the case of brief quotations embodied in critical articles and reviews. For information, address HarperCollins Publishers, 195 Broadway, New York, NY 10007.

HarperCollins books may be purchased for educational, business, or sales promotional use. For information, please email the Special Markets Department at SPsales@harpercollins.com.

FIRST EDITION

Designed by Diahann Sturge

Title page and part photograph © mpaniti / Shutterstock

Library of Congress Cataloging-in-Publication Data has been applied for.

ISBN 978-0-06-313590-1

23 24 25 26 27 LBC 5 4 3 2 1

This book is dedicated to Cheryl Nason. Thank you for all the lovely luncheon discussions. The world is a brighter place because you're in it. Thank you for being my friend.

PART ONE

THE WEDDING

CHAPTER 1

When I saw you, I fell in love, and you smiled because you knew.
—Arrigo Boito

The first time Samantha Riley married into the Ginelli family, her fanciful in-laws called it the "Lightning Strike."

In reverential tones, Nick's parents, Marcella and Tino, told romantic tales of legendary ancestors who'd been hit by metaphorical love-lightning. Generations of Ginellis had fallen madly in love at first sight and ended up in solid, long-lasting marriages, and they had the genealogical records to prove it.

There wasn't a single story of the Lightning Strike gone awry. Legend had it, once you got walloped by the one-two punch of predestined love, in Ginelli-land you were mated for a happily-ever-after life.

She'd fallen in love with the entire Ginelli clan as surely as she'd fallen in love with their youngest son. The Ginellis represented everything she'd longed for as an orphaned child—a loving tight-knit family who always had her back. They might be a little meddlesome at times, but it all came from a place of genuine love and respect.

Samantha met Nick on the first day of her high school junior year.

Her foster family, the Dellaneys, had just moved from Houston a month earlier, as her foster father, Heath, had taken a position working with the Moonglow Cove Chamber of Commerce. After years in a high-pressure corporate human resources job, he was ready for the slower pace of a small beachside tourist town.

Piper, Samantha's foster sister and best friend in the entire world, declared the town b-o-r-i-n-g, and she was pouting as they walked into Moonglow Cove High School together, unsure of where the registrar's office was or how to find their classrooms.

"Hey, look. What a cute mascot," Samantha said to cheer up her pal, and pointed at a chubby-cheeked chipmunk painted on the wall. Chipmunk Charlie had his head thrown back in raucous laughter, his white teeth flashing and big tail thumping.

"Seriously? A ground squirrel? That is so lame."

"But look at his beautiful grin." Samantha widened her own smile in effigy.

"Chipmunk Charlie would be an amuse-bouche for Ivan." Piper studied her fingernails with their chipped chartreuse polish.

In Houston, their mascot had been a tiger nicknamed Ivan the Terrible. Cheesy? Oh yeah, but Piper was right. Fierce Ivan would make short work of cheerful Charlie.

"A school the size of Moonglow Cove wouldn't scrimmage our old high school."

"Gawd, don't be so literal." Piper rolled her eyes. "Let me guess. Their class song has to be that silly Chipmunks song." In a voice that sounded like she'd been inhaling helium, Piper sang a few bars of the Christmas tune by Alvin and the Chipmunks.

Samantha interlaced her fingers and brought her hands to her heart. "Please try to like this place . . . for me?"

"Okay, sure." Laughing, Piper slipped her arm through Samantha's and pulled her into a skip, and they bounced jauntily down the hallway. People turned to stare as they skipped past. Boldly, Piper stuck out her tongue as Samantha's face heated up.

"We're really doing this on the first day?" Samantha asked, feeling self-conscious.

"Yeah, baby. Flying our freak flag. Let 'em put that in their Zig-Zags and smoke it."

They rounded the corner, and a thick stream of students came pouring in through the side door, forcing them to halt abruptly.

Piper blinked. "Okay, Miss Spreadsheet, where do we go from here?"

"Come on." Samantha led the way to the registrar's office. "Where's your normal sunshiny self?"

"Back in Houston. Dad ruined my life dragging us to Podunk, USA."

"How can you say that? We're living at the beach! I feel like I've died and flown to heaven."

"You're so easily amused. Now I feel all guilty and shit."

Someone jostled Samantha's elbow, and she fumbled with her phone, almost dropping it.

"We're gonna get trampled. We gotta move." Piper took hold of Samantha's arm and dragged her back into the foot traffic.

Samantha pulled the school handbook from her purse to read it, as if more knowledge could save her.

"It says here that . . ." Samantha glanced up to show Piper the handbook and watched horrified as her friend approached a folding ladder erected below the Moonglow Cove High School sign. A maintenance guy stood on the top rung tightening down the "M" with a power drill.

Terror shot adrenaline through Samantha's veins. "Piper, no! It's bad luck!"

"What?" Her bold friend stopped directly underneath the ladder and turned to look at Samantha. Piper extended her arms wide, touching both sides of the ladder. "It's an old wives' tale."

Samantha took a giant step forward, grabbed Piper by the wrist, and yanked her from underneath the ladder just as the maintenance person bobbled the power drill and it fell right where Piper had been standing two seconds earlier.

Thunk.

"Holy cow." Piper peeked at the drill that would have conked her on the head. "You saved my life."

They stared into each other's eyes as the maintenance guy jumped from the ladder to retrieve his drill, apologizing profusely.

"Yipes. I won't mock your crazy superstitions again," Piper said.

"I'm just glad you're okay." Samantha wiped sweat from her forehead, then linked her arm through Piper's again and skirted her around the ladder.

"This school is out to kill me. I told you I didn't like it here and—" Piper stopped dead in her tracks, and Samantha was two steps ahead before she realized Piper had stayed rooted.

"What is it?"

"Changed my mind. I *love* this place."

Samantha pushed her glasses up on her nose and squinted at her friend. "Huh?"

Piper nodded toward the water fountain. "Pinch me. I must be dreaming."

Samantha followed her foster sister's gaze and—*bam!*—it was like something from the romance novels she read in secret so Piper wouldn't tease her.

There, in the illuminating glow from the overhead skylight, stood a handsome, dark-haired student in a letterman jacket. He was tall, around six feet, broad of shoulders and narrow of waist. His teeth were straight and white. Dude could have modeled for a toothpaste commercial. In his left cheek, a dimple deepened with his expanding grin. He wore tight jeans, Converse sneakers, and a fitted black T-shirt. His skin was beach-bum tan, the color of cinnamon-soaked peaches. His nose crooked slightly, as if it had been broken, as if he wasn't afraid of a fight. His good looks had a Mediterranean vibe. What was his ancestry? Italian? Greek? Spanish?

Samantha studied him, intrigued. *Italian,* she decided before she ever found out his last name.

Her heart did a crazy bump and grind, stalling her breath in her lungs. Her hormones blistered a trail from her cheeks, down her neck, and around her spine to lodge squarely in her stomach before spreading electric shock waves straight to her pelvis. She met his dark brown mischievous eyes and welcoming grin.

And Samantha was a goner.

Mine, she thought greedily.

This one was heaven-sent just for her. *This* was what she'd waited for her entire life. Her nerve endings tingled, and her brain locked up as saliva filled her mouth. She hopped right onto the high-speed train to Sexy Danger Town and didn't look back.

Piper poked her in the rib cage, and she didn't even notice. With his stare latched tightly on to hers, the Italian Stallion sauntered toward Samantha.

"Oh my gawd, oh my gawd, oh my gawd." Panting, Piper fanned herself. "He's coming over."

Samantha stood frozen to the spot, unable to move or speak. Finally, she understood what people meant when they said someone was caught like a deer in the headlights. Her—doe. Him—eighteen-wheeler.

Everything evaporated except *this* guy.

She couldn't have run if there'd been a zombie apocalypse. Illogical words exploded in her brain.

Fate. Destiny. Kismet.

Her foster sister extended a palm toward the handsome guy and grinned like a loon. "Hello, my name's Piper, what's yours?"

He never broke eye contact with Samantha, just peered right over Piper's head. "That was really intuitive of you. Pulling your friend to safety just before the janitor dropped his drill."

"You saw that?"

"You've got keen survival instincts."

"It's more that my foster sister is superstitious as all get-out than anything else," Piper said. "Me? I don't have a superstitious bone in my body. I'll walk under ladders all day long if it leads to you."

Nick slanted a look at Piper, then quickly dismissed her as he turned back to Samantha. "Hi, I'm Nick Ginelli."

"Sa-Sa-Sa . . ."

"Sa-Sa-Sa?" he teased. "Unusual name."

"I . . . um . . . Samantha. My name is Samantha Riley."

"You're new here."

"I am."

Lightly, he nudged Piper to one side with his elbow and came closer.

Piper frowned and sank her hands on her hips. "Hey, hey. I'm not the invisible woman."

"Excuse me." Nick didn't even glance at her foster sister.

"Huh, maybe I *am* invisible?" Piper patted herself.

Nick's focused attention sent a sweet shiver through Samantha's solar plexus. Intoxicating stuff for a girl who'd spent a lifetime rolling from one foster home to the next.

When Samantha was three, her parents were killed by a tornado as the ceiling in their bedroom collapsed on them while they'd slept. By some miracle, tucked in her trundle bed, she'd been spared. Samantha remembered nothing from that time, but there'd been news clips about it, and dozens of people had wanted to adopt her when they discovered she'd had no immediate family to take her in.

A childless couple who already had foster experience, Frank and Joy Pursell, won the honor of caring for her. She'd lived with them until she was six, and they were in the process of adopting her, when Frank left Joy for his best friend, Oscar. The betrayal sent Joy into a mental health crisis, and she relinquished Samantha back to the foster care system.

By then, Samantha was no longer a cute cuddly toddler. Because of the instability in her life, Samantha developed some challenging behaviors that caused her to act out, and this discouraged other foster families from taking the step of adoption.

It wasn't until she ended up with the Dellaneys three years ago that she'd finally felt safe enough to let down her guard and trust them to have her back.

And yet somewhere deep inside of her lurked the vulnerable little girl who'd lost everything and everyone she'd ever cared about. It didn't take much to raise her hopes and fire up happily-ever-after fantasies of a traditional home and family.

Samantha's heart pumped hard, thrilled that Nick had come over to her instead of Piper.

Boys swarmed her friend like honeybees to flowers. Pretty, perky, and profane, Piper possessed qualities boys seemed to enjoy. Guys were rarely interested in bespectacled, overly organized bookworms. Unless they were begging her to write their term papers.

Nick extended his hand.

Nervous, Samantha pushed her glasses up on the bridge of her nose and caught a whiff of his fragrance.

His touch was electric, and she lost her breath completely.

"You heard it, too, didn't you." Statement, not a question.

"Wh-what?"

He didn't let go of her hand, kept his gaze locked on to hers. "That unmistakable *click*."

Oh yeah, she had heard the snap inside her brain like the missing piece of life's puzzle clicking into place, and her mind filled with romantic *what-if* scenarios revolving around her future and this boy.

But she wouldn't admit that to him. Far too scary.

"You felt it." He paused, continuing to hold her hand and staring deeply into her eyes.

"Mm . . . um . . ."

"Like cobalt-blue lightning jumping from the sky and shooting straight through your heart."

"Y-yes." She blinked, both impressed and confused by his insight. "How did you know?"

"I felt the same thing. When you know, you know."

Know what? she wanted to ask, but her tongue wasn't working.

"When the lightning strikes, the lightning strikes, and there's nothing you can do but climb aboard the ride."

Mixing metaphors, but okay. *Sign me up!*

The crowd in the hallway thinned out. Soon it was just her, Piper, and Nick left standing. And the maintenance guy folding up his ladder.

Piper elbowed Samantha. "C'mon. We're gonna be late."

Lateness. It was a terrifying thought for a good-girl people-pleaser, but Piper's warning didn't even make a dent in her brain, gone all mushy from Nick's warm touch.

"Go on without me."

"Oh, hells to the no, cupcake. No woman left behind. We're a team. You're here. I'm here. All for one and one for all."

On the whole, Samantha appreciated Piper's loyalty and friendship, but not today. Today, she ached to tell Piper to buzz off. Which wasn't like her. What had this guy done to her in under five minutes?

"Goodbye now, Mr. Ginelli, we gotta go." Piper tugged on Samantha's sweater.

A lone student came running down the corridor, shouldering a heavy backpack, wide-eyed and panic-stricken, chanting, "I'm late, I'm late," as if he was the White Rabbit in *Alice in Wonderland*.

Samantha couldn't resist mentally adding, *For a very important date.*

Except she wasn't late. Her very important date was standing right in front of her, looking at her like she was a magical unicorn.

Nick's hand was still hot on hers, his eyes aglow like twin flames burning just for her. "We're fated, Samantha Riley. You and me. I know it. You know it. And the Lightning Strike knows it."

From anyone else, at any other time in her life, this might have sounded super corny, and maybe even a little creepy. But at sixteen, eager for adventure and yearning for her first boyfriend, it was the coolest thing she'd ever heard.

In her head, Kylie Minogue was singing "Love at First Sight," and just like that, Samantha was lovestruck.

And from that moment forward, there was no one else for her but Nick Ginelli until the day he died.

CHAPTER 2

I fell in love the way you fall asleep: slowly, and then all at once.

—John Green

Now that Samantha was set to marry into the Ginelli family a second time, she felt doubly blessed. Despite all she'd been through, providence had smiled on her again, and she was madly in love for the second time around.

Although, this romance was the complete opposite of her first.

After losing Nick, she was no longer starry-eyed about marriage, but the slow burn she'd first felt for Luca Ginelli since he'd moved back home last year had grown stronger each passing day. What started as a flicker was now a raging blaze, and she couldn't wait to marry the second love of her life.

Nick might have been her Lightning Strike, but Luca was her soul mate. Nick had been an adventure, whereas Luca was a destination. With Nick, she'd been swept away, helpless as flotsam on the ocean's tide. With Luca, she had her eyes wide open. Nick had been an imperative, Luca a choice.

A joyful choice she was thrilled to make. In Luca's arms she'd found the thing she'd searched for her entire life.

The steady heartbeat of her true home.

She didn't worry that Luca would ever leave her, and for the young girl inside of her who'd lost so much, that trust was irresistible. Her life was full. What more could she ask for? She had the world on a string, and nothing could possibly go wrong.

On this balmy Friday evening in late May, that grateful attitude led Samantha, latched on to her fiancé's arm, into Mario's Bistro on Moonglow Boulevard.

She'd entered this building almost daily for the past fourteen years, ever since she and Piper started waiting tables at the restaurant after school and on weekends. The eatery had been passed down through three generations of Ginellis, and it was the go-to spot for authentic Italian cuisine in quaint Moonglow Cove.

After high school, Samantha had started community college and gotten her associate degree in mathematics before she and Nick married. Piper had entered the Coast Guard Academy with Nick. Piper and Nick had even ended up as partners in their installation. Losing Nick had been almost as big a blow to her foster sister as it had been to Samantha.

Now, at thirty, Samantha wanted only one thing. To rebuild the life that gut-wrenching circumstances had stolen from her. She would do whatever it took to provide a safe, happy environment for her seven-year-old daughter, Destiny.

And Luca was the key.

She couldn't wait to be his wife. Couldn't wait for the wedding night and their first time together.

They'd started dating ten months earlier, after Luca left his marine biology career in Alaska to come home and take over the restaurant when his dad, Tino, had a stroke. Tino had recovered for the most part, but he wouldn't ever be able to work full-time again.

She and Luca had been holding off from having sex until they received Nick's death certificate, seven years after he disappeared at sea, and their sexual tension was off the charts. Each touch, each glance, each whisper between them lit Samantha on fire.

Sexual fantasies kept her up at night as Samantha anticipated what it would be like with Luca. The only person she had to compare him to was his younger brother. Nick had been her one and only, and after he was gone, she'd had a newborn to raise so romance had been completely off the table. If Tino hadn't had the stroke, she and Luca probably wouldn't have ever gotten together.

Of the two brothers, Luca was the better kisser, and if that was any indication of what was in store for her in the bedroom, *whoo-ee*, they'd have one heck of a honeymoon.

Staying celibate for ten months hadn't been easy. Not only did they work together at the restaurant six days a week, but they also lived across the street from each other. She treasured their closeness, but it had been torture keeping Luca at arm's length, and they'd scheduled the wedding for two days after the court hearing officially declared Nick deceased.

They'd pushed the sexual envelope as far as they could without going all the way, and if Luca hadn't been so adamant about waiting, Samantha would have caved.

How hungry she was for him!

Luca interlaced their hands, and with kind eyes and a tender smile, guided Samantha to the large private dining room where the wedding party had gathered for the rehearsal dinner. The air smelled as it always did of onions, garlic, and simmering tomato sauce. The fragrance she most associated with home.

"Happy?" he asked.

"Ecstatic." Samantha's pulse fluttered strangely.

Why?

She knew and loved everyone in the room, and she'd just seen them all at the seaside chapel for the wedding rehearsal, but early ripples of anxiety played along her nerve endings. It had taken her eighteen months to wean herself off a Xanax dependency after Nick vanished in a squall, and she never wanted to go back.

Luca inclined his head toward the dining room. He possessed an uncanny ability to pick up on even the most subtle shifts in her mood. He was the sort of man who paid attention to details, which was one of the qualities that kept Mario's prominently featured in *Texas Monthly* as the finest Italian restaurant on the Texas Gulf Coast.

"Do you need a breather before we go inside?"

Through the glass panels, Samantha could see her foster parents, Heath and Ruth Dellaney, talking to Luca's folks. "I'm fine. Just butterflies."

"Seriously, sweetheart, if you need to take a moment, they'll wait for us." Luca rubbed his thumb across her knuckles.

She angled her head to meet his steadfast gaze.

Luca was a good three inches taller than his younger brother had been, and almost a foot beyond Samantha's five-three-and-a-half-inch height. He stood out in any crowd, just as Nick had, but for completely different reasons. Nick had been the life of the party, Luca the one who stayed behind to clean up the mess.

"Second thoughts?" His tone was light, but she spotted a hint of worry in his dark brown eyes.

"About the wedding?"

He nodded.

"*Never.* I can't wait to start our lives together. Our time has finally come."

"And these last-minute jitters?"

Why was she feeling unsettled? Samantha paused, considering. She patted the handbag hooked over her left shoulder. "It just dawned on me that I still have Nick's death decree in my purse."

Luca flinched.

"I should have put it in the keepsake box."

"It's a stressful situation. Completely understandable that you're conflicted." His voice was kind, thoughtful.

She studied his dear face. "Do you ever regret falling in love with me?"

"No." His response was instantaneous and certain. He paused with his gaze locked on hers. "Do you?"

"Sometimes," she whispered because it felt disloyal to say out loud what she'd often thought to herself. "I regret not meeting you first . . . but if I had, I wouldn't have Destiny."

"You *had* to marry Nick. It was fated."

"I thought you didn't believe in superstitious signs from the universe," she teased. "Despite your family indoctrination."

"I don't," he said. "But you do and so does my family. I can honor and respect your beliefs, even if I don't share them."

She reached up to cup his cheek. "I know it seems silly——"

"Shh," he said. "Shh. I get it. I understand. You don't need to say anything else."

Yet despite his reassuring words, Samantha couldn't pretend she hadn't seen the flicker of pain in his eyes. She feared the Ginelli family legend made Luca feel second best. Falling in love with each other had complicated both their lives.

At first, she and Luca resisted the pull, but in the end, they couldn't ignore the strong feelings knitting them together, and when they'd finally admitted their feelings, his family had been happy for them.

"I love you so very much." She squeezed his hand.

Luca tugged her into an alcove between the dining room and the bustling kitchen. They'd sneaked their share of kisses in this spot, and he kissed her now, hot and passionate.

This strong, solid relationship was far better than any Lightning Strike. With Luca she felt safe in a way she hadn't felt with his brash brother. That thought made her feel disloyal to Nick, and she quickly shoved it aside. She'd once confessed those same feelings to the therapist she'd started seeing after Nick's disappearance.

The woman had asked her why she felt that way. Nick was dead. What was she holding out for? Was she expected to mourn Nick to the end of her days? Was her anxiety keeping Luca at arm's length? Samantha denied it, but the fears crept in when she least expected them.

"We're so lucky to have each other." She stroked his cheek.

"So damn lucky." His lips vibrated against hers. His mouth moved to the curve of her jaw, and he nibbled lightly. "I can't wait for tomorrow night."

"Mmm," she purred, and ran her hand through his hair. "Me either."

He nuzzled her neck, and her entire body tingled as a longing sigh escaped her lips. She closed her eyes so she couldn't see the photographs lining the walls, pictures that included snapshots of Nick.

Luca's kiss was sweet but urgent and his mouth set her body simmering, and in that lovely moment, Samantha surrendered and let Luca soothe away every ounce of doubt.

* * *

"Luca! Samantha! Leave something for the honeymoon." Piper's teasing voice punctured their love bubble.

Simultaneously, Luca and Samantha turned to see Piper heading toward them with a pale-skinned man of medium height.

Luca scowled and felt his protective instincts jump to alert. Who was this guy and why had Piper brought him?

The man didn't look like Piper's usual type. He had a willowy build, wore black-framed glasses and stylish clothing, and had an air of superiority. Samantha's foster sister usually dated bodybuilders, MMA fighters, and other extreme athletes, or fellow Coast Guard members.

"You brought a date," Luca said.

"I hope that's okay." Piper put a hand to her throat and her hazel eyes widened. "Sammie said I could have a plus-one."

"For the wedding," Samantha said gently as she stepped back from Luca. "But of course, it's fine. We have plenty of food. This is Mario's."

Luca extended his hand to the stranger. He might not trust the guy, something about him gave off nefarious vibes, but he was a gracious host. "Hi, I'm Luca, the groom."

"Oops, my bad." Piper put a hand on the man's shoulder. "This is Victor . . . er . . . what's your last name again?"

"Jorge," the stranger said, an odd gleam in his eyes.

"We met on Brushfire," Piper said, referencing a hip new dating app.

"Nice to meet you both." Convivially, Jorge shook first Luca's hand and then Samantha's, offering a slick, polished smile that further fueled Luca's negative first impression.

Samantha shot Piper a look. "You two just met recently?"

"Yep. Just now." Piper raised her shoulders and her palms.

"You know I hate going stag. Vic was up for a wedding rehearsal dinner. Win-win."

Samantha took the curve ball in stride. "Well, it's nice to have you, Victor. Come on in and meet our noisy gang."

His bride-to-be opened the door to the private dining room and waved Jorge and Piper inside. Luca plucked at her sleeve, urging her to hang back.

"Yes?" She blinked up at him with those sweet blue eyes that took his breath away.

"Do you want me to get rid of that guy?" Luca asked. "It wasn't fair for Piper to ambush you."

"No, no. It's all right."

"You sure? This is *our* time. It's okay to put yourself first for once."

"That's darling of you to offer, but truly, it's okay."

"Your call. But give me a sign and I'll jettison that joker so fast, he'll feel like *his* brush caught fire."

Samantha giggled, which was what he'd been aiming for. She went up on her tiptoes to kiss his cheek. "I adore how you leap to my defense."

The pressure of her lips against his skin calmed Luca, but he didn't drop his wariness of Piper's date. "I've got your back, Sammie. Always."

"Let's mingle." Samantha turned to the wedding party milling around the long dining table and made a beeline for Destiny.

Luca touched his face where her lips had landed and smiled as he watched her walk away.

She'd sent her daughter on to the restaurant with his folks while the two of them had stayed behind to wrap up last-minute details with their priest. After a round of hugs and hellos, as if the wedding party hadn't all just seen each other at the chapel a half hour ago, Luca and Samantha took their assigned seats at opposite ends of the table.

He winked at her.

She blew him a kiss.

Luca pretended to catch it and press the invisible kiss to his heart.

"Aww," one of the bridesmaids said. "You two are like bread and butter. You just *go* together. I want a love like that someday. You are so lucky."

"Yes, we are," Luca said, holding tight to Samantha's steady gaze.

And it only took us fourteen years to get here.

CHAPTER 3

Superstition, like true love, needs time to grow and reflect upon itself.

—Stephen King

Piper sat to Samantha's left, and the waitstaff brought an extra place setting for Victor Jorge, who'd parked himself on Samantha's right. She'd wanted Destiny to sit in that spot, but she let it go.

She glanced down the table at Luca. He raised his eyebrows, inclined his head toward the door, and she could swear she could hear his mental cogs whirling. *Say the word and Brushfire guy is toast.*

Grinning, she shook her head.

Music piped through the speakers mounted at the four corners of the room, and the ubiquitous Dean Martin crooned "That's Amore." The table was covered with a red-and-white-checkered tablecloth and the equally omnipresent Chianti-bottle candles flickered, casting a soft glow over the fresco walls. The song changed, still Dean, this time singing "Everybody Loves Somebody."

It was the song that had been playing when Luca kissed her for the first time in the walk-in pantry after they'd worked long into the night doing inventory.

Remembering, Samantha sent her husband-to-be another meaningful look to see if he'd noticed the song.

Luca's gaze held hers. Of course, he'd noticed. This was Luca, who noticed everything. He stared at her as if she was the only person in the room, smiled softly, and mouthed the words to the romantic song.

She placed a hand over her heart and felt her eyes get misty. She could look at that man forever and never get tired of seeing him.

Someone snorted.

Loudly.

It was the odd man seated at her right.

Samantha turned her head. "Do you need something, Mr. Jorge?"

"No, thank you. I'm good."

"How about a beverage?" Samantha lifted an index finger to one of the three servers waiting on the wedding party.

Yolanda Perkins was a perky young coed and Mario's employee of the year. She'd just come through the door with water for the group, and after passing out the tumblers, she hustled over to Samantha, the serving tray held against her chest.

"Beer," Jorge said.

"Bring Mr. Jorge the Moonglow," she told Yolanda. "And I'll have iced tea."

"No peach Bellini?" Yolanda asked, knowing it was Samantha's favorite.

"I want to keep my head clear," Samantha said. "I've got so much to do tomorrow. I can't afford a headache."

"Got it." Yolanda finished taking the drink orders from the others at the table, and after shooting the stranger an assessing glance, she left.

Mr. Jorge leaned in too close, and it was all Samantha could do not to retract from his breath, which smelled faintly of weed. "You're the brains of this operation."

"Not at all," Samantha said smoothly, and sent Piper a "help me" look, but her foster sister was conversing with Marcella and didn't catch her eye.

"Piper said you're CFO."

"No, she overstated. I'm just the bookkeeper."

"So, the groom . . ." Victor Jorge shot a look at Luca. "I understand he's your dead husband's brother?"

Samantha's upper lip started to tingle the way it did whenever she felt put on the spot. "Yes, Luca is my brother-in-law."

"Wow." Jorge smirked. "Biblical."

The hairs on her arms lifted. "It's not like that."

"No?" He studied her as if he had some kind of agenda, and Samantha's gut twisted. Something was off about this guy.

"Not at all," she said, hoping to shut him down.

"So, tell me." He settled his elbow on the table and leaned in even closer. "What's that like going from one brother to the other?"

Normally, she would have simply ignored unwanted comments rather than confront them, because she liked to give people the benefit of the doubt, especially on such a happy weekend, but when it came to her family, that was a boundary she didn't allow people to cross. Piper's Brushfire stranger was entirely too nosy.

"That's really none of your business, Mr. Jorge."

"Ouch." He laughed. "The kitten has claws. How does Mr. This-Time-Around feel about getting his brother's sloppy seconds?"

Samantha froze, unable to believe the obnoxious man had just asked her that. Curling her hands into fists, she dug her fingernails into her palms and hauled out a polyurethane smile. She wouldn't let this poseur ruin the rehearsal dinner.

"If you'll excuse me," she said. "I need to see to my other guests."

"That question was rude. I apologize and retract it."

"Thank you." She relaxed a little.

Jorge put a hand on her wrist, and her guard shot right back up. "I have a better question. Why do you feel such a need to play Cinderella?"

"Excuse me?"

"You're searching for a fairy tale. Wise up. You're deceiving yourself. Thinking *this* time love will finally save you."

Samantha tried to pull her hand away, but Victor Jorge hung on. She glared at him. "I feel sorry for you."

"Why is that?"

"You've clearly never had a grand love." Her heart was pounding so hard, she was certain everyone in the room could tell.

"Keep your pity. You gotta wake up from the dream sometime, Sleeping Beauty." Victor Jorge looked positively Machiavellian.

Oh, he was up to something, the scoundrel, but she had no idea what it was. Her hand twitched to slap his smug face, but she wouldn't act on such an impulse. Then again, she didn't have to.

Luca practically teleported from the opposite end of the table, moving so swiftly that Samantha barely registered what was happening.

"Get your hand off my fiancée," Luca growled low in his throat. *"Now."*

Every eye in the room swung their way. Samantha cringed. So much for a glitch-free rehearsal dinner.

"Ahh," Jorge said to Samantha, and he was no longer whispering.

"I'm starting to get the picture. This one was in love with you long before you married his little brother."

His comment was absolutely ridiculous. Samantha had barely known Luca before he came back to run the restaurant. He was four and a half years older than Nick, finishing college when she and Nick had been in their junior year of high school. Luca had moved to Alaska not long after she and Nick had started dating, and he'd only come home for short visits during the holidays and for special family events.

"Out!" Piper hopped to her feet, snapping her fingers at the man and pointing toward the door. "Get out now!"

But Luca wasn't waiting for the creep to vacate under his own steam. He took the man by the scruff of his neck, tugged him from his chair, and muscled him efficiently toward the door.

Samantha's heart was pounding so hard, she could barely swallow. She darted a glance at Destiny, who watched wide-eyed.

"Mom?" Her daughter's voice was shaky.

"It's okay, honey. Everything's fine," Samantha soothed.

"Who was that weirdo?" Destiny nibbled a thumbnail.

"A mistake," Piper said to Destiny. Turning to Samantha, she said, "Sammie, I am so, so sorry."

"It's all right." Samantha's smile wilted. She couldn't blame Piper for her date's bad behavior.

Returning to the dining room, Luca dusted off his palms and headed their way. Yolanda entered the room behind him, carrying a tray of beverages.

Samantha tracked his journey. Luca didn't possess his younger brother's bulky muscularity, but he did have a fit body and he moved with an easy, self-assured gait. His pace was steady, rhythmic. Whenever she watched him, her pulse kicked into overdrive. Luca was a man comfortable in his skin, in contrast to Nick, who'd given off an electric, uncontainable energy with his fast, long-legged strides. Nick had always seemed in a hurry to get somewhere.

You gotta stop comparing him to Nick. There is no comparison. Luca's here and Nick's not.

Luca stopped beside her chair. "You okay?"

"Yes, thank you for dispensing with Mr. Jorge."

Luca leveled an assessing glance at Piper. "Just who was that guy?"

Piper's face reddened. "I really have no idea."

"Why," Yolanda said, sliding the beer the man had ordered onto the table beside Samantha, "I thought you'd invited him here on purpose."

"We did not," Luca said.

Yolanda touched the tip of her tongue to her upper lip. "You guys don't know?"

"Know what?" Samantha asked, confused.

"Victor Jorge is a YouTube influencer from Houston who specializes in wedding scandals," Yolanda said.

"Why on earth would we invite him on purpose?" Samantha blinked at her.

Yolanda shrugged. "I figured publicity for the restaurant maybe . . ."

"What does that mean?" Marcella asked. "I don't understand."

"It means the jerk targeted Piper on a dating app in order to get close to our family, Ma," Luca said.

"An influencer specializing in wedding scandals?" Ruth scratched her temple. "Where's the scandal?"

"He's just trying to stir up trouble." Piper patted her mother's shoulder. "You know, because of Nick. Jorge figured there must be a juicy scandal in there somewhere."

"And he was using you to do it, Piper?" Ruth clicked her tongue. "What an unsavory fellow."

"This feels like a bad omen." Marcella hissed in a breath through clenched teeth.

"Ma, please don't get superstitious," Luca said. "The guy is a troll, but he's got nothing to do with Samantha and me. Everything'll be just fine. He's gone. Let's get back to our celebration."

"A toad," said Tino Ginelli, whose speech was still glitchy after the stroke, raising his wineglass.

Samantha raised her glass of iced tea and smiled across the table at Tino. "A toast. To family."

"To family!" Everyone clinked glasses and drank and laughed and ate and forgot all about the odious Victor Jorge.

Except for the niggling little voice of doubt in the back of Samantha's brain insisting that Victor Jorge *was* a bad omen. The same little voice that followed her from foster home to foster home until she finally found her safe place with the Dellaneys and the Ginellis.

The little voice whispered, *Trouble's brewing.*

To quell the anxiety tightening her chest, Samantha shook a few grains of salt from the shaker on the table into her palm and tossed them over her shoulder. Just in case.

CHAPTER 4

Love is friendship that has caught fire.

—Ann Landers

I thought that went really well." Luca sprawled out on Samantha's couch with his feet propped on the ottoman. "Once we got rid of Piper's awful Brushfire date."

There Luca went, looking on the bright side. Optimism. His best trait in her book, although she couldn't deny his rocking-hot body. Her husband-to-be looked so handsome that her heart skipped a beat. She couldn't wait to have him sitting there every day for the rest of her life.

Luca was her tonic. Her safety net. He wouldn't walk out on her during an argument without telling her where he was going.

Samantha had just finished putting Destiny to bed after reading her a chapter from *Harriet the Spy*. Pulling the pins from her bun, she let her hair fall loose past her shoulders and ran a hand through it to tame the curls. She stuck the hairpins into her pocket and curled up beside Luca on the couch.

Ahh. Her favorite part of the day. Unwinding with her man.

"You were magnificent by the way." Luca reached to interlace their hands.

She curled her fingers around his. "Thanks. So were you. I got all fluttery when you dispensed of Mr. Jorge. My hero."

"Anytime, babe, anytime."

"Why do you suppose that guy was snooping around us?"

"Trying to dig up a story. Piper oughta be more careful. That jerk took advantage of her free spirit."

"She's a big girl. She can take care of herself."

"Piper is tough as an old boot, and she can see whomever she wants, but when her shenanigans impact you, that's when I get upset."

"Piper is who she is. I accept her, flaws and all, and she does the same for me."

"Still . . ." Luca shook his head. "I worry she'll hurt you one day."

"If she does, she does. It's not like I haven't survived my share of heartbreak. I couldn't love her more if she were my biological sister."

"I know." He gave her an indulgent smile.

"She didn't mean to cause problems, Luca."

He looked as if he might say something but thought better of it. In the shadowy light from the industrial-style table lamp, he looked so much like his younger brother that Samantha startled. Nick had been the one to pick out the table lamps, and it occurred to her that maybe it was time to redecorate.

Or move.

They hadn't fully discussed what to do about merging their households. Wedding prep had taken precedence, and they'd tucked away the topic for the not-too-distant future.

"So," she said, sliding her legs underneath her on the cushion and turning her body to face him. "Have you given any further thought to where we'll live when we get back from our honeymoon?"

"We both have great houses, but yours is bigger."

"Yes, although . . ." She waved a hand. "Memories."

"Yeah." He dropped her gaze and picked up the remote control, flicked the TV to local news.

Avoiding the topic? she wondered.

"Maybe we could go take a look at the new housing development on the west side of the bay after we return from Fiji?"

"Sammie, we've got the rest of our lives to figure out where to live. Tomorrow is our wedding day, let's focus on the here and now."

"You're right."

Luca was so down-to-earth. Such a far cry from Nick's impulsive personality. She'd often wondered how they'd come from the same set of parents. She rested her head on his shoulder, savoring his calm strength.

He wrapped his arm around her, pulling her closer. "Shh, just relax. We'll be up at dawn, going like gangbusters."

On the television, the station cut from commercial back to the newscast, but Samantha barely noticed. The volume was low, and she was too enthralled with the feel of Luca's hand gently stroking her neck.

Mmm.

"In a case of life imitating art," the announcer said, "early this morning, an American citizen was discovered marooned on an uninhabited island off the coast of Mexico. Just like Tom Hanks's character, Chuck Noland, in *Cast Away*, the man had been living shipwrecked alone for many years. Details are sketchy, but here at KTRK Houston, we'll bring you the latest developments as the story unfolds. And now, let's go to Clarissa for the weather."

"Thank you, Tim," Clarissa, the gorgeous weather forecaster, said. "Tomorrow will be perfect for your outdoor plans. A balmy seventy-five degrees, light winds, and blue skies."

"Did you hear that?" Luca asked, nuzzling her neck. "Perfect day for our wedding. God is smiling down on us."

"I can't wait to be your wife."

"I can't wait for our wedding night." He wriggled his eyebrows. "Ten months is a long time."

"It'll be worth it. Wait until you see my honeymoon trousseau." She batted her lashes.

"What's a trousseau?"

"A stockpile of sexy lingerie."

"I like the sound of that. Are black lace and silk involved?" His voice lowered along with his eyelids, and a seductive smile crossed his lips.

"Count on it."

Luca groaned. "You're killing me, woman."

"One more day," she whispered. "One more day and we can have all the sex we want."

"We'll never leave the honeymoon suite."

"Fine by me." She giggled.

He kissed her then, long and deep and passionate, until every nerve cell in her body revved high. They smooched for several minutes until things started getting hot and heavy. Finally, Luca pulled away, sighing. "Gotta slow that down."

"Hmm . . . to be continued tomorrow night."

"Even though I can't wait to be with you, let's not put too

much expectation on the wedding night. It's a big day and we might be too exhausted for anything but sleep."

"We'll see about that." She walked two fingers over his chest, felt the honed muscles beneath his shirt. "Piper and I went to Victoria's Secret yesterday."

"Easy." He chuckled. "My self-control is not as strong as you give me credit for."

A lock of sandy-brown hair had fallen over his forehead, giving him a boyish air. She liked that he wore his hair a little longish, and she enjoyed running her fingers through the silky strands.

"Lie back and put your feet in my lap," Luca invited. "I'll give you a foot rub."

Luca gave the best foot rubs on the planet, and he seemed to enjoy doing it. Eagerly, she sank against the seat cushion, pulled the throw blanket to her chin, and propped her feet against his hard-muscled thigh. It felt so good to have his fingers knead the soles of her feet.

And to think she had a lifetime of this ahead of her!

He started talking then, about what he liked in a house—cozy, a big backyard with lots of Moonglow pear trees, maybe a place near the beach if they could find something affordable. His low voice relaxed her.

Samantha yawned and before she knew it, she'd drifted off to sleep.

* * *

IT WAS A graveyard wedding. Nuptials among the tombstones. Odd that the ceremony was at midnight. Whose idea was that?

Samantha picked up the skirt of her bedraggled wedding gown

and moved through the rolling mist toward the altar. Underneath a crescent moon, someone waited for her. His shoulders were broad and sturdy, but because of the midnight sky she couldn't see his face.

It was Luca, of course, who else would it be? They were getting married today.

But why in a graveyard?

What had happened to the chapel by the ocean? Where were the guests? The minister? Their family?

Frowning, Samantha stopped. Something was wrong. The surrounding tombstones were not uniformly lined up, but instead sprouted from the ground higgledy-piggledy.

Startled, Samantha began running, anxious to get to Luca, desperate for the safety of his strong arms. Her shoes were stuck as if in mud, sluggish and slow. What was happening? She looked down and could no longer see her feet. The mist was just too thick. A shiver of fear spread up her arms. Luca, she had to get to Luca.

But Luca was gone.

Vanished.

Just like Nick had vanished seven years ago.

She swung around, stumbled, fell, and hit her shin. *Oww.* Glancing up, she saw that she was face-to-face with her parents' tombstone, John and Lidia Riley buried side by side.

Her heart wrenched and tears sprang to her eyes. The wound that wouldn't fully heal. On this, her wedding day, she missed her parents more than she could say. Parents she had never really known, but she felt certain they would have loved Luca.

Luca, where was he? And why was it so dark?

She yanked her feet from the muck, staggered forward, tripping over a tombstone and banging her shin again as she went down. On her belly in the mud, she crawled. The wedding dress was utterly ruined. She tried to call for Luca, but even though her mouth opened, no sound came out.

Her elbow whacked into granite at just the wrong place, and the blow sent a bolt of electric pain shooting all the way up to her shoulder. With a howl, she rolled over, clutching her arm, and saw the tombstone etched with her late husband's face.

Nicholas Antonio Ginelli
Born: May 3rd, 1993
Died: May 14th, 2016
SEMPER PARATUS
BORN READY

That's when Samantha shrieked.

* * *

"Sammie, Sammie, wake up, sweetheart." Worried by Samantha's terrifying scream, Luca shook her gently, while on TV the late-night host was interviewing the starlet du jour.

Gasping, Samantha sat upright on the couch, yanking her feet from Luca's lap and clutching the throw blanket in her fist. "Wh-what happened?"

"You were having a nightmare."

"Oh." She blinked. "Oh."

Luca gazed down at his bride-to-be, tenderness filling his heart. Reaching for her, he eased her into his arms and gently kissed her forehead.

She rested her head on his shoulder, and he stroked her hair.

"Shh, shh," he soothed. "It's okay. I'm here. I'll always be here for you, no matter what."

"You promise?"

"I will never leave you, Samantha, not until my dying breath. Not ever." He knew they were words she needed to hear. Losing her parents so young and growing up in numerous foster homes left her fearful of abandonment, and his brother's disappearance had only compounded the problem.

She burrowed her face against his skin. He tightened his arm around her and held her for a long time.

"Do you want to talk about your nightmare?"

"What time is it?"

"Just after midnight."

She sucked in a breath. "Oh no, no. You've gotta go."

"Now?"

"Yes, yes. Right this minute! We're getting married today. You're not supposed to see me before the wedding. It's bad luck."

"Says who?"

"We can't afford bad luck. I'm serious, please go home." She pushed against his chest, breaking free of his embrace, and hopped off the couch.

He reached for his phone on the coffee table.

"What are you doing?" she asked.

"I'm looking it up."

"Huh?" She ran a hand through her mass of curls, finger-combing the tangles.

"The origins of that superstition. Well, well, what do you know," Luca mused, studying his phone screen.

"What?" She leaned over to see what he was looking at.

"The practice of the groom not seeing his bride on the wedding day goes back to arranged marriages where the bride's family worried the groom would back out if he saw her before the wedding."

"No kidding?"

Luca tugged her into his lap and, laughing, she wrapped her arms around his neck as he planted soft kisses over her cheek, enjoying the salty taste of her skin. "I've already seen you and I'm bowled over. I'm not going *anywhere*."

"But you will go home, right? I don't want to take any chances. I've had enough bad luck to last a lifetime. I know it's a silly superstition but humor me, please."

Luca chucked her under her chin and gave her an indulgent smile. He found her superstitions endearing and understood that she needed them to feel in control. He wouldn't burst her bubble. "My little traditionalist."

Lightly, he settled her onto the cushion, got up, and strolled to the door. He paused with his hand on the knob. "Our wedding will be wonderful, Samantha, our marriage even better. You and me? We might not have the Lightning Strike, but we've got staying power. Count on it."

"With you, everything feels possible."

"Sleep well," Luca said. "And no more bad dreams."

"No more bad dreams," she echoed, and got up to kiss him one last time before he left.

"Lock the door behind me," he instructed.

"Of course."

He stepped out onto the porch and waited to hear the click of the dead bolt before he started across the street to his house. His body was charged from all the kissing. He'd waited so long for Samantha, and he couldn't believe that in less than twenty-four hours they would be sharing a bed as husband and wife.

The magnitude of their future fully hit him as his lungs filled with the sea air. The streetlamps cut through the light fog, guiding his way to the house he'd bought just to be near her. He'd loved Samantha from the moment he'd seen her when she'd walked into Mario's with Piper to apply for a job. He'd come into the dining room where his mother was interviewing them to ask her about the morning's vegetable delivery. He'd taken one look at her and *wham!*

Like a bolt from the blue, all the pleasure centers in his brain lit up and his heart careened sideways in his chest and his mind had hollered, *Lightning Strike!*

Honestly, he couldn't believe it was happening because on Monday, Nick had come into the house after school bubbling over with the news that he'd found *his* Lightning Strike. What were the odds that both Ginelli brothers found their soul mates in the same week?

Or at all.

Growing up, tales of one true love had been the dominant mythology in his family's household and, truthfully, his cynical side thought it was all baloney, but then he'd seen her, and just like that he was a believer.

It wasn't simply Samantha's girl-next-door cuteness that captivated him either. Her smile sparkled brighter than the sun, and when she flashed it, she turned stunningly beautiful in his book. Then he spoke to her—a simple hello—and she'd leaned forward with all her attention locked on him as she returned his greeting. Her gaze was curious and open, as if she was eager to hear more about him, and he'd yearned to pull up a chair and talk to her for hours.

Luca remembered everything about that first meeting, including what she'd been wearing. Simple red V-neck tee, the color complimenting her hair; denim shorts that showed off her legs but kept something to the imagination; and white sandals that revealed toes painted with pink polish and a cheeky toe ring on her left big toe. She'd had her hair pulled back in a fancy braid, and dark-framed eyeglasses lent her a scholarly air.

But she was too young for him, still in high school, while Luca worked at the restaurant on weekends in his last year of college at Texas A&M in Galveston. He'd been twenty-one to her sixteen.

He'd been an adult and she was still a teen. He couldn't be thinking about her in *that* way.

Then Nick had swept into the restaurant and made a beeline straight for Samantha. He'd pulled her from the chair where she sat next to Piper filling out the job application, slung his arm around her shoulder, and announced, "Luca, Ma, I want you to meet Samantha, my Lightning Strike."

CHAPTER 5

Love is something sent from heaven to worry the hell out of you.

—Dolly Parton

Samantha couldn't shake the bad dream gloom.

While she and Nick had had something special, at least in the early days, it was long gone, and clinging to those memories wouldn't serve her new marriage. She owed Luca her whole heart.

How could she exorcise the ghosts of the past? How could she give herself to Luca one hundred percent? How could she finally let go of old history and step into her future unshackled?

Her mind toyed with the questions as she took a shower, brushed her teeth, and did her nightly facial routine.

A ritual. That's what she needed.

Rituals gave spiritual context to everyday moments, lending structure and balance to the bumps and bruises of life. Often Nick had pooh-poohed her need for tradition, teasing her for "sticking to the script."

"I need to fully release you, Nick," she whispered as she massaged night cream into her skin. "Once and for always."

That didn't mean forgetting about Nick. She could never do

that—he was the father of her child—but she needed to let go of the emotional charge around him.

She stared at herself in the mirror, her hair pulled into a messy bun, her face shiny with moisturizer. "Before you marry Luca, you need a final symbolic ritual."

"Agreed," her reflection said.

But what? And how?

Samantha picked up her cell phone and searched "rituals for letting go," and the first thing that popped up was a burning ritual. The article suggested burning photographs or letters from a dead romance.

Hmm. She could burn their wedding photographs, but Marcella had copies, and that felt too drastic anyway. She didn't want to *erase* Nick, just completely accept that he was gone for good, so she could move on without regret or guilt.

The next entry she came across suggested chanting a mantra. She'd tried that in the past and it hadn't really worked. Instead of emptying her mind of Nick, the mantra had filled it with him.

Another article suggested a moon ritual, but that required a waning moon and tonight was a new moon. One method suggested smudging, which she was open to trying, but she didn't have the tools required for that either.

She thought about texting Piper to ask her opinion. She even started a message, but then thought better of it. Piper would be sound asleep by now.

Turning back to her internet search, she stumbled across a website advocating a cord-cutting ritual. This one seemed doable. All it required was a strand of black yarn, which she had. Ruth had taught Piper and her to knit, and to this day, Samantha knitted to keep her hands busy whenever she felt anxious.

The article instructed taking two photographs, one of her and one of Nick, and tying them together with a strand of yarn. She also needed a candle and a lighter to burn through the yarn.

She found the yarn, photographs, candle, lighter, and a hole punch and then she went through her photo albums to select the right pictures.

The picture she chose of Nick was one of her favorites. It had been taken in high school, not long after they'd started dating. He was mugging for the camera, showing off his biceps, and giving her a sultry-eyed stare. For herself, she picked her senior year cap-and-gown picture. Her choices captured who they'd been back then. Him, the cocky, irresistible jock. Her, the studious good girl.

Now, studying their youthful, smiling faces, Samantha's heart wrenched. They looked so innocent and unsuspecting. They had no idea what fate held in store for them.

Pausing a moment to dab away tears, she pulled Nick's old bathrobe from the back of her closet and put it on over her pajamas. It was the one piece of his clothing she'd held on to. The robe was threadbare and soft and, in her mind at least, still smelled of him.

Following the instructions, she punched a hole in each of the photographs and tied them together with the black yarn. Now, she needed to find a quiet place and visualize her connection to Nick.

Easy enough. She meditated every morning on her back porch swing, a practice her therapist had taught her for managing anxiety. Carrying the items, she padded outside, feeling the cool flagstones underneath her bare feet. The air smelled of the ocean, which was only a few blocks south.

Settling onto the swing, Samantha closed her eyes and stilled her mind. She visualized how she and Nick used to be. How certain they were of the world and their love for each other. It seemed so idealistic now.

Melancholia pushed at the seams of her heart as a montage of memories flashed through her mind, starting with that first day in the corridor of Moonglow Cove High.

Nick's charismatic self-assurance and her fluttery pulse. The day he strolled into Mario's, where she was applying for a job, and announced to his family that she was his Lightning Strike.

Marcella had opened her arms wide and said, "It's like we were just waiting for you to walk through the door."

Tino had come from the kitchen to pump her hand and pat her back and welcome her to Mario's. Luca had congratulated her and Nick. The Ginellis had made her feel so special. As if she belonged. And for a girl who'd spent most of her life not fitting in, their ready acceptance was a dream come true.

She recalled their first date at the skating rink when he'd put his hand on her elbow to steady her. His bold touch and her quivery stomach. Their first kiss underneath Paradise Pier amid the delighted screams from passengers on the Juggernaut, the wild roller coaster that they'd just ridden. His firm mouth; her swoony knees.

Let go.

That was water under the bridge. A new future awaited her with Luca. There was sadness for what they'd all lost, yes, but also much optimism and hope too.

She'd been in limbo for seven years, waiting on the courts to declare Nick dead, while at the same time holding on to the hope that somehow he would return. Even after the Coast Guard had found a piece of his shipwrecked sailboat four years after he'd gone missing, she'd hung on, terrified to face the truth.

Nick was dead and he wasn't ever coming back.

Let go.

She opened her eyes and crawled off the swaying porch swing to sit cross-legged on solid ground. She lit the candle and inhaled the scent of lavender, then picked up the two pictures attached by the black yarn.

Nick's photograph was in her left hand, her own in her right. Her late husband smiled at her. This bygone boy she'd once loved so much.

Samantha stretched the yarn above the flicking candle and watched as, one by one, the strands of yarn snapped from the fire until a thin single string remained.

Let go.

She held her breath, waited, and yet that last tie didn't break.

That's when Samantha realized she'd unconsciously lifted the photographs higher from the flame to preserve that one last precious thread.

"Mommy," Destiny called from the back door. "What are you doing?"

Startled, Samantha stuffed the photographs—still connected by that narrow fiber—into the pocket of Nick's bathrobe. Feeling guilty, but not really knowing why, she blew out the candle and hopped up.

"Sweetheart, what are you doing up?" Embarrassed, Samantha rushed toward her daughter.

"I went to the bathroom and looked out the window and saw you crying."

Had she been crying? Samantha put a hand to her face, surprised to feel her cheek was damp.

"What's wrong, Mommy?"

"Nothing, nothing. Scoot off to bed." Lightly, she swatted Destiny's bottom.

"What's the candle for?"

"I just needed a little time to catch my breath, and the candle helped my meditation." That wasn't an outright lie. "Come on, we have a big day tomorrow."

Destiny paused at the foot of the stairs. "Mom?"

"Yes?"

Destiny grabbed her in a bear hug. "I love you."

She kissed the top of her daughter's head and hugged her right back. "I love you too. Now, let's get you to bed."

She tucked Destiny in for the second time that night and then went to her own bed. Just as she was dropping off to sleep, she remembered the photographs and the ritual left unfinished.

* * *

LONG BEFORE DAWN, a restless Luca woke and couldn't go back to sleep. Today was the biggest day of his life, and while he was a practical man who generally took life's ups and downs in stride, he understood the meaning of "pins and needles."

Anticipation tingled throughout his entire body, but underneath the tingling was the strange heaviness he always felt this time of year because it was both Nick's birthday month and the same month he'd disappeared in the Gulf.

Rolling out of bed, he padded to the bathroom, wondering if perhaps they should have waited until June for the wedding. May was the earliest they could get married after Nick had finally been declared dead, and so they'd seized on the first weekend after the decree came through.

He dressed in jogging shorts and running shoes, stuck his cell phone in his back pocket, and took off on his morning run an hour and a half earlier than normal.

He still missed Rex, the chocolate Lab he'd rescued when he lived in Alaska, and hoped, once things settled down, they could adopt another dog, with Destiny's input. He was an animal lover and it just felt weird not having a pet.

Running with Rex had saved his sanity in the early days of his move to Alaska. He'd gotten out of Moonglow Cove as soon as he graduated with a degree in marine biology and accepted a job offer in Anchorage. He could have stayed home and gone to work for the state of Texas, but he'd wanted to get far away from Samantha and his unrequited feelings for her.

It killed his soul to see her with his brother, and since Luca found accepting reality was generally less painful in the long run than hoping against hope, he'd left, determined to get Samantha out of his head.

And it had worked.

He'd moved on, dated, and had a couple of semi-serious relationships. He'd enjoyed his job and his life in Alaska. He returned home twice a year, at Christmas and the Fourth of July, and whenever he visited, he did his best to keep from being alone with Samantha.

But then Nick disappeared, and the hope Luca had thought he'd conquered came surging back. His desire for Samantha stirred his guilt and shame over lusting after his brother's wife, and he'd continued to keep his distance.

Though he did come home more often to check on his parents, Samantha, and Destiny in his brother's absence.

It wasn't until his dad had a stroke last summer that he'd returned for good and taken over the day-to-day operations of the restaurant. His family had needed him, and he couldn't abandon them. Without any misgivings, he gave up his career in Alaska to invest in the family legacy.

He wasn't going to lie. He did factor in that Samantha was now running the front office and they'd be working side by side.

Their romance was slow and gentle as they took it in stages. He knew she was fragile after losing Nick, and he wouldn't rush her no matter how hot his passion burned. They went from co-workers to dating to engaged over the course of ten months. They got along so well, and they'd never had an argument.

Oh, they disagreed of course, like any couple, but they afforded each other respect and validation, and their differences of opinion didn't devolve into fights.

Sometimes, he wondered if that was bad. If they were missing that passionate spark that caused couples to get into knockdown drag-out arguments. But usually, about the time he was having such thoughts, Samantha would tell him how relieved and grateful she was that they didn't get into daily spats the way she and Nick had done.

Even so, the specter of his larger-than-life brother lurked in the background. Nick had died young and made himself a legend, and Luca couldn't compete with that.

His feet pounded the pavement as dawn edged up the eastern horizon, and he pushed himself harder, faster. Leaving the neighborhood, he headed for Moonglow Boulevard and the seawall. He passed by Mario's. The restaurant was closed today because of the wedding. From the Moonglow Bakery, he inhaled the scent of fresh-baked cinnamon rolls that mingled with the fragrance of the ocean.

He had no real destination, just a jog along the beach to clear the cobwebs before the day's activities ratcheted up, but he found himself drawn away from the seawall and touristy glut of shops and restaurants.

Turning toward the center of town, he was the only pedestrian on the streets, and he didn't fully realize where he was headed until he spied the black wrought-iron fencing and ornate gate with scrolled lettering:

MOONGLOW COVE CEMETERY

Luca paused to catch his breath as the palm tree fronds rattled in the breeze and he stared through the fence at the well-maintained plots. The grass was mowed, the flowers were in decorative vases, and the gravestones were free of debris.

If you had to be dead, he supposed, this was a pretty good place to rest.

The gate creaked loudly when he pushed it open, and Luca's caretaker mind jumped to WD-40 and the Neil Young album *Rust Never Sleeps*.

"Well, Nick, you sure burned out, no rusting for you," he mumbled past the ache in his chest.

He traveled along the brick pathway between the tombstones, his mind filling with memories of childhood with his little brother. He'd been four and a half the day Nick was born, and he still remembered when Ma and Pop brought Nick home from the hospital. He'd been so intrigued by the squirmy newborn, and when he peered at him, Luca swore Nick looked him right in the eyes and smiled. Although, his mother had said newborns were too young to smile with intention and he probably just had a gas bubble.

"You're the big brother now," Ma said. "It's up to you to look after your little brother."

Luca had taken that responsibility seriously and ran interference for Nick on more occasions than he could count. If anyone dared to bully his little brother, Luca was there with raised fists. When Nick came into his room uninvited and messed with his toys, Luca didn't yell at him. He was a little kid. How mean would that have been? Truthfully, he'd adored Nick and let him tag along wherever he went.

Memories circled in his head, precious moments of childhood—chasing the ice cream truck down the street for Italian ices, fishing off Sandrin Pier with Tino and their uncles, skateboarding along the seawall. He'd taught Nick how to use a pocketknife, start a campfire, beachcomb, whistle, and snap his fingers.

By the time he reached the family plot, Luca's eyes were misted over with unshed tears. If he hadn't been so caught up in the past, he would have noticed the guy sooner, but it wasn't until Luca was within a few feet that he recognized Victor Jorge holding a video camcorder and filming Nick's grave.

What the hell?

Instant anger exploded inside Luca's body. How dare this jackal use the Ginelli family's tragedy for clickbait fodder.

Clenching his fists, Luca sprang forward growling, "What are you doing?"

Jorge startled but didn't stop filming. He spun around and trained the camcorder on Luca. "Free country. Public cemetery. I'm allowed."

By nature, Luca was a stoic man, and it took a lot to ruffle his feathers, but when it came to family, all bets were off. He thrust out his chest and stepped forward. "There's nothing for you here. No scandal to uncover. No rumors to monger. Move on."

He anticipated Victor Jorge shrinking in fear—Luca was certainly scowling fiercely enough to scare him—but instead of backing off, Jorge motioned him forward, eager to fuel Luca's rage.

The sleazeball was trying to provoke him for the camera.

That realization was enough to stop Luca in his tracks. Dropping his pugilistic stance, he turned and started walking away.

"What?" Victor Jorge goaded, running around to get in front of him. "You're just going to turn tail and run?"

The temptation to smash the man's smug face was overwhelming, and it took everything that Luca had in him to keep his hands loose at his sides. "Step off, buster."

"So, tell me, how does it feel?"

If his eyes could shoot bullets, Victor Jorge would be hemorrhaging from a dozen bullet holes.

"Oh shit." Jorge blinked and smirked. "You don't know, do you?"

Luca shouldn't rise to the bait. The man was a master manipulator, but he couldn't resist. "Know what?"

"No, no." Jorge shook his head and hooted. "I'm not about to be the one to tell you, but I do aim to be there when you find out."

If Nick had been in Luca's shoes, he would have grabbed the man by the throat, slammed him up against an oversize tombstone, and threatened his life.

The urge was there. The anger generated a lot of heat in his gut, but Luca simply wouldn't give the creep the satisfaction. This was his wedding day, and he wasn't going to let anything get in the way of his happiness.

Instead of answering, he left the cemetery and pulled out his cell phone to text the wedding planner that they needed to beef up security.

CHAPTER 6

Have enough courage to trust love one more time and always one more time.

—Maya Angelou

While Luca was facing off with Victor Jorge, Samantha read over her wedding checklist a half dozen times and confirmed that everything was in order before she woke Destiny at dawn.

Now, her daughter sat yawning at the kitchen table over a bowl of oatmeal and fresh strawberries straight from her grandmother's garden. Marcella raised award-winning, farm-to-table fruits and vegetables for the restaurant, and her family reaped the rewards.

Destiny rubbed sleep from her eyes. Her honey-colored hair, two shades lighter than Samantha's own, was mussed and sticking out all over. She looked so adorable that it was all Samantha could do not to tousle the silky strands. Her daughter was starting to assert personal boundaries, and Samantha wanted to respect as many of them as she could. Destiny was growing up, despite her Supergirl pajamas.

"We have to stay on task today," Samantha reminded her. "We have hair and makeup appointments at nine."

"Where's Uncle Luca? He usually has breakfast with us."

Samantha tucked her hands underneath her thighs, a self-soothing gesture she was barely aware she did. "Not today."

"Why not?"

"The groom isn't supposed to see the bride on her wedding day."

Destiny cut her eyes at Samantha. "For real?"

"It's tradition."

"Sounds wack to me."

Samantha watched Destiny blow on the oatmeal to cool it. There was something she'd been meaning to bring up with her daughter but hadn't found the right time. Shifting forward in her chair, she pressed her palms together in front of her heart.

"Sweetheart, maybe it's time you stopped calling Luca your uncle."

"Why?" Destiny popped a strawberry into her mouth. "He *is* my uncle."

"He's about to become your stepfather."

Destiny looked petulant. "Am I expected to call him 'Dad'?"

"Don't you want to call him 'Dad'?"

"I dunno. I don't want to forget *my* dad." She stabbed the oatmeal with her spoon.

"Look at me. You never knew your real father."

Destiny darted her a quick glance but dropped her gaze just as swiftly.

"Is there a reason you don't want to call Luca 'Dad'?"

Destiny poked her tongue against the inside of her cheek and didn't answer.

"It's a hard mental shift, I understand."

A long silence fell between them, and just when Samantha was about to get up, Destiny said, "Kids at school make fun of me."

Samantha stilled, waiting. If she gave Destiny enough space, usually she'd open up, but if Samantha jumped in with too many questions too soon, her daughter clammed up.

It took Destiny a few more pokes at the oatmeal before she continued. "Kids say it's weird that my uncle is gonna be my dad."

"Oh, honey, why didn't you tell me?" Samantha reached over to hug her.

Her daughter pulled away, shrugged.

"Luca wants to legally adopt you. Do you not want that?"

"I dunno."

"Destiny—"

"I don't wanna talk 'bout it."

Samantha leaned back in her chair, feeling gut-punched. She'd overheard a few snide comments in the community about her marrying her husband's brother. Just last week, a couple of neighbors had been whispering about her in the produce aisle at the H-E-B grocery store as she'd turned to pick from the stack of Hass avocados.

One of the women said to the other in a judgy voice, "Luca is only marrying her because he feels *obligated* to take care of his brother's widow."

The memory burned.

Samantha knew the gossip wasn't true. She knew Luca loved her unreservedly, but such comments still hurt. Shame on those kids for teasing Destiny. It was none of their business, and it was unfair that they judged her daughter for something Samantha was doing. Moonglow Cove was a fairly small town and people did love their gossip. If she'd had time, she would have pressed Destiny, dug deeper, and gotten to the bottom of what was going on in her child's head, but they had a tight schedule, and that conversation would have to wait.

"You're a very lucky girl. So many people love you. Luca, Gramma, Poppy, Piper, me."

"Mom."

"Okay, all right. I'll hush about it." Samantha filched a strawberry from her daughter's dish. "Are you nervous about being flower girl?"

Destiny rolled her eyes. "I'm too old to be a flower girl."

"On their website, the Knot says a flower girl should be between four and eight years old. You're the exact right age."

"People expect to see a little kid flinging rose petals."

"Do you not want to do it?" Samantha's heart sank. She'd been looking forward to having Destiny in the wedding party.

"I'll do it." Destiny gave a long-suffering sigh. "Just don't blame me if it looks super dorky in the wedding pictures because I'm so tall."

Samantha bit down on her bottom lip, trying to decide the most appropriate way to respond when her cell phone rang.

Was it Luca? She didn't know who else would be calling so early, but Luca almost always texted instead of phoning. It was another thing they had in common. They both preferred texting— or, better yet, speaking in person—to phone conversations. She pulled her cell from her pocket and checked the screen.

It was the florist.

"Hello, Helen," she answered cheerfully. "Good morning to you."

"Samantha . . ." Helen inhaled audibly, and the sound sent a ripple of dread up Samantha's spine. "We need to talk."

"Oh dear, what is it?" she asked, bracing herself.

"I'm afraid I've got unfortunate news."

Samantha's heart sank to her stomach. "Yes?"

"There's been . . . a . . . er . . . mix-up. I don't know how it happened. I came to work early to make sure everything was running smoothly."

Just cut to the bad news. "Of course, you did."

Helen ran her words together in one long, anxiety-soaked exhale. "The box of flowers arrived late last night, and I didn't immediately open them, just stuck the box in the cooler. I should have opened the box, but I didn't, that's on me."

Samantha used her thumb and index finger to massage the bridge of her nose as she waited for Helen to collect herself, even while her own anxiety chanted, *Bad omen, bad omen, bad omen.*

"Instead of the white roses, dahlias, and peonies we ordered," Helen said, "I received stargazer lilies, carnations, and spider mums."

Funeral flowers.

Oh dear. This wasn't good. She thought of that wretched YouTuber, Victor Jorge, and her graveyard nightmare and the fact Luca had seen her after midnight on the day of their wedding. She thought of Destiny catching her in the middle of the letting-go ritual and the photographs still in Nick's bathrobe hanging from a hook in the bathroom. The wrong flowers were buttercream icing on the bad omen cake.

Don't be ridiculous. Mentally, she shook herself. *Snap out of it.*

"It's a terrible mistake, awful, dreadful. I am so, so sorry," Helen said.

Samantha sighed softly, dropping her chin to her chest as disappointment pushed through her. She refused to let this defeat her. They were just flowers after all. She and Luca would still have a beautiful wedding.

"Mom?" Destiny asked. "Are you all right?"

Samantha raised her head, forced a smile. "I'm okay, sweetie. No biggie. Just a mix-up with the flowers."

"I'll do my best to make these flowers more festive," Helen said, still speaking in a frantic rush. "I'll add lots of greenery and ribbons and some pink Gerbera daisies since I have a bunch of those on hand and—"

"And you'll give me a significant discount." Samantha's accountant brain kicked in. She knew how to stretch a dollar. Being a single mom would do that for you. She might be nice, but she wasn't a pushover.

"Oh, yes, yes, yes. The Ginellis are such good customers, absolutely yes. Ten percent off."

"Twenty."

"Um, Samantha, that'll skin me to the bone. Twelve percent?"

Samantha worried her bottom lip with her top teeth. She didn't want to hurt Helen's bottom line, but the woman *had* messed up. "Eighteen."

"Fourteen?"

"Fifteen."

"I can do that—it is all my fault. I know this is your special day and I've ruined it."

"The day isn't ruined," Samantha said.

And it wasn't.

She refused to let some flower mix-up destroy her happiness. Or let her daughter see her having a meltdown over something that couldn't be helped. She was setting an example here.

But she'd no more ended the call and asked Destiny to wash out her breakfast dishes and put them in the dishwasher when her phone rang again. This time it was the wedding planner, Freida Kravner.

"Samantha," Freida said. "We've got a problem."

Almost afraid to ask, Samantha bit down on the inside of her cheek. "What is it?"

"Father Costa fell down the stairs last night and hit his head."

Samantha splayed a hand over her heart. "Oh my goodness. Is he all right? What happened?"

"He tripped over his little Maltese, Coco, and he has a mild concussion."

"That's awful. How is Coco?"

"The dog didn't suffer any injuries and Father Costa will be okay, but the doctor absolutely forbade him to work for the next several days. If you want Father Costa to perform the ceremony, we'll have to postpone."

"And if we don't want to wait?"

"If you can think of anyone willing to officiate, they can get ordained online in a matter of minutes. Do you know anyone who might do it?"

"I'll see who I can find." Heavens, what a scramble. She got off the phone with Freida and sent an SOS text to Piper.

Piper: On it.

Instantly, Samantha felt calmer. Piper was a Coast Guard lieutenant. She was accustomed to handling stressful situations with ease.

Corralling her anxiety, she sent Destiny upstairs to get dressed for their hair appointments while she wiped down the kitchen counters and sink. She thought about texting Luca but decided to wait until she heard back from Piper.

In the primary bedroom she'd once shared with Nick, she made the bed and found herself softly whispering, *It'll be okay, it'll be okay.*

The phone in her pocket buzzed, and she pulled it out to see Luca's number. He was calling and not texting? Something else must be up.

"Hello, beautiful," his warm, low voice murmured in her ear. "How are you this morning?"

"I'm okay."

"What's wrong?" he asked, instantly picking up on her mood.

"Nothing to worry about. It's all being handled."

"I've got some big, strong shoulders, Sammie. Unload on me."

She told him about the flowers and what happened to Father Costa. "But Piper's on it."

"I can check on Father Costa, if you'd like me to do that," he offered.

"Oh, would you? That would help so much."

"Anything else I can take off your plate?"

"Could you double-check our travel plans? Just to ease my mind?"

"Already did it. Gotcha covered."

In that moment, he sounded so much like Nick, in his tone and turn of phrase, Samantha caught her breath. "Thank you."

"Anything for you. Anytime. Anyplace."

"My rock." Her heart fluttered. It felt good knowing she had a man she could always count on. Her phone beeped. "Got another call. I'll let you go."

"Text me if you need anything else. Love you."

"Love you too." Samantha ended the call with Luca and accepted the call from Piper. "Hey."

Tucking the phone between her cheek and shoulder, Samantha finished smoothing out the bedspread, stepping gingerly over her packed luggage. Her bags sat ready for tomorrow morning, when they would catch their flight to Fiji.

"It's settled," Piper said.

"Who'd you find?"

"Mom."

"Ruth's going to perform the ceremony?"

"She's getting ordained online as we speak."

"Oh, what wonderful news." Relieved, Samantha sank down on the foot of the bed.

"She's thrilled to pieces. Apparently, performing a wedding was on her bucket list. Who knew?"

"I do hate that Father Costa hit his head, but I am really glad Ruth will do it. It's perfect, actually."

"After the flower mix-up, you deserve a break. We're officially past the glitches. Everything else will be easy-breezy," Piper said.

"Promise?"

"Absolutely."

While Samantha appreciated her friend's optimism, she couldn't shake the feeling that something was about to go terribly wrong, and she had absolutely no good reason for her irrational fear.

But just to be on the safe side, she knocked three times on the bedside table.

CHAPTER 7

You don't marry someone you can live with; you marry some-one you cannot live without.

—Unknown

It's a beautiful day for a wedding." Piper turned from the window of the bell tower overlooking the Gulf of Mexico.

Built in 1858, the bell tower was attached to the stone chapel constructed by the town founders long before the seawall was built around it. The chapel no longer held regular church services, and instead it served as a popular wedding spot because of the spectacular view.

She and Luca had invited two hundred guests to the ceremony, and to accommodate them all, they were holding the ceremony in an elevated gazebo on the long stretch of beach in front of the chapel. The reception would be held at the Moonglow Inn, right down the beach.

Dressed in her wedding gown, Samantha glanced from her reflection in the vanity mirror, where she'd been reapplying her lipstick after her makeup appointment that morning, and smiled at her foster sister.

"The weather is in our favor," Samantha said. "Seventy-two degrees with a light breeze. We're so blessed."

"Look, I want to apologize again about that dickhead Victor Jorge. I ruined the rehearsal dinner."

"You didn't. It's okay, Piper. Luca sent him packing. Mr. Jorge is long gone and forgotten."

"Thank you for being so understanding. I hated that I caused turmoil." Piper gave her a grateful smile. "Just so you know, I deleted my Brushfire account."

"There was no need to do that."

"Yes, there was. I haven't found one decent guy on that app."

"Minor blip."

"But then your flowers got screwed up." Piper shook her head. "I have to say Helen did work magic with the flowers, and despite the overwhelming fragrance of stargazer lilies, your bouquet looks fantastic."

"Luca and I don't need flowers to prove our love. I keep reminding myself we saved on the flowers because of a tiny hiccup."

"You know how to go with the flow, Sammie. I'd be having a fit, and yet you're smooth as butter. I'm jealous."

"I'm smooth because Luca is so chill, and he rubs off on me. Don't think I didn't have a moment of panic, but then I reminded myself all these little glitches will make a great story for our grandchildren someday."

"How much gratitude journaling did you do to achieve this lofty Zen state?" Piper chuckled.

"You know me too well." Samantha picked up the pen and small journal sitting beside her makeup brushes on the vanity, opened it up, and wrote, *Today, I am beyond grateful for my dear sister-of-the-heart, Piper. She keeps me grounded and real.*

Piper peered over her shoulder. "Aww! I'm grateful for you too!"

Samantha closed the journal and rested it in her lap. "I can't imagine how my life would have turned out if your folks hadn't fostered me."

"You mean the world to us. Dad is overjoyed that you asked him to walk you down the aisle. We're so happy you found love again after Nick. The man was a tough act to follow, but Luca is perfect for you. You've both been through so much, it's a joy seeing you happy together."

Samantha settled the pen and journal on the vanity and stood up. "May we talk?"

"Mmm, sure."

Samantha took Piper's hand and led her to the small love seat underneath the open-air cutout designed to look like a castle tower window. When she and Piper came here as teens, they pretended to be twin Rapunzels while their true lovers waited below.

She paused to look out at the Gulf of Mexico and fully appreciate the moment. In the far distance, she spied a Coast Guard vessel headed into the bay and it stilled her heart. It could have been the vessel Nick had worked on once upon a time. How many times over the past seven years since Nick's disappearance had she climbed up here on the off chance she'd see his fellow guard members escorting him home?

A hundred easily.

In the beginning, she'd climbed the steps every single day. Then as the weeks became months, she returned less and less. Four years after Nick went missing, the authorities found the wreckage of his sailboat, and the family had to accept that Nick was gone.

After that, Samantha's trips to the bell tower dwindled to special occasions, and now she went more out of habit than anything else. She came up here on Nick's birthday, their anniversary, and the date he'd gone out to sea and never returned.

Once she and Luca started dating, she'd accepted the hard reality and stopped coming entirely.

Shaking off those tough memories, she sat down and settled onto the love seat beside Piper. Afternoon sunlight, falling through the opening, cast her friend's features in a soft glow. Piper was an outdoorsy tomboy, and that's why the Coast Guard suited her so readily. Even though some might argue that her friend's loose-cannon approach to life was in opposition to a rule-following career, Samantha understood that at the core of Piper's behavior was the need to always be prepared. The Coast Guard gave Piper what she lacked inside herself—a clear role, responsibilities, and a chain of command to follow.

Honestly, the Coast Guard had supplied the same thing to Nick—parameters of acceptable social conduct. Both her husband and her friend had greatly benefited from the structure of such an organization, and Samantha thought it was wonderful that they'd found where they fit so early in life. She wished she'd been more focused as a youth.

Then again, she could say that the Ginellis had been her North Star, as opposed to a career. She'd gone into accounting simply because she'd been good at math, not because it offered her personal enrichment. She depended on her family for that.

Piper kept her auburn hair in a cute pixie cut that suited her facial structure, and she rarely wore cosmetics. Seeing just how beautiful her foster sister looked, enhanced by the wedding makeup, was a little startling.

"You look gorgeous in rose blush," Samantha said.

"Me? *Pfft*. You're the gorgeous one. You're glowing."

"I'm supposed to. I'm the bride."

"The last time you looked this happy was on your wedding day to Nick." Piper fingered the gold Coast Guard necklace at her throat that spelled out *Semper Paratus.*

Nick had bought the necklace for Piper when they graduated from the Coast Guard Academy together, and Piper had given Nick a Coast Guard pinkie ring. Coast Guard colleagues jokingly called Piper Nick's work wife. Some members of their family thought that was weird, but Samantha was thrilled that her foster sister and husband had gotten along so well.

Nick had been one of a kind, but then again, so was Piper. Whenever Samantha had stood between the two most colorful people in her life, she'd often felt like a plain little wren.

However, she had Luca now, and in his eyes, she was always the most important person in the room. With Luca, she felt special in a way she hadn't felt with anyone else, including Nick, and for an orphan, that was a huge deal.

"What did you want to discuss?"

Samantha cleared her throat and broached the topic she'd been hesitant to bring up before. "You knew Nick better than just about anyone. Do you think he would be upset that I'm marrying his brother?"

Piper took both of Samantha's hands into her own and squeezed them. "Listen to me. You and Luca were meant to be. Okay, maybe not in that batshit-crazy Ginelli Lightning Strike way, but you guys are two peas in a pod. Honestly, I haven't ever seen two people more in tune with each other. You fit like puzzle pieces."

"We do, don't we?" Samantha smiled and glanced down at her hands clasped between Piper's palms.

"You've got so much in common. You and Luca are simpatico

in a way that you and Nick weren't. I mean, sure, you guys had off-the-charts chemistry, but Nick was a maverick who had to do things his own way."

"You really think so?"

"You don't?"

"I guess I just needed confirmation."

"Look, it doesn't matter what Nick would have thought about you marrying his brother. He doesn't get a vote. He's the one who went off sailing solo and never came back."

"After we'd had a terrible fight." Samantha paused and closed her eyes against the swift sweep of grief. She did not want to remember that awful day. "A fight I started."

Piper put a hand to Samantha's cheek, and Samantha opened her eyes to peer into her dear sister's face. "You've beaten your-self up enough over that, sweetie. You gotta let it go. You weren't to blame. Nick is the one who went out in the Gulf knowing a squall was on the way. He made that choice. He took that risk."

"He was angry. If I hadn't—"

"Nope. I'm not listening to that. Live your life, Samantha. Be happy with Luca. Stop beating yourself up over the past."

"I wish I could but . . ." Samantha paused, met Piper's under-standing gaze.

"But what?"

"Nick still haunts me." She told Piper about the nightmare. "It's not the first time I've had that graveyard dream either."

Piper stood up. "I feared this might happen."

"What? Nightmares?"

"No, I worried that your guilt would get the better of you, and you'd start overthinking things like you sometimes do."

"You nailed that."

"Hang on. I picked up something from Shelley this morning, in case of an emergency." Piper went over to the vanity where she'd left her purse.

Shelley, and her husband, Sebastian, ran the Moonglow Inn. Shelley was nice as pie, and she did have something of a woo-woo bent that Samantha found intriguing. Shelley dressed in drapey fabric, jangly bracelets, and went barefoot most of the time. She smelled like a flower garden because she made soaps, creams, and candles from essential oils and sold them in the gift shop of their B&B. Shelley had once been involved in a yoga cult in Costa Rica, but Samantha wasn't one to judge people for past mistakes. Shelley had found her way back home to Moonglow Cove, made peace with her sisters, Gia and Madison, and now she was living her best life on her own terms. Kudos, Shelley.

But that didn't make Samantha any less wary of what Piper was digging around for in her purse. She trusted her friend, but Shelley had some off-the-wall beliefs. At least to Samantha's more conventional way of thinking.

"What are you up to?" Samantha ventured, her curiosity getting the better of her.

"Ghostbusting." Piper held up a white sage smudging stick and lighter as she dropped her purse on the sofa beside Samantha. "Ta-da!"

"You're a mind reader." She told Piper about the letting-go ceremony she'd tried to have in the wee hours of the morning. "I didn't get a chance to fully break the thread."

"Now's your opportunity. Nick is gone. His opinion on your marriage to Luca doesn't matter, but since you can't stop worrying . . ." Piper could be a force of nature when she was intent on something she wanted, just like Nick had been. "Stand up."

"I'm in awe of your preparedness."

"Honey, did you have any doubt? I'm Coast Guard. Always ready. Now, arms outstretched." Piper lit the smudge stick.

The acrid smell of burning sage wafted from the smoldering bundle. Samantha's nose twitched.

"Close your eyes."

Eagerly, Samantha extended her arms and shut her eyes. What a blessing if a smudging ritual could banish Nick's ghost once and for all.

Piper waved the smoking sage above Samantha's head and intoned, "May your mind be cleansed of troublesome dreams."

Well, she couldn't argue with that. Her nightmares were unsettling. Samantha opened one eye a slit so she could watch what her friend was up to. She hoped peeking wouldn't negate the ritual.

Piper moved the smudge stick in a figure eight over Samantha's right shoulder, down her arm, around the tips of her fingers, and back up to her armpit. When she finished, she moved to Samantha's left arm.

"May your shoulders be cleansed of unnecessary burdens." Fanning the smoke, Piper shook the sage around Samantha's throat. "May your throat be cleansed so you can speak your truth."

"The truth is you're more than just my foster sister, you're a terrific friend as well, Piper. Thank you."

"Shh. This is sacred . . . and you're staring at me."

"Oops." Giggling, Samantha shut her eyes again.

Piper cleared her throat. "You done laughing yet?"

"Mm-hmm." Samantha pressed her lips together and bobbed her head.

Piper stepped closer. "Actually, I like your lightheartedness."

Samantha could feel her friend's body heat and the overpowering scent of burnt sage. The stench would get into her clothing. Darn it. She should have taken her wedding dress off before the smudging.

"May your heart be cleansed of ghosts," Piper murmured.

When Nick and Samantha were in high school, he took her stargazing on Moonglow Hill. Of course, she'd known stargazing was a euphemism for making out—savvy Piper had clued her in to that. What she hadn't expected was for Nick to bring a telescope and show off a detailed knowledge of the constellations.

That surprised her. Stargazing seemed too sedentary a hobby for such a magnetic dynamo. At seventeen, she'd peered through the telescope lens at Orion's Belt while kneeling on a blue chenille blanket in the bed of Nick's pickup truck and watched a falling star flare through the midnight sky.

"Wish upon a star," she'd said, filled with the romance of the moment.

"Why should I wish on space debris?" Nick laughed.

"So that your wish will come true."

"My wish has already come true." He knelt beside her, tenderly brushing away the lock of hair that had fallen across her face. Then Nick had pulled her into his arms and kissed her, and that was the night she gave him her virginity, the only man she'd ever had sex with.

"Cold feet?" Piper asked.

"About Luca? No way."

"Ahh, but maybe you're not yet ready to banish Nick's ghost?"

"It's been seven years." Samantha notched up her chin and ignored her churning stomach. "It's past time."

"Keep going with the smudging?"

"Keep go—" Samantha didn't get the word out.

The door she was standing in front of suddenly flew open, whacking her hard in the butt and shoving her into Piper.

"Oof!" Samantha flailed, trying to right herself, but wobbled in her high heels and crashed against Piper, sending them both to the floor.

"Oh my goodness!" Marcella exclaimed. "I should have knocked before just busting in. That goofy door sticks, and I'm used to shoving hard to get it to open. Someone should have it lathed."

Her mother-in-law stepped into the room to circle the Samantha-Piper heap. "Are you two all right?"

The woman who was to become Samantha's mother-in-law a second time hovered above them. She wore an ankle-length burgundy beaded evening gown with tulle godets. The dress was a little too formal for an afternoon wedding, but Marcella complained she had cankles and didn't like showing off her legs. Marcella favored slacks or maxi dresses. Samantha thought her mother-in-law was beautiful and far too hard on herself.

"We're okay. Just took a spill." Piper reached out a hand. "Boost up, Marcella?"

Marcella grabbed Piper's hand and tugged her to her feet and then turned to help Samantha up. Crinkling her nose, she sniffed the air. "What's that smell?"

"We were burning sage," Samantha said at the same time Marcella let out a horrified gasp.

"Smudging is an energy-clearing ritual," Piper rushed to explain as she bent down to pick up the still-smoldering sage stick. Smoke curled through the room as she took the sage to the sink in the corner, dropped the stick into the bowl, and turned on the water.

"No, I'm not talking about that." Marcella leaned over to touch Samantha's waist. "Your beautiful dress is ruined."

"What?" Startled, Samantha glanced down and saw a small dark hole in the center of the dress just above her belly button. "Oh no!"

"Oh shit, oh damn!" Piper danced around with both hands pressed against her mouth. "Oh, Samantha, I am so, so sorry."

If the accident was anyone's fault, it was her own. Samantha was the one who hadn't bothered taking off the dress before the smudging ritual, but that didn't stop misery from spreading through her.

"I am sorry too," Marcella said. "I should have knocked. Why didn't I knock?"

Both women were twisted up over the incident. Samantha's immediate instinct was to comfort and reassure them, but she was transfixed, staring down at the hole that was the diameter of a pencil eraser.

It was definitely noticeable.

"What's done is done," Samantha whispered past the anvil in her throat. "Laying blame doesn't change anything. It happened. It's over."

"I'll pay for the dress." Piper wrung her hands.

"No, I will." Marcella covered her eyes with her palms as if not looking at the hole could change things.

The sense of doom she'd barely been keeping at bay ever since Victor Jorge showed up at the rehearsal dinner last night bowled Samantha over. The impulse to give into despair was strong, yes, but no one had died.

It was just a dress.

Okay, her *wedding* dress, but still just a piece of cloth. And yet, the sense of loss pushing against her chest was real and painful.

"It's not about the money," Samantha murmured. "What am I going to wear to the wedding?"

Piper and Marcella looked at each other and then eyed the hole again.

"Maybe we could affix some kind of pin or brooch," Piper said.

"In the dead center of my waist?"

"A sash or tie?" Marcella glanced around the room as if a solution would magically appear.

"It was such a beautiful dress." Samantha sighed, mournfully smoothing a hand over the spot and accidentally spreading soot over the surrounding material.

"Maybe you could keep your bouquet positioned over the hole throughout the ceremony?" Piper raised a hopeful eyebrow.

"How would that work?" Marcella asked. "Luca has to take her hand to put the ring on her finger."

"No clue." Piper blew out a breath. "I'm grasping at straws."

"I can't even run down to the bridal store and buy a new one," Samantha said, her heart sinking to her shoes. "The wedding is in thirty minutes."

"We could stall," Piper said.

Samantha paused, considering it.

"There is one possible solution," Marcella said, "but I don't think you'll like it."

Hope bloomed. "Yes?"

"You could wear the dress you wore when you married Nick. It's in a box in our attic. Remember when you asked us to store it when you two first moved into that tiny apartment on Doge Street?"

"You're still the same size," Piper pointed out. "It *would* fit."

The suggestion was reasonable. More than reasonable. It was her only real solution. And yet it felt so unfair to Luca.

Samantha hesitated. Would wearing her old wedding dress put their marriage on rocky footing?

"The clock is ticking," Marcella said.

"The guests are arriving." Piper pointed out the window toward the parking lot.

They were right. Marrying Luca was all that mattered. Everything else was fluff. No wedding scandal reporter, no graveyard nightmare, no flower mix-up, no concussed priest, no sage-burn hole in her dress would stop Samantha from marrying the man she loved.

She could allow her superstitious nature to convince her these things were bad omens, or she could detach any negatively charged meaning to the obstacles and do what she knew in her heart of hearts was right.

Luca was waiting for her.

"All right," Samantha told Marcella. "Go get the dress."

CHAPTER 8

True love comes quietly, without banners or flashing lights. If you hear bells, get your ears checked.

—Erich Segal

Twenty-five minutes later, dressed in the wedding gown she'd worn when she married Nick, Samantha waited on the seawall outside the chapel with her foster father, trying not to fret about bad omens.

Members of the wedding party lined up in front of them on the stone stairway leading from the chapel to the beach. The path to the gazebo was festooned with billowy white window sheers. The wedding planner and her crew had stretched a sand-colored carpet over the ground for the wedding party to walk down, and the area was roped off from tourist traffic. Hired security guards stood sentinel to thwart lookie-loos.

Both sides of the gazebo were filled by guests seated on white wooden folding chairs. On Sandrin Pier, the stone fishing jetty to the left of the gazebo, a harpist, dressed in a flowing dress the same color as the azure sky, plucked "The Wedding March" in high, blithe notes. The setting was like something from a movie, and despite the numerous hiccups to get here, it was a magnificent day.

Relief eased Samantha's tension. Everything was just fine.

In the distance, boats bobbed on the Gulf of Mexico, including several sailboats and the same Coast Guard vessel she'd spied from the bell tower. The craft was much closer now as it cruised toward the marina farther up the bay.

"Hey," her foster father said. "Look at that. The Coast Guard ship is a sure sign that Nick's looking down from heaven and signaling his approval."

"You think so?" Samantha wanted so much to believe that. Would Nick have given his blessing for her to marry his brother? She didn't know, but she liked to think that he would.

The wedding planner, Freida Kravner, nodded at Luca, who waited at the bottom of the stairs below the seawall. Luca hadn't yet seen Samantha, and she worried what he'd think when he saw her dress and realized it was the one she wore when she'd married Nick.

Nervously, she worried her bottom lip, but made herself stop before she smeared her lipstick.

Luca started down the aisle, soon followed by Tino, who was serving as Luca's best man. Her groom towered above everyone else in the wedding party.

She admired his broad shoulders, his self-assured stride, and the proud tilt to his head. In his tuxedo and fresh haircut, Luca took her breath away. Her heart went pit-a-pat. Soon, this dear man, who lit up her life, would be her husband.

Luca and Tino stepped to their places at the altar, where her foster mother, Ruth, stood as the officiant. Luca turned his head and his gaze fixed on Samantha as if she was the only living creature on the planet. He gave no indication that he recognized the dress.

Her hands trembled so hard that her bouquet shook, scenting the air with roses and stargazer lilies.

Funeral flowers. Another bad omen.

Stop it. Pay attention. This moment is precious.

The three groomsmen, all of whom were waitstaff from Mario's, officially opened the processional, strolling down the carpet stretched over the sand. The breeze blew in a raft of clouds that covered the sun and offered a pleasant respite from the late afternoon heat.

The bridesmaids came next, with Piper, her maid of honor, at the end of the processional.

Freida handed Destiny a wicker basket filled with rose petals.

Beside Destiny stood the four-year-old ring bearer, Joey, the son of a Ginelli cousin. The boy carried the white satin pillow as if he was a Templar tasked with protecting the queen's gold. He looked adorable with his bow tie askew, and Samantha wanted to kiss his sweet little cheek.

Destiny leaned over to whisper something to the boy, and he peered up at Destiny with goo-goo eyes. Her daughter glanced over her shoulder at Samantha and gave a thumbs-up.

I love you, Samantha mouthed. *You're doing a great job.*

Smiling, Destiny prodded Joey, and they started down the aisle toward the altar. Reaching into the basket looped over her arm, Destiny scattered rose petals in their wake. Samantha's daughter looked like sunshine in her bright yellow dress.

Too bad Nick couldn't be here to watch Destiny grow up. He'd missed out on so much. His daughter had been a newborn when Nick went missing. How different life would have turned out if he hadn't climbed into the sailboat that tempestuous day.

"You okay?" her foster father asked, patting her arm. "You're crying."

"Tears of joy. Destiny is so poised."

"You did a good job with her." Heath pulled a new handkerchief from his jacket pocket and passed it to Samantha.

Laughing, she dabbed away her tears.

Destiny reached the midpoint, and Freida signaled it was Samantha's turn. Samantha passed the handkerchief back to Heath and noticed all eyes were fixed on her.

This was it. The moment she and Luca had been waiting for. Today they would become husband and wife, and their lives together would begin in earnest. They'd waited a long time, and now it was finally happening.

Her foster father held on tight. "You ready for this, kiddo?"

She smiled at the man who'd become her template for what a good father should be. "So ready."

"Ruth and I are thrilled you found happiness again. You're so resilient, Samantha, and Luca is a lucky man."

"Thank you." Her foster father's touching words gave her courage. "I feel like I'm the lucky one."

"Here we go." Heath stepped forward, escorting her toward the ocean.

And Luca.

Samantha glanced at the panoramic view of Moonglow Bay, her second time getting married in this same location. Gentle whitecaps rode the waves. Seagulls circled overhead, catching an updraft. A colorful windsurfer swooped and swirled in the distance.

The afternoon sun warmed her scalp, and she felt a bone-deep sense of déjà vu, remembering ten years earlier when it had been Nick waiting for her in the gazebo.

It occurred to Samantha that maybe they should have found a different location for their service, but she and Luca hadn't even discussed alternatives. They both loved this beach, and it was just across the street from Mario's. Getting married here seemed natural.

Until now.

The Coast Guard vessel bobbed closer, but it wasn't headed for the marina as she'd supposed. Instead, the ship sailed straight for Sandrin Pier, which jutted out over a mile into the Gulf. Why would they come ashore there instead of the marina?

She had no idea unless there was a problem—as a former Coast Guard wife, the ship's movements seemed odd to her.

Whatever was happening over there was none of her business, she reminded herself. *Be present.*

Her feet glided over the rose petals that her daughter had strewn, and the floral fragrance drifted up from each footstep. Ahead of her, she studied Piper standing on one side of the aisle and Luca on the other.

Everyone she cared about was here. Love and tenderness overwhelmed her. These precious moments were so fleeting. She committed each face to memory as she passed by them—cousins, employees, customers, high school friends, and family.

What a blessing! What an honor!

Destiny finished her walk and turned to face the seawall. Samantha winked at her daughter and telegraphed a reassuring smile. *You did good, sweetheart.*

Beaming, Destiny sat in the front row beside Marcella.

With her daughter squared away, Samantha gave Luca her

undivided attention. She was almost at his side. Just a few feet away now.

Beneath the gingerbread cupola, Luca waited with his hands clasped in front of him, supreme love for her shining from his dark eyes. Samantha's pulse quickened, and she held his gaze, sending him a tender look to let him know exactly how much she loved him in return.

He was her rock. Her world. Her everything.

Smiling proudly, Ruth stood with her back to the Gulf, a tablet computer clutched in one hand and a microphone in the other, eager to assume her role as a newly ordained officiant.

Samantha's early life had been fraught with heartache, but she'd struck gold twice and happily ever after was just a few yards away. Floating on harp music and the ocean's lullaby, each step she took was a celebration of life.

Luca's gaze locked on hers, leading her straight to him like a laser beam. He looked serious and responsible but overjoyed as well.

When she and Heath reached the gazebo, her foster father stopped.

Smiling at her husband, Ruth said, "Who gives this woman in marriage?"

"Her mother and I." Heath grinned back at his wife and stepped away to take his seat in the front row.

Luca reached for Samantha's hand.

She turned to pass her bouquet to Piper and, as she did so, smiled at the audience, sending them thoughts of love and gratitude for sharing this special day with them.

And that's when she saw *him.*

Lounging on the steps of the chapel, his back against the

chapel door, he was holding a camcorder and had an insouciant grin on his face.

Victor Jorge.

* * *

"SAMMIE? YOU OKAY?" Piper whispered.

Her friend's voice broke through her trance. How long had she been standing there unmoving, staring at the creep who was filming the proceedings with a self-satisfied smirk?

She met Piper's eyes and leaned in to whisper as she passed her the bouquet. "Check out the chapel."

Piper's gaze swung to the church, her eyes narrowed and her mouth puckered, but she kept her voice low. "That son of a bitch."

"What's wrong?" Ruth asked.

Another bad omen?

There was nothing she could do to chase off Victor Jorge without making a scene. He was outside the boundary of the cordoned area and free to film away. She wasn't about to let the scoundrel ruin her wedding by making a big deal of things, even if she secretly wanted to punch him in the throat. She would be the bigger person.

Luca scowled at the man too.

They were giving the creep too much power. Squaring her shoulders, Samantha turned back to Luca, dialed up her loving smile, and sent him a message with her eyes: *If that YouTube weasel wants to film our wedding, so be it. We won't give him anything salacious.*

Ruth rested her tablet on the thin Lucite lectern so she could read from it as she adjusted the microphone. "Dearly beloved, we have gathered today to celebrate the marriage of two of my most favorite people in the whole world: Luca Tomaso Ginelli and the daughter of my heart, Samantha Elizabeth Riley Ginelli."

The wind whipped Ruth's hair into her face, forcing her to pause and tuck the loose strands behind her ears so she could continue. From the corner of her eye, Samantha spied the Coast Guard ship docking at the far end of Sandrin Pier, but it barely registered. She held tight to Luca's hands.

He was her lifeline. Her anchor. Her second chance at happiness.

"Luca," Ruth said. "Ten years ago, we all gathered in this same spot as Samantha married your younger brother."

Luca and Samantha stared at each other, then shifted their gazes to Ruth. She'd gone off script, deviating from what Father Costa had planned to say. Samantha hadn't had time to go over the officiating in any depth with Ruth. Her foster mom had reassured her she had everything under control, so why was Ruth throwing this curve ball about Nick?

Samantha cleared her throat and shot her foster mom a look.

But Ruth was on a roll and didn't even glance up from the tablet. She couldn't see that Samantha and Luca were uncomfortable with the weird direction the ceremony had taken.

"With a mournful heart, we stood at Nick's graveside three years ago as we said goodbye to an honorable servant of God."

Luca looked as alarmed as Samantha felt. Was it just them or did other people also find Ruth's oration strange?

Searching for impartial feedback, Samantha peered out at the crowd and noticed Victor Jorge crouching in the sand to the far side of the gazebo filming everything. He'd slipped under the security guards' radar.

Good grief, the jerk was relentless.

"Nick's death upended our close-knit community as we realized the powerful jaws of death are never far away," Ruth continued.

Behind Samantha, she heard Piper snort, and she could feel her friend's body shaking. Was she laughing or crying? Piper had a wicked sense of humor, and perhaps she found the whole thing hilarious.

Or maybe her friend's heart was breaking afresh over losing Nick. Piper and Nick had been close friends and worked together. Honestly, Piper had spent as much time with Nick as Samantha had.

Worried that Piper might be sobbing, she dropped one of Luca's hands and reached behind her to clasp Piper's.

Her friend took her hand and clung to it.

Now she was in a weird position. Her right hand clutching Luca's, her left attached to Piper.

"The Lord works in mysterious ways. He took Nick from us far too soon, but he also brought Luca and Samantha together."

Oh, thank heavens, Ruth was finally getting to the point.

Ruth scanned the crowd. "If there is anyone here who knows any reason why these two beautiful souls should not be joined in holy matrimony, please speak now or forever hold your peace . . ."

With a clenching in the pit of her belly, Samantha peered at their families sitting in the front row. Marcella sniffled into a tissue. Tino patted his wife's arm. Destiny picked her thumbnail. Half the guests were dabbing their eyes.

Samantha held her breath.

The past twenty-four hours had been insane with complications, and she was terrified someone would stand up and claim that she shouldn't marry Luca for some illogical reason.

The short pause felt like an hour.

Every muscle in her body tensed.

She could feel Luca's gaze hot on her face. To reassure him that no one on this earth could tear them apart, she let go of Piper and grabbed on to him with both hands.

Luca peered into her face, his grasp firm and strong, calm and reassuring as always. There was nothing fiery or dangerous about this man. He was good, decent, and understanding.

"Very well," Ruth said. "Now for the exchange of vows. Luca, you may go first."

Luca locked his eyes on Samantha and gave her a look that made her feel cherished to the depth of her soul. He loved her. Of that she had no doubt.

"Samantha," he said. "Marrying you is not the end of my freedom, it's the beginning."

"Aww." The crowd gave a collective sigh.

"We might have had an unconventional start. We might not have had the famed Lightning Strike, but you and I have something far richer than mythology. We have a love honed by friendship and respect, by mutual admiration and caring. I don't need to be hit by a legendary weather pattern to know that you and I were meant to be. When I wake up in the morning, you are the first thing on my mind, and when I close my eyes at night, yours is the last face I see."

Samantha's heart melted to a gooey puddle.

"Samantha, you are the love of my life, my best friend, my guiding light, my partner in every way."

Her smile trembled. What a lovely vow!

"We had to wade through a lot of tragedy to get here," Luca said. "But the obstacles have only strengthened our bond."

Samantha's world narrowed to two points.

Luca's adoring eyes.

The crowd around them disappeared. Ruth blurred into the background. The Coast Guard ship docking at Sandrin Pier evaporated. That stupid Victor Jorge actually vanished as two security guards finally noticed him and strong-armed him off the beach.

In the moment, no one else existed and nothing else mattered.

Luca rubbed his thumbs along her knuckles, his voice heartfelt and earnest. "I promise to honor and cherish you to the end of my days. Through thick and thin, through sickness and health, richer or poorer, for now and always, I vow to be at your side. With you, my love, my life is complete."

She could feel the strength of his enduring love. It radiated off him like sunbeams. She could see it in his eyes and hear it in his voice, and she felt the same for him. This was finally their happy ending, and all was right in Samantha's world.

Ruth turned to her. "Now your turn, Samantha."

Blinking, she came back into her body, fully aware of the wind in her hair and the salty sea spray on her face. Still gripping Luca's hands for all she was worth, Samantha drew in a deep breath, moistened her lips, and stared deeply into her groom's dark eyes.

"Nick, you are my—"

A gasp went up from the crowd, and it was only then that Samantha realized she'd called Luca by his dead brother's name.

CHAPTER 9

'Tis better to have loved and lost, than never to have loved at all.

—Alfred, Lord Tennyson

*N*ick.

Luca took the artillery hit. Felt the pain ping-pong throughout his body, a pinball crashing into vital organs—brain, stomach, liver, heart.

Samantha had called him by his dead brother's name at the most crucial moment of his life. This was far more than a mere Freudian slip. It was an epic tumble into the abyss of her psyche. No matter how much she might protest otherwise, Samantha still wasn't over Nick.

Luca was second best. Now and for always.

Struggling to cover his wounding, he kept the smile frozen on his face. He couldn't blame her. He couldn't blame anyone. Life had thrown them both curve balls, and they only had two choices.

Accept reality or deny it.

Painful as the truth might be, Luca picked the former over the latter. Samantha loved him, of that he had no doubt, but she would always and forever love Nick more. And there was simply no competing with a ghost.

Looking horrified, Samantha slapped a palm over her mouth. "I-I . . ."

"I understand," Luca said, eager to erase the shame from her eyes. He didn't want her to feel badly over this. The gaffe was unintentional. He knew that. "Slip of the tongue. Nothing to get worked up over. Happens to the best of us."

"I am so sorry," she whispered.

"Shh," Luca said. "It's okay."

But he could feel her body trembling and the crowd had gone silent, the guests leaning forward in their seats.

Waiting . . .

"Start again," Luca said, taking hold of her hands once more. "Forget everyone else. Just look at me. Speak your heart to me and me alone."

Samantha cleared her throat and began her vows anew. "Luca, you are my beloved. My heart was broken, and you helped me pick up the pieces and put them back together."

Luca nodded, encouraging her to continue.

"You've been a father to my daughter and a calm port in stormy seas. You've been both a balm to my soul and a blessing to my heart."

He heard a few *oohs* and *aahs* from the audience.

"You've given me strength and courage when the world looked so incredibly bleak. You brought me to a place of peace and acceptance. Thank you, Luca, thank you."

Sniffles came from the guests. Tissues dabbed eyes. Samantha's mistake was forgiven in the sweet rush of wedding love. Luca felt the shift, in the guests and in himself. Everything would be okay. Healing took years, but the family had gotten here together. Whatever else cropped up, they'd handle it.

"And now," Ruth said, tears shimmering in her eyes, "the exchanging of the rings."

Luca's father came forward with Samantha's ring and gave it to him and then Tino stepped back.

Shouts came from the opposite end of the mile-long Sandrin Pier where the Coast Guard ship had docked, but to Luca the noises sounded as distant as the seagull caws. Just part of the scenery. Nothing that deserved their attention, but several beachgoers who'd been standing on the quay watching the ceremony turned and headed toward the commotion.

Holding the wedding band between his thumb and finger, Luca lifted Samantha's left hand and slipped the ring onto her third finger. This was it. The moment he'd dreamed of since he was twenty-one.

"With this ring, I do thee wed," Luca said.

"Samantha." Ruth nodded. "It's your turn."

Weak-kneed, Samantha turned to accept the ring Piper pressed into her palm, and then she shifted back to Luca. "With this ring, I pledge my undying love."

More commotion on the pier, more people walking toward the ship. Luca tuned it all out as Samantha slipped the simple gold band on his finger.

They peered into each other's eyes, enrapt. Everything would be just fine. It would all work out. Their love could and would survive anything.

"I now pronounce you husband and wife," Ruth said. "Luca, you may kiss your bride."

Luca wrapped his arms around Samantha and drew her to his

chest. No half measures. He was all in. His mouth came down on hers and he kissed her with everything he had in him, and she kissed him back just as fervently for a good long time.

The crowd loved it and cheered them on.

"Woo-hoo!"

"Go, Luca!"

"That's some kiss!"

Grinning, Luca bent Samantha backward and kept on kissing her. Finally. At long last, she was his and he was hers. They were married.

And it was the happiest moment of his life.

*　*　*

"BEFORE EVERYONE SCATTERS, we have a few housekeeping announcements," Ruth said into the microphone, her voice booming out across the beach.

Samantha and Luca stood with their hands locked. They couldn't stop grinning at each other.

She was so deeply grateful that he'd readily forgiven her for calling him by Nick's name. She just hoped she could forgive herself as easily.

"We need the wedding party to gather for photographs." Ruth waved in the direction of the photographer. "Please meet up at the seawall in front of the chapel. The rest of the guests can proceed down the beach to the Moonglow Inn. We've provided flip-flops in your wedding-favor bags so you can walk in the sand if you choose."

The wedding planner, Freida, doled out seed packets and directed the congregation to where they could stand to shower Luca and Samantha with birdseed as they left the altar.

"Before the reception begins," Ruth said, "Luca and Samantha hope you'll join us in a unity ceremony. We're having a sky lantern lighting at dusk on the beach in back of the Moonglow Inn. The wedding party will meet you there after the photographs. Y'all have a great time."

Luca took Samantha's hand, and together they walked down the carpet toward the photographer and the seawall as the harpist strummed the recessional song, "Ode to Joy."

Samantha searched for Destiny and found her daughter talking with Gia Straus, Shelley's younger sister.

Gia was a kite maker who had studied in Japan under a master kite maker, and she'd transferred those skills into creating handcrafted sky lanterns for weddings. The lanterns had been expensive, but Luca had wanted a unity ceremony, so Samantha crunched the numbers and made it happen. She was glad now she'd agreed. The guests seemed excited about lighting the lanterns.

Well-wishers lined the carpet, gently tossing birdseed at Luca and Samantha as they held hands and laughingly tolerated the friendly onslaught. The breeze had picked up, dusting them with ocean spray, and they could hear snippets of conversations of the people they passed by.

In the gathered crowd, she heard a woman say, "When Samantha called Luca by Nick's name, I just about had a heart attack."

Samantha winced but kept her smile in place, as birdseed pinged off her head. Luca tucked her against him and braced her with his arm, trying to shelter her.

"It was just a slip of the tongue," another woman said.

Samantha recognized the voices of two local women, Harper Cooper and her sister, Flannery Charbonneau. They ran a bread-making website called "The Flower Dough Sisters."

"Major oopsie on Samantha's part," Harper said.

"Luca took it in stride," Flannery added.

"No man takes something like that in stride. Not even someone as chill as Luca Ginelli."

"Don't project your opinion onto other people, sister dear," Flannery said. "Everyone has their own point of view."

"You know what? Even before Samantha's flub, I half expected Nick to come sailing up to holler, 'Stop the wedding!'" Harper said. "I mean, surely I wasn't the only one thinking it. They never did find his body, just his sailboat. Nick might not be dead after all."

"Shh," Flannery shushed her sister, then added softly, "This isn't a soap opera but, honestly, the same thought crossed my mind."

Samantha tried to ignore the women's comments. She liked Harper and Flannery, and they were having a private conversation, not being malicious. Too bad that darn wind was blowing their words into her ears. Then again, maybe the reason she was so aware of the sisters' exchange was because she felt so wretched for calling Luca by Nick's name. She would do her best to make it up to him.

At the seawall, the photographer waved the wedding party over. Luca held tightly to her hand and guided her toward the gathering group.

Compelled, Samantha tried to apologize again. The last thing she ever wanted was to cause Luca pain. "I really am so sor—"

"Honey, it's fine. People like to gossip. Let them think what they want. We know the truth."

"Are you sure——"

"Sammie, it's okay." He dropped her hand and slipped his arm around her waist as they ducked underneath the tulle-draped archway and the final round of birdseed splattered over them. "Please, just drop it."

He was right. She'd goofed. The ceremony was over. They had their whole lives ahead of them. No reason to cling to past mistakes.

The photographer waved Luca and Samantha toward the seawall. The rest of the wedding party was already there as Freida Kravner and Gia Straus herded the guests toward the Moonglow Inn. Everything was squared away. Nothing for Samantha to do but follow instructions.

She reached for Destiny, who was standing next to Marcella and Tino, drawing her daughter closer as everyone settled in for the wedding photos. "You did such a good job with the rose petals. Thank you, sweetheart."

"It wasn't as dorky as I thought it'd be."

"You were top-notch, kiddo," Luca told her.

Destiny beamed.

"Scooch in closer." The photographer motioned with the first two fingers of each hand for the group to move inward.

Everyone packed together, getting cozy. Luca's shoulder was against hers on the right, Piper to the left, and Destiny was standing right in front of her. Sand filled Samantha's shoes, and she wished for a pair of the wedding-favor flip-flops.

As the photographer snapped away, Samantha inhaled the moment, breathing in the scent of cologne, flowers, ocean, and funnel cakes drifting on the wind from Paradise Pier. A sweet mix of heavenly smells. She heard familiar sounds, ocean waves, excited voices, and the roller coaster clacking on wooden tracks. The peaceful lulling melody of home. She saw her loved ones dressed up in suits, ties, tuxedos, and silk dresses.

Even the hubbub at the end of Sandrin Pier didn't disrupt her happiness. Whatever was going on over there had nothing to do with them.

Luca squeezed her elbow. She lifted her gaze to her new husband. His encouraging smile sent an arrow straight to her heart.

He leaned down to whisper in her ear. "I'm right here. I've got you. No matter what. *Always*."

"Say cheese and crackers." The photographer snapped away.

They grinned for the camera as the photographer reeled off shot after shot. Slowly, the photographer started dismissing people from the group. Groomsmen and bridesmaids were relieved of their duties, and they split off to join the others at the Moonglow Inn. As the sun settled on the horizon, the assembly dwindled to just Luca, Samantha, and Destiny.

Then finally just Luca and Samantha were left as Freida returned to escort Destiny to the reception.

By the time the photographer finished, the sun had faded to an orange-purple-pink smear above the Gulf. Along with the dying of the light came a cooling of the air, and Samantha shivered in the evening breeze.

Luca took off his tuxedo jacket and draped it over Samantha's shoulders. It swallowed her up, and she found that comforting.

"Thank you, husband."

"You're welcome, wife." He paused, looked her up and down. "Hey, isn't that the same wedding dress you wore when you married Nick?"

Samantha's cheeks burned. Honestly, he was such a detail-oriented person, she was surprised that it had taken him this long to notice. Quickly, she filled him in on what had happened with the dress. Luca inhaled deeply and she watched his face, trying to gauge his feelings, but he was pretty good at keeping his emotions under wraps.

"That's a shame," he said.

"I'm glad your mom kept the dress, though."

"Lucky," he said, his tone mild, but there was a firm set to his shoulders that belied the word. "And you got to wear something old."

She nodded. It was the same thing she'd told herself. "You're not upset?"

"The dress doesn't matter. All that matters is the person inside of it." He always knew what to say to make her feel better.

"Thank you."

"No, thank you for agreeing to be my bride." He kissed her lightly, a soft brush against her forehead.

The photographer and his crew packed up their equipment to move to the reception. Beaming, Luca took Samantha's hand and guided her down the beach toward the Moonglow Inn. They didn't speak, just enjoyed the stroll and each other's company.

Hermit crabs scuttled in front of them, headed for the ocean. Tidewater lapped at sandcastles left by departing families. Patio lights came on in the shops and restaurants along the seawall.

Such a peaceful place, Moonglow Cove.

"If you'd told me seven years ago I could ever be this happy again, I wouldn't have believed you," Samantha said.

Luca gently pinched the skin on the back of her hand, whispered, "Believe it. This is real."

"We went through so much."

"Nothing but good times ahead."

She leaned into his body, and Luca wrapped his arm around her shoulder. By the time they reached the Moonglow Inn, she was in a blissful trance, spellbound by the magical day.

Piper came to greet them, carrying her maid-of-honor kit.

"C'mon," Piper said, taking Samantha's hand from Luca. "You need a potty break before the unity ceremony."

"Bye." Samantha gave her groom a lazy wave and loopy smile. She loved this feeling of relaxed peace and contentment, and wondered how long she could stretch it out.

"Wait." Luca gave her another lingering smooch.

His lips were as warm and sweet as fresh honey. She couldn't wait until they were alone tonight and could finally explore each other's bodies. Delaying sex until after the wedding had sharpened her desire for him to a heated, intense point.

"Shoo," Piper said to Luca. "Go circulate. I'll bring her back to you in a few minutes."

Luca kissed the back of Samantha's hand like Prince Charming. "I'll be right here, my love, forever and always."

Feeling like the luckiest woman in the world, Samantha put the hand he'd kissed to her heart.

"Come along, starry-eyed bride." Piper hauled her past the guests and ushered her into the inn. "Pace yourself. We've got a long night ahead of us."

CHAPTER 10

In real love, you want the other person's good. In romantic love, you want the other person.

—Margaret Anderson

Fifteen minutes later, Samantha and Piper returned to find the guests lining up at a rectangular table covered with a white satin tablecloth that was sitting parallel to the beach.

Delicious smells from the kitchen wafted into the backyard as Sebastian and Shelley prepared a reception dinner for two hundred. Twenty round tables, that seated ten each, were set up in that yard and along the beachfront patio. Romantic lighting illuminated the trees, and soft music played from strategically placed speakers. Waitstaff moved through the crowd, offering hors d'oeuvres on gilded trays.

Piper snagged a pollo asado mini-taco from a passing server and popped the whole thing in her mouth. "Oh, yum," she said around the bite. "You want one?"

"No, thank you."

"You should have one. They turned out delicious." Piper had gone with her to the wedding food tasting, and they'd both fallen for the mini-tacos.

"Maybe after the unity ceremony."

"Then it'll be time for the meal."

Samantha scanned the gathering. "Can you see Destiny?"

"Looks like Freida put her to work." Piper waved toward the ocean, where Destiny was handing out the black and white lighters that had Luca's and Samantha's names and their wedding date inscribed on them.

Once she knew her daughter was accounted for, Samantha searched for Luca and saw him on the beach demonstrating how to open the biodegradable paper lanterns and light them. He'd rolled up his slacks to his knees and looked absolutely fetching.

Samantha's heart skipped a beat. In just a few short hours, she'd have this man in her bed. She could hardly wait to kiss him all over and explore every inch of his body.

Destiny broke away from Freida and scurried over to Luca. She lifted her wrist up to him, and that's when Samantha noticed her daughter's bracelet had broken. Luca immediately stopped what he was doing to give Destiny his undivided attention. He worked his magic, repaired the bracelet, and knelt to put it back on Destiny's wrist.

When he finished, Destiny kissed his cheek and ran back to help Freida. Luca straightened up with such a sweet smile on his face that Samantha's heart got soppy all over again.

Once the guests had received their lantern and lighter, Freida directed them to the water's edge to wait for everyone to get supplied.

Picking up the skirt of her wedding dress so she didn't trample it with the flip-flops Piper had given her in the restroom, she headed toward the gathering. Piper had decorated her special bridal flip-flops herself, using a hot glue gun to zhuzh it up with white plastic peonies and beaded lace. Her friend was the ultimate maid of honor.

She spied her in-laws hanging out with her foster parents and waved. Ruth, Heath, Marcella, and Tino smiled and waved back.

Samantha was truly living a Cinderella fairy tale. She'd gone from orphaned waif to being part of the finest family anyone could ask for. She'd found love twice, and although losing Nick had been the greatest tragedy of her life, she'd healed and had a brand-new happy ending.

Luca looked up and caught her gaze as an effervescent grin overtook his handsome face. "Here comes my beautiful bride."

People parted to let her by, turning to give compliments and smiles. Everything was low key and peaceful. Samantha couldn't help comparing this event to the raucous party that was her wedding reception when she married Nick. That had been a wild and crazy night, such a contrast to this relaxed affair.

"You ready?" Luca asked, handing her the oversize lantern with their names and wedding date imprinted on it.

Goodness, she'd been woolgathering about the past and hadn't noticed what was right in front of her. All the guests had congregated at the water with their lanterns and lighters and stood waiting for Samantha to join them.

"Yes." She took the lantern from him. There remained one last paper lantern lying folded on the table. It was oversize like the one she held, as opposed to the smaller lanterns distributed to everyone else. "What's this?"

"I hope you don't mind." Luca looked a little worried.

"Mind what?"

Hauling in a deep breath, Luca leaned across the table and flipped the lantern over. Printed on it was a one-word name.

Nick.

Along with the date that he'd disappeared.

A chill blasted through her bones. Samantha raised her gaze, locked eyes with Luca. "Why?"

"So that we can let him go together and move out of the dark shadow of his death and into our bright new life."

Her hands trembled. This was the perfect letting-go ritual that she'd been searching for. The yarn severing and the smudging had fallen short, but this time, it would be her and Luca carrying out the ceremony together. Finally, saying goodbye to Nick once and for always.

"I think it's a lovely idea. Are your folks aware?" She wanted to be sensitive to Marcella's and Tino's feelings.

"It was Mom's idea." He nodded toward his mother, who was walking toward the beach holding hands with his father.

"Which of us releases Nick's lantern?"

Luca held her gaze. "I think it should be you."

* * *

Luca stood at the lapping tide with his back to the Gulf. He was barefoot and windblown, the long sleeves of his white shirt rolled up to the elbows, and the faces of the people standing around him were cast in spooky shadows from the ambient lighting.

In one hand he held their sky lantern, in the other a lighter. He looked at his new bride and felt love swell his heart to twice its normal size.

Facing the crowd, Luca said, "Thank you all so much for coming to share this tender day with us. We treasure your presence. Please, launch your lanterns after Samantha and I have released ours."

He held out his hand to Samantha, and when she came close, he tucked his arm around her waist and whispered, "I'll hold the lantern while you light it."

She took the black lighter he passed to her.

Luca waved to Ruth to join them as the officiant of the unity ritual. In the same robe she'd worn for the wedding ceremony, Samantha's foster mother came to stand next to them.

"Samantha and Luca," Ruth said. "The lighting of this sky lantern symbolizes the joining of your individual flames into the partnership of marriage."

Luca smiled at Samantha as he held the lantern aloft for her to light. She peered into his eyes and gave a tiny private smile meant just for him. How many times had she smiled this way at him across the restaurant as they worked together? Thousands. The familiarity felt special. They had so much more than any ridiculous Lightning Strike. They had a deep and abiding friendship along with their passion for each other.

Staying celibate during their engagement had been a worthy idea and he was glad they'd waited, but now he was so starved for her, so desperate to feel her body merged with his that Luca worried everyone could tell what he was thinking.

Samantha's hands shook so badly, she could barely flick her lighter. It sparked but did not flame. What was the emotional charge behind her trembling?

"Here," Luca said in a low voice, and handed her another lighter, this one white. "Try this."

With a wry laugh and a shy glance at the audience, she lit the lantern and stepped back to watch as Luca let go of it. Majestically, the lantern rose into the sky, quickly carried high by the night breeze.

Ruth cleared her throat. "As each person lights and releases their own lanterns in celebration of Luca and Samantha's marriage, we send our hopes and prayers for their long and prosperous union together."

The guests began lighting and releasing their lanterns, and soon the sky was dotted with the ephemeral flickering lights representing Luca and Samantha's love. Gratitude brought a misting of tears to his eyes. The ceremony was beautiful.

From the dance floor, the deejay played Tim McGraw's "Please Remember Me."

"Luca and Samantha will release one final lantern," Ruth said, passing the lantern labeled *Nick* to Samantha. "In memory of the lost husband, father, son, and brother. Nick won't be forgotten, as we release him now into God's hands."

This time, Samantha held the lantern while Luca ignited the wick, and she was the one to open her hands and let Nick fly away from her.

Nick's lantern caught an updraft and flew higher and faster than the others, speeding away into the darkness, disappearing far too soon. That lantern was like Nick himself. Eager to go. Always ready to roll.

Luca reached out to take her hand and squeeze it. He understood her mixed-up emotions as he was overcome with feelings himself.

A tear rolled down her cheek, and Luca's heart stammered. She turned her head away from him, sniffling.

Luca turned to see what Samantha was looking at and saw Piper standing ankle-deep in the water. There were wet tears streaking down Piper's face, dribbling over her chin as she watched Nick's departing lantern growing smaller and smaller.

He and Samantha weren't the only ones hurting. Tough, head-strong, irreverent Piper was literally sobbing her heart out.

For Nick? After all this time? He knew his brother and Piper had been close, but this seemed like something more. Had Samantha's foster sister been carrying a torch for his brother all this time?

Something jagged, like broken glass, spiked through Luca's body, poking him in odd places and slicing the breath right out of his lungs. It felt like stumbling across a particularly hateful Yelp review written by someone you'd considered a friend. Or learning your credit card had been stolen by a loved one. That stomach plummet, that hot-flush panic of snapping safety cords, sent him freefalling like a sky jumper with a malfunctioning parachute, hurtling thousands of feet toward the earth . . .

And oblivion.

"I need to go to her," Samantha whispered to Luca. "She needs me."

"Maybe give her some space?"

Piper saw they were watching, swiftly scrubbed her face with her palms, and turned her back to them.

"She loved him too," Samantha said.

"I know." Luca wrapped his arm around her shoulder and whispered, "It's okay to put our happiness first. This is our wedding day."

"Yes." She bobbed her head. "Yes."

"It's time for dinner, my love."

The last strains of the Tim McGraw song begged, "Please remember me." Shelley and Sebastian came to the water's edge to usher the guests to the buffet.

"Let's hang back a minute," she said. "I want to watch the sky lanterns."

"Okay." He waited beside her patiently.

Her head was tilted back, her eyes on the sky. "They're so lovely."

"Not as lovely as you." Luca took her hand and led Samantha through the wedding arch the attendants had brought from the beach. They crossed the sandy threshold and walked into their new lives together, the past put to bed at long last.

* * *

LUCA AND SAMANTHA sat together at the long table with the rest of the wedding party stretched out evenly on either side of them.

Samantha savored every second of the reception. The menu she and Luca had carefully curated was a huge hit as Sebastian and Shelley outdid themselves with the two entrée choices of grilled lamb and herb-roasted chicken. Everything flowed smoothly, and it turned out to be the perfect wedding reception Samantha had always dreamed of.

The toasts were lively and fun. Piper's speech was particularly heartfelt but with her usual degree of snark to counterbalance the emotionality. Dancing followed and the deejay was at the top of his game, riffing with the guests before the songs and working up the crowd.

For the first time as husband and wife, Luca and Samantha danced as Elvis crooned "Can't Help Falling in Love."

Samantha rested her head on Luca's shoulder and followed his lead as he waltzed her around the dance floor.

"You're such a good dancer," she murmured, running her fingers up the nape of his neck to tangle in his soft, wind-tousled hair. "How'd you get to be so good at dancing? Nick had two left feet and was proud of it."

Luca leaned his head back and looked down the length of his nose at her, paused for just a second too long. "I didn't tell you?"

"No."

"Hmm. I guess we do still have a few secrets we've kept from each other."

"Oh, now I'm intrigued. You saved some secret scandal to spring on me at our wedding reception?" she teased, not the least bit upset. Luca was an open book. Any secrets he possessed wouldn't be shocking.

"I did, indeed."

"So, who taught you how to dance? Some mysterious older woman?" Samantha wriggled her eyebrows at him and lowered her tone. "Was she married? Did you once have a secret lover?"

"*He* worked for Arthur Murray."

"You actually took dancing lessons?"

"I did."

"So why the secrecy? Are you embarrassed about your twinkle toes?"

The song finished and another started, "Grow Old with You." Samantha grinned at him. "When did you ask the deejay to play Adam Sandler?"

"Weeks ago." He twirled her away from him.

"So back to the dancing lessons."

"Yes?" He spun her close, and she lost her balance and bumped right into his chest. Just touching his body sent a blast of heat rushing through her.

He righted her. "It's fun seeing you cut loose like this. You're normally so focused."

"You can thank two glasses of champagne for that." She licked her lips and gave him a coy glance. "What motivated the dance lessons?"

He held her eyes. "A woman."

"Ooh, things are getting really juicy now. What was her name?"

"Do you really want to know?"

"Your darkest secret? You bet. Yes, sure, lay it on me."

He leaned in, brushed his lips against her ear and whispered, "*You.*"

"What?" She turned her head.

"You're the reason I learned how to dance. I learned to dance for you."

"But you could dance long before Nick and I ever got married."

"I know."

Samantha stopped dancing. "I don't understand."

Destiny bounced onto the dance floor as "I Gotta Feeling" came over the speakers. Destiny's eyes sparkled as she looked up at Luca. "It's my favorite song. Will you dance with me?"

"I would like nothing more," Luca told her. To Samantha, he said, "Sorry, babe, a princess has asked me to dance. When royalty calls . . ."

"You gotta go where your heart leads." Blowing them kisses, Samantha backed off the dance floor and crashed into Piper.

Samantha put out a hand to steady her friend. The shine in Piper's eyes told her that she'd had a bit to drink but not too much. Just the right amount of tipsy.

"Whoa." Piper laughed. "Good save."

"I need to pee again. Can you come help me deal with this train?"

"Absolutely." Piper patted the maid-of-honor tote kit she'd slung over her shoulder like a cross-body handbag.

They went to the bathroom on the ground floor of the inn, and after Piper assisted her with the dress, they both touched up their makeup.

"Do you know what?" Samantha asked, reapplying her mascara.

"What?" Piper plunked down so hard on the closed toilet lid that Samantha readjusted her assessment of her friend's inebriation level.

"Luca said he learned to dance because of me."

"That's sweet." Piper got up and leaned over Samantha's shoulder for a better look in the mirror at her lipstick application and dabbed at the corner of her mouth with a pinkie finger.

"No, you don't get it. He already knew how to dance long before Nick and I got married."

Piper cocked her head, blinked. "Mmm, okay."

"I mean, a man doesn't learn how to dance to impress a woman if he isn't interested in her, right?"

"You seem upset. Most women would love for a guy to learn to dance for them."

"Piper, do you know what this means?"

"Um, no."

"This means Luca had a crush on me for years. Back when I first started dating Nick, in fact."

"Sure, he did." Piper shrugged. "Everybody knows that."

"What?"

"You seriously didn't know?" Piper capped her lipstick and stuck it back in her makeup bag.

"How would I know? No one told me."

"Your tone took a turn. Are you accusing me of something?" Piper stepped back and eyed Samantha up and down.

"Of course, my tone took a turn. I just found out my best friend of seventeen years didn't tell me when she knew a guy had a serious crush on me." Samantha couldn't believe the words were coming out of her mouth, or that she was hurting over it as much as she was. She didn't want to feel this way, but she did.

Why?

"What does it matter? You and Nick were meant to be from the moment you laid eyes on each other and the Lightning Strike hit you. Luca knew the rules and accepted his fate, and that's why he never told you how he felt."

"But he took dancing lessons to impress me."

"Hope springs eternal, right? And look, it paid off. Now you have a lifelong dance partner."

"But I knew none of this." Samantha felt confused and strangely a little betrayed.

"Why would you know? You were besotted with Nick. No one else existed for you but him. You even forgot I was around a lot of the time. It was Nick, Nick, Nick, twenty-four/seven."

Stumped, Samantha stared at her friend. "I did that?"

"Hey." Piper patted her arm. "I understood. Most people never get a Lightning Strike. I wasn't going to stand in the way of your one true love."

"Apparently, neither was Luca," Samantha mused, trying to make sense of this new information.

"It's old history. It doesn't matter. This is your wedding night. You've waited a long time for this. You let go of Nick's sky lantern and you put the past to bed. That's a lot for one day."

"It seems Luca's been waiting a lot longer than me."

"Are you mad at him for being crazy about you?" Piper asked. "'Cause it sounds like you're mad at him."

Samantha wasn't sure how she felt about it. She hadn't had time to fully absorb the idea that Luca had been enamored with her for years. "Do you think that's why Luca accepted a job in Alaska after Nick and I started dating?"

"*Duh.*"

"I don't know how to react to that."

What if she and Luca could have been together all along?

No, that wouldn't have worked. Then she wouldn't have had Destiny. Any remaining anger leaked from her lungs on a long sigh.

"My advice? Go get your man, take him home, and screw his brains out. Do it. You'll thank me later." With that, Piper snapped her compact closed, dropped it in her tote bag, and sashayed out the door.

CHAPTER 11

Where there is great love, there are always miracles.

—Willa Cather

Two hours later, the party was in full swing as guests twisted and flapped to a techno version of the "Chicken Dance."

Everyone looked so funny that Samantha laughed out loud. Destiny was especially into the number, vigorously flapping her arms as she danced between Marcella and Tino. Her two sets of grandparents would swap out caring for her while Luca and Samantha were on their honeymoon. But already, Samantha was missing her daughter, and they hadn't even left yet.

"I'll get us some water," Luca said, when the dance was over and they'd settled in at their table once more.

While Luca was gone, Freida came over. "It's time to cut the cake."

"Already? Aww, that means the night is almost over."

"No, no." Freida winked. "It just means it's time for the good stuff."

Laughing, Samantha felt her cheeks turn pink as Shelley and Sebastian came out of the inn pushing the wedding cake on a wheeled cart to the dance floor. It had been baked by Anna Drury, who owned the Moonglow Bakery and was Shelley's sister-in-law by marriage.

The guests *ooh*ed and *aah*ed and chanted, "Cake, cake, cake."

Freida hustled Luca and Samantha over to the cake and handed Luca the knife while everyone gathered around. The photographer snapped pictures as Luca sliced the cake using precision strokes.

Watching him, Samantha remembered how Nick had hacked at their wedding cake willy-nilly, sending crumbs and frosting flying.

Luca settled the first perfectly cut piece onto the plate that Samantha held out for him. Her gaze met his, and she gave him a smile, suddenly swamped by shyness.

Soon they would be alone. Soon they would be making love. Sexy images of a naked Luca filled her brain. Goodness, she couldn't wait.

He handed her a fork, and they each cut from a corner of the slice. Simultaneously leaning in, they fed each other a bite of cake.

At her first wedding ten years earlier, Nick had ignored the forks and grabbed a handful of cake in his fist, laughing as he smeared it over Samantha's face. Although she hadn't cared for that, she'd good-naturedly gotten into the game, scooping up a handful, giving as good as she got.

It had been titillating at twenty to let go of decorum and act like a barbarian. Something Nick excelled at. At thirty, she preferred Luca's dignified adult version.

"This cake is unbelievable," Luca said. "Want another bite?"

"Oh, yes."

They finished off the slice, feeding each other bite for bite. Afterward, they had the garter and bouquet toss. At her first wedding, rascally Nick had stuck his entire head underneath her dress, diving for the garter in a comical way that kept everyone entertained.

Luca, on the other hand, was reverential, getting down on one knee as Samantha sat in a chair. He treated the removal of the garter as if it was a sacred act. He kept his gaze hooked firmly on hers the entire time his magical fingers slid up her thigh to find the garter and slip it down her leg.

Once he'd edged the garter over her foot, he waited until she'd settled her skirt before he stood, turned to the crowd, and shot the garter off his index finger to the gathered crowd.

The garter flew over heads and landed somewhere off into the darkness. People scrambled to look for it, but Shelley's dog, a golden retriever named Neo, came trotting up to Samantha with the garter in his mouth. That drew a collective chuckle.

Samantha applauded. "Looks like there's love in Neo's future."

"Neo! How did you get out of the side yard?" Shelley scolded the dog. Then to the guests she said, "Sorry, y'all, I'm fostering Neo until I can find him a good home, and I'm in the middle of training him."

Shelley took the garter from Neo, handed it to Luca, and hustled the golden back behind the doggy gate.

"Should I throw the garter again?" Luca asked.

"Toss it with the bouquet," someone in the crowd suggested.

Piper brought over Samantha's bouquet. Samantha picked up the garter and wrapped it around the clutch of flowers. Amid speculation of who might snag the bouquet, she climbed the porch stairs for a better vantage point as Piper gathered the singletons below her.

"Ready?" Samantha called over her shoulder.

"Ready!" Piper confirmed.

Samantha launched the bouquet over her shoulder, aiming for Piper. Her friend had caught the bouquet at Samantha's first wedding, but this time, she jumped aside to get out of Yolanda's way as the trustworthy Mario's employee went at the flowers like a shortstop trying to get a runner out on second base.

The deejay started up the music again. Shelley and Sebastian rolled the cake off the dance floor as a few people went back to dancing, while others gathered up their things, ready to depart. Samantha and Piper sat side by side on the porch steps, watching the guests.

"You didn't want the bouquet?" Samantha asked.

"Didn't do me any good the last time, so I figured, why try?"

"Patience is a virtue."

"I'm not interested in getting married." Piper shook her head. "Not anymore."

"Not ever?"

"Nope."

"Come on, really?"

"We're not all as lucky as you, Sammie. Finding not one, but two great guys in a lifetime. I think you took my share."

Samantha didn't know how to react to that. Her foster sister knew the grief she'd gone through to carve out a little happiness. "It's better to have loved and lost—"

"No. No, it's not," Piper said. "No love is worth the kind of pain you suffered when you lost Nick."

Before Samantha could respond, Piper launched herself off the porch and dashed across the lawn to throw herself onto the dance floor, writhing joyfully to "Uptown Funk." Piper was running away from something. Samantha could see that plain as day, but damn if her best friend didn't hide from her demons with stylish panache.

Chuckling at her exuberant foster sister, Samantha got off the steps, dusted her palms, and glanced up to see Luca standing there in the darkness with his hands in his pockets, watching her with awestruck eyes.

"Hi."

"Hey."

"Seems we're spending more of the reception apart than together," he said.

"Lots of people to talk to. Everyone wants to share in our happiness. That's a good thing."

"I miss you," he said.

"I'm right here." She held her arms wide, and he scooped her up and spun her around twice. When he finally let go, she staggered a little, dizzied from the whirl.

"I still can't believe you're finally mine," Luca said, reverence shining in his eyes. "I feared this day might not come."

"It's here. It's now. And I'm all yours."

"How much longer until we can get out of here?" he whispered against her ear. "I can't wait to get you alone."

The deejay cued up "Save the Last Dance for Me."

"Ask and you shall receive, Mr. Ginelli." She held her hand out to him.

Luca interlaced his fingers with hers and led her to the dance floor. People were getting out of the way so they could have the spotlight.

"It's been an amazing night," he murmured.

"The best of my life," she whispered.

"Oh, no, sweetheart," he said. "We're just getting started. The best is yet to come."

The photographer's video crew caught their last dance on film as Samantha gazed into her new husband's eyes. It was true. The very best was yet to come.

After the last dance, they made the rounds, bidding everyone goodbye. Samantha gave Destiny a hug and told her to be a good girl for her grandparents. Her daughter was going home with Marcella and Tino tonight. Freida passed out sparklers, and the guests waved them goodbye with a shower of fireworks.

They paused for one last photograph before Luca escorted Samantha into the awaiting limo. Once the door shut behind them, they sank against the seat, holding hands and grinning moony-eyed at each other.

At her first wedding, they'd had an after party that lasted long into the wee hours of the night. This time, the after party was just the two of them.

Luca leaned over to cup her face between his palms and gaze deeply into her eyes. She felt cherished and seen. Then he kissed her, and it was the most perfect kiss in the entire world. Sweet and warm and firm. A kiss filled with so much hope and promise.

The driver let them off at Samantha's door. Luca tipped him big, and he drove away with a grin and a jaunty toot of his horn.

"Well, wife," Luca said as they stood on her front porch in their wedding attire. "May I have your housekey?"

Feeling giddy, Samantha dug in her clutch purse to produce the key. "Here you go, husband."

Luca took the key, unlocked the door, pocketed it, and then

peered down at her. The streetlamp cast shadows over his face, and for a second he looked like a stranger.

Who was he really? This man she'd just married? The man who'd learned to dance for her years ago, and she hadn't known. What other secrets had he kept?

Her pulse leaped and her breath caught on the inhale.

Then he moved and she could see his familiar eyes, and when he smiled, the weird strangeness vanished.

This was Luca. Her husband. Her heart.

He bent to scoop her into his arms. The poofiness of her satin, tulle, and lace wedding dress billowed around her body. Eager anticipation spun her head, and her senses swirled as she wrapped her arms around his neck and felt the quickening beat of his heart that matched her own escalating tempo.

Luca stepped over the threshold and into the darkened hallway. The house was silent except for the hum of the fish tank apparatus from the aquarium in the living room and the sound of the air conditioner clicking off. The hallway's electrical outlets had night-lights built in, and these tiny beacons guided his path to her bedroom.

The bedroom she'd once shared with Nick.

A sensation of wrongness washed over her. They shouldn't have come here. They should have gone to Luca's house instead. There were no memories in that home.

With the tip of his whole-cut oxfords, Luca bumped open the door and carried her inside. He stopped by the light switch so she could turn it on, and then he set Samantha on her feet beside the bed, his attentive gaze fixed on her.

To be fair, she couldn't stop looking at him either.

They stood staring at each other for what seemed an inordinate amount of time, before Luca pulled in a shaky breath.

"Well," he said. "Here we are."

"Here we are," she echoed.

"Are you as nervous as I am?"

"Yes," she admitted.

Everything between them was about to change. She *wanted* it to change, ached for it. But still, change was change, and she was the type to hesitate before leaping into anything, just as Luca was. Hesitation wasn't a sign she had regrets.

On her wedding night to Nick, he'd carried her into that hotel room, tossed her onto the mattress, and fell on top of her.

Not fair to compare, she reminded herself. She'd barely been twenty when she'd married Nick. So young and naïve. The things she hadn't known!

"May I undress you?" Luca asked.

Nodding, Samantha turned her back to him and lifted her hair off the nape of her neck so he could get to the zipper.

His fingers were cool against her skin as he eased down the zipper, but his breath was warm on her neck. A dual sensation of heat and chill had her shivering again.

Behind her, she felt him dip his head and press his lips to her spine, blazing a trail of hot kisses that followed the zipper's descending path.

Goose bumps dotted her exposed skin. They'd been holding back for so long that she wasn't fully prepared for the onslaught of feelings pouring over her like a thunderstorm. It had been over seven years since she'd had sex with anyone, and her body ached raw with need for him.

When he reached the end of the zipper, Luca slipped his hands around the parted material to cup a palm over each of her hip bones covered by lacy lingerie. He inhaled audibly and rested his forehead against her back.

In a low murmur, he whispered, "My God, but you are beautiful, Samantha. Let me just absorb this minute."

She got it. She had dreamed of being with him like this for ten months. Her senses were heightened, her body sensitive with building need.

Lowering the dress from her shoulders, Samantha turned in the white lace bustier to face Luca.

His eyes widened and his lips parted, his gaze tracking from her eyes to her lips to her heaving chest. "I want you."

"I want you too." Her knees quivered, and she thought she might just sit right down on the floor. It was that hard to hold herself up.

"I can't promise I won't be too quick," he said. "It's been so long for me."

"Luca, my love, we have the rest of our lives. Don't worry. If we don't get it right the first time, that's just more reason to practice, practice, practice."

He stroked his knuckles over her cheek. "I want to please you."

"You already have, in so many ways."

The urgency growing inside Samantha spread low and hot down her belly, a heavy liquid flame, dense and incendiary. She wanted to feel this man inside her. Wanted her body to awake from hibernation. She'd spent too much time in grief.

They both had.

She couldn't wait to fly into a million pieces, shattered by his lovemaking and lying breathless beneath him. Her need was feral, clawing at her insides.

"Please," she said, letting her dress fall to her knees and stepping out of it so she could stand before him in nothing but the bustier, thong panties, and white stockings. "I need you. I need you *now*."

"Sammie, Sammie." Luca pulled her to him, kissing her long and hard, telegraphing his own fiery desire.

His touch was magic, carrying her to a place she'd only found in fantasy. She didn't know if it was just the waiting and the yearning, but her hunger for Luca was so desperate, she could taste the umami richness at the back of her tongue. If her desire had a flavor, it was earthiness.

Her frantic hands flew to the buttons of his shirt, fumbling as she tried to flick them open, but the shirt was new, the buttons stiff.

"Argh!" She gave a cry of frustrated desperation and, with uncharacteristic impatience, grasped the shirt's material in each fist and yanked.

Buttons popped, flying across the room. One jumped up to smack her cheek.

Luca gave a low chuckle. "I would give anything to see how you ripped open your presents on Christmas morning when you were a kid."

"Oh," she said, flattening her palms along his bare torso and spreading her fingers wide. "I took great care with my presents because I wasn't sure I'd ever get another."

"I forget sometimes," he murmured, "what a rough childhood you had before you ended up with the Dellaneys. You're so well-adjusted, it's easy to forget."

"Believe me, that wasn't always the case," Samantha confessed. "I was a train wreck in middle school, picking fights, getting detention, sneaking out of my bedroom at night to run around the neighborhood."

"Wow." Luca looked impressed. "My unexpected hooligan. That doesn't sound like you at all."

"Remember, I have a secret wild side," she said, wrapping her arms around his neck and tugging his head down so she could kiss him thoroughly.

Luca made a pleasant noise of encouragement low in his throat and kissed her so fiercely that her toes curled in the beach flip-flops she still wore. Suddenly aware of her footwear, she pulled back from his lips just long enough to kick the shoes off.

He gathered her close and kissed her again, this time her toes digging into the plush carpet, her mind fully wedged in the moment. She wanted to savor every second of her first time with Luca, but her need overpowered her again.

Her hand dropped to his waistband. The closure of his trousers. The zipper.

Luca was practically panting as she rubbed her palm against his hard erection. "Babe, babe, slow down, slow down. We've got all night."

"We've waited so long," she whispered. "I can't wait anymore."

"Sammie—"

She didn't give him any more time to protest. She captured his bottom lip between her teeth and sucked.

Luca groaned.

Laughing, she sank to her knees and pulled his pants down in the process. When she had his trousers around his ankles, she moved to untie his shoes, but he'd double-knotted them, and it took her a moment to get them undone.

"We should have gotten you slip-ons!"

"Wow, Sammie, you're blowing me away. Who knew you were this fiery in the bedroom?"

"You ain't seen nothing yet, Ginelli." She got his laces undone and his shoes off.

He stepped from his pants, and she shoved them aside. He stripped off his dress shirt, twirled it on the end of his finger, and let go, sending it flying across the room to land squarely in the doorway.

Samantha laughed, giddy and gleeful.

"C'mere," Luca said, reaching down to draw her to her feet.

She looked up at him.

He cupped her cheeks with his palms and peered into her eyes. "I am the luckiest man on the planet."

"We're going to have the best life together."

"Yes, we are."

"What we've been through has only made us stronger."

"Our bond gets tighter every day."

"And we're about to take a huge step forward." She crooked a finger at him and reached her hand back to pat the mattress.

"You ready for bed?" he murmured.

"I've been ready for ten months."

Samantha thought of what Luca had revealed to her at the reception. That he'd wanted her for a lot longer than the ten months they'd been dating, and she hadn't even known he'd been carrying a torch for her. At the time, she'd been so wrapped up in Nick and the legend of their Lightning Strike that she hadn't even considered anyone else.

Nick was her first love and the only man she'd ever been with. The weight of that hit her like an avalanche. She was thirty years old and had had sex with only one man, and now she'd just married that man's brother.

It felt Shakespearean.

Had she fallen for Luca simply because he was Nick's brother and the closest she could ever get to having her first love back?

A sobering thought. One that had been hovering at the back of her mind for some time. In marrying Luca, had she been trying to recapture the magic of what she'd had with Nick?

Luca was gazing at her with such happiness on his beautiful, dear face, she jammed those disloyal thoughts to the laundry hamper of her mind.

Did it matter what her secret motivations might have been in choosing Luca? Nick was gone for good, and she and Luca had something solid, unshakable. She felt that truth in the very center of her chest.

"I'm glad we released a sky lantern for Nick tonight," she said.

"Me too." The light in his eyes shifted and a somber expression tugged at his mouth.

Damn it, why had she brought up Nick?

Luca reached out and tucked a strand of her hair behind her ear. "This is me and you now, Samantha."

"Yes." She nodded, agreeing wholeheartedly.

"Just the two of us are climbing into that bed together. Let's leave old history at the door."

"I like that idea."

"I like *you*." His smile was a warm bath, heating her in all the right places. He picked her up again, and she loved how supported and cared for she felt in the circle of his strong arms.

She nuzzled his neck and ran her tongue along his jawline, took satisfaction with the moan she pulled from his throat.

"Oh, you just wait, missy. You're gonna get as good as you're giving."

"What a lovely promise."

She giggled as he placed her on the bed. When he stood above her, looking down with such love in his eyes, she knew this was exactly where she belonged.

Outside, she heard a noise on the deck but ignored it. There was a family of raccoons who showed up every now and again to use the pool as their watering hole. Her focus was on one thing and one thing only.

Luca.

He sat down on the mattress beside her and slowly started undoing the lace bustier, his fingertips brushing her breast, sending magical tingles spreading through her nerve endings.

The giddy sensation reminded Samantha of her first summer with the Dellaneys when they took her and Piper to Disney World. This moment had that same heady feel. The incredible awestruck disbelief that such a place existed and the exalted realization that it was true. In a sea of worldly troubles, an oasis of pleasure beckoned.

Luca kissed the bare flesh he'd exposed as he parted the lace. Her nipples hardened, eager to experience his warm, wet tongue.

Intoxicated, she threaded her hands through his lush, thick hair, enjoying the silky feel as the strands slipped around her fingers. She clung to him like a lifeline. Thrilled to be here. Fully engaged. Understanding this sweet moment was as good as life got.

She had it all. A handsome, hardworking husband. A loving family. A precocious daughter who excelled in school. A loyal best friend. A job she loved, working alongside people she enjoyed. A lovely home in a fun beach town. The best in-laws ever. She was living a Hallmark card life, and she was so very grateful for her blessings.

Luca's hands were all over her body, and she was kissing him as if tomorrow would never come. They were swept away, blinded by their escalating foreplay, racing toward the special moment when their bodies joined for the very first time.

Blood was pumping so hard through her ears, that her mind didn't register the footfall in the hallway until it was too late.

And then a raspy tortured voice spoke into the darkness of the bedroom and shattered everything.

"What the hell are you doing in bed with my wife, *brother?*"

PART TWO

THE HOMECOMING

What we have once enjoyed we can never lose. All that we love deeply becomes a part of us.

—Helen Keller

Samantha's hysterical screams rolled long and loud throughout the night, arriving one on top of the other and ricocheting around the room.

That terrifying sound grabbed hold of Nick Ginelli's soul and wouldn't let go.

Nick watched as his shocked wife leaned over the side of the bed, snatched up a fancy white dress that was lying on the floor, and clutched it to her bare breasts as she sank back against the headboard.

It was a wedding dress, his stunned brain registered. The same wedding dress she'd worn when she'd married him.

It took Nick a hot second to calculate that his wife had just married his brother, as evidenced by the strewn tuxedo and the beach wedding he'd seen when the Coast Guard ship pulled up to Sandrin Pier.

What he'd witnessed must have been *their* wedding.

His wife and brother had gotten married in the exact same spot where he and Samantha had held their ceremony. The impact literally knocked Nick backward and had him shaking from head to toe.

Maybe he was hallucinating the whole thing. Maybe his entire rescue had been just another delusion his damaged brain cooked up.

A few weeks into his isolation on the island, Nick had started hallucinating. In his peripheral vision, he would see people or animals, and think they were real, but when he'd whip his head around, nothing was there.

At times he got a weird sensation as if he'd been shot in the chest by pellets. At other times, his fingertips felt electrified, and whenever he touched something, the jolt would blast through his nervous system, leaving him fried and too fearful to move. For several months, it was a horror show as his brain played tricks on him and reality was totally distorted. Eventually, he recognized that his mind had gone haywire with the seclusion, and he was the only one who could salvage his sanity.

To keep the madness at bay, he sang to himself. He made musical instruments from coconuts, sticks, and stones. He composed songs and played air guitar, putting on concerts for the rats, birds, and insects. He made pets of them, giving them names and making up origin stories. Physical activity also helped, and he performed calisthenics for hours a day once he regained his strength after finding a regular supply of food and water.

But what kept him hanging on was the faith that his fellow Coast Guard members would keep searching for him no matter how long it took. He believed without question that he would be rescued one day. Holding that belief was the only way he survived.

Crippled by the inability to trust his own brain, Nick staggered against the open bedroom door, palm slapped over his chest, knees wobbly as a newborn foal. Of all the reunion scenarios he'd imagined over the past seven years, this one hadn't entered his head.

His older brother marrying Samantha.

It was a knockout punch and one that left Nick thinking he should have died on the island. Everyone would be better off, including him. Dry tears shook his body like an earthquake. Sorrow devoured him.

Luca, wearing nothing but black boxer briefs and a pugilistic expression, jumped between Samantha on the bed and Nick at the door. His fists cocked, ready to defend her with his life.

"Who the hell are you?" Fury contorted Luca's features as he roared in the harshest tone Nick had ever heard thunder from his brother's throat.

That question rocked Nick to his core.

Honestly, he did not know. Seven years alone on a desert island, without even a damn volleyball named Wilson as company, had rusted his social skills, shrunk his hubris, and splintered his identity. He was a shell of who he used to be, and he feared no matter what he did to heal, he couldn't fully recover.

The damage was simply too great.

Just like Nick, Samantha was trembling from head to toe. Their gazes locked, and in her eyes, he saw the most gut-wrenching expression he'd ever seen.

Samantha mumbled like a long-term psych ward patient, "It's not possible, it's not possible, it's not possible."

"What? What is it?" Luca appeared utterly confused. How could he not recognize his own brother? Had Nick changed that much?

Luca spun his gaze from Nick to Samantha and back again.

"We let you go," Samantha wailed with haunted eyes. "We released you. You're not here. You can't be here."

"Who *are* you?" This time, his older brother sounded utterly terrified.

Nick had handled this all wrong. Walking into the house, using the key he'd lovingly cherished for seven years as a talisman to keep from despair. He unlocked the back door, climbed the stairs, entered their bedroom, expecting nothing to have changed, assuming Samantha would just be waiting . . .

How many times had he envisioned Samantha falling into his arms, so very grateful that he'd returned? Raining kisses over his face, as she told him how much she loved and missed him. A million times, easily.

What a stupid, self-centered fool he'd been. He could not bear to imagine her moving on, so he simply hadn't.

He should have called first. Should have found a gentler way to break the news that he was very much alive. Actually, he had tried to call, borrowing a cell phone from one of the Coast Guard officers who had rescued him, but Samantha had changed her cell number, and when he'd tried to phone his parents, that call had gone to voicemail.

Understandable in retrospect. They'd been attending a wedding.

A fresh batch of sadness blew over him in icy blasts as he absorbed the cutthroat realization he'd only been minutes away from preventing his brother from marrying his wife. Two Coast Guard officers had escorted him down the stone pier as people lined up to watch, but Nick had been so out of it, he'd barely noticed the wedding party posing for pictures at the chapel.

Nick had been so desperate to see Samantha, to gather her into his arms and beg her forgiveness for leaving her. Fantasy and joy had ridden with him in the Coast Guard ship as they'd sailed away from that tiny Mexican island.

The island that had been his prison for seven years. He'd been so filled with gratitude for his rescue.

But now, here, this minute, reality bit hard.

While he'd been away, life in Moonglow Cove had not stood still awaiting his return. The world had moved on, and any hopes he'd clung to, those dreams of Samantha greeting him with wide-open arms and an overjoyed smile, vanished like smoke in a hurricane.

"N-Nick?" Luca stammered, dropping his arms and unclenching his fists. "Is it really you?"

For the first time, Nick caught sight of himself in the full-length mirror mounted on the wall near the closet. He squinted at his reflection, shocked by what he saw.

While he'd viewed his face in the bathroom mirror on the Coast Guard ship after his rescue, this was his first time seeing his entire body. He was dressed in a spare Coast Guard uniform they'd given him, because his own clothes were nothing but threadbare rags. It was the smallest size they could find, and still far too large on him.

A long scruffy beard covered his face, but facial hair couldn't hide the hollow of his cheeks. His eyes were sunken deeply into his head, and his body looked thin to the point of emaciation. There were bug bites on his skin, along with nicks and cuts on his arms and legs.

The Coast Guard had whisked him from the ship, down the pier, to an awaiting vehicle that delivered him to Moonglow Cove Memorial Hospital, where he'd been examined in the emergency room. That's where he'd been for the past several hours.

The ER doc had checked him out, done blood work, and given

him intravenous therapy, then urged him to get to his regular physician as soon as possible. The doctor had actually wanted to keep him overnight for observation, but Nick had refused. All he'd wanted was to go home and sleep in his own bed.

Nick stared at the skeletal man in the mirror, stunned at what he'd become.

A survivor.

No wonder Luca didn't recognize him. He didn't recognize himself.

Once upon a time, he'd been a burly bodybuilder. This scrawny version of himself was untenable to Nick's self-image. He knew he'd lost a massive amount of weight and muscle, but to see himself so gaunt was a shock, labeling the excruciating extent of his losses in stark visuals.

Silence descended over the room.

No one spoke.

Or moved.

One look on his dear wife's face and Nick Ginelli knew he'd lost her, and not just because she'd gone and married his older brother.

That could be easily annulled.

What couldn't be annulled was the way she was staring at Nick. Not overjoyed as if she'd spent the last seven years pining for their reunion the same way he had. She'd thought he was dead, and she'd moved on.

With his brother.

Luca and Samantha were transfixed, mouths open, frozen to the spot. It was up to Nick to break the spell. He was the interloper in his own home.

Give them time to process this.

"Get dressed," he said in a voice that came out thin and raspy, his vocal cords weakened from lack of practice.

Hand on the doorknob, he stepped into the hallway and shut the door closed behind him. It took all his mental, physical, and emotional strength to perform that simple act.

He closed his eyes, heard scrambling noises on the other side of the door and frantic whispering. He took a deep breath to steady his nerves.

What would happen next?

Another question. What should he do? Wait in the hall? Go downstairs to the kitchen? He was hungry even though they'd fed him before he'd disembarked the Coast Guard ship and they'd given him hyperalimentation at the ER. Was it impolite to rummage through the fridge that used to be his? He had been so long without human contact that he'd forgotten the rules of civilized society.

He stared down at the bandage on the back of his hand where the IV had been and felt stupid standing there waiting for his wife and brother to open the door, so he turned and crept downstairs.

In the kitchen, he flipped on the lights and was shocked again to see nothing was the same. Samantha had completely renovated the kitchen. Where had she gotten the money?

His life insurance? Coast Guard benefits?

Pushing aside that distressing thought, he sat down at the kitchen table and wondered what else had changed. Had she gotten rid of his motorcycle? His free weights? His pickup truck? His autographed baseballs?

Tightness screwed a hole in his chest. Two days ago, he'd been alone on a tiny island, spending his days gathering coconuts and catching fish. Even though getting home had been his goal for seven years, now that he was here, it felt eerie and surreal.

Maybe he *was* hallucinating.

He heard lowered voices coming down the stairs, closed his eyes, and braced himself for a conversation with his loved ones.

No dream.

He *was* home, but he was also a stranger in a strange land. Nick no longer belonged here. The world had moved on without him, not just Samantha. He heard the front door open and then click closed.

"Nick?"

He opened his eyes and saw Samantha standing in the door-way wearing a summery ankle-length dress and an expression of gobsmacked disbelief. Her feet were bare, and her brown hair tousled.

Inhaling sharply, Nick stared.

His wife was still the most beautiful thing he'd ever seen, and she took his breath away. Her hair was still done in a festive hairdo, although somewhat mussed now. She rubbed the toes of her left foot against the shin of her right leg and pulled one corner of her bottom lip up between her teeth. That hadn't changed. The un-conscious gesture that signaled she was nervous.

Nick didn't blame her. He was nervous too.

His eyes met hers. She blinked and dropped her gaze in that sweetly shy way of hers. That hadn't changed either.

His mind flew back to that long-ago Saturday morning when his mother had hired both her and Piper to wait tables at Mario's. Even though they had first met that Monday in the high school hallway, he'd been so busy with football practice, he'd been unable to fully explore the insta-attraction between them. He'd gotten her phone number and given her his, and they'd done some tentative texting and he'd chatted her up in the hallways between classes. He hadn't wanted to overwhelm her with that Lightning Strike business, but he'd known from first sight that she was The One.

When she applied for a waitstaff position, she hadn't known his folks owned Mario's, and when he'd come from the kitchen, flour dough clinging to his chef's apron, to ask his mom a question about the night's menu specials, he'd seen Samantha standing in the empty dining room with his mother, Piper, and Luca.

Luca had been staring at Samantha as if she was a bright supernova lighting up the night sky. His brother had looked like Nick had felt when he'd first seen her.

Awestruck.

No, no, no, his competitive teenage brain had yelled. *She's mine.*

"Nick," his mother had said. "Come meet our new employees, Piper and Samantha. They start tonight."

"This is your mother?" Samantha asked, looking delighted. "You and I will be working together?"

Nick had zipped across the room, draped his arm over Samantha's shoulder, and declared while locking eyes with his brother, "Luca, Mom, I want you to meet *my* Lightning Strike."

The memory brought a smile to his lips, but that was so long ago. So much had changed.

Samantha stayed in the doorway, hugging herself, barely meeting his gaze.

"Where's Luca?" he asked.

"He went to go get your parents and Destiny. Unless you don't want him to break the news to them. Should I text him and tell him to come back?"

Nick considered it. Which was better? Having Luca break the news or springing it on his parents and his daughter himself? Neither option seemed optimal but forewarned was forearmed. "I thought he'd at least stay and talk to me first."

"He said you and I needed time alone." She paused to draw in a deep breath and gestured in a northerly direction. "Luca lives across the street."

"Where? At the Wheelers' house?"

She nodded. "They downsized once their kids graduated from high school."

How freaking inane, talking about the neighbors at a time like this. "When did Luca move back from Alaska?"

"Almost a year ago, after your dad had a stroke."

"Dad had a stroke?" Rattled to his core, Nick stood up from the table, but arose too fast. His head spun and he had to grab hold of the kitchen counter to stay upright. What else had happened since he'd been gone? What other things had changed? He was terrified to find out.

"Your dad's okay now. Tino had months of rehab and had to step back from running Mario's and your mom went part-time. That's why Luca came home. To take over the restaurant."

And apparently, Samantha's heart.

"You and Luca run Mario's together now?"

"We do."

Nick slowly let out his breath through pursed lips, trying to wrap his mind around all the changes. On the island, the concept of time had ceased to exist as one day blended seamlessly into the next without variation. He'd lost track of exactly how many days, weeks, months, and years had passed since he was stranded. He'd only known it was seven years because the Coast Guard had told him so. Reorienting to this new reality was difficult.

"I went back to school to finish my bachelor's degree in accounting," she said, and put a hand on the doorframe. "I keep the books for the restaurant now."

"Good for you. You always did have a knack for math." That sounded so mundane, but he didn't know what else to say.

She nodded again and a long silence stretched out. All he heard was the ticking of the stove clock and the sound of his own breathing.

The distance between the kitchen countertop and the doorway where she stood was less than ten feet, but it felt like ten thousand miles. Nick wondered why she wasn't pelting him with a million questions the way the Coast Guard crew had. No doubt she was reorienting too.

"It really is you," she whispered.

"It's really me." He clenched his hands at his sides and waited for her to fly across the room and embrace him in a heartfelt hug the way she used to do when their love was fresh and new.

"We had a memorial for you."

"Yeah?" Nick rubbed the thumb of his right hand over the bandage on his left where the IV had been and drew comfort from the achy sensation. Pain was nature's way of letting you know you were still alive.

"Over five hundred people came to the service. We held it in the new megachurch on the outskirts of town because nowhere else could accommodate a crowd that large. You were much loved, Nick. There wasn't a dry eye in the place. Your death wrecked us all. Luca had to pull me off your coffin so they could lower it into the ground."

"You buried an empty coffin?"

"Yes. Coffin. Cemetery plot. Tombstone. The whole nine yards. It's what we all needed, some kind of closure. But the coffin wasn't empty. We made a time capsule of it. Put in the pieces of your sailboat that they'd found and some of your favorite things."

"Wow."

"Your folks added in your first baseball mitt, your baby teeth, and a lock of your hair. I put in the T-shirt you were wearing the day we met, your Mario's apron, and a copy of our wedding photo. Piper contributed a model of that Ferrari you always wanted, ticket stubs to a football game the two of you attended together, and your Coast Guard cap. Luca included the PlayStation you'd given him for Christmas one year, and a copy of *The Godfather*."

Nick winced. "My life in a nutshell."

"How are you feeling?" She took a step toward him.

His heart thumped, waiting . . .

But she stopped and went no farther.

There was so much more he wanted to say to her, but he had no idea of how to start a conversation that complicated. Not just because it was a tough topic, but because his brain simply wasn't as sharp as it once was, his memory hazy of what they'd even fought about that fateful day.

"I wish I could have been there . . . for the memorial service, I mean." He laughed too loudly, too shrilly. He sounded drunk or high. He supposed he *was* high on the adrenaline rush of his rescue, but the exhilaration was quickly wearing off as reality slapped him hard.

Samantha cringed. "Oh, Nick, what we've all been through!"

"So, you and Luca . . ." He threaded his hand through his long, shaggy hair.

"We got married tonight."

Hearing her confirm it was like an ax to his heart, and he still hadn't fully absorbed the reality. In his absence, his older brother had married his wife. He felt a fresh stab of betrayal even though he knew he had absolutely no right to feel that way.

He was the one who'd left. Samantha had done her best. He knew that, but it didn't quell the primal feeling of being karmically ripped off.

"Nick, you need to know that Luca and I . . ."

"Yes?"

"We—" She cleared her throat. "Well, we haven't slept together yet."

She hadn't slept with Luca! Hope, that fire-breathing dragon of possibilities, burned a blaze up his neck, as his cheeks flushed and his scalp tingled.

"Y-you haven't?"

"No."

"Why not?" If the roles had been reversed, Nick sure as hell would have bedded her. Or at least the old Nick would have. This new Nick was numb.

Samantha still wouldn't meet his eyes. "It just felt wrong not to wait until we were legally married, considering everything."

"Out of loyalty to me?"

"Partially." She nodded. "And we had your family and Destiny to consider, and it didn't seem right to either of us until you were officially declared dead."

"When was I declared legally dead?" he asked out of morbid curiosity.

"Two days ago."

"The day before I got rescued." Wow. They might not have had sex, but they hadn't let the ink cool on his death certificate before getting married.

C'mon. That's not fair.

"Really?" Her face paled. "What awful timing."

"Why did it take so long to get a death decree?"

"Even though we found the wreckage of your sailboat three years ago and held your funeral, the Texas courts said legally we had to wait seven years from the time you first disappeared."

Nick searched her face, trying to figure out what she was feeling, but she remained so stoic. Not at all like the openhearted Samantha he recalled. Then again, she'd been widowed, or had believed she was, and she'd raised their daughter on her own.

His gut wrenched for what she'd gone through, for everything they'd both lost. He wanted to go to her, gather her into his arms, and work to repair everything. But he no longer trusted his impulses. Seven years alone and he'd lost the ability to read people. Should he hug her? Keep his distance? Ask her what she wanted?

Samantha put a palm over her mouth and eyed him.

"What is it?" he asked, unnerved by the expression on her face.

"You look so thin." Concern knitted the spot between her eyebrows. "Are you hungry? Do you want something to eat?"

"Not right now, no." He moistened his weather-roughened lips with his tongue. "Can I . . . would it be acceptable for me to give you a hug?"

Various shades of emotions crossed her face as he watched her go from anxious to hesitant to afraid. "Of course."

She moved across the kitchen toward him, placing each foot deliberately in front of the other, as if she was a condemned inmate on execution day. This was not how he wanted her to feel. He wanted her to be thrilled to see him and thrilled to have him back.

Instead, she just seemed scared to death.

Of him.

Fair enough. He had just returned from the dead. He had to manage his expectations of what a joyous homecoming looked like.

He moved toward her, too, but his legs were shaking so hard, he didn't get far.

Slowly, she closed the gap between them, her gaze focused on his face. She looked uneasy, like a sailor studying a bloodred dawn.

"What's wrong?" he asked.

"I'm afraid I'm going to hurt you," she said. "You're just so thin."

His mouth twitched as he tried to smile and failed. "Ahh, Sammie, I screwed up bad."

Her arms went around him then and, to Nick's horror, he began to sob. He wanted to hug her back, but he couldn't move his arms for fear he'd topple over.

Samantha cradled his head against her shoulder and swayed with him in her arms, soothing him as if he was a baby. She smelled so good. He'd missed her fragrance so much. His tears dampened her dress, and he curled his fingers around her upper arms and held on for dear life.

She pressed her mouth to his ear and whispered, "Shh, shh, it's okay, it's okay. It's all over now. At long last, you've come home."

CHAPTER 13

True love stories never have endings.

—Richard Bach

Nick trembled in her arms, his thin shoulder blades sharp as knives against her palms. He was so different from the robust, cocky man she'd once known. Living isolated on a desert island had changed him in the most fundamental ways.

He might be home, but he was still lost, and she didn't know if he would ever find his way again.

Love for him poured from her heart, but it wasn't the crazy, so-hot-for-him-I-can't-stand-it kind of love that had brought them together. This feeling was more akin to her love for her daughter— rich and nuanced and unconditional.

Nick would forever and always hold a place in her heart, if not her life.

She wanted to wipe away his tears, tenderly kiss his forehead, and tell him everything would be all right, but that was a lie, wasn't it?

What had happened to him, to all of them, was a gaping wound that would divide the family for the rest of their lives. As much as she cared about Nick and wanted the best for him, she was with Luca now and that was a reality everyone had to accept.

Stepping back from her embrace, Nick swiped at his eyes and avoided her gaze as if ashamed of his tears.

"It's okay to be emotional," she said. "Perfectly acceptable."

He gave her a grateful smile and turned back to the table. That's when she realized how weak he was and that he needed a chair.

She sat down with him, heart in her throat. She had no idea what to say or do. The fixer in her wished for a magic wand so she could erase the past seven years and go back in time.

But if she did that, she wouldn't have Luca, and he was so much better for her than Nick had ever been.

The magnitude of what they were facing hit her hard, as a dozen different emotions of varying shades and intensity ebbed and flowed through her as strong as the Gulf tides.

She reached for his hand and held it.

Finally, he looked her in the eyes, his gaze filled with sorrow and regret. "I thought of nothing but you and Destiny and my family for seven years. The only thing in my mind, other than survival, was getting back home to you. But now that my dream has come true . . . I understand how shortsighted I was."

"It's nothing like you imagined." Woebegone, she squeezed his hand. "It's the same for me. Your homecoming is nothing like I envisioned either. In the beginning, before they found the wreckage of your sailboat and I had to accept that you were gone forever, I fantasized constantly about how it would be when you finally walked through that door."

Remorse was a bullet shooting from his eyes straight into her heart. "I caused this. It's my fault. I ruined us."

"You didn't cause the squall."

"No, but I went into the ocean without checking the weather.

In a fit of anger, I acted like an immature jerk, and we're both paying the price."

"You were only twenty-three, Nick. Still a kid."

The fact that he took responsibility for his actions impressed her. The old Nick wouldn't have admitted he was wrong.

Nick leaned in, closing the distance between them. He had a look in his eyes that said he wanted to kiss her.

Alarmed, Samantha jumped up, pulled her hand away, and hustled to the kitchen counter. "Do you want some coffee? I need some coffee."

He settled against the back of the chair. "Sure, I'll take a cup."

"That must have been so hard," she said, "going cold turkey from caffeine." Nick used to guzzle several cups a day.

Immediately, she realized it was such an inane thing to say and wished she'd kept her silly mouth shut.

"So many things were hard," he said. "Coming off caffeine was nothing compared to everything else."

"Of course, of course." She pressed a palm to her forehead.

She had so many questions about his time away but wasn't sure she was prepared to hear the answers. To mask her uneasiness, she got out a coffee filter and lined the basket, aware that Nick was tracking her every move.

"It's stuffy in here," he said. "I'm used to the open air. Do you mind if I raise a window?"

"Not at all. Switch off the AC first, though."

He got up to head for the hallway where the thermostat was located, and as he went by, his elbow brushed lightly against the middle of her back.

Intentional? she wondered.

His touch wasn't electric like it had once been. In fact, the slight contact made her feel adrift and lonely, as if cut from her moorings. She listened to his footfall in the hallway and the click of the air conditioner shutting off.

He returned to the kitchen, went to the windows, and struggled with the latches. "I think I've lost my fine motor skills."

"The latches are probably just stuck from the humidity and lack of use. I don't open them often."

When the noisy coffeemaker fell silent, Samantha poured two mugs of coffee, black for him, cream and two sugars for her, and carried the mugs to the table, where he'd sat back down after he'd pried the windows open.

She joined him at the table once more, but this time she sat at the far end instead of right beside him. She told herself it was so she could see him better but, honestly, she didn't know what she'd do if he tried to kiss her, and she wanted to remove the temptation.

They sipped in silence for a moment, but then it felt too weird not to talk. "Tell me about the island you were on. How big was it?" *What a stupid question, Samantha.*

"About the size of Moonglow Cove."

"Did you have shelter?"

"I built a hut. It took me over a month to construct with only a utility knife. Plus, I kept thinking I'd be rescued and why waste the time and energy . . . but when days became weeks, and the rainy season started, I knew I was in it for the long haul." He laughed, a dry, rusty sound. "Little did I know just how long."

"Oh, Nick, I am so sorry this happened and so very glad you're home."

"Are you?" He studied her with serious intent.

"I am. Truly, I am."

He stared at her down the length of the small kitchen table, his gaze drilling into her, and the room seemed to shrink. An overwhelming sense of foreboding shoved against her chest, and she had a sudden urge to sprint from the house they'd bought together, jump into the car, scoop Destiny up from her in-laws, and just drive until she ran out of road.

The one thing she'd wanted for her entire life—a loving home and family of her own—was in grave jeopardy, and the man across from her, a man she still loved on some level, was the cause.

Wind billowed the curtains, and the chill sent goose bumps up her arms. The sound of the pounding ocean waves filled her ears, and the earthy scent teased her nose.

Nick took a sip of coffee, closed his eyes, and sighed. "Such a simple thing. A good cup of coffee. I used to take it for granted." He opened his eyes, found her gaze again. "I took so much for granted."

"Do you want something to eat?" she asked, feeling dumb because she already asked him once, but she didn't know what else to say. In the Ginelli family, food equaled love. "Although, since we were leaving town for two weeks for our honeymoon, I cleaned out the fridge. But I could find something . . ."

"Really, don't worry about it. I'm not used to eating much and my stomach has shrunk. Plus, they gave me supplemental nutrition at the hospital."

"When?"

"Tonight."

While she and Luca were at their wedding reception. "I remember when you could eat two Big Macs, a chocolate shake, large fries, and still be hungry an hour later."

"Yeah." He gave an embarrassed half smile. "I was a glutton."

This was not the man she'd married. Never in a million years would the old Nick have recognized his central flaw and accepted it as fact. He *had* been a glutton. He'd possessed a relentless craving for adventure and a willingness to put his hungry desires above everything else. He'd always wanted more—a faster car, a louder sound system, a bigger house.

The old Nick would have dug in to his justifications and rationalizations, proudly arguing that he needed more calories because he was Coast Guard and went to the gym every day. When his clothes got too tight, he would complain that she used too hot of water in the wash and had shrunk them.

Timid little mouse that she'd been, Samantha wouldn't have contradicted him. Her need for a loving family was so great, she'd feared rocking the boat, and so in everything, she'd acquiesced to Nick.

He was her Lightning Strike, after all.

It occurred to her then just how much the old Nick had enabled her helplessness and how much she'd changed as a consequence of living without him. She'd learned to be independent and self-sufficient. She'd raised a child on her own, and she'd discovered just how strong and resilient she really was. Once upon a time, she'd needed him. Now, Samantha Riley Ginelli could take care of herself.

"You're different," he said.

"So are you."

They stared at each other. He had fresh tears in his eyes.

As did she.

And then the back door slammed open so loudly, Samantha and Nick both jumped up from their seats.

Piper blasted into the kitchen, red-faced and breathless. "Nick! Gawddam! You mother trucker! You're alive!"

Samantha watched Nick smile as if the sun had come out after forty days and forty nights of torrential rains.

Piper's eyes were wild and wide as she looked Nick up and down. "Gawddam, Nick, good gawddam."

"Hey, Piper." Nick gave her a sheepish grin.

Piper flung her arms around him and held on tight. "I could squeeze the stuffing out of you! You're alive, you're alive, you're gawddam alive." She pounded his shoulder and hooted. "You tough son of a bitch."

He laughed. "I got lucky."

"We need to take you to Vegas and run the blackjack tables. Hot dog! You're back!" Piper did a little victory dance. "We have to *celebrate*! You got any hooch in the house, Sammie?"

"Nick's folks and Destiny are on their way over. Maybe we should hold off on the liquor," Samantha said.

Piper's gaze searched Samantha's face. "How are *you* holding up?"

Samantha shook her head. "It feels like a dream."

"She's stunned," Nick said.

"Hell, who's not?" Playfully, Piper swatted his shoulder and met his eyes again, a helpless grin overtaking her face. "Nick Ginelli, as I live and breathe. You survived, you old dog!"

"How did you find out about Nick?" Samantha asked Piper.

"From the guards who rescued him. It's not every day we find an island castaway. Never mind a castaway who's one of us."

"I'm confused how you got from the ship to the ER to the house, especially since you had no money or a phone," Samantha said. "I saw the ship in the bay but couldn't imagine you were on board."

"Four Coast Guard members escorted me down Sandrin Pier," Nick explained. "They had called ahead to have a car meet us at the seawall, so we didn't have to navigate all the way around to the marina on the opposite side of Moonglow Cove. Especially since the hospital and our house are so near Sandrin Pier. At the hospital, the Coast Guard driver stayed with me until I was released." To Piper, Nick said, "The guy wasn't anyone I knew. No one on the vessel was, but they all knew of me."

"It was Pete Griniere. He's a probie."

"Yes. Pete took me home from the ER and dropped me off at the curb. He offered to come inside with me, but I declined."

"The logistics aren't important. What's important is that you're home." Piper enveloped Nick in another hug. "I'm so damn glad you're alive."

"Me too."

Piper ruffled his hair and laughed. "Shaggy."

He beamed at her. "Maybe I'll let you cut it."

"Sammie, you got any scissors?"

"I do, but it's after midnight and Luca's bringing Marcella, Tino, and Destiny here as we speak," Samantha said.

"Later then. Do you want to talk about what happened to you, or is that just too much too soon?" Piper asked Nick.

"CliffsNotes version. A squall blew up while I was sailing in the Gulf. I battled hard. Got knocked overboard, but I had a life vest on. I passed out, and then when I woke up, I was on the island. I spent seven years trying to signal to passing boats and aircraft. Finally, it paid off and the Coast Guard rescued me." Nick said it fast, his words falling one on top of the other.

"That's putting it in a nutshell. Guess you'll leave the rest for therapy, huh?" Piper laughed.

Yes, Samantha thought. They would all need therapy. Nick most of all.

Nick shrugged as if his ordeal had been no big thing. "The sun rose and the sun set. Rinse and repeat. Somehow, I made it through."

"I can't imagine what that must have been like for you. Not having anything to distract you from yourself." Piper patted Nick's arm.

Going through Coast Guard training with Nick and then working side by side with him for years, Piper knew Nick well. Maybe more than Samantha did. Nick hadn't been a contemplative guy, and he'd had seven years to do nothing but think.

"Well, I better scoot," Piper said. "Just had to come by and hug your neck. We'll debrief later. Maybe while I give you a haircut."

"Don't leave!" Nick grabbed for Piper's elbow.

He sounded desperate to keep Piper in the room. Was he that afraid of being alone with her?

"I mean," he amended, "don't go too far away. You're right. We *do* need to celebrate."

"Sammie? Do you want me to go, or should I hang around for moral support?"

"You're family," Samantha said. "Of course, we want you here for the family reunion if you want to stay."

No sooner had she said that, than they heard the sound of Luca's vehicle pulling into the driveway.

"They're *herrre*." Piper drew out the last word and made a comical face.

Nick looked as if he might throw up.

"What can I do to help you prepare for meeting your daughter?" Samantha asked, realizing she needed to speak to Destiny before the child met her father for the first time. Luca might have told her daughter about Nick, but it was her job as a mother to make sure Destiny was truly prepared for this moment.

"Turn back the clock seven years." Nick's tone was mournful.

"I wish I had a magic wand," Samantha said. "But I don't. Please give me a minute with our daughter before everyone comes barreling in."

With that, she walked out the back door, leaving Piper and Nick alone in the kitchen.

CHAPTER 14

It is a curious thought, but it is only when you see people looking ridiculous that you realize just how much you love them.

—Agatha Christie

Samantha went outside to intercept the Ginellis before they entered the house. Luca was leading the way, carrying Destiny,
her head resting on his shoulder, her little arms looped around
his neck.

"Hey," Luca said.

"Hey."

They stalled in the driveway, just looking at each other as his
parents came up behind them.

"Could you put her down?" Samantha asked Luca. "I need to
talk to Destiny before she meets her father."

"Sure, sure." Luca set Destiny on the ground.

Her daughter was sleepy-eyed, and her hair was mussed. Samantha wanted to hug her tight to her chest and never let her go,
eager to protect her from the fallout she knew was coming and
couldn't keep from happening.

"Is it really true?" Marcella asked, coming around Luca and
carrying a covered dish with her. "Nick is alive?"

"He's alive."

All the air left Marcella's body in a loud whoosh, and for a second there, Samantha feared the diminutive woman would topple right over. Samantha moved to slip her arm around her mother-in-law's waist.

"Are you all right?" Samantha asked.

"I've never been more right." The wobble in Marcella's voice hit Samantha like a visceral punch as she tried to imagine how she would feel if she believed Destiny was dead only to learn she was alive. The rapture would overwhelm her.

Marcella shoved the covered dish in Luca's hand. "Take this. I gotta go see my boy."

Luca accepted the dish and stood there looking out of his depth.

Marcella took off for the back door, with Tino trailing behind her as Samantha turned her attention to her daughter. She took Destiny's hand and guided her toward the patio table.

Luca hovered. He seemed uncertain whether to stay with her or go with his parents.

Samantha smiled tenderly at him. "Go on inside with your folks."

He gave a nod and went into the house.

"Destiny . . ." Samantha took both of her daughter's hands into her own. "How are you feeling?"

Her daughter gave an uncertain shrug, moving one shoulder forward and the other back. "I dunno."

"What did Luca tell you?"

"That my daddy's not dead like everybody thought. That he was living by himself on a faraway island all this time."

"What's happened is very unusual. It might feel weird for you. It feels weird for me too."

Destiny nodded. Samantha shook her head, trying her best to put herself in her daughter's shoes. How would she feel if she learned her parents hadn't died in that tornado? She believed she'd be overcome with joy, but there would be fears and uncertainty too.

"Do you have any questions for me?" Samantha asked.

"Are you still married to my dad and not Luca?"

Samantha blew out her breath. "I don't know. We'll have to talk to a lawyer."

"Will we still live here?"

"For now. Yes."

"What am I supposed to do?"

"Nothing. You don't have to do anything you don't want to do."

"I don't have to hug him?"

"You do not."

"Do I have to call him 'Dad'?"

"No, but you might want to. Give him a chance, Destiny. He is your father." She felt like she was walking a tightrope stretched across the Grand Canyon.

"But he left us."

"Not intentionally. He didn't mean to."

"What if I don't like him?"

"It's okay to be unsure. Just give it time. Things will be all right, I promise. I'll be with you. I'll be right by your side like always."

"But, Mommy . . ." Destiny hesitated.

"Yes?" Samantha gently squeezed her daughter's little hands. "You can tell me anything."

"What if he doesn't like *me*?"

* * *

His mother was the first one through the door—moving like a supersonic bullet, she shot straight for Nick, her arms outstretched.

"Ma!" Nick grabbed his mother and swept her into a hug.

Speaking in rapid-fire Italian, she told him how much she loved him, how happy she was that he'd come home, how very much she'd missed him. They were both crying, tears streaming down their cheeks.

She enveloped him in the heartiest of hugs and patted his cheeks. "This is the happiest day of my life!" she exclaimed. "My boy! My bambino! You've come home to us! You've come home!"

Once she'd finished hugging and kissing him, Marcella moved out of the way to stand beside Piper as his dad came next.

His father was sobbing almost as much as his mom. Nick noticed Pop's mouth drooped a little on the left side. Tino clapped him on the back in a warm embrace while his mother danced around them, giving anxious commentary.

"You are far, far too thin." His mother went up on her toes to pinch both of Nick's cheeks. "We must fatten you up."

"I missed your cooking something terrible, Ma," he said. "I used to dream of your lasagna and chicken Alfredo and pasta e fagioli."

"We must have a party." His mother clapped her hands, excitement wreathing her face. "A homecoming feast. I will make all your favorites."

"And we will invite all your friends," Pop added.

Luca came through the door, and his parents stood on either side of him as his older brother came over for his hug.

Things felt simultaneously weird and wonderful.

Silence fell, then everyone spoke at once, and then they all fell silent again. That's when the door opened one final time, and Samantha entered holding the hand of a precious seven-year-old girl.

This had to be Destiny.

My daughter.

Nick felt as if God's fist had reached from the heavens and punched him dead center in the heart.

The girl looked at Samantha, then dropped her gaze, obviously nervous about meeting this scarecrow of a man with shaggy hair and a long scruffy beard.

"Hello," he said, moving toward his daughter as everyone fell out of his way. "You must be Destiny."

Destiny bobbed her head. She looked so much like he had as a child that it was downright freaky.

It suddenly hit Nick exactly how much he'd lost. Seven years of this child's life, instead of being with her, he'd been cracking open coconuts, spearfishing with a sharpened stick, and trying his best not to die.

And it was all his fault.

As he looked at her, twin electrical bolts exploded inside him. One white-hot, the other stone-cold. They ricocheted in different directions, streaking a trail of contrasting temperature throughout his body. One bolt was self-recrimination, the other self-acceptance. One bolt led to his brain's black hole. The other drove away from that dark impulse, led to hope and salvation.

To this girl.

His bright sweet light.

Nick could either give in to despair and wallow in all he'd lost. Or he could find his way back to life. He glanced from his daughter to Samantha, who was standing right behind Destiny, hands on her shoulders, watching him with cautious eyes.

She smiled encouragingly, love glistening along with her tears.

Nick saw his answer there. Samantha and Destiny were worth fighting for. He wouldn't allow his emotional and mental despair to get the better of him. He'd keep the black moods and hopelessness at bay. He'd do his best to heal.

For them.

A crumb of real hope roused him from his pit of despair. Despite all the odds stacked against him, he'd made it back home. If he could accomplish that, surely he could win back Samantha's heart and repair their marriage. They had the Lightning Strike after all. It would take a lot. He knew that, but he and Sammie were meant to be. The universe had brought them together again. There was a grand divine plan for their lives.

As for Luca?

He cringed. He hated that his brother was caught in the middle, but Nick and Samantha were destined. Luca knew that. And yet, the last thing Nick wanted was to hurt his brother.

Too late for that.

"Do you remember me?" Nick asked, squatting in front of his daughter.

Destiny shook her head, looking wary. What a stupid thing for him to ask. Why would she remember him? She'd only been a few weeks old when he'd gone out in that boat.

"I'm your daddy."

"My daddy died."

"People thought I was dead," Nick told her. "But I wasn't. They searched and searched and searched for me, but they couldn't find me."

"You must be really good at hide-and-seek."

"Indeed. I'm the hide-and-seek champion."

Destiny eyed him. "Do I hafta hug you?"

Slowly, he shook his head. "No. Not until you want to. Not until you're ready."

"Okay." His daughter looked relieved, and her relief stung, but he couldn't choose to wallow in that—no matter how deep his damage, he wouldn't make this about him. Destiny had a lot to process. As they all did, but they could do it together as a family. He was optimistic about their chances except for . . .

Luca.

Nick looked up at his brother. His eyes burned Nick's face like hot coals.

"Brother," Nick said. "Could I speak to you outside?"

Luca nodded.

"Let's go into the kitchen," Samantha said to the rest of the family. "And heat up those leftovers."

While everyone else went into the kitchen, Luca and Nick stepped out into the temperate night. Just seven short hours ago, Luca and Samantha had been on the beach saying their "I dos."

He and his brother stood on the back patio, gazing up at the stars and saying nothing. Complicated emotions closed a fist around Nick's heart. There were a thousand snarky, unkind things he could say to his brother, that he *wanted* to say, but he bit down on his tongue. Pettiness was the wrong move, plus he'd been away for seven years. Presumed dead. He had no right to be upset.

Instead, Nick turned and opened his arms to his brother. "Can I have another hug?"

Luca's face cracked open as his grin split from ear to ear, and he reached for Nick. "C'mere, baby bro."

They clasped each other in a back-slapping embrace, and damn if a tear didn't spring into Nick's eye. To compensate for the maudlin emotions, he punched his older brother lightly on his upper arm the way they'd done as boys in their pugilistic play.

"I'm so glad you're alive," Luca said, his own eyes shiny in the glow from the backyard security light. "After they found the wreckage of your sailboat, we all gave up hope."

"*I* never gave up hope," Nick said. "I knew I was coming home to Samantha and Destiny, or I'd die trying."

Luca stepped aside and the awkwardness charged back at full force.

"I want to thank you for taking care of Samantha and Destiny while I was gone," Nick said, feeling oddly out of breath.

"Of course."

"This is gonna be hard for us. Sorting out our lives."

Luca jammed his hands into his slacks. Slacks that had been part of his wedding tuxedo.

"It sucks."

"Everything's changed."

"Yeah."

"How'd you survive on that island?" Luca asked.

"I had the Swiss Army knife you gave me for Christmas when I was in high school. I used it for everything from filleting fish to building a shelter. I don't think I would have survived without it. Thanks for the gift, big brother. You saved my life."

Luca met his gaze. They studied each other intently. Nick wondered if his brother felt the same wariness creeping up the back of his spine. How could his brother have courted Samantha? It felt like such a betrayal.

You were dead to them, numbskull. You should be thanking him for looking out for your family.

"What'd you do for water?" Luca tightened his arms over his chest.

Nick stared at his brother's bunched biceps. Luca was strong and robust whereas he was just the opposite.

It was a switchback.

Growing up, Nick had been the burly one. Now, with his muscles in a dwindled state of starvation, Nick was weak, and he hated it. He'd always depended on his body to carry him through life's challenges, and honestly, if he'd been a little less fit before the shipwreck, he probably wouldn't have survived.

"Collected rainwater, dew, anything I could. Finally, it dawned on me to follow the birds, and I discovered a freshwater source on the island."

"Great survival skills."

"I learned a few things in the Coast Guard."

"It must have been crazy hard for an extrovert like you to be alone for so long."

"After a while, the mental survival was harder than the physical," Nick said.

Nick wasn't feeling sorry for himself, just stating facts. He'd done what needed doing. He'd had a singular goal. Stay alive so he could get home to his family, and damn if he hadn't achieved it—but now that he was here, he was starting to realize just how shortsighted he had been. He hadn't thought about what would happen next.

"What are we going to do about this?" Luca asked, clenching his hands at his sides as if he was considering punching something.

But Luca was even-tempered. Nick could count on the fingers of one hand the times he'd seen his brother truly upset, and none of those instances had been directed at Nick. It was more than just the clenched fists that concerned him. It was the look in Luca's eyes.

Or rather, lack thereof.

His brother was staring blindly through Nick as if he wasn't even there, as if he was a ghost. Which, he supposed, until now, he had been.

He tried to put himself in Luca's shoes. How would he feel if the situation was reversed?

Nick gulped.

Only one of them could win, and the odds were in Nick's favor. Not only was he the one legally married to Samantha, but she was also his Lightning Strike, and nothing could stop fate. He felt sorry for Luca but not at his own expense.

And then something else occurred to Nick, something that shook him to his soul.

What if Samantha didn't want him back?

CHAPTER 15

Your task is not to seek for love, but merely to seek and find
all the barriers within yourself that you have built against it.

—Rumi

Staring up at the Big Dipper, Luca marveled at the expansive-
ness of the universe and hauled in a deep breath. He was a
man yanked in opposing directions. His new wife on one side of
the equation, and his little brother on the other.

And there was no easy fix.

Legally at least, as far as he knew, Samantha still belonged
with Nick. The family legend underscored it. Samantha and Nick
had enjoyed a fated love, and Luca was out in the cold.

Except Luca knew in his heart of hearts that he and Samantha
were a far better match than she and Nick had ever been. He
was thrilled beyond joy that his little brother had returned. How
could he ever regret that?

But with Nick's return came the loss of Luca's new bride.

By nature, Luca was a cautious man. He thoroughly researched
Consumer Reports before buying big-ticket items. Nightly, he
checked the weather to prepare for the next day. He insured everything, and he even had prepaid funeral arrangements. He held
a spotless driving record and yearly maxed out his 401(k) contri-

butions. Fiscal responsibility came as easily to him as breathing. Luca kept his bank statement balanced, his automobiles maintained, his lawn clipped at regulation height, and his emotions in check.

Except right now his feelings were coming out hard—shocking and blindsiding him with unexpected explosions.

Sweat had pearled on Luca's upper lip, and he swiped it away with the back of his hand. "I'm so happy you're home, little brother."

"Are you?" Nick's tone was flat, dead.

"You doubt it?" He cast a sidelong glance at Nick as they stood on the brick patio. A patio he'd built for Samantha. In his head, Luca heard the slow crank of a handle and the strains of "Pop Goes the Weasel."

"Samantha looks good," Nick said, husky-voiced and tentative. "Really good."

Pop! Jealousy. The old green-eyed monster.

Luca stuffed his envy back down—damn it, he was *happy* Nick was home—and shut the lid tight. *All around the cobbler's bench . . .*

"When she hugged me, I just about came out of my skin because it felt so good to be held in her arms again."

Pop! Fear. That hand-wringing anxiety.

Jamming the implications of Nick's return as far into the box as it would go, Luca imagined inserting a key and ticking the lock. But the song's refrain still echoed. *The monkey chased the weasel . . .*

"It was like no time at all had passed," Nick went on. "She smelled exactly the same."

Pop! Grief. The tear-flowing, snot-slinging sense of loss.

Luca wrestled with his sadness but couldn't quite corral it. He could feel Samantha slipping through his fingers, and that deepened his bereavement. How selfish was he? His little brother had been through hell and back, and Luca was thinking only of how it impacted him.

Pop! Shame. Cheek-burning, stomach-churning, I-don't-deserve-to-draw-breath shame. A good person wouldn't think like this about his own brother.

You're still being selfish, bucko, focusing on your bad feelings. Kicking yourself doesn't change a thing. Stop it.

"Thank you for taking care of my family while I was gone. It means the world to me."

His brother was so thin, it was scary. He was a frail copy of his former self. "What did you want to say to me in private?"

"It's weird being around people again. My social skills are nonexistent. Hell, listen to my raspy voice. I'm not even used to talking."

"You didn't talk to yourself out there?"

"After a while I got pretty sick of listening to me . . . That's when I started singing Simon and Garfunkel's 'Sound of Silence' over and over again."

"Dad's favorite."

"Mom wouldn't let him play it at the restaurant because it wasn't on brand, but he'd blast S and G at home."

"Cheers to Simon and Garfunkel for helping you keep it together."

"Hello, darkness." Nick gave a shudder.

Luca folded his arms over his chest, felt his skin tighten and his scalp tingle. "So . . ."

"So?"

"What was it *really* like?"

"What do you mean?"

"You got kicked in the teeth hard by Mother Nature. Did you gain any insight on life? On mortality?"

"I didn't think about it much. It's different for y'all. You guys thought I was dead, but I knew I wasn't."

"Did you experience a crisis of faith? Or a moment where you realized *aha*, this is why we're all here? Any pithy takeaway from the experience?"

"You want to know my take on the meaning of life after seven years in isolation." Nick studied him with a hard-edged gaze.

"Yeah."

"Do whatever you have to do to survive. Set traps for rats so you can skin 'em and eat 'em. Swallow fish eyeballs for extra protein. Earthworms taste pretty damn good when you're literally starving to death."

Luca winced, wishing he hadn't asked and wondered why he had.

"I learned that life isn't about grabbing the brass ring or making bank or being the best at what you do," Nick said. "When you're totally alone in nature, everything has a cost—food, water, sleep. Life revolves around the tremendous effort it takes to meet your basic needs. There's no energy to squander on philosophy or esoteric musings."

"I suppose you're right. I hadn't thought of it like that."

"I pray to God you're never in a situation like that. You learn to fight for everything—every breath, every bite, every bathroom break. It's all precious because it can slip through your fingers in a heartbeat. You *have* to struggle. Every single minute of every day. From the second your eyes open in the morning, you're in a battle. You battle the weather, the wildlife, the boredom, and your own freaking mind. All while realizing that I would most likely die out there. I can't tell you how many times I almost gave up."

Luca felt a knife stab inside his heart. "What kept you going?"

"Thoughts of Samantha," Nick said. "And Destiny."

"I can't wrap my head around it."

"No. No, you can't. Not really. Not until you've been there. Winning, losing, victory, despair. It's all ongoing, coexisting at the same moment."

"Wow, it sounds to me like you learned a lot."

Nick leveled a hard gaze at his brother. "Fair warning, brother. I'm winning her back."

"Wh-what?" Luca blinked.

"Just so you know. She's *mine*."

"Shouldn't you let Samantha decide that?" Luca asked, keeping his voice measured and his eyes steady on his brother.

"She wants me," Nick said.

"You don't know that."

"I'm her Lightning Strike."

"You've been gone for seven years. The same amount of time you knew her before you left."

Growling low under his breath, Nick stepped closer and toed off with him. His Coast Guard–issued shoes touched the tips of Luca's sneakers. "I didn't survive for seven years just to let you walk away with her."

Luca hardened his jaw. "I was here for her. You weren't."

"I was lost at sea. Not. My. Fault."

"You took the sailboat out without checking the weather. That *was* your fault."

"So, it's all my fault that you stole my wife?"

"No," Luca said. "It's your fault because you walked out on her in the first place. You acted like an entitled spoiled brat. Fatherhood was tough, you got in an argument, and you went out recklessly. You didn't act responsibly . . . and really you never did."

"You're not going to step aside? I've returned. She's my wife. Get out of my way."

Luca held up his left hand, flashing the wedding band on his finger for Nick to see. "I'm married to her too."

Nick stared down at his bare left hand. "I may have lost my ring, but I don't need it. I married her first. Legally, she's mine."

"Samantha's not a possession," Luca said. "She's a fully grown, living, breathing woman. She's smart and loyal and kind, and she deserves to be treated with the utmost care and consideration."

Nick puffed out his chest, dropped his shoulders, and lifted his chin, his familiar cock-of-the-walk stance. But what had worked on a robust twenty-three-year-old looked downright silly on an emaciated thirty-year-old.

Luca laughed.

Nick scowled. "And you don't think I can deliver?"

"I know you can't." Luca's voice turned flinty. "You're too selfish. You didn't put her needs first. Well, I *do* put Samantha above all else, and she's gotten used to being treated with respect. You're gonna find that a pretty damn hard act to follow, brother."

Nick grunted. "You're right."

"Huh?" Luca relaxed the fist that he hadn't even realized he'd clenched.

"I was a selfish prick. Leftover legacy from being the star quarterback in high school, I guess."

"The Golden Boy."

Nick locked eyes with Luca. "I'm not the same guy I was."

Luca held his brother's stare. "You don't look the same, granted, but when it comes to your behavior, that's something you'll have to prove."

"I'm winning her back."

"See? That right there tells me you haven't changed one bit. Samantha's not a trophy to be won, and I won't play these childish macho games with you, Nick. Too much is at stake."

"You may have the lead right now, but I'm coming for her, Luca, and fair warning: I've spent seven years relying on my wits and cunning."

"Wait, did you hear that?" Luca cocked his head. In their conversational pauses, he thought he'd heard something digging in the trash cans. A raccoon or an opossum or a stray cat.

"What?"

This time, Luca clearly heard the metal rattle.

Nick jumped back and craned his neck, his eyes wild and his breathing rapid. He grabbed a tree branch off the ground and cocked it over his shoulder like he was batting cleanup. The veins at his temples bulged, and he charged toward the noise in the dark.

Running after his brother, Luca thought, *He's got PTSD.*

* * *

THE SHOCK OF the camera flash sent Nick stumbling backward, as he dropped the tree branch to raise his arms defensively and cry out. He was back on that island and the rats were coming after him again.

"Hey!" Luca shouted from behind him. "Stop that! You're trespassing!"

His brother was coming to help him. Warmth spread through Nick's body. Luca had always taken up for him.

There were bugs crawling on him, bugs, bugs, everywhere. Nick swatted wildly at himself, trying to get them off. He tripped over a broken flowerpot and fell backward, whacking his head against the concrete.

Luca rushed over. "Nick, Nick, are you all right?"

"Bugs!" Nick heard the terror in his own voice. "Get them off me!"

"Nick." Luca was on the ground beside him, holding Nick in his arms and rocking him. "You're off the island, you're home, you're home."

"I-I'm home?"

"You're home, buddy, you're home. There are no bugs on you."

* * *

Someone shone a flashlight in Nick's eyes, and Luca could see the man behind the light with a video camcorder resting on his shoulder.

"Jorge," Luca growled through clenched teeth. "What do you want?"

A giddy laughter. "Got all I need. Thanks."

They heard footsteps sprint down the driveway and then the sounds of a motorcycle starting.

"Damn it," Luca muttered.

"What is it?" Nick asked. "What's going on?"

"That was Victor Jorge, an attention hound with over a million followers on his YouTube channel featuring wedding scandals," Luca said. "Hold on to your sanity, little brother. Your rescue is about to go viral."

CHAPTER 16

My wish is that you may be loved to the point of madness.

—André Breton

By five in the morning, the adrenaline of learning that Nick was alive had worn off and everyone was drained. They'd spent the past few hours listening to an encapsulation of Nick's seven years on the island and devouring appetizers left over from the wedding that Marcella had wisely packed when they'd driven over with Luca.

In a strange way, it felt like old times.

A bittersweet nostalgia settled over the family, and no one wanted to leave. Finally, Piper bid them goodbye and went home. Destiny was passed out on the couch.

"Ma, Pop, why don't you sleep here?" Samantha asked. "Luca can drive you home after we've all had some rest."

"That sounds good." Marcella nodded and nudged her husband. "Come on, Tino. Let's head to the guest room."

Tino linked his arm through his wife's, and Luca watched his parents make their way down the hallway to the spare room on the first floor. Leaving Luca, Samantha, and Nick to sort out who was sleeping where.

More than anything in the world, Luca wanted to stay with Samantha. They were all three sitting on the living room couch, with Samantha in the middle, Nick to her right, Luca to her left.

"I need to put Destiny to bed," Samantha murmured, gazing at her daughter. She got to her feet, yawned, and stretched.

Luca noticed Nick was watching Samantha with hot longing. "You'll bunk at my house."

His brother frowned. "I'll sleep here."

"Not in Samantha's bed," Luca growled.

"No, no, of course not." Samantha shook her head. "We can't just go back in time."

"You're throwing me out of my own house?" Nick sounded hurt.

Luca met Samantha's gaze. She looked so conflicted. He felt her angst like a bullet passing through the center of his chest.

"I'll put the blow-up mattress in the home office," Samantha said. "It's really comfortable."

Nick pressed his mouth together in a tight line, as if he might protest. "Sure."

Luca blew out a breath.

"Nick, could you carry Destiny upstairs to her bed?" she asked.

"Sure thing." Nick hopped up quickly, but in his haste, lost his balance and had to grab hold of Samantha's arm to stay vertical.

"All you all right?" Samantha asked.

Nick winced. "Just got up too fast and spun my head. It happens."

Luca's gaze locked on Samantha's hand wrapped supportively around Nick's elbow.

Pop! Jealousy.

"I'll carry Destiny," Luca said to Nick. "You're in no shape. If you get dizzy while you're climbing the stairs with her, you'll both go down."

"I'm fine now," Nick said.

"You don't look like you could carry a sack of sugar much less a healthy seven-year-old." Luca stood and pulled his spine up to his full height, three inches taller than his little brother.

Nick narrowed his eyes.

Luca jutted out his chin.

"Tell you what." Samantha moved to where her daughter was sleeping. "I'll carry Destiny."

"You're my family," Nick said. "I'm coming upstairs with you."

Samantha put up a palm. "No."

Pop! Schadenfreude. *Pop!* Guilt over the schadenfreude. Luca was not a person who took pleasure in the struggle of others.

Right now, you are.

The smile fell from Nick's lips. "Please?"

"Honey . . ." Samantha said.

Pop! Right back to jealousy.

"You're getting ahead of yourself. Right now, we all need time to adjust to our new circumstances. And the best way to do that is to get enough sleep, eat right, stick to a routine, and let things settle down."

Luca feared Nick might protest. His face clouded and he grunted, but then he nodded and accepted Samantha's rules.

"All right," Nick said. "I understand."

Samantha gave Nick a wistful smile.

Pop! An aching sense of loss.

Luca couldn't just accept his fate as second best. He had to do something to pull ahead in the fight for Samantha's affection. He loved her too much to give up just because Nick had come first.

Before Samantha could stop him, Luca gathered his sleeping niece in his arms and started for the stairs.

* * *

SAMANTHA WATCHED FROM the doorway of her daughter's room as Luca settled Destiny into her bed. Her emotions were all over the place, flying from one thought to another, from one brother to the other.

Initially, she was irritated with Luca for carrying Destiny upstairs after she made it clear she'd do it but, honestly, she was just so tired, she had no energy for an argument. Right now, all she wanted was to fall into bed and sleep for twenty-four hours solid.

Luca pulled the covers over Destiny and turned to leave the room. Closing the door behind them, he asked, "How are you holding up?"

"I don't know." She paused. "How about you?"

"I don't know either." He shrugged, but his eyes looked haunted. All she wanted to do was wrap her arms around him and tell him everything would work out, but she couldn't do that because she was still trying to convince herself.

"I'm happy Nick's back," she blurted.

"I am too, I am too," Luca said in a rush as if he feared she doubted him.

"It's tough," she said. "For all of us."

He nodded, his mouth twitching at the corners the way it did when he was trying to keep his feelings in check. "It's going to get even tougher once this hits the national media."

"I know."

"That damn Victor Jorge."

"If it wasn't him, it would be someone else. It's a unique story. No matter what we do, we'll be bombarded."

There was such hunger in his eyes, and fear too, lurking there. She didn't blame him. She experienced the same conflicts.

"We should be boarding a plane to Fiji right about now," he said.

"I know."

"Is it bad that part of me wants to grab our bags and just flee?"

"Luca," she said, too overwhelmed with her own inner turmoil to soothe him. "Please don't say things like that. I can't make sense of this right now."

"Hopefully we can get our money back because of a family emergency since we have travel insurance. I'll call the airlines and hotels and excursions and let them know we'll be canceling," Luca said.

"Thank you for taking care of that. It never even crossed my mind in the midst of the biggest upheaval of our lives."

He reached for her then, and she let him draw her to his chest, eager for comfort. For the longest time, he just held her, and she let him.

She breathed in the scent of him, this man who'd come to mean so much to her, curled into his warmth and tried to still her wildly jumbled thoughts.

Tightening his grip on her arms, Luca pressed his forehead to hers. "I love you."

"I love you too."

And she did! So much. But she also loved Nick and had no idea where her loyalties lay. None at all. She wanted Luca. They were so good together. But Nick was her Lightning Strike and the father of her child. He seemed deeply changed . . . and for the better.

Did she owe it to Nick to honor their marriage vows? What about her vows to Luca? What would Nick's return do to their entire family?

"I want you," he whispered against her ear. "More than ever."

"Oh, Luca." She wrapped her fingers around his arm and squeezed so that he understood she was too conflicted right now to deal with this.

She didn't want to hurt either brother, but there was no safe harbor. Nothing that would spare them all pain. There were no easy answers here. No right or wrong. Just complexity and complications.

"Sammie . . ." He raised his hand and cupped his palm against her cheek, his voice loaded with intensity, his dark-eyed gaze drilling into hers.

"Luca." Her heart ached at the situation they found themselves in.

"We'll figure it out," he whispered. "Together. You and me."

"What about Nick?"

It came back to that, the thorn in their sides. Immediately, she felt guilty for even thinking that. What a wonderful miracle that Nick had returned. It *was* a miracle, and eleven months ago, his return would have been the greatest gift from God.

But now? The timing couldn't have been worse. They were all going to get damaged, and there was no way around it.

And that was it. The crux.

Luca caressed her jaw with a knuckle. "We were so close, almost there . . . but deep down inside, I knew it was too good to be true."

"No." She shook her head. "No. It wasn't."

He enfolded her in his arms, and her treacherous body responded instantly to his touch. She rocked her hips against his.

A ragged groan escaped from his chest and pushed up into his throat. *"Sammie."*

His hand slid into her hair at her neck, his fingers splayed, cradling the back of her head as he peered into her eyes for what seemed like eons. He wanted to make love to her, she could see it in his hungry gaze, and she ached for him equally.

Luca lowered his head.

She didn't protest or back away.

He was going to kiss her and, God help her, she wasn't going to stop him. She shouldn't do it. She knew that. Letting him kiss her would make an already byzantine situation worse, but she needed to feel the heat of his mouth on hers, craved something to sear away the doubts and fears and turmoil churning inside of her.

For one sweet agonizing moment, she tasted the honeyed lips of her groom.

Slowly, he tugged her closer, deepening the kiss. Instinctively, she pressed her body into his, clinging to him like a life preserver, taking a brief respite in this moment, knowing full well a category-five hurricane was on the way.

His hand in her hair, he tilted her head back, giving him deeper access to her mouth. His body swayed into hers as he edged a muscular thigh between her legs, his knee triggering her most sensitive spot.

A soft moan slipped from her as she inhaled his breath and swallowed the warm taste of him. How could something feel both wrong and oh-so-right at the same time? She had done nothing wrong—this man was her husband and this was her wedding night—and yet she felt so horribly guilty.

Kissing him was exciting and bone-thrilling, so daring and brash. Heaven help her, she was lost. Swept away in heat and passion.

The primary bedroom was so close, just across the landing from Destiny's room. Half a dozen steps and they'd be there.

Luca nipped lightly at her bottom lip, and his hands roved over her body. He kissed the little valley between her lip and her nose, traced her upper lip with his tongue, then nibbled at her chin, her earlobe, her throat. His mouth explored her, teasing, coaxing, driving her crazy with throbbing need.

Frantically her heart galloped in her chest, desire sweeping her body in waves of heat. She allowed herself the indulgence, knowing that this could be the last time they ever kissed, considering what was happening to their family.

It wouldn't go past kissing. She knew that. Luca had so much self-control and honor—but, oh, how she wished they could.

A fresh wave of guilt knocked her back. What would Nick think if he walked upstairs right now and caught them like this?

No.

This was wrong.

She spread her palms across Luca's cheeks, fingers splayed, and pushed. "We have to stop."

"I know." He looked devastated.

She felt the same way. "Luca . . ."

He reached up a finger to brush away the tear trickling down her cheek, his own eyes misty and forlorn. "I need . . . I need . . ."

"To know if I'm going to choose you or Nick?"

Mutely, he nodded.

"I-I can't."

"Can't choose?" he asked. "Or can't be with me?"

She shook her head, another tear tracking down her other cheek. "It's all too much to absorb. You've got to give me some space."

"Sammie."

Trembling inside and out, she stepped from his embrace.

He reached for her, but she eluded his grasp. "Don't you still want me?"

"Can't you tell?" Her chest heaved with the heaviness of her emotions.

"But you want him too."

"I don't know," she said. "I just don't know."

"I'm here to help you figure it out, and if you choose Nick, I'll accept it." He reached for her again. "But you have to know, Nick isn't right in the head." He told her what had happened outside the house when Victor Jorge snapped Nick's picture. "I fear he has PTSD."

"I wouldn't be surprised."

"I don't want him alone here with you and Destiny. Not until he's had a thorough mental and physical examination."

"Agreed."

Moistening his lips, Luca reached for her again.

She shied away. "Please," she begged. "Please just go."

He looked as if he wanted to say something more. To press the issue, maybe? But that wasn't Luca's style. Instead, he kissed the top of her head, whispered, "Sweet dreams," and then walked downstairs and out the front door.

Samantha stayed stock-still, listening to his footfall on the stairs and staring at herself in the wall mirror as misery crawled through her.

Who was she now? The woman staring back at her.

Who did she want to be?

This morning, she'd wanted to be Luca's wife more than anything in the world, but that was shattered. All she knew was that she couldn't go back to being the naïve girl who'd first married Nick. Too much had changed. But how could she move forward with Luca when things were so complicated?

No matter what choice she made, they would all get badly wounded, and there was simply no way around the pain.

CHAPTER 17

Maybe love was superstition, a prayer we said to keep the truth of loneliness at bay.

—Leigh Bardugo

After several restless minutes, Samantha fell into an uneasy sleep. She had the graveyard nightmare again, except this time, when she fell against the tombstone, Nick arose from the grave and zombie-grabbed her.

And she woke up screaming.

"Sammie, Sammie, it's okay, it's okay, you're all right." Piper's soothing voice broke through her terror. Her foster sister sat on the edge of the mattress and gathered Samantha into her arms.

"Wh-what are you doing here?" Confused, Samantha blinked and tried to wrap her sleepy brain around her new reality.

"I came to check on you."

"Why?"

"Um, because of last night. Don't you remember?"

"Is it true?" She clung to her friend. "Is Nick really alive?"

"Yes. He's still asleep."

Feeling more grounded now, she wriggled from Piper's embrace and sat up to press her back against the headboard. "Destiny?"

"Marcella and Tino took her home with them. They figured they'd get out of the way while you and Nick and Luca sort things through. Although Marcella is expecting us all to come over for a big celebration dinner tonight."

"That was considerate." Although none of this would be easily sorted and the ramifications of Nick's return would have a devastating ripple effect she was just now beginning to understand.

"What day is it?" Time was a blur.

"Sunday."

"Really? It seems a decade since last night."

"I know." Piper patted her hand.

"If it's Sunday, that means we can't even talk to a lawyer yet and figure out our legal options."

"You mean about annulling your marriage to Luca?"

"Actually, I suppose the first step is making Nick undead." Samantha kneaded her temples. "This is such a mess."

"But you're happy Nick's back, right?" Piper gave her a cryptic sideways glance.

"Yes, of course. I'm just overwhelmed."

"So's Nick."

"I'm sure . . . you and Luca are as well." She thought about telling her friend that she'd kissed Luca in the wee hours of the morning but decided against it. She ran a hand through her hair, still stiff with hair spray from her fancy wedding hairstyle. "What time is it?"

"Noon. When did you go to bed?"

"Dawn."

"You should go back to sleep."

Shaking her head, Samantha threw off the covers. "I need to see Destiny and make sure she's okay."

Piper put a restraining hand on Samantha's arm. "Maybe you should give her some time to process this."

"You mean without me?"

"Put your own oxygen mask on first, Sammie. Then you'll be strong enough to be there for Destiny."

It made sense, but every motherly instinct she possessed was pushing her toward her daughter.

"Self-care," Piper said. "Want to go to Sunday brunch at Mc-Gillicutty's?"

"It feels weird to go without the family," Samantha said.

"If you ask me, the Ginelli family needs some breathing room from each other. You guys are always up in each other's grill. While it's nice to have support, sometimes boundaries are in order."

Samantha wasn't going to lie. She wanted to do the exact opposite of what Piper suggested. Like Marcella, she needed to gather everyone for a big celebration of Nick's return.

"There's time enough for a party," Piper said, reading her mind. "I told Marcella the same thing."

Samantha reached for her phone on the nightstand. "Let me just text—"

Piper grabbed the phone away from her and stuck it into her hip pocket. "Nope."

"Hey!"

"As maid of honor, I'm pulling rank. You need clarity. Let's go."

"I'm not up for the crowd at McGillicutty's," Samantha said, grateful for Piper's intervention. Her friend was right. Samantha's emotions were piling up hard and fast, and she could barely think her way through the fog.

Nick was back. Luca had kissed her. Samantha had let him. Not only let him but encouraged it. Oh! This was miserable.

"Fine. We'll hit a food truck and walk the pier." Piper held out her hand.

Her friend was a force of nature. When Piper got it into her head to make something happen, it happened, and Samantha was in no mood for a battle. Resigned, but appreciative too, she sank her hand into Piper's and let her friend tug her off the mattress.

* * *

As Piper and Samantha were strolling the pier, Nick, alone in the house that used to be his, showered and put on his old terry cloth bathrobe that he'd found hanging on a hook in the bathroom.

He fingered the material. Samantha hadn't thrown his old robe away—that had to mean something, right?

The bathroom mirror was fogged. He'd stood so long underneath the hot water, trying to sort through the horde of emotions ganging up on him and failing miserably.

He rubbed a hole in the mirror mist with his terry-cloth-covered elbow and stared at his reflection. Gaunt features. Weather-roughened skin. Haunted eyes. Shaggy beard.

He didn't know this stranger in the mirror.

How could he expect Samantha to know him? Or want him back? Gut-punched, his knees wobbled, and he sank against the wall to keep himself upright. No wonder she'd shrieked when she'd seen him. He looked awful.

Nick had survived seven years on a desert island by himself and he'd made it home.

But to what?

The man in the mirror said, "Maybe you should just walk away. Be the bigger man. Leave her and Luca alone. They're happy. Don't ruin it for them."

And do what with his life?

Live in the same town with them? Work with them at Mario's? Sit across the dining room table with them on holidays and pretend that it was okay that his brother had stolen his wife?

Not fair. You know that's not fair.

Luca had been looking out for Samantha and Destiny. He should be grateful, not jealous. Yeah, "should" was one thing, truth was another.

Nothing about this mess was fair. To any of them. Not one single thing. Grief-stricken, Nick jammed his hands into the pockets of the bathrobe and touched something in the right pocket.

Curious, he pulled it out.

And found himself staring at two photographs of him and Samantha, attached to one another by black yarn burned almost through. A single thread was still holding them together. The yarn was sooty and smelled of smoke.

Nick sucked in his breath so loudly, the sound echoed in the confines of the bathroom. He didn't know what this was about, but the message was clear. Samantha had been trying to separate them through some kind of ritual, but she hadn't completed the severing.

Why not?

And why had she left the pictures in the pocket of the robe?

Did he still hold a piece of her heart?

Shifting his attention back to his reflection, Nick notched up his chin and met his own eyes. "You can't give her up without a fight. Come hell or high water, you've got to win her back. No matter what it takes."

Win Samantha back!

The imperative lit up Nick's brain like a favorite song. He was behind the eight ball on this one, but he'd had seven years to think of ways to make amends. He'd been petulant, taking his sailboat out when he was angry and not checking the weather. What kind of Coast Guard officer didn't check the weather before he went to sea?

A foolhardy lunkhead. That's who. A young dumbass who thought he was stronger than any weather pattern. A cocky jock who arrogantly believed he could handle whatever Mother Nature threw his way.

Ha!

Yes, he'd paid a high price for his folly, but he couldn't surrender his marriage without a fight.

Win Samantha back!

Nick left the bathroom wearing the bathrobe, realizing he had no clothes to put on and no phone to call anyone to take him shopping.

Feeling out of step with the entire world, he flopped down onto Samantha's bed, the bed that used to be theirs, overwhelmed by her scent on the covers, and just sobbed, so very grateful to be home at long last.

Then he heard the front door open and Luca calling his name.

* * *

WHILE NICK WAS having a meltdown, Samantha and Piper ambled the boardwalk, noshing on soft tacos. Being outside in the ocean breeze banished Samantha's drowsiness, but now everything seemed fraught with meaning.

Cumin on her tongue had never tasted so earthy and warm.

The chugging of the roller-coaster car laboring up the incline and the excited screams of passengers as it rushed down had never sounded so thrilling. She watched a family—mom, dad, and young daughter—shoot water guns at balloons on the midway and thought about all the times Nick hadn't been with her and Destiny for the simple things. The events he'd missed out on from Destiny's first step, to her losing her first tooth, to her first day of school.

The old pain cut into her heart as fresh as the day the Coast Guard found the remains of Nick's sailboat. The day she'd finally given up all hope that he'd return home to them.

That was when she realized she couldn't count on her in-laws forever. She had to take charge of her future. That was when she'd gone back to finish her accounting degree. On Nick's urging, she had dropped out of school when she'd gotten pregnant with Destiny. He'd promised to take care of her so she could be a full-time mom.

After Nick's memorial service, she'd tried her best not to think of him, but that was impossible. Working at Mario's and being so close to her in-laws kept him foremost in her mind. Nick was woven into the fabric of her life, and she'd learned to live in the shadow of grief.

Grief that had changed and molded her, just as it had them all.

Reclaiming her own interests, which she'd packed away when she'd met Nick, had helped her mute the sorrow into acceptance. And now, she was expected to do a one-eighty and change her mindset and her orientation to the world.

Within seven years, she'd gone from young wife and mother, to widowed single mom, to an accidental bigamist. Samantha had emotional whiplash, and her brain was idling in neutral.

"You were right, I needed to get out of that house." She finished off the taco, wiped her fingers on a napkin, and flipped it in a nearby trash can.

"Never doubt the wisdom of a Coast Guard officer," Piper said sagely.

Unless he goes out in a sailboat without checking the weather. "I wonder what Nick will say when he learns you outrank him now?"

"Nick has bigger concerns than competing with me."

"Oh yeah," Samantha said, as more implications of Nick's return occurred to her, and she thought about what Luca had told her last night. Did Nick have PTSD? She certainly wouldn't be surprised to learn this was the case. "He can't just return to work, can he?"

Piper stared at her. "Hello? Cleopatra, is that you?"

Samantha crinkled her nose. "What are you talking about?"

"That river in Egypt you're paddling down."

"Denial?"

"Big-time. What Nick went through changes a person forever. Look at him. He's trashed. His mind is shot. It'll take *years* for him to come anywhere close to normal, much less hold down a full-time job as demanding as the Coast Guard."

Reality was a hammer knocking at Samantha's skull. *No easy way out.*

"Resuming his old life will be an adjustment. It's gonna take time . . . lots of time."

It felt so daunting. Not just for Nick, but for the entire family.

Piper leaned over the rail and tossed the last bite of her taco to the seagulls. One scavenger bird caught it, and the others chased the bold guy, trying to get their share. Piper watched the gulls for a moment, then turned her head to eyeball Samantha. "If you and Nick even *want* to resume your old life."

"God, it's so complicated." Samantha sighed and touched her lips, remembering Luca's kiss and battling the wall of guilt building higher by the moment. "Things are such a mess."

"At least Nick came back before you and Luca had sex. That makes things easier in that regard."

Samantha rarely kept secrets from her foster sister, but she wouldn't tell her about kissing Luca this morning. Not that she feared Piper would judge her, but because she was ashamed of herself. She should have been stronger. Should have resisted.

Piper rested her hand on Samantha's. "It'll all work out the way it's supposed to."

"Easy for you to say. You don't have two husbands."

Laughing, Piper slung her arm around Samantha's shoulder and leaned in to touch their heads together. "My friend the bigamist."

"Piper, what am I gonna do?"

"What do you *want* to do?"

"I have no idea. Last night, all I wanted was to marry Luca and build a great life together. Now . . ."

"Are you unhappy that Nick came home?"

"No! He's the father of my child. His death almost killed me . . ."

"But?"

"It's been seven years. He's changed. I've changed. We're strangers to each other. Piper, we were apart as much time as we were a couple."

"So, you might choose Luca?" Piper asked.

Was that a hopeful note in her voice? Did Piper think she should choose Luca? Or was Samantha merely projecting her own wishes onto her friend?

"What's your opinion?"

"Oh, no, no." Piper raised both palms and backed up. "Don't drag me into deciding this."

"But you've been there since the beginning, and you know me better than anyone else. I really want to know what you think I should do."

"Not going to weigh in."

Blowing out her breath, Samantha glanced down the boardwalk at the happy couples holding hands. She spied a sandwich-board sign sitting next door to the Wall of Funhouse Mirrors. The sign featured an Eye of Horus logo levitating over a crystal ball and the name Madame D'Veaux in goth scroll lettering.

Clichéd to be sure, but Madame D'Veaux targeted tourists who expected a traditional aesthetic from their vacation fortune-tellers.

"I know," Samantha said. "Let's go see Madame D'Veaux."

"That old fraudster?" Piper snorted.

"She confirmed that Nick was my Lightning Strike, remember?" Fourteen years ago, fresh from her encounter with Nick in the high school hallway, she and Piper had come to Paradise Pier after school that same day, Samantha still aglow from her insta-crush.

If Madame D'Veaux hadn't been treading water in an end-of-summer financial slump and offering two-for-one readings, they wouldn't ever have even considered going in. Twenty-five dollars for sixteen-year-olds was a budget-buster. As it was, giggling and giddy, they scraped up twelve-fifty apiece, grabbed each other's hands, and stepped through the beaded curtains into the dark interior of the psychic's inner sanctum.

After the reading, Samantha had emerged one hundred per-

cent convinced she and Nick were meant for happily ever after. Now, standing in front of the sign, with the memory of how
elated she felt after that visit, Samantha interlaced her fingers
through Piper's.

"Her prices have doubled since our first reading. That's ridiculous."

"Let's do it anyway. Let's go in."

"Okay, but this is just for fun. You don't really believe she has
psychic powers, right?"

"I don't believe, but sometimes you just need someone to tell
you something that you already know deep in your heart, but
can't see the forest for the trees."

"Hmm, I gotta have a moment to wrap my head around that."

"So, you'll do it?"

"No, but I'll watch you have your cards read or whatever."

"Yay." Samantha gave her friend a spontaneous hug. "Thank you."

"Lead on." Piper waved at the tent. "But remember, the old gal
knows just how to manipulate."

CHAPTER 18

They say a person needs just three things to be truly happy in this world: someone to love, something to do, and something to hope for.

—Tom Bodett

Inside, they found the wizened woman wearing a lavender mantilla wedding veil, layers of gauzy black and purple fabric, rings on every finger, and numerous jangling bracelets. A lifetime of coastal living was etched in every road-map line on her face, her tanned feet were bare, and her toenails painted midnight black.

The room smelled of soured washrags and patchouli, just as it had the first time they'd visited.

The psychic looked a bit like Yoda if the Star Wars character had been purple instead of green and told fortunes on a boardwalk in Moonglow Cove. She possessed that same kind of mysterious wisdom. On a small card table in front of her sat a crystal ball, a deck of tarot cards, a melted black candle in a dish with dragon heads on it, and a dispenser of hand sanitizer.

"Come in, come in." She waved languidly, her bracelets clinging together in a melodious sound. "Madame D'Veaux sees all, knows all."

"Except the importance of sunscreen," Piper whispered behind her hand to Samantha.

Samantha widened her eyes at Piper, sending her a signal to knock off the snide comments, and lightly tapped the tip of her sandal against her friend's ankle.

"Sit," Madame D'Veaux commanded, nodding at the two metal folding chairs positioned in front of the table.

Samantha eased into the chair directly in front of the woman and rubbed the leather strap of her purse with her thumb. Okay, yes, she was nervous.

Madame D'Veaux held out her hand. "Fifty dollars, cash, card, or Venmo accepted."

Piper held up her palms. "I'm not here for a reading, just moral support."

Madame D'Veaux scowled. "Then you must leave. Your sister's reading is not fodder for your entertainment."

A chill went up Samantha's back. How had Madame D'Veaux guessed they were sisters of a sort? She and Piper didn't resemble each other in any way.

"I'm not leaving." Piper folded her arms, brought her right ankle to her left thigh, and tipped back in the chair.

"Then no reading." The shriveled woman scooped up the tarot cards. "Negativity disturbs the spirits."

"*I'm* the negative influence?" Piper raised her eyebrows.

Madame D'Veaux pinned Piper with an unblinking stare. "There is a darkness in you the spirits don't like."

Piper? Darkness? Her friend was the bubbliest person Samantha knew.

"Yeah," Piper said. "It's called a healthy skepticism. C'mon, Sammie, let's get out of here."

Samantha knew her friend was just trying to help, but Piper's combative stance ruffled her own feathers. "Please, could you just wait outside?"

"Seriously? You're still going to do this?"

"Don't judge me. I'm in a tailspin."

"And you just loaded the gun for this faker. Now she doesn't even have to do a cold reading. Mark my words, she'll tell you to embrace the chaos or some such nonsense." Piper shook her head, arms still folded tightly across her chest, her scowl deepening.

In that moment, Piper looked so much like Nick—or at least the way Nick used to be—cocky and so secure in her own rightness, that Samantha was taken aback.

"Piper, please."

"Fine, fine." Piper flung her hands into the air. "I'm leaving, but I'm not going far. I'll be outside making faces in the funhouse mirrors."

"Thank you." She gave her friend a grateful smile.

Piper left, and the tent flap made a sucking noise as it fell closed behind her.

"Fifty dollars." Madame D'Veaux's open palm extended to Samantha's face.

Samantha hesitated. Was this worth fifty dollars? Feeling slightly stupid, but still aching to know which way to go, she dug in her purse for one of the hundred-dollar bills she'd gotten from the bank for honeymoon travel. Dropping the bill into the woman's withered hand, Samantha waited for her change.

"Tarot, palm reading, or crystal ball?"

"Tarot," Samantha said. It's what she'd done the first time, and she liked sticking with the tried-and-true.

"Very well." Madame D'Veaux picked up the deck of strange-looking cards and began to shuffle. "Now, you must clarify your intention and expectations."

"What does that mean?"

"What do you want to know, and why do you want to know it?"

"I want to know if—"

Madame D'Veaux put up her palm. "Wait, don't tell me, just think it."

"Okay." She wanted to know which husband to choose because nothing was more important to her than her family.

"Got the question clear in your mind?"

"I do."

After a few more shuffles, Madame D'Veaux put down the deck. "Cut into three stacks."

Samantha cut the deck and watched the woman reunite the cards and deal them out. On the black velvet cloth covering the table, she fanned out all the cards.

"Pick three. These cards represent your past, present, and future," she said. "Take your time. Run your hand above the cards, and when your fingers start to tingle, pick that one."

Samantha nodded and slowly selected three cards.

When she was done, Madame D'Veaux turned over the card representing Samantha's past. It was the Page of Wands and depicted a dapper young man holding a staff. Samantha took one look at it and thought, *Nick.*

"This card stands for someone who has strongly influenced your current situation."

That was sure true.

"It can indicate new beginnings, or a wrong path taken in your past. Since the card is in the past position for this reading, it most likely means the latter, but not necessarily." Madame D'Veaux picked a piece of lavender lint off the black velvet and let it drift to the ground.

Honestly, it could be both. Nick was her path in the past, but she could have a new beginning with him.

And leave Luca behind?

The thought sent a rush of panic surging through her veins.

Madame D'Veaux turned over the "present" card that Samantha had selected. The Five of Wands. It featured five men, each wearing a different style of clothing and carrying raised sticks as if they were shaking them at a protest rally.

"The meaning of the Five of Wands is conflict, disagreements, competition, tension, and diversity. It's chaotic," said Madame D'Veaux.

Chill bumps popped out on her arms. The card nailed her current situation to the wall.

"How will the conflict end?" Samantha asked, rubbing her palms over her upper thighs.

"Let's look into your future. This card shows what's just around the corner for you." The woman flipped the remaining card.

The Four of Cups.

Depicted on it was a young man seated beneath a tree with four cups in front of him, and one of the cups was being offered to him via a cartoon cloud.

"What does this one mean?"

"The Four of Cups represents a strong emotional retreat from the discontentment you will soon experience. A new opportunity will present itself. Your challenge is not to retreat as you have done in the past, but to accept the opportunity life is offering you and move forward."

"What does that even mean?"

Madame D'Veaux shrugged. "That is for you to decipher."

"Can't you give me any better answer than that?" Frustrated, Samantha tugged on a lock of her hair, just as she'd done as a kid when she landed in a new foster home.

"Listen to your heart. It knows the way."

So not helpful. "Um, thanks. Could I have my change please?"

"Would you like to buy a love talisman?" From a black box on a side table, Madame D'Veaux took out a necklace with a pendant of two lovers locked in an embrace. She arranged it on the card table in front of the crystal ball.

"What's it supposed to do?"

"Protect you in love." The elderly woman paused for effect. "It will prevent you from making poor romantic choices and keep your heart safe and help you break old destructive patterns and find a new way of being in the world."

Way too late for that. "What makes you think I need it?"

Madame D'Veaux stared at her, unblinking as a lidless lizard, and repeated her tagline. "I see all, I know all. If you want a better life, you have to change. There is no other option."

Samantha ran a finger over the pendant necklace, surprised by the quality. She'd expected some trinket made in China, but the medallion of the lovers was hand carved, and the chain was real silver. "How much?"

"I only offer this deal to my most loyal customers."

"But I'm not a loyal customer," Samantha said.

"You have been here before."

Wow, Samantha was impressed that the elderly woman remembered. "Yes, but that was long ago, when I was in high school."

"And now you are back." The woman smiled. "That makes you a loyal customer."

"How much is the necklace?"

"For you . . ." The old woman slanted a speculative glance at Samantha.

"Fifty dollars," Piper hollered from outside the tent at the same time Madame D'Veaux said, "Fifty dollars."

Piper stuck her head around the flap. "See? I'm psychic too."

Madame D'Veaux left her seat, drew herself up as tall as she could, and pointed a bony finger at Piper. "Out! Get out right now."

"Not without my friend." Piper marched inside, grabbed Samantha's arm, and yanked her from the tent.

Samantha was still holding that talisman. "I guess I just bought this."

"You want to go get your fifty dollars back? I can handle that."

"No, no."

"The old bat was suckering you. Trying to wring out every bit of that hundred dollars. Surely, you can see that."

She didn't get upset with Piper often, but when her foster sister horned in and started taking charge of Samantha's life, that's when she got irritated.

Samantha glanced over her shoulder at the fortune-teller's tent. "I like the pendant."

"Do you? Or did you just like the idea of it?"

"You were eavesdropping."

"Of course, I was. I don't trust that creature any further than I can throw her, although considering how much I can dead lift and how tiny she is, that might be quite far."

"While I appreciate your concern and know you only have my best interests at heart, I can fight my own battles, thank you."

"I know, but sometimes you're just too nice."

"Sometimes," Samantha said, "you cross boundaries."

"Okay, I'm the asshole, but that old woman was taking advantage of your vulnerability. You're not in a good place right now and you're grasping at straws. I should have been more respectful."

"Yes, you should have."

Piper reached out both hands. "Forgive me?"

Her foster sister spoke with such heartfelt conviction, that Samantha couldn't stay mad.

She placed her hands in Piper's. "I forgive you."

"Whew, 'cause it'd kill my soul if anything ever happened to our friendship."

Samantha felt the same way. She'd known Piper and her family longer than she'd known anyone.

"Turn around. I'll put that pendant on you," Piper said.

"Thanks."

Was Madame D'Veaux right? Were her ideas about love holding her back? It was a startling concept, and her mind jumped on *what if*.

What if she and Nick hadn't been destined after all? What if the Lightning Strike was nothing but a fun fable? What if the Ginelli clan were all involved in a multigenerational delusion and she'd just jumped on board?

It was a radical idea, shedding off the skins of an old belief system that had once served her so well. She wasn't the same person, and Nick's homecoming had simply magnified that truth. Should she go back in time and try to be who she used to be? Or should she move toward a future with Luca? What would she need to do to resolve things? How would her actions affect her family?

What she needed was a sign. A directive from the universe about which path to take.

There you go with the magical thinking again. Open your eyes. See reality right in front of you. Accept it.

No matter what she did, she couldn't win. The one thing she'd worked her whole life to achieve—a stable, loving home—was about to go up in smoke.

And she didn't need a psychic to tell her that.

CHAPTER 19

Love makes your soul crawl out from its hiding place.

—Zora Neale Hurston

Whdat shall we do now?" Piper asked. "Wanna go on the Juggernaut? Get the juices flowing. The line's short."

"I need to get back," Samantha said, fingering the necklace at her throat. "I've been away for too long. Things are up in the air, and I need to check on Destiny. I need to find out how all this is affecting her."

"Sure, sure."

"May I have my phone back?" Samantha held out her palm.

"Oh yeah, I forgot I had it." Piper dug around in her pocket for Samantha's phone and passed it to her.

Samantha turned the phone on and saw dozens of texts. From Luca. From Ruth. From Marcella. From friends and acquaintances. News was getting out about Nick, and her phone had blown up.

"Ugh," Samantha muttered.

"That bad?"

"It's just going to get worse." From the long list of texts, she saw one that might have been from Nick and scrolled to it.

Luca took me clothes shopping & 2 get a phone. Wanted
U 2 have the #.

That was it. Sent ten minutes earlier. Nothing else from him.
"Nick's got a phone," she said to Piper.

"I know, he texted me while you were in there with Madame
D'Veaux, and I told him we were at the pier. He must have gotten our numbers from Luca."

"C'mon, let's get out of here." She stuffed her phone into the
pocket of the new summer dress she'd planned to wear in Fiji and
turned toward the wedding chapel parking lot where they'd left
Piper's SUV.

As they neared the chapel, Samantha heard someone calling
out over the noise of the amusement park.

"Help! Please help me!"

Samantha looked at Piper. "Did you hear that?"

"Sounds like a kid."

They looked for the child, but the wind picked up the little
voice and swirled it around, and they couldn't tell what direction
it came from.

"Help! Help!"

"Let's split up," Piper said. "I'll search the parking lot. You go
to the side of the chapel."

Scanning the area, Samantha scuttled around the corner of
the stone building as Piper went toward the parking lot.

"Up here!"

Samantha glanced up.

There, on the window ledge of the bell tower, twenty feet
above the ground, crouched a young girl about Destiny's age. The

girl lifted her hand to wave but tottered precariously and plastered herself back against the side of the church, stark fear on her little face.

Samantha's heart stuttered. The child was going to fall!

"Don't move!" Samantha hollered. "Stay right there."

"Help me! I'm stuck."

Samantha didn't stop to think. She simply reacted, running to the side door, charging through the entryway and into the stairwell. She could still hear the girl's cries ringing in her ears.

Help me!

She raced up the stairs, taking them two at a time, heading for the bell tower, the vein in her forehead pounding. Yesterday, she'd been in that same room with Piper having her wedding gown smudged.

Had it really been less than twenty-four hours ago?

Forget that. It's gone.

A single imperative pushed her forward.

Save the kid, save the kid, save the kid.

With each thundering step, her mission reverberated inside her brain. Samantha reached the door to the bell tower, grabbed for the knob, and pushed inward.

It didn't open.

"The door's stuck," the girl called.

"Hang on, honey," Samantha shouted so the child could hear her through the thick door. "I'm coming."

Samantha leaned back, cocked her leg, and kicked at the door. It didn't budge.

She switched legs, kicking and kicking and kicking, and yet the door refused to yield, hung up on the corner swollen by salty air.

What was she going to do?

Frantically, she looked around for something she could use as a battering ram, but there was nothing.

"Help! The ledge is cracking. I'm gonna fall!"

"You are not going to fall. Don't even think that way."

"The ground is really far off." The girl sounded on the verge of full-blown panic. "I'm gonna get hurt."

"Don't look."

"There's another lady down there now."

Must be Piper, but there was no time to waste. She had to act.

Samantha stepped back several paces, getting enough distance for a running start, and slammed her shoulder into the door as hard as she could.

The door shook and gave a little bit but didn't fully open.

The pain that shot through her right shoulder was excruciating, almost more than she could bear. Samantha cried out, closed her eyes, and swallowed hard against the pain.

"It's not working," the girl said. "The door is still stuck."

Samantha took a deep breath and had another run at the door, this time leading with her left shoulder.

Finally, the door popped open upon impact, and the momentum sent her stumbling into the bell tower room. She tripped over the tip of her sandal and fell, barely able to catch herself with her left arm before she face-planted onto the stone floor. She couldn't move her right shoulder, and the joint was on fire with pain.

Grunting, she staggered to her feet.

That's when she saw it.

One of the sky lanterns they'd released the previous evening was in the room, and printed on it, in white scroll lettering against the black background, was a single name.

Nick.

She had asked the universe for a sign. It didn't get much sign-ier than this.

"Are you okay, lady?"

"I'm fine, fine." Ascribing meaning to sky lanterns would have to keep. She had a kid to rescue.

Ignoring the pain in her right shoulder as best she could, Samantha gritted her teeth and rushed to the window opening and poked her head out. Sick to her stomach from the relentless pain, she glanced down to see Piper standing below.

"Fire department is on the way." Piper waved her phone with such calm reassurance that Samantha thought she might be over-reacting. "They'll be here any minute."

In the distance, Samantha heard the wail of sirens. *Don't freak, don't freak. Help is on the way.*

She turned her attention to the girl, and that's when she recognized her. Her name was Allie Montgomery, and she was in Destiny's class at school. Allie was locked in a squat on the ledge that was no wider than the bedazzled sneakers the girl was wearing. Numerous fissures ran through the century-old stone and grout.

Bile rose in Samantha's throat. She was not overreacting.

Allie had backed onto the far corner of the ledge, trying to brace herself against the crook of the building, and she was well out of Samantha's reach, even if Samantha was able to reach the girl with her banged-up shoulder. The intense pain was almost blinding, but she couldn't let Allie see that. She had to keep the child calm.

Gritting her teeth, she said, "Hi, Allie, it's me, Mrs. Ginelli. Destiny's mom."

"Hey, Mrs. Ginelli." The girl shifted and a small piece of mortar broke off and hit the ground beside Piper.

"Easy does it," Piper hollered.

"Allie, please be as still as you can," Samantha said. Tears burned her eyes. The shoulder pain was overwhelming, almost more than she could bear. She must have dislocated it.

Buck up. You had twenty hours of natural childbirth. You can get through this.

Allie peered at the ground. "It's a *long* way down."

"Honey, don't look, keep your eyes on me. Got it?"

"Okay," Allie said in a wavery voice.

"Where's your mommy?" Samantha kept her gaze locked on to the girl's eyes. Prayed that the fire department would arrive on time. She could feel her pulse throbbing at her throat, in her ears and her brain.

"She's on the beach. We were having a picnic and she fell asleep. I got bored."

"And you decided to go exploring?" Samantha studied the distance between herself and the girl, trying to figure out a way to reach her without putting added pressure on the crumbling ledge.

"I followed the balloon."

"Balloon?"

"It was caught in a palm tree, and the breeze grabbed it and sent it flying into the tower. I wanted to see it, so I came up here."

Oh, she must be talking about the sky lantern.

"But after I shut the door, it wouldn't open," Allie said. "And I thought I could climb out the window and grab on to the tree and shimmy down, but I couldn't. Then when I tried to crawl back in, the ledge started breaking apart and I was scared to move."

"You did good. You are so, so brave, and we're going to get this figured out. I won't let you fall."

Just then another chunk of the ledge broke off.

"Eek!" Allie's eyes grew wide, and in the softest, most heart-wrenching little voice she whispered, *"Help."*

"Hang in there," Piper yelled up at them.

But there was nothing for Allie to hang on to.

A crowd had gathered, gawking and taking cell phone pictures, but Samantha couldn't spare a glance for them. It was all she could do to battle past the pain in her shoulder and keep the little girl steady.

"If I stretch my arm out, do you think you can reach my hand?" Samantha asked, gauging whether she'd be able to pull the child to safety with her left arm.

Her right side, her dominate side, was completely useless. Luckily, Allie was perched to the right of the opening. If she'd been to the left, Samantha would have had to reach for her with her right hand, and there would be no way she could have done that.

"I can try."

"Be very careful. If you don't think you can do it, then don't try."

"Okay." Allie licked her lips. "Let's try."

Grimacing against the pain, Samantha widened her stance, planted her feet solidly, and put her left arm out of the opening as far as it would go, but Allie was still over a foot away from her reach. Right before her eyes, Samantha saw the cracks in the ledge widening, but she couldn't let the girl see her fear.

Forcing a smile, she said, "Now try to inch forward until you can grab hold of my hand. But keep looking at me. Don't look down."

"All righty." Allie shifted from the crouch and went onto her knees, but the ledge wasn't wide enough for that maneuver and her right leg slipped off the ledge.

Samantha gasped and Allie shrank back, her light blue eyes filled with terror.

The sirens were getting louder. Soon, very soon, help would be here, but would the ledge hold in time?

"The firemen are almost here, Allie."

The child cowered, whimpering, "I'm gonna fall, I'm gonna fall."

"Shh, shh, it's okay. You're all right," Samantha soothed. Her right shoulder had gone completely numb and her arm felt like an alien chunk of wood attached to her body, but at least the searing pain had lessened. "Everything is going to be just fine."

Sirens wailed into the parking lot. Doors slammed. A commanding voice barked orders.

Allie glanced over. "The fire trucks are here."

Thank God.

"Don't look down, remember? Eyes on me, Allie."

More pieces of the ledge flaked off. Bigger pieces this time, chunks of stone mixed with the grout. It wasn't going to hold. The ledge was falling apart right underneath Allie.

Anxiety clenched Samantha's chest. No, no, she could not let Allie fall. She couldn't let this little girl die before her eyes. Guilt swamped her. If they hadn't let the sky lanterns go, this would have never happened. Allie wouldn't have come up here if she hadn't been chasing the lantern.

Stop with the self-blame. It serves nothing and gets in your way.

"Allie!" a terrified woman screamed from the ground.

"Momma!" The girl looked down at her mother and immediately started wobbling wildly.

"Allie, Allie, look at me, look at me," Samantha said, trying to keep the panic from her voice as the bile rose higher in her throat.

Oh God, she was going to vomit. Gulping, she swallowed it

back. From her peripheral vision, all she could see was a swirl of red from the arriving fire trucks and a muddle of melted faces in the gathering crowd. Was she losing her eyesight?

She heard pummeling footsteps charging up the stairs. Help would be here soon, but would it be soon enough? The cracks were getting wider and wider as more of the ledge crumbled.

Do something! Now!

But what?

Allie shrieked as a huge piece broke off. The ledge wasn't going to last. The firemen weren't going to make it in time. Too late. They were too late.

The crowd gasped. Allie's mother screamed. The firemen were rushing to get their extra-long ladder propped against the bell tower.

Too late! Too late! The whole ledge was going.

Samantha stuck half her body out the window, reaching as far as she could without losing her own balance, and prayed she wouldn't tumble over in the process. "Allie, grab my neck! Do it, do it now!"

Allie leaped just as the last bit of ledge collapsed, and she grasped on to Samantha's neck. Immediately, Samantha wrapped her left arm around the child, pulling her close to her chest.

But Samantha's own purchase was unstable.

She wavered, more of her body weight outside the opening than inside the room, and she was unable to correct her balance because of her useless right shoulder.

More horrified gasps from the crowd. She couldn't imagine how terrifying their situation must look from the ground, but it was exceedingly scary from her end.

Behind her, she heard someone burst through the door, breathing heavily, but she didn't dare look around. It took everything she had inside of her to hold tight to Allie and not fall out the window. The child was so heavy against her.

The firemen are too late, she thought. *We're going over. We're going to die.*

That's when strong arms went around her waist, yanking her and Allie backward into the room. She and Allie fell atop their rescuer as all three of them landed safely on the floor.

Thank God for the fireman. Thank God, thank God. But when she turned to express gratitude to their savior, she saw it wasn't a fireman at all.

Instead, she looked into the dear face of her husband, Luca.

Then she glanced over and saw Nick standing helplessly in the doorway, staring at the sky lantern with his name on it, and coming up the stairs behind him was Piper leading a charge of firemen.

* * *

A POLICE OFFICER took Samantha's statement in the back of the ambulance as a paramedic popped her dislocated shoulder back into place and put her in a sling with instructions to see her family doctor for a follow-up.

The pain, which had come rushing back once the adrenaline and endorphins wore off in the wake of pulling Allie to safety, quickly ebbed as soon as the paramedic finished putting the ball of her arm back into the shoulder socket and she was left with only a mild soreness.

Luca and Nick sat beside her in the ambulance. One on either side of the gurney.

A crowd had formed around the ambulance, and the police kept having to shoo people away. Piper stood off to one side with Allie and her mom, as another paramedic checked Allie's vital signs.

Allie's mom had been so grateful to Samantha and asked if they could plan a playdate for their daughters when Allie returned from summer camp the weekend before the Fourth of July, and Samantha had agreed. It seemed far enough away to give her time to deal with everything that had fallen in on her. Samantha's motherly heart couldn't say no.

Basking in the media's attention, the little girl chattered up a storm about how Samantha had saved her life.

A bevy of cell phones flashed pictures, and at the center of the fanfare was that slimy Victor Jorge.

CHAPTER 20

There is only one happiness in life, to love and be loved.

—George Sand

Following Samantha's rescue of Allie Montgomery, the next two and a half weeks were chaos as the Ginellis found themselves caught in the torrential current of over-the-top publicity about Nick's return, and he had the added complication of resuming his life after being declared legally dead.

Everyone wanted to interview him. The family fielded calls from *Dateline*, *20/20*, and *60 Minutes*. Book publishers and movie producers phoned, wanting rights to his story. Reporters and paparazzi camped outside all their homes.

His mother took him shopping for clothes since his shopping trip with Luca had been cut short. Everywhere they went, media ghouls waylaid them. One nutty reporter even crawled under the dressing room stall at Kohl's to get his attention.

The onslaught was exhausting.

In between dodging the brouhaha, Nick visited his physician, who insisted on a mountain of tests to assess his overall health. After that, all the Ginellis saw a family therapist to help guide them through the process of putting their lives back together. Nick also had private sessions with the therapist. He'd wanted marriage counseling with Samantha, but the therapist told him that for now, it was best to focus on his own personal healing.

When Nick received a diagnosis of complex PTSD, no one was surprised.

They'd also made an appointment with a lawyer, who started the legal process of having Nick's death decree reversed. That was something else that would take time. For the foreseeable future, Nick was in limbo.

Nick spent the nights in his childhood bed at his parents' house, and even though he'd much rather have stayed at his house with Samantha and Destiny, he couldn't complain. Any mattress underneath a roof was a cherished luxury, and when he'd first slipped beneath the soft flannel sheets smelling of fabric softener and his mother's love, he actually teared up.

During that time, the two people he most wanted to be with didn't seem to want to hang out with him. Destiny was standoffish, and when he tried to connect with her, she wouldn't look him in the eyes. It killed him to see that his own child was leery of him, but his daughter had grown up without him, and he couldn't expect her to greet him with open arms.

This, too, would take time.

As for Samantha, she avoided being alone with him. If they found themselves alone in a room together, she'd invent an excuse and make a clean getaway. She invited Nick's mom to go with them to the doctor's and lawyer's offices, and when it came to visiting the Coast Guard outpost to check in with his old employer, she begged off, asking him to take Piper with him instead.

Which is where he and Piper were now headed on this Wednesday morning, two and a half weeks after the Coast Guard plucked him from the island.

Piper pulled up to the guard shack of the Coast Guard Galveston sector, a thirty-minute drive northeast of Moonglow Cove, and flashed her badge at the attendant.

Nick didn't know the fellow in the booth who waved her through. "What happened to Ross?"

"He retired a couple of years ago and moved to Florida."

"I feel so out of touch. Nothing's the same."

"You'll get used to things eventually. It's been a long time. It'll take a while to find a new normal."

Nick ran a hand over the top of his head, unaccustomed to his old flattop hairstyle he'd gotten on Monday. "Even my haircut feels weird."

"Lookin' damn fine to me, Ginelli." Piper shot him a crooked grin. "A little skinny, but your ma will fatten you up soon enough."

"Not so bad yourself, Dellaney. I swear you look younger than you did seven years ago. Got a fountain of youth hidden somewhere?"

"I lost a little weight," she said. "Helps my chipmunk cheeks not look so chipmunky."

"You don't have chipmunk cheeks."

"Tell that to my high school yearbook."

She parked and they got out of the vehicle. Nick paused, blinking in the bright sunlight and scanning the place where he used to work. It was a memory-lane visual of what he'd left behind—the docks, the seagulls, the boats, the hub of activity . . .

His old partner.

Holding out a hand, Piper motioned for him.

It was only after he took her hand that Nick realized she'd simply been beckoning him forward, but once he'd put his hand in hers, Piper smiled and interlaced their fingers as she led him inside.

Not gonna lie. It felt nice.

Right off the bat, he noticed they'd painted the walls. No longer sky blue, they were now a pancake-batter yellow. Piper led him to the meeting room and pushed open the door.

Peering inside, Nick halted at the threshold.

Before desert island living, he'd been a gregarious extrovert, but so much time alone had rewired his brain, and the sight in front of him threw Nick into full-blown anxiety. What was he supposed to say to all these people?

His chest tightened and his throat closed off, and if his legs hadn't been loose as overcooked noodles, he would have run out of there.

His old boss, Captain Jeff Martindale, and the other Coast Guard officers stood on the dais at the front of the room. The familiar faces weren't so familiar anymore. Oh, the people were the same, but unlike Piper, seven years had visibly altered their appearance. Some had gone paunchy. Others were balding. The changes were startling, but what really had him hanging at the entrance of the standing-room-only crowd was the cluster of cameras filming his reaction.

He'd been ambushed.

The second the audience spied him, they got to their feet and stood at attention, his comrades saluting him.

Salutes were a punch in the gut.

He didn't deserve this. He glanced over at Piper, who was

softly smiling at him with tears in her eyes, and that's when he realized he was still clinging to her hand.

The entire room burst into applause, and someone started singing "For He's a Jolly Good Fellow," and quickly other voices joined in.

Nick stood frozen, overwhelmed.

Piper squeezed his hand. "S' okay," she whispered. "You're among friends. You're home."

He gulped, uncertain if his legs would move him to the podium where Captain Martindale was waving him forward.

"Smile," Piper urged.

Nick forced the corners of his mouth upward as best he could. It had been so long since he'd smiled that he'd almost forgotten how. Piper let go of his hand and put her palm to his back, propelling him forward.

He saw his parents in the crowd, then Samantha and Luca. His brother and his wife were standing close together as if they were a couple, as if they were meant to be, and Samantha had her hand resting on Luca's shoulder.

When Nick caught her eye, Samantha quickly dropped her hand.

Pain arrowed straight through his heart, and he couldn't tell if it was emotional or physical. He had lots of odd aches and pains, and the doctor had warned him that some of his symptoms were due to malnutrition.

Someone started a slow, steady clapping that built as everyone joined in.

He turned to Piper. "I don't know if I can do this."

She winced and her eyes filled with regret. "It was clueless of me not to think how it would feel in your shoes. When Captain

Martindale suggested a ceremony, I thought it sounded wonderful. We shouldn't have sprung it on you. Luca warned me that you might not be up for this, but I thought he was just being a worrywart. I can see now it's too much, too much too soon. I'm so sorry, Nick. You wanna leave? Say the word and we're out of here."

Nick gulped. Did he? It would be so easy to run away.

And leave everyone, with their good intentions, confused?

No. He could do this. He'd been selfish for far too long. Head up, Nick climbed the three short steps to the dais. Piper hung back at the bottom of the stairs, giving her support but staying out of his limelight.

Limelight he didn't want.

This so was different from the way he used to be.

Fact. Seven years ago, Nick had been an attention hog and, in hindsight, somewhat inconsiderate in his drive for validation and admiration.

Standing at the podium, looking out into the sea of faces, most of whom he knew, overwhelmed him. But damn it, he was here, he was alive, he'd made it back. People wanted to honor him, and he would tuck away his own feelings and think of others for once.

Captain Martindale was talking, addressing the audience, giving them a rundown on how Nick had survived seven years alone in complete isolation. Nick barely listened. His mind was still hobbled, his senses hypervigilant, his body on high alert for danger.

Nick forced a grin and a wave and tried to resurrect the old personality that had withered in isolation. Slowly, he roused, uplifted by the kindness and camaraderie all around him. He knew he might never work for the Coast Guard again, but in this moment, he was one of them once more, and that made all the difference.

"Welcome home, Nick." Captain Martindale adjusted the mic to Nick's height and then stepped out of the way, giving Nick the floor.

Heat suffused his body and he felt oddly breathless, like an unexpected prom queen, thanking the crowd for their votes.

"Gosh, I'm . . . wow . . ." He pressed a hand to the back of his neck. "This is so . . . thank you. Thank you so much. It's . . . well, I dreamed about this every night as I fell asleep beneath my palm-frond blanket."

That drew a laugh from the crowd, and for a moment, Nick felt like his old self again, making jokes and cutting up, the life of the party.

"I see a huge sheet cake at the back of the room," Nick said. "Is that for me?"

"You betcha! It's German chocolate," Piper hollered. "Your fav. But you gotta share."

The crowd chuckled.

"Before we get to the cake," Captain Martindale said, "we have a presentation for this unprecedented moment. Lieutenant Dellaney, since you set this up, would you like to do the honors?"

Nodding, Piper joined Nick onstage. It felt extraordinary having Piper beside him again. Just like the old days when they'd been partners. She was quickly turning into his emotional support person. It was a role that should have gone to Samantha but hadn't.

Piper picked up the remote control that rested on the podium and turned her back to the audience as she queued up a video on the big screen behind the dais.

A slideshow unfolded, capturing Nick's life. From infancy, to childhood, to teen years, to his wedding, to his graduation—along with Piper—from the Coast Guard Academy, to his memorial service.

That's when he realized the video must have been from his memorial service and Piper had just added to it to bring it up-to-date. That was how she'd put this thing together in only two and a half weeks. The highlight from the memorial service was the appearance of the Ceremonial Honor Guard. Watching the guard respect him with military pageantry and listening to the reading of the Honor Guard's creed brought a lump to his throat.

"I will Honor all Coast Guard men and women both living and dead," the service members on the video recited.

The hairs on Nick's arms rose. He was witnessing his own funeral.

The camera panned out from the Honor Guard and scanned the crowd with hundreds of people at his graveside. It was powerful and moving. While they'd been having his service, he'd been on an island struggling to survive. He didn't know if that idea made him feel better or simply broke his heart. This whole thing seemed like it was from a far-fetched movie.

On the video, the camera narrowed in on Samantha, dressed all in black, and sitting front and center. His parents were seated to her left, and to her right sat Luca, a four-year-old Destiny on his brother's knee. Seeing his daughter looking so young hurt Nick like a lifelong ache, but what seized up his lungs and cut off his oxygen was the expression on Luca's face as he settled his arm around Samantha's shoulders, and she leaned into him for comfort.

The look in Luca's eyes was one of pure, desperate love. His brother had wanted Nick's wife even then.

Knocked for a loop by the video, Nick sought out his brother in the crowd and found Luca staring at him intently. His brother knew that Nick now understood Luca's feelings for Samantha were long-standing.

"You okay?" Piper touched Nick's arm softly, and it was enough to bring him into the moment and return his focus to the presentation.

The video shifted from the memorial service, leaving Nick with his hands clenched at his sides and his pulse pounding swiftly in his ears. These photographs were new to the slideshow. Pictures of him on the island, stumbling to the Coast Guard ship, hairy, sunburned, wasted away. It was shocking to see his rescue laid out so visually.

The presentation finished and Captain Martindale stepped back to the podium.

"On the occasion of your triumphant return." The captain held up a paver brick with Nick's name on it, the date of his birth, and the date he was lost at sea. "Seven years ago, we set this brick in the wall of fallen Coast Guard members. Yesterday, it was our honor to chisel it out."

The moment was surreal, and for an instant, Nick wondered if he was back on the island merely caught in a sweet dream. But Piper was there, reading his mind and gently pinching the fleshy part of his upper arm. A subtle message.

You're not dreaming. This is real. You're home.

He might have been gone for seven years, but he and his work partner were still on the same wavelength. Piper understood him in a way no one else did.

Including his wife.

His gaze went to Samantha, who was watching him with misty

eyes. A stab of guilt went through him, and he sent her an encouraging smile and silently mouthed, *I love you.*

Samantha smiled gently, but that was all.

Captain Martindale kept talking, but Nick's emotions whipped in a dozen different directions. He was on overload.

Perspective, Nick reminded himself. It was all about perspective. He could still be sitting on the island with nothing but birds and sand crabs for company. This was a helluva lot better than that. Besides, all he had to do was give her a sign, and Piper would whisk him out of here.

"Nick has experienced epic challenges, and I can't imagine just how lonely that must have been," Captain Martindale said.

No, no you cannot.

"That level of isolation eats at a person's soul. It's not often someone returns from the dead, but Nick is our own modern-day Lazarus."

Deafening applause.

"Nick, we're your family, and our hearts overflow with the joy of your resurrection." Captain Martindale extended the brick to Nick. "It is our honor to present you with this brick and to welcome you home."

"I . . ." His voice creaked like a rusty door hinge and his knees wobbled. Could he do this? Swallowing his fear, he tried again. "Hang on a sec. I've spent seven years without seeing a single human being, and all your lovely faces are kind of overwhelming."

That pulled a few "*awws*" and murmured sympathies from the crowd. The brick was far heavier than Nick expected, and his thin wrist hurt from holding it aloft for the camera.

Surreptitiously, Piper took the brick from him and smiled brightly for the audience.

Nick curled both hands around the podium to hold himself steady. "I thank you for your support and concern and your prayers for my family while I was gone. Thank you so very much. Words simply can't convey the depth of my gratitude."

He paused, every eye in the place on him.

"It's more than I can process. I hope you'll forgive my rough edges. You never think something like this could ever happen to you and then it does. I missed this place so much. I thought of you all often, and I regretted not telling you at the time how much you meant to me."

Cell phones clicked pictures. A few people dabbed tears from their eyes. Then everyone jumped to their feet, clapping wildly.

A standing ovation.

One Nick didn't deserve. All he'd done was survive. He wasn't particularly courageous. Or smart. He'd just managed to live despite the odds aligned against him.

Living was good. He was happy he'd survived, but so much had changed. He was ready to get off this stage. Ready to go home.

He turned to Piper and said, "So can we have that cake now?"

That brought laughter and a lessening of wound-up emotions as everyone headed for the cake at the back of the room, including Captain Martindale.

"German chocolate is my favorite too," he said to Nick.

"Sir?" Nick put a hand on his boss's forearm. "Can I have a word?"

Momentarily, Captain Martindale looked disappointed that he couldn't immediately go after that cake. "What's up, Ginelli?"

Squaring his shoulders, Nick found the courage to ask for what he wanted. "What steps do I take in order to return to work?"

Captain Martindale clamped a hand on Nick's shoulder. "Heal. You need to heal. Until you heal, we can't have that conversation. Healing is your top priority."

CHAPTER 21

Love does not begin and end the way we seem to think it does.
Love is a battle; love is a war; love is a growing up.

—James Baldwin

Sitting in the passenger seat on the way back to Moonglow Cove, Nick watched as Piper cut in and out of traffic, jockeying from lane to lane in her bid to pass everyone who wasn't traveling at least five miles over the speed limit.

Once upon a time, Nick's driving skills had been just as aggressive if not more so, but now, seeing the cars flying around them at top speed put his teeth on edge.

"Where's the fire?"

"Huh?" Piper whipped her head around to stare at him.

"What's the rush? Life's short. Why be in such a hurry to get it over with?"

"Oh yeah." She looked a little sheepish, reduced her speed, and slipped into a slower lane. "Sorry. I bet the freeway looks pretty woolly to you after seven years without being behind a wheel."

"That and I've learned to appreciate whatever moment I'm in as the only scrap of time we truly have."

She darted another glance in his direction. "Wow, you really have changed."

"I didn't have a choice." He studied her profile as Piper gripped the steering wheel like a NASCAR driver skirting a wipeout pileup.

"Be here now. Mindfulness. Zen. I get it." Piper sped up to dodge a dump truck and slid like a ninja into a small opening between cars.

"You gotta live every day like it's your last." Nick grabbed the handgrip. "Because one day it will be."

"Deep thoughts, Little Mary Sunshine. You really didn't have much to do on that island but think, did you. That must have been excruciating."

Yeah, it had been. Nick took in a deep breath to steady his nerves.

"I can't imagine. Oops, hang on. The exit is coming up and everyone's in my way." She goosed her SUV and zoomed ahead to cut through two lanes of traffic, leaving raised middle fingers in her wake.

Nick closed his eyes and imagined his favorite spot on the island—the top of a hill next to the freshwater supply where the wildlife gathered.

"Sooo," Piper said, taking the exit ramp. "I heard you talking to the captain. You really want to come back to the Coast Guard?"

Nick opened his eyes and looked over at her. "It's all I ever wanted. It's all I really know."

"I beg to differ. You know what it's like to be shipwrecked on a desert island. That's a rarefied skill set. You could become a motivational speaker. It'd pay a helluva lot more than the Coast Guard."

"Food for thought."

"You'd be great at it. You've got so much energy . . . or you used to. You'll rehab and get your vim back. You're such a people person."

"I used to be a lot of things. I haven't for sure made my mind up about returning to the Coast Guard. First things first. I gotta discuss the future with Samantha. Figure out how we're going to move forward."

"You haven't already talked about it?"

"Not just the two of us. We've been so busy with appointments and the media being in our faces. We did have that family therapy session, though it didn't much go anywhere. All any of us really want is to not hurt one another, but no matter what we do, there'll be pain."

"Is Samantha hanging out with Luca?"

"Honestly, I don't know."

"Want me to find out?"

Nick paused, considering it, but shook his head. "It's none of my business."

"You're not jealous?"

"Hell yes, I'm jealous." Nick grunted. "But thinking about it is more than I can deal with right now."

"Is it weird that you drove with me and she's with Luca?"

"There are a lot of things that are weird right now. Besides, my parents drove with them. They're not alone together."

Nick stared out the window at a line of cars sitting at a Mc-Donald's drive-through. He used to put away an unhealthy number of those burgers. Nostalgia washed over him. "Could we stop for a Big Mac?"

"Dude, yes." Piper did a U-turn in the middle of the street and headed for the fast-food restaurant.

"When I was on the island," he said, "I literally dreamed of Big Macs."

"You want fries?"

"And an apple pie. The works." He knew he wouldn't be able to eat it all, rather he yearned for the ubiquitous emotional comfort of a McDonald's meal.

"Chocolate shake?"

"Yep."

Piper joined the line. "So anyway, I've been thinking . . ."

He waited for her to continue and when she didn't, he prodded, "About . . . ?"

"While you were gone, I took training courses in kinesiology and physical therapy to become a personal trainer on the side."

"Why?"

"You know me. I can't stay still, and my friends kept bugging me to train them. I figured why not earn extra money since I was at the gym every day anyway?"

"Um, okay."

"What I'm trying to do is offer you my services, completely gratis. If you want help, that is."

"That's kind of you." Piper as his physical trainer? That was a thought.

"Of course, after this splurge," Piper said, inching the SUV forward in the line. "You're gonna have to give up the Mickey D's."

"I laid off them for seven years. I think I can manage."

"It'll be harder this time. You're home with all the temptations of modern society."

"I'm committed to reclaiming my old life."

Piper turned her head to meet his gaze. "You sure that's what you want? If there was ever time for a fresh start, it's now."

"What does that mean?"

Piper chuffed as the vehicle ahead of her moved, and she pulled up to take their turn at the speaker box. The sunlight caught the strands of her auburn hair and glimmered like gold. "Nothing . . . I just . . . well, if there was ever any reason you wanted to start over from scratch, it's prime time—"

"Are you saying I should get out of Luca's way and let him have Samantha?"

"I'm not about to tell you what to do, Nick. All I'm saying is that there are a lot of people who missed you far more than you can know and any number of them could be pining for you a lot more than Sammie is in my estimation."

That pulled Nick straight up in his seat. "Piper, are you saying—"

"I'm saying, it's time to get your health back so you can make the best decisions for your future."

"A future without Samantha?"

"I'm not saying that . . ."

"What *are* you saying?"

"Things have changed. That's all."

His chest tightened all over again. "Does this have anything to do with—"

"No," Piper cut him off. "It absolutely doesn't have anything to do with *that*."

From the speaker box a grainy voice greeted them, "Welcome to McDonald's. I'll take your order when you're ready."

* * *

AFTER HIS CONVERSATION with Piper, Nick set an immediate goal for putting his life back together. First on that list, get

Samantha alone for a private conversation about their future. Once he knew where they really stood, he would accept Piper's offer of physical therapy and move forward with his healing. Until then, he was in limbo.

Piper dropped him off at Samantha's house, just as Luca and Samantha pulled into the driveway. Yolanda was babysitting Destiny at the restaurant. Marcella and Tino planned to pick his daughter up from there and take her to their house, so Nick could spend time with her that afternoon.

"Need moral support?"

"I'm okay." He smiled at Piper and unbuckled his seat belt. "But thanks."

"I'm serious about helping you with rehab, 'kay? Let me know what you decide."

"Will do."

"Nick?"

He stopped with his hand on the door handle and raised his eyes to meet hers. "Yes?"

"If you ever need to talk, I'm just a text away."

"Thanks." He shut the door and Piper drove off.

Luca was already out of Samantha's SUV and moving in the direction of his own house across the street. His brother waved. "I'm off to the restaurant to work. It was a great party. Good to have you home, buddy."

"Thanks for coming." It felt trite, the silly pleasantries, when there were so many weighted unspoken emotions stewing between them.

Luca nodded.

Nick nodded back.

Samantha waited in the driveway, hugging herself the way she did whenever she felt vulnerable. In the past, her "fragile flower" vibe would have had him riding to the rescue, white knight style. Big and strong and ready to fight to the death for her.

But he wasn't so strong anymore, and Samantha was anything but defenseless. Truth be told, she'd thrived in his absence, blooming into a capable, confident woman.

The Big Mac he'd eaten sat like an anchor in his belly. He just wasn't used to that kind of food anymore. At least that's what he told himself. Safer to blame the food than the knowing look he'd seen pass between his brother and his wife.

Samantha looked so beautiful with the ocean breeze ruffling her hair over her shoulders that Nick couldn't resist staring. Once upon a time, he'd taken her for granted. He'd been a stupid fool.

"Hey." Samantha looked as shaky as Nick felt. She tucked a strand of errant hair behind her ear, and that's when he realized her ring finger was bare.

She wasn't wearing either his or Luca's ring.

Wedding rings.

What an odd custom, he thought.

Using compressed carbon to claim someone. Like an emperor penguin giving a pebble to its mate. Until the island, Nick hadn't been prone to pondering social constructs, but for the last seven years, he'd had nothing to do but survive . . . and think.

He supposed, in some ways, he was a better man because of the harrowing experience—but, damn, what he wouldn't have given to have skipped it. Yes, he'd certainly changed, but so had Samantha.

She was much calmer than she'd been as a young bride, more mature and down-to-earth. The wide-eyed anxiety through which she'd once viewed the world had ebbed, and now he saw a woman who could withstand life's storms. He'd put her through hell and back, but she'd grieved him and moved on, while Nick had been in limbo.

It was, he realized, the first time they'd been completely alone since the talk they'd had in her kitchen on her wedding night.

"We should talk."

"Yes."

"A walk on the beach?"

"That sounds nice."

He extended his elbow for her to take his arm. She hesitated a beat, as if reluctant to touch him. Nick drummed up the kindest smile in his arsenal. Her eyes turned tender, and she looked so damn vulnerable, it just about broke his heart.

Tentatively, she reached for his arm, and he let her take hold of him rather than the other way around. Once upon a time, he might have been a little too grabby, a little too possessive, but not now. Not today. He wanted to show her how much he respected and admired her. Something he'd been pretty shabby at doing seven years ago.

Face it. He'd been a cocky young jock who believed he'd had the world on a string. Now, he was a man who'd been slapped hard by life.

No one was invincible. Everything could disappear in an instant, and that wasn't a lesson he could ever forget.

They walked the six blocks to the seawall without speaking, and the tension between them was as palpable as the humidity.

During the middle of the week, the boardwalk was quiet. A few people strolled the seawall, and there were two elderly couples in a fringed surrey pedaling in the opposite direction. The cloudless sky was deep azure, but the sun wasn't too hot.

Nick guided Samantha down the stone steps toward the beach. On the sand, a group of young adults were flying colorful kites, and another group played beach volleyball.

He could hear the *clackety-clack* of the roller coaster from Paradise Pier a half mile away as it whizzed around the wooden track. Mario's was across the street on the opposite side of the seawall. He'd grown up with Paradise Pier as a constant backdrop. How he'd missed the sound.

Samantha stopped when they reached the beach and held on to his shoulder for balance as she slipped off her sandals and hooked the straps over her fingers. She turned to face the ocean and took in a slow, deep breath.

Fortifying herself?

"How are you doing?"

The air whipped through her clothes, billowing her gauzy yellow dress around her firm thighs. Nick tried not to stare, but, damn it, she was his wife and he'd been so long without a woman's touch.

Used to be your wife, bub. Everything had changed.

"I'm all right. You?"

"Overwhelmed . . ." he said. "Scared."

"Of what?" She tilted her head, and the sun cast extra light on her eyes, giving her an ethereal, otherworldly appearance.

"About what's gonna happen to us."

"Oh." She didn't say anything else, just walked closer to the water's edge and stood there letting the tide wash over her bare toes.

If anxiety had a dial, the expression on her face would have notched his up to warp speed. He waited patiently—rushing her to speak wouldn't serve him, but it was hard not to prod her.

The old edgy Nick was still in there somewhere, prowling like a caged lion.

Samantha looked as if she'd gambled big in Vegas and gone bust, and it was his fault, Nick realized. *He* was the cause of her suffering. Because he'd come home, he'd ruined things between her and Luca.

"I think I want to return to the Coast Guard," he said, not even realizing that's what he was going to say.

"Is that even feasible?" She walked heel-toe down the beach, leaving footprints that touched each other in the sand.

He remembered the first time he'd seen her make the pattern. It was on their first date, and he'd been endlessly fascinated by her and the things she stirred in him. The fire of young love was long gone. Worn away by time and distance. He appreciated her. Cared for her. Loved her still, in the way of childhood things. And yet, there was a gaping psychic wound in his heart and no way to fill it.

"Nick?" She'd stopped walking and was studying his face, snapping him back to the present.

"What? Huh? Oh yeah. Captain Martindale says I have a chance of returning, but I need to rehab first, and there are other hoops to jump through, but yeah."

"I see."

"Piper offered to help me rehabilitate."

"Is that really what you want?"

"Honestly, until I know where you and I stand, I can't make any decisions about anything else."

"So, you're hooking your life on what I want?"

"Yes."

"Why?"

"You're my wife."

"It doesn't really feel like it," she said, so softly he could hardly hear her. "Does it?"

"I want to repair my life," he said. "I want that more than anything. And I want it to be with *you*."

"What about Luca?"

"Do you love him?" It was hard for Nick to ask the question that was like a sharp new ax placed tight against his throat. He knotted his hands into fists, trying to steady his emotions.

"I do."

"More than you loved me?"

"I don't know the answer to that, Nick. This is a very difficult situation. I once loved you with every fiber of my being, but now I don't know if that was real love or just a fanciful story we told ourselves about love."

"What's the difference?" he asked, feeling panicky.

"When we were together, it was over the top and out of this world. The stuff of fairy tales."

"Yes. I know. That's what I miss."

"In retrospect, I can see that kind of frantic passion isn't all that healthy, Nick. It was too intense. We were out of balance."

"No." Nick shook his head, staunchly denying what was right under his nose. "We were *meant* for each other. We were entangled. I didn't know where I stopped and you started, and vice versa."

"That was the problem, Nick. We didn't have good boundaries."

He didn't agree with her. He'd thought their love had been perfect. Yeah, okay, they'd had their ups and downs, but that was just part of life, right?

"So, you're saying you don't want to be married to me anymore?"

"I don't know what I'm saying. I can't snap my fingers and decide just like that. It's not as simple as picking you. There's so much to consider. Not just for you and me, but for Destiny, for the entire family."

She wasn't wrong about that, but part of him ached for the girl she'd once been. The one who'd thought he'd hung the moon and stars and who couldn't get enough of kissing him and flinging herself giddily into his arms.

"Remember the first night we came here together? You snuck out of your bedroom window and met me right here in front of Panama Pete's." Nick waved at the little open-air beach bar a few yards down the beach.

She grinned. "It was the most thrilling night of my life."

"Have you forgotten—"

"I remember." Her cheeks flushed red, and she dropped her gaze.

"Our first kiss," he said.

"Blew me away."

"Me too." He reached for her hand. She didn't resist, although she looked conflicted. He pulled her closer. "You tasted like wild strawberries."

"It was my lip gloss."

He lowered his head.

She looked up into his gaze and interlaced their fingers, squeezed his hand softly the way you'd do with a mourner at a funeral.

"Can we recapture the past? Do we have any hope of rebuilding our marriage?"

"I don't know."

"Do you *want* to recapture the past?"

"I don't know that either."

"Samantha," he whispered her name. "We were each other's one and only."

"Until we weren't." She shrugged and that broke his heart.

"We lost our way."

"Yes, we did."

"The Lightning Strike is forever. It never goes away."

"Nick, I don't even know if there is such a thing as a Lightning Strike."

He heard himself grunt, unable to believe she'd said that. If they didn't have the Lightning Strike, their entire marriage had been built on shifting sands. Without the Lightning Strike, they had no anchor, nothing to bind them together.

"You can't deny how we felt about each other," he said.

"It was teenage lust. There is nothing wrong with that, but it isn't magic. It's hormones. Chemistry. Not really the firm foundation on which to build a solid life."

He couldn't accept that. It went against everything he believed. She just needed reminding. It had been so long, she'd forgotten how combustible they were together.

"It *was* magical, and you know it."

Tenderly, he reached out and hooked his thumb underneath her chin, lifted her face up to meet his, and there, with the backdrop of the pounding surf and brilliant blue sky, Nick kissed Samantha with every ounce of passion he had in him.

CHAPTER 22

Love is a superstition. Understanding is reality.

—Karan

Stunned, Samantha took the emotional one-two punch to the solar plexus as all the air leaked from her body.

Nick's kiss took her completely by surprise. She'd been avoiding him as much as possible for the past two and a half weeks, anguishing over the situation that had her twisted inside out for this very reason.

Once upon a time, they'd shared what they both believed was a rarefied love, but in Nick's absence, Samantha had grown up. And once you stopped believing in things like Santa Claus and the Easter Bunny and the Tooth Fairy and Lightning Strikes, it was impossible to go back.

Now, she understood that magical moment in Moonglow Cove High School over fourteen years ago had been teenage hormonal stew mixed with her desperate need to feel special. Around Nick, she'd felt like a princess, and then when the Ginellis had welcomed her with open arms, she'd sunk into his family's embrace like a feather pillow.

And there was absolutely nothing wrong with the kindness she'd found with them. The Ginellis were good people, lovely folks with hearts of gold. The Ginellis, like the Dellaneys, had offered a safe haven for an orphaned girl who'd often struggled with her self-esteem. She'd surrounded herself with a loving tribe, built the life she'd always dreamed of, but now, with Nick's return from the grave, her tribe had been thrust into chaos. Not that she didn't want him alive. Far from it. She was thrilled her daughter would get to know her father, but there were so many complications, so many land mines to navigate.

And Samantha wasn't so sure she was strong enough to work through this in a mentally healthy way, despite all her resources.

Nick's lips moved over hers and she sighed softly.

Being in his arms again felt surreal. So many empty nights she'd imagined his homecoming, had prayed intensely for this very thing. She threw coins into fountains and blew out birthday candles and crossed her fingers and made requests of wishbones, all for his safe return, but now that it had finally happened, now that he was home, she felt . . .

Lost.

She didn't know this man who was kissing her. His body had changed alarmingly, going from muscular bulk to skin and bones. He smelled and tasted differently too. Or maybe she simply couldn't remember what he'd smelled and tasted like before. What they'd shared once upon a time had shifted into a foggy memory that went more out of focus the harder she tried to recall it.

The man kissing her was essentially a stranger. Nick had changed that much. And it just felt weird. She didn't want to feel this way about him, but she did.

Nick let go, looking surprised and then worried. "You didn't kiss me back."

"I . . ." She stepped away from him and pushed her windblown hair from her face. "I can't do this, Nick."

"I'm sorry. I shouldn't have kissed you." He dropped his arms. "I just thought a kiss might remind you of who we used to be."

"It's too soon, Nick." She stepped back, putting distance between them. "We can't just pick up where we left off seven years ago. You're expecting too much of me. Of all of us."

He pressed his forehead against hers, wrapped his arms around her again. "Because of Luca."

"And Destiny and your parents . . . and *I've* changed too, Nick. I'm not the fluff-headed teenager I used to be."

"I can see that." He nodded. "But you were never fluff-headed."

"I'm not the sweet young wife you once knew, dazzled by your looks and sexual prowess and the fact that *you* wanted *me*."

He gulped visibly. Somewhere down the beach a child screamed with delight, and Samantha felt the tension inside her twist tighter.

"I get it." He stepped back and she could breathe again.

"My feelings aren't a switch I can turn off and on at will. I can't suddenly go back to who I used to be." Samantha squared her shoulders, raised her chin, and met his gaze like a head-on collision. "I don't *want* to go back. I finished my schooling, Nick. I got my bachelor's degree. I don't need a man in order to be fulfilled."

"Everyone needs love," he said. *"Everyone."*

"I'm not saying I don't love you. I do love you. Fiercely. But not in the way I once did, and my heart is shattered to pieces over this, but it is what it is."

He smacked the heel of his palm against his forehead, turned away from her, and stared out at the ocean. "I shouldn't have come back. I shouldn't have fought so hard to get back. I should have died on that island."

Did he mean it? Or was this a pity play? When she was younger, Nick had been pretty adept at manipulating her empathy, but if any circumstances deserved pity and regret, this was it.

She drew in a breath and fought off her natural people-pleasing tendencies to placate and soothe him. She'd learned a lot in the therapy she'd undergone after Nick was lost at sea, and she didn't judge him for his attempt to reclaim his old life. If she was in his shoes, she'd pull out every stop to claw her way back to him.

"Nick," she said kindly. "That sounds petulant, and while you have every right to feel marginalized and forgotten, you don't get to make me feel guilty for moving on."

"With my brother."

Aha, they were getting to it at last. She waited, arms crossed, unsure how to respond.

He hung his head. "I'm sorry. I hear myself now. I sound like a victim."

"We've been apart as long as we were together."

"We were supposed to be forever. Through sickness and in health—"

"Until death parted us. I thought you were dead, Nick. I had to get on with my life. I had to raise our daughter. You can't blame me for that."

"So, there's no chance we can find our way back to each other?" He looked so forlorn that it tore her right in two.

"I—"

A guy trotted up to them. "Hey! Hey! Mister, you're him. You're that guy! The desert island dude. Mr. Real-Life Cast Away."

Simultaneously, she and Nick turned to see that the entire

group of young people who'd been playing volleyball on the beach a few yards away had stopped their game and were coming toward them. Before Samantha could react, they were surrounded by the curious onlookers.

In the past, Nick would have lit up at such attention and maybe even preened a little at the notoriety. But now, he shook his head and put up his palms.

"Not me."

"Yeah, yeah, it *is* you." The ringleader, a buff, tanned guy in his early twenties, insisted. "We saw the rescue on social media."

"You're mistaken."

Samantha noticed Nick put himself between her and the volleyball players. Safeguarding her. He had been protective of her, that hadn't changed. With his head held high, for a second he looked like the self-confident, in-charge guy she'd married, and her heart slammed sideways in her chest.

"It is you," said a young woman in a red string bikini. She held up a cell phone playing a YouTube video.

Samantha couldn't really see the woman's phone screen, but she could hear the social media influencer speaking.

"I'm here in Moonglow Cove, Texas, coming to you with an extraordinary Robinson Crusoe story of Nick Ginelli, who was lost at sea for seven years in a breathtaking case of life imitating art. Nick lived the same situation as the Tom Hanks character in *Cast Away*."

She recognized that voice.

Pulse quickening, Samantha stepped from Nick's shadow so she could see the video on the woman's cell phone.

The woman spied her and held the phone closer, confirming Samantha's suspicions. The YouTuber was Victor Jorge.

After their security guards had thrown him off the beach during the wedding, he must have hotfooted it to the pier, where he'd interviewed a dazed-looking Nick as he'd stepped off the Coast Guard ship. She had to give Jorge props. He was relentless.

"Nick survived shark-infested waters! An uninhabited island! Subsisting on survival skills he learned in the Coast Guard. For seven years he lived alone, eating whatever he could forage from the trees and seas. Without even a volleyball for companionship."

Samantha stared at her bedraggled husband in the video. Nick looked like Rip Van Winkle awakening from a seven-year nightmare.

Oh God, he'd been through so much. It literally hurt her insides to think of all Nick had suffered, the loneliness, the isolation, the deprivation, the starvation.

"Tell us, Nick . . ." On the screen, Victor Jorge thrust the microphone in Nick's face. "What was going through your mind during those endless days and nights?"

"My family," Nick croaked on-screen. "It's all I ever thought about. Getting home to my family."

Wretchedness washed over Samantha. All Nick had wanted was to come home to her, and she'd moved on. She shouldn't have given up hope.

"Excuse us." Nick took Samantha's hand. "We have somewhere we need to be."

"It *is* you, isn't it?" the guy who'd first called to them insisted as the interview played on. "You shaved and got a haircut, but it's you."

"Can we get an autograph?" Another of the volleyballers produced a pen and cocktail napkin.

Nick sighed. "Please, my wife and I just want to be alone."

My wife. Samantha wasn't sure how she felt about him calling her that.

On-screen, a Coast Guardsman whisked Nick away from Victor Jorge, but the awful man wasn't done.

Staring into the camera, he said, "Little does Nick Ginelli know, that just down this very beach, at this very moment, his wife is marrying his brother."

* * *

"THAT WAS BRUTAL," Samantha said as they headed back to the house. "I'm sorry about all that."

"Not the first time. It won't be the last."

"Still, it's gotta hurt."

"Seven years on an island by myself and I've learned pain is a way of life."

"That's over now. It's gone."

He stopped. "It's not, Samantha. Humpty-Dumpty fell off the wall, and there is nothing we can do to put him back together again."

"In this analogy, who or what is Humpty-Dumpty?"

"Me. You. Luca. Destiny. My parents. All of us."

She reached for his hand.

He pulled back. "No. Don't."

She dropped her arm, embarrassed.

"If you don't think we can rebuild our lives together, then please don't encourage me," he said, and added in a raspy voice, "*please.*"

"Nick, I have to be honest, I just don't know what to do or

how to feel." Currently her emotions were all over the place, vacillating between pity, hope, grief, joy, and a hundred different shades of other feelings she hadn't had the chance to explore and dissect.

"Me either, Sammie." He paused. "If only I'd arrived just one day sooner. If only I'd gotten here before you married my brother."

"It wouldn't have made a difference."

"To me it would have."

"This is going to rip our family apart, isn't it?"

"I don't see how it can't."

"Maybe it would be better if Destiny and I moved away from Moonglow Cove," she said. "Made a new start somewhere else."

"You're considering taking my daughter away from me?" He looked as if she'd pulled out a chain saw and cut his heart to ribbons. "After everything I've been through?"

"No . . ." She clutched her head in her hands. "I don't know. I just thought maybe I should give you and your family the space you need to heal and for me to get some perspective."

"I don't need space, Samantha. I've had a lifetime of space. I need my wife and daughter."

"And Luca? What about him?"

A dark expression clouded Nick's face. "Your marriage to Luca is invalid. The lawyer said as much."

"But my feelings aren't."

He was facing her, the seawall at his back. "You love him."

"I do."

"More than you ever loved me?"

"There's no comparison, Nick. We had the sizzling white-hot heat of first love. Nothing can ever compare to that."

"So why isn't this clear-cut? The courts have me declared alive, and we renew our vows and life goes back to the way it was."

"You don't understand. Once upon a time, you were my one and only. I couldn't imagine life without you."

"I felt the same. I still do." He reached for her again.

She shied from his touch. "I'm sorry, Nick. I can't go back."

"Why not?"

"The girl I used to be no longer exists."

"Tell me how can I turn back the clock?"

Samantha sucked in her breath. "I'm not sure you're prepared to hear my answer."

"Yes, yes, I am. I can't fix things if I don't understand what's broken."

"I can't go back because I wasn't happy, Nick."

"Wh-what?" His face paled.

"I was miserable in our marriage. I still loved you, sure, but you were rarely home after I got pregnant with Destiny."

"I was working overtime to provide for my family!"

"C'mon, you used work as an escape from fatherhood, because when you weren't at work, you were mostly hanging out with your friends. I was pregnant and wanted you to hang out with me, but you were too cool for the mundane details of marriage and parenthood."

"I was dumb. I screwed up. I didn't understand what I had. I was a fool."

"That fight we had—"

"No reason to rehash it now. I was wrong. I was an ass. I shouldn't have left. That is on me. I don't blame you for anything, and I am sorry that I wasn't the husband you deserved."

She stared into his eyes, heartsick. "We were both so young, and whether we want to admit it or not, we were trapped by your family's legendary mythology. Don't get me wrong. I adore your family. They're the best, but the Lightning Strike tied us up. We had no wiggle room. No space for possibilities."

"And Luca makes you happy in a way I didn't?"

"He does. He *enjoys* hanging out with me. We do the Sunday crossword puzzle together. We garden and take long walks on the beach and go see Shakespeare in the Park. You didn't want to do any of those things with me."

"That's not true."

"Isn't it?"

"No."

"Well, it felt that way to me."

"Then fine, it's a no-brainer. Get legally untangled from me and go be with Luca. You have my blessings. Because that's all I want, Samantha. For you and Destiny to be happy, and if you're happier with my brother than with me, then I accept it."

Despite what Nick had said, this wasn't a no-brainer. It wasn't anything that could be handled easily or waved away or excised.

This was the most complex and challenging situation of Samantha's life. Emotions kept shifting and churning through her. Some she could embrace; some she couldn't look at too closely for fear of collapsing, hurt mixed with longing, mixed with regret, mixed with shame.

Yes, in her heart she felt ashamed for having given up on Nick.

Seven years, whispered a voice in the back of her mind. Seven years is a long time to hold on to hope when even the court system agreed it was time to let go.

Nick turned and walked away from her, climbed the metal steps of the seawall, headed toward Mario's.

"Nick, wait."

He paused at the seawall and glanced over his shoulder, his face filled with angst.

She rushed toward him, her heart leading the way.

Hope lit up his eyes, and for an emotion-filled second, they were back in that hallway in Moonglow Cove, and she was sixteen again and they were each other's destiny.

She flew up the steps.

He opened his arms.

She flung herself into his embrace.

He squeezed her tightly, lifted her off her feet.

She clung to him. "I don't know what's going to happen, and this will take time to sort out . . . a lot of time."

"What are you saying?" He settled her onto the ground.

"I want us to be a family, but I don't know what that will look like. We'll have to start from scratch. You'll stay living with your parents or get your own place. You'll focus on your healing. You'll see Destiny often and form a solid loving relationship with her. You'll take Piper up on her offer to help you rehabilitate—"

Lines pulled at the corners of his eyes. Lines that hadn't been there seven years ago. "And you and me?"

"I can't answer that."

"I'm not complaining, mind you," Nick said. "But it sounds like I'm the one doing all the work. Doesn't seem quite fair."

She looked at him, a bit stunned, both because he made a good point and because he was the one who'd chosen to take the sailboat out in an impending storm. "Do you for one second think your disappearance was easy for me?"

He raised both palms. "No, no. That's not what I'm saying."

"This is a difficult situation for us both, Nick. You don't get to play the victim."

"Is that what I'm doing?"

"It feels like you're trying to make me feel guilty for setting ground rules around our relationship."

"Then I expressed myself poorly. That's not how I meant to come across. You have to remember I haven't been around people in a very long time and I'm rusty at this."

She took a deep breath, noticing how fear tightened her chest. "I apologize if I sounded defensive. We're both doing our best to navigate a difficult situation."

"Do I get to have ground rules too?"

She nodded. How could she say no? But those tense chest muscles squeezed even tighter. "What are your rules?"

He seemed taken aback. "I-I don't know yet."

The smell of funnel cakes, snatched from Paradise Pier, rode the air. The playful senior citizens in the bicycle surrey tooted their horn at them and waved as they cycled past. Reflexively, Samantha smiled and raised a hand in greeting.

"Sammie?"

"I don't know if you and I have a future together, Nick. This isn't some fairy tale where everyone gets to live happily ever after."

He winced. "Okay, here's *my* ground rule: You can't keep being around Luca while we're trying to put our lives back together. You have to at least give *us* a chance."

"Nick, that's completely unreasonable. Luca and I work together at the restaurant. He lives across the street."

"I meant seeing him romantically."

"My feelings aren't a water faucet I can turn on and off at will."

Nick looked as if she'd cut him to the quick. "It feels like you turned them off for me pretty fast."

"What did you expect me to do? Spend the rest of my life pining for a dead man? Never finding love again?"

The quick flash of anger that passed through his eyes told her that yes, on some level, part of him thought just that, but he managed to tuck his emotions away behind a civil veneer. He'd been through a lot. She could understand why he was angry. He'd been caught in a time warp, and he'd come home unprepared for the changes.

"You were my Lightning Strike."

"Do you know the problem with that?"

"No. I don't see loving you as a problem."

"It's not the love that's the problem, it's the magical thinking. We weren't special, Nick. Tons of other people feel something similar. I'd hazard to say most people feel something similar when they're falling in love. We were young. We were attracted to each other. It was our first big crush. You were raised on fairy-tale fantasies, and I was an orphan desperate for whatever love I could get. It was easy to believe our love was heaven-sent, that we were meant to be, but here's the thing. Lightning strikes are a destructive force. They obliterate everything they hit."

He gave a soft moan, as if he was shocked to the core, and she supposed he was. She'd rocked the very foundation of his belief system. She'd had seven years to form a new, more rational view of love. He was still caught up in the fantasy.

"So, you've already decided. You've made up your mind to be with Luca."

"I'm not saying that."

"What are you saying?"

"I'm saying that it's going to take a long time to untangle this mess, and there are no guarantees we'll come out on the other side of this as a couple."

"But there is a possibility?"

"Anything is possible, Nick." Her heart was split down the middle.

"So, where do we go from here?"

"One step at a time."

"But what's our end goal?"

"I can't make any promises. Things aren't clear-cut. There's no right answer. We're figuring this out blind."

"What about Luca?"

"What about him?"

"Are you going to break the news to him, or shall I?" He paused. "Or maybe we should do it together. Perhaps at a Ginelli family meeting? Get the folks to weigh in."

Samantha couldn't imagine a worse scenario. She refused to put Marcella and Tino in the middle of this. "I'll talk to Luca."

"Today?"

She nodded. "Yes, I'll go talk to him right now."

PART THREE

THE SPLIT

CHAPTER 23

Thinking of you keeps me awake. Dreaming of you keeps me asleep. Being with you keeps me alive.

—Unknown

Walking into the kitchen at Mario's was like stepping into a different time and place.

From the brick pizza ovens to the replicated Tuscan decor to the wooden rustic kneading table to the cloves of garlic suspended from the ceiling, Samantha could have been teleported to turn-of-the-twentieth-century Italy.

It was one of the things she liked most about the place. The timeless appeal of hearty delicious preparation. Feeding people was how Marcella and Tino showed love, and three generations of Ginellis had been showering love on the townsfolk of Moonglow Cove for over sixty years.

Activity buzzed around her. Servers came in and out of the kitchen. Dishwashers hummed. Professional-grade mixers toiled as the staff prepared for the upcoming dinner rush. Stockpots bubbled on the stove, emitting welcoming smells, and everywhere there was bread. Fresh-baked loaves graced cooling racks. Stale bread was cut into cubes for homemade croutons. Sliced rounds for garlic cheese toast, coated with olive oil, minced garlic, and Parmesan cheese, waited in line for the ovens.

Jericho Beinot was the stoop-shouldered baker who'd worked for the Ginellis since they'd opened the restaurant in 1962. He used a large wooden peel to slide a pepperoni pie into the pizza oven. He was closing in on eighty but had the agility of a man twenty years younger.

Luca stood at the kneading station, elbow-deep in semolina flour. He often helped with the baking when things got too busy for Jericho to handle it all.

When Samantha walked in, Luca was staring into space, seemingly mesmerized by the Zen-like process of kneading dough. He wore a white T-shirt that fit snugly over his muscular biceps, black jeans, and a green apron emblazoned with the red Mario's logo. All three garments were dusted with flour. He radiated such serenity that Samantha paused in the doorway to study him, awestruck by his good looks and laser focus. He was so different from his flashy younger brother. Or at least the way Nick used to be.

"Luca," Jericho called.

"Huh?" Blinking, Luca glanced up from his work.

"You got company."

The second he saw her, Luca's face lit up. The dread that had been living deep in Samantha's stomach since their wedding night rose up, and she felt a little sick.

He looked her up and down as if she was a royal feast. Goose bumps spread across her chest. His warm, lazy smile traveled all the way to his eyes. "Hey."

"Can we talk?"

"Sure, sure." He reached for a kitchen towel and set it over the top of the dough he'd been working and went to the sink to wash his hands.

Samantha came closer.

He turned back to her, and he must have seen the truth on her face because he said a little too lightly, "You've been with Nick."

"I have."

"You two had a long talk."

"How did you know?"

"I saw you on the seawall," he said.

"There's something I need to tell you, and I hope you won't get mad."

Luca's face paled and he looked shaken. "Just don't hide things from me, Samantha. That's all I ask. I can handle the truth."

"That's why I'm telling you."

"What happened?"

"Nick kissed me."

Luca's jaw clenched and he looked cut to the quick.

"I didn't kiss him back."

"But you didn't stop him either."

"Luca, he was hurting. I tried to comfort him. Nick mistook it for more than it was, and I set the record straight."

Tension plucked at the corners of Luca's mouth. "I've got to get back to work."

"Luca, I love you."

"But you loved him first."

"It's not like that. Nick is not the same person, and my feelings for him are complicated."

"I understand, but you need to understand something too. Nick has powerful emotional and mental struggles that he could pull you and Destiny into. While I love my brother, I don't trust him. Not yet. Not until he's proven himself to be a safe person."

"Um . . . maybe we should have this conversation someplace private?"

Everyone in the room had stopped what they were doing and were staring at Luca and Samantha. It felt like they were in the middle of a soap opera. Which, she supposed, they were.

Luca clapped his hands. "Back to work, people."

The employees returned to their chores. Luca reached for Samantha's hand, but she was afraid to take it. Fearful that his touch would stir more feelings of sadness and longing and fuel the gossip she knew was spreading about town like wildfire.

"The VIP dining room is empty."

She nodded and he led the way out of the kitchen. The dining room seemed cavernous without people in it, and their footsteps echoed against the terra-cotta tiles as they entered. Luca closed the door behind Samantha, and then turned to face her.

In the windowpane, she could see their faint reflections as if they were a ghost couple.

"Where do you and I stand?" He looked as if he wanted to touch her again, and it was taking everything he had inside him not to do so. "And be honest."

"I can't . . . I haven't . . . I'm so . . ."

"Yes?"

"Conflicted."

"Do you love me?"

"I do," she said. "Desperately."

"And I love you." Luca drilled his gaze into hers. "Unconditionally."

"I know." She felt utterly wretched. Shaken, she pulled out a chair and plunked down.

Luca moved to sit beside her, and she watched torment play across his face. "But you married my brother first."

"I did."

Luca pulled off his chef's hat and tossed it on the table. "I feel like Nicolas Cage in that movie he did with Cher."

"*Moonstruck.*"

"Yeah," he said. "That movie had a fictional version of the Ginelli Lightning Strike."

"The Lightning Strike is fictional too, babe."

"But not my feelings for you, Samantha. You and Destiny are my heart and soul." Melancholia filled his eyes.

"Is this the part where I tell you to snap out of it?" she asked, struggling for levity, trying to recall the romantic movie she'd seen only once about a woman in love with two brothers. Except in Samantha's case, the brothers' roles were reversed, and there was no lost-at-sea element in the movie to further complicate things.

"I think of you day and night, Samantha. I can't get you out of my head, no matter how much I try. I understand that I'm the loser in all this. I know the family comes first. Destiny comes first. She has to."

"Destiny doesn't even know Nick. You've been her father figure since you came back from Alaska."

"But I'm *not* her father, and I can't come between a father and his child." He got up to pace the length of the dining room like a caged animal.

She jumped up and paced alongside Luca.

Luca stabbed his fingers through his hair. "I see the truth of it."

"What truth is that?"

"My brother and I can't fight over you like dogs over a ham bone. Although I'm not going to lie, there is some latent caveman gene in me that wants to do just that. But you're not a possession. You're an autonomous human being, and before you can make any kind of decision about the future, you've got to let Nick and me go."

"Wh-what?" Samantha put a hand to her throat. "You're giving up on us without a fight?"

He kept pacing. "My brother has been through far too much. My parents have been through too much. *You've* been through too much."

"So have you."

"I can't be the thing that stands in the way of you rebuilding your marriage to Nick." He quickened his pace, walking faster as he covered the length of the dining room. "If that's what you want to do."

She hurried to catch up with his long-legged strides. "What about *our* marriage?"

Luca stopped pacing and she almost plowed into his back. He spun to face her. "Our marriage wasn't even consummated, Samantha. *Our* marriage doesn't exist. Nick got you first. You owe it to him, to yourself, to your child, to try and pick up the pieces."

"But what about you?"

He clenched his jaw but didn't answer.

"Oh, Luca. This is awful." She wrung her hands.

The muscle at the front of his ear jumped, and his voice came out tight as a vise. "Our timing was just off. We have to accept that."

"No, we don't."

"Don't we?"

"Please, it's not cut-and-dried. Nick is basically a stranger to me now. He's changed so much and, as you said, he's got a lot of challenges ahead of him before he's healthy enough to be in a romantic relationship with anyone and . . ." She hesitated, unsure of whether she wanted to reveal the secret she'd been keeping from him for seven long years.

"And?"

It felt too disloyal to Nick to confess at this point. She bit her bottom lip, debating. She'd stayed silent all this time to not upset the family, but she wanted Luca to know that all was not lost for the two of them.

Except the look on his face said it was. Her heartstrings unraveled, a spiral of messy, complicated tangles. Could she ever knit her life back together?

Biggest question.

Which life?

"Samantha?" His voice was tender, but the anguish in his eyes was hard to bear.

She dropped her gaze and picked at the thumbnail of her left hand. Her ring finger was bare. She'd taken off Luca's ring the night that Nick had come home, dazed, confused, and adrift.

"If there's something you don't want to talk about, don't feel like you have to tell me right now." There he was, being so understanding, so kind. His steadfastness was what had drawn her to him, in complete opposition to his impulsive younger brother.

"The day Nick went out in the sailboat, we had a huge fight," Samantha blurted. "I'm the reason all this happened. I'm the reason Nick got lost at sea."

"And you've been holding this in for seven years?" Luca's voice lowered, gentled.

She nodded.

"You've been racked with guilt, thinking you were the cause of his disappearance."

"Yes."

"Aww, sweetheart." He opened his arms, and she flew to him, desperate for the comfort of his embrace. "Why didn't you tell me?"

"I was so ashamed."

He wrapped his arms around her like a snug cocoon. Held her close and kissed the top of her head. She entangled her arms behind him, pressed against him as hard as she could, wishing she could enter his body and be inside his skin with him.

After several minutes, Luca let her go and stepped back. "What was the fight about? Wait, don't answer that. It's none of my business."

"I don't mind telling you. I had postpartum depression, and Nick kept trying to force me to go out and party. I just couldn't do it. So, he went and had fun, and I started to resent him. Dirty dishes and laundry were stacking up, and I was fed up with having to do everything."

"You were both so young and had a lot of responsibilities."

"Too young to get married and start a family. I know that now."

"You had a newborn. There was a lot of pressure for you both."

"Don't try to make me feel better. I was wrong."

"Everyone makes mistakes." His kind voice was meant to soothe, but it only agitated her. She deserved punishment, not empathy.

"You don't understand. That day Nick had planned to go rock climbing with friends, and I asked him to please take out the trash on his way out and . . ."

Samantha hiccuped, remembering that awful day in a flash of

hot images. Nick looking sporty in his climbing gear, whistling at the top of his voice. Happy to be going out. Leaving her home alone as resentment toward him stewed.

"He said he'd take out the trash when he got back. The soiled diapers were stacked on the floor. Destiny had colic, and neither she nor I had slept that night."

"A lot of things piling up on you."

"Luca, I lost my shit. Totally. I screamed at him like a madwoman. I called him worthless and lazy. I didn't even know myself. I ranted like a lunatic."

"But did you really? Or were you just a young woman pushed to the brink by an immature man who'd put you in the position of being the responsible grown-up in the relationship? You were at your wit's end. It wasn't your fault. You weren't to blame for his actions."

"Luca, Nick had asked me for a divorce."

"What?" Luca looked genuinely shocked.

Samantha had been carrying that secret for so long, it felt so good to unburden herself to someone as accepting and validating as Luca. She felt as if a boulder had rolled off her chest.

"I really wish you'd told me before, but this isn't about me. This is about you beating yourself up for seven years."

"I felt like such a failure. I blamed myself for chasing Nick away."

"How could you have been responsible for his choices?"

"I didn't live up to his fantasy of me."

"That's on him, Samantha. He's the one who walked out on you. He was the one with the unrealistic expectations of married life. Not to diss my brother, but Nick had an irresponsible streak."

"I know," she said. "It was one of the things I liked about him.

I was serious and practical, and Nick's spontaneous playfulness opened me to adventure, and it was *wonderful* . . . until we became parents and reality set in, and I was the only one shouldering the load." Her eyes met Luca's. "And then came *you*."

"Don't," he said, a croak in his voice. "Please don't."

"Don't?"

"I can't come between you and Nick. I won't."

"It's not like that. Nick is coming between you and me, not the other way around."

"Samantha," he said, his voice so soft she could barely hear him. "I have to step back."

"St-step back? What does that mean? Are you breaking up with me?"

"No, I'm giving you your freedom."

"That's the same as breaking up with me!"

"No, no. I'm getting out of your way, that's all. I'll still be here. I'm always in your corner, but right now, I'm listening to what you're telling me."

"What am I telling you? I don't even know."

"That right there, sweetheart. You don't know what to do. You're mixed-up and confused. You can't get clarity as long as you feel trapped." His jaw clenched and she could see the muscles working beneath his skin.

"I don't understand. What are you saying?"

"Maybe it's time you found another job. Maybe it's time you took a break from the Ginellis."

Nothing terrified her more than losing her family, and her throat muscles spasmed so hard it took a moment before she could swallow and speak again. She considered what Luca was telling her and tried to imagine not working at Mario's, not being with the Ginellis every day, and she simply couldn't wrap her mind around it.

"B-but what about Destiny? I can't take her away from her grandparents, her dad, her uncle."

"It's not permanent. From the way I see it, you need time to figure out who *you* are. For half your life, you've measured yourself by the Ginelli yardstick. And while my family is pretty darn awesome, perhaps this is your opportunity to find out who you are without us."

"I love your family! I don't know who I am without them."

"That's the problem. You don't know who you are deep inside. Loosen your grip a little bit. Let go and see what happens."

"That's like asking me to walk off a cliff."

"And maybe that's exactly why you should do it. Define yourself by your own standards, Sammie, not ours."

"What will you do?"

"Maybe it's time I went ahead and sold my house. We were going to do it anyway. If things eventually work out between us, then we'll be ready to buy a place of our own together, and if they don't work out, I won't be right across the street."

He was asking the impossible and, besides, she saw no need for it. Enough of her life was in freefall, she couldn't intentionally unmoor herself from everything that she depended on.

"Give it some thought. Talk to your therapist. I think you'll see this is the healthiest move."

The idea of getting a new job was too overwhelming, and the notion of Luca moving off her block had her wanting to curl up into a ball and cry her eyes out. She needed him. Needed the Ginellis.

And that's exactly his point, whispered a voice in the back of her head. *You depend on them too much.*

"Luca, you're my best friend. I don't know what I'll do without you."

"I'll be around. I've forever got your back. I just won't be underfoot constantly. And you've got Piper and Ruth and Heath. You'll be okay. You're the most resilient person I know. You just don't seem to know that about yourself."

"It's not the same. You get me inside and out. We don't even have to talk. We understand each other that well. You brought peace to my life. Wholeness. I don't know who I'd be without you."

"We still have that. This doesn't change how we feel about each other."

"I choose you, Luca. I want you. I'll tell Nick."

He shook his head. "No. I can't."

Fear soaked her body, and she was cold at her core and hot on the surface of her skin. "Why not?"

"Because no matter how badly I want to take you up on that offer, it's not in your best interest. You need to love yourself first, Samantha. I'm giving you the space you need to sort your life out. Please take it as that and not as a rejection."

Silence fell.

The air conditioner kicked on, and the sound was deafening in the empty room. The red-and-white-checkered tablecloth on the table directly under the vent rippled in the breeze. The Chianti-bottle candles were snuffed out. There were breadcrumbs on one table. Whoever had closed up last night had missed a spot.

It all sounded so rational, logical, just like Luca himself, but that's not what she wanted. Right now, she wanted him to declare his undying love and tell her he would do anything to have her. That he would fight tooth and nail to claim her. That she belonged to him and to heck with Nick and his recovery.

But Luca didn't do that. He simply looked at her as if his heart had shattered. "I have to get out of your way and let you find your way back to you."

CHAPTER 24

Ever has it been that love knows not its own depth until the hour of separation.

—Kahlil Gibran

L uca." She reached for him, her eyes beseeching. "Please . . ."
He stepped from her grasp because if he didn't, he'd pull her into his arms and kiss her so hard he'd forget all his good intentions and beg her to choose him over his brother. "You've got to find you before you can be with anyone."

A whimper escaped her. She rubbed her left foot against her right calf. She was nervous. He'd upset her and that wasn't what he'd wanted to do.

Looking into that dear face he'd loved for almost fifteen years, Luca wanted to cave. To stay with her in this limbo land no matter how badly it hurt. He loved her. Loved her deeply. But trying to continue the relationship until she'd sorted herself out was simply too painful. He needed to save his dignity, and she needed time to clear her head and he would give it to her.

She stared at him, eyes wide, bottom lip trembling, and he knew in her mind she'd gone back to some old hurt from a screwed-up childhood. A moment when she'd had to say goodbye to yet another foster family.

Luca reached out for her then and almost touched her, but in the end, he clenched his hand into a fist and pulled it back against his chest. He wouldn't complicate things for her any more than they already were.

How had his life upended so abruptly? One minute he was the happiest guy on earth, the next his world was falling apart.

They stared into each other's eyes, whiplashed by circumstances beyond their control. If only things were cut-and-dried, Luca tried to rationalize. But they weren't and never would be. He and his brother loved the same woman, and there was no easy solution.

"I know this feels overwhelming and it is, but I'm not abandoning you. I'll be here. I'm simply getting out of your way." Luca's heart was a sledgehammer pounding inside his chest.

"I don't want you to get out of my way." Samantha's teary eyes pleaded with him.

He couldn't take it anymore. He was just a man who'd waited over fourteen years for her. He had his limits, and this was it.

He stepped closer, risking undoing everything he'd just said, torn between common sense and his foolish heart. *"Samantha."*

She notched up her chin, and he saw the pulse at the hollow of her throat twitch. How he wanted to press his lips there and feel the heated throbbing against his mouth. "Luca."

He dipped his head, hovered above her lips.

She didn't move. Didn't react. But her pupils widened.

He took it as a green light and dropped his head even lower. They'd kissed in this room before, many times, but this time seemed particularly weighted.

Her blue eyes stared into his, and Luca almost caved, almost waved the white flag and told her what she needed to hear.

Luca brought his mouth down on hers in the fiercest, most

demanding kiss he'd ever given her. He put all his passion into it. Every last drop of his desire. Pushed on by the deep ache in the pit of his soul and burning sexual need, Luca parted her lips with his tongue.

Samantha moaned and leaned into him, pressing her body against his.

He put everything he had into that kiss, drawing every bit of pleasure he could extract from her lips, because he had no idea if he would ever kiss her again.

And she was kissing him back, matching his tempo with heartfelt zeal. He wasn't imagining it. She did want him as much as he wanted her. Or at least her body wanted his.

As for her heart and her mind? He had no idea.

Abruptly, Luca broke off the kiss and stepped back, panting. Unable to believe he'd lost control like that. He didn't like being impulsive—it made him feel small and lost. He'd been wrong to kiss her. It only made this more difficult.

"Wh-what did you do that for?"

He noticed she was trembling. Good. So was he. "Because I want you to know what's waiting for you when you are really truly ready for me."

* * *

FLABBERGASTED, SAMANTHA STUMBLED out of Mario's, blinking in the blinding sunlight. She couldn't believe that Luca wanted her to distance herself from his family. She couldn't have been more shocked if he'd outright fired her.

Was he right? Did she need to distance herself from the Ginellis?

Every fiber of being shouted, "No!"

The Ginellis were her salvation. Her rock. Even if she took both Nick and Luca out of the equation, Marcella and Tino had been so very good to her. They were her family too, as much, if not more, than Ruth and Heath.

And there was Destiny to consider. How could she tell a seven-year-old that it was time to take a break from her grandparents and uncle? How confusing that would be for her daughter.

No. Luca was wrong. Separating from her main source of strength and comfort was the wrong move.

Just because she and Luca had run into some serious complications in their relationship, it didn't mean she should bail. In fact, if anything, she should dig and hold on to the family as tightly as she could.

And what of Nick? How did he figure in to all this?

Now, she'd come full circle, back to the same problem. How did she resolve her feelings for the two brothers without tearing the family apart?

Feeling lost, she pulled her cell phone from her pocket and texted Piper.

Samantha: Hey.

Piper: S'up.

Samantha: Can U hang?

Piper: Mom & I R @ the Yarn Nest.

Samantha: Can I meet U there?

Piper: Sure.

Samantha: C U soon.

Oh, this was good that Piper was with Ruth. Two heads were better than one, especially when she was relatively certain they'd both be on her side. Resolved to come up with a solution to her dilemma today, Samantha headed down Moonglow Boulevard toward the yarn shop and the family who'd welcomed her before she'd ended up as a Ginelli.

* * *

SAMANTHA FOUND RUTH and Piper at the back of the store, visiting with the shop owner, Ted Harris, as he restocked the bins. Ted was a thirty-something gay man who'd moved back home to Moonglow Cove from Houston to take over his mother's yarn shop when she grew too infirm to run it. Truth be told, he had a more artistic eye and better business sense than his mom, and the shop had thrived under his management.

They were the only customers in the store. As Samantha walked up, Ruth added three skeins of yellow alpaca yarn to the shopping basket looped over her arm.

"Hi, sweetie," Ruth said. "I'm gathering supplies to knit that cute little octopus Destiny wanted for her birthday and—"

Her emotions must have been written on her face because her foster mother and sister rushed over.

"What is it?" Ruth asked. "What's wrong?"

Surrounded by yarns of every color and material, Samantha

shook her head. It was hard to find the right words to express what was happening inside her.

"Sammie?" Piper touched her shoulder. "What is it?"

"Nick and Luca . . ."

"Are they okay?" Piper leaned in.

Ruth clicked her tongue. "What have they done now?"

"They're both fine, they just . . ."

"What?"

"They kissed me."

"Both of them?" Piper's eyebrows shot up on her forehead.

"At the same time?" Looking flustered, Ruth pressed her fingers over her mouth.

Ted straightened and eyed Samantha with interest. Gossip traveled fast on Moonglow Boulevard, and Ted was a renowned chin-wagger.

The last thing she wanted was to fuel the already-buzzing grapevine. Samantha stared at Ted, sending him a message that she'd like some privacy, but he wasn't picking up on what she was putting down. Absentmindedly, he rubbed the fingers of his right hand over his sternum, drawing her eyes to the T-shirt he wore, imprinted with fanciful lettering that declared: MAKE YOURSELF AT HOME IN THE YARN NEST.

He mistook Samantha's stare as interest in his T-shirt. He said, "I made it myself. I have the equipment in the back. I'm starting a side business printing merch. If you want anything for Mario's just let me know."

"Thanks." Samantha smiled at him. "I'll give it some thought."

"I would be happy to give you a twenty-five percent discount since—"

"Ted," Piper said. "I think Sammie wants to talk to us in private."

Ted's eyes got round. "Oh, I'm just standing here running my mouth, aren't I? I'll be in the break room. If you ladies need anything, just give a holler."

"Thank you," Samantha said.

Ted gave a little wave and headed for the exit. Once Ted was gone, Samantha said, "I'm feeling a little wobbly, can we sit?"

"Sure, sure." Ruth led the way to the knitting circle table on the opposite side of the store. The chairs scraped against the vinyl plank flooring as they pulled them out and sat down.

"Okay," Piper said as they settled in. "Spill it. Tell us everything."

Quietly, Samantha told her foster mother and sister what had transpired between her and the Ginelli brothers.

"So, Nick wants you back?" Piper asked, her voice sounding tight, as if she was a bit put out with Samantha for some reason.

"And Luca wants to let you go?" Ruth took a knitting project from her tote bag and began to purl the sky-blue yarn around bamboo knitting needles.

"That about sums it up." Samantha rested her elbows on the table and dropped her face into her hands. Her life was unraveling, and she was helpless to knit it back together again.

"Then choose Nick," Ruth said. "He's your first love, the father of your child—"

"But Nick has PTSD. It will take him a long time to dig out from that, and Sammie's already put him in her rearview mirror," Piper said. "Why go back?"

"He needs her."

"What every woman wants, a clingy husband."

"Piper," Ruth said in a chiding voice. "All marriages have ups and downs, and each partner has different needs at different times. If we gave up on marriage when problems crop up, no one would stay together."

"Sammie's been through so much. She deserves some happiness, and she has the best chance of that with Luca."

Samantha's nose twitched as she inhaled the lanolin scent of high-quality yarn and the lavender-fragrance plug-in near the table. It was a peaceful smell that she normally enjoyed, but today the aroma irritated her. This was not what she'd come into the store expecting.

What did you expect? That they could offer real answers?

Yes. Yes, she had.

You're giving up your power again. It was Luca's voice in her head. Pointing out in absentia what he occasionally called attention to in her life. The times she allowed other people to direct and guide her rather than turning within for answers.

"I think we're forgetting something in this debate," Ruth said to Piper.

"Yeah?"

Ruth set down her knitting and reached across the table to place her hand over Samantha's. "What is it that *you* want?"

"I honestly don't know. I'm too conflicted."

"You need to get quiet and listen to what's in here." Ruth patted her heart.

"Luca said something along those same lines," Samantha mumbled.

"See, that's why you should choose Luca," Piper said. "He's looking out after your best interests. He'd rather set you free than risk hurting you. It's like that story in the Bible with King Solomon and those two women claiming to both be the mother of a baby."

"Samantha's situation is nothing like that story at all," Ruth said, picking up her knitting again. "There's no baby here."

"No, but there is Destiny to consider. Which is why Sammie needs to pick the guy who'd be the best father and that's Luca."

"Come on, sweetheart," Ruth said. "Nick is Destiny's real father. When he gets finished healing, he's the best one to raise his own child."

"*If* he can heal, maybe, but that's a big *if*." Piper folded her arms over her chest.

Yep. Asking their advice was looking more and more like a big mistake. Samantha's thinking was more muddled now than when she'd walked through the door, and it had been pretty darn scrambled then.

The bell over the door clanged, and two older women wearing fanny packs, sun visors, and Bermuda shorts entered. The tourists took off their sunglasses and started browsing the bins, commenting on the beautiful yarn.

"Well," Samantha said, realizing the conversation was going nowhere. "I better get going. I need to pick up Destiny."

"She's with Marcella and Tino?" Ruth asked.

"Yes. Nick wanted to spend a little time with her, but he's not well enough yet to care for her on his own." *And I'm not ready for him to hang around the house with us.*

"How is Destiny doing with all this?" Ruth asked.

"As well as could be expected. The family therapist said it'll take some time before we figure this out." Samantha noticed that the tourists had come around the aisle and were staring at them. She was ready to get out of there.

She heard one of the women whisper to the other, "I think

that's the woman from the news. The one with the dead husband who came back from the grave."

Great. She'd been spotted. Definitely time to get out of here. This unwanted fame was hard to get used to. Maybe Luca was right after all. Maybe she should distance herself from the Ginellis and Moonglow Cove until the mess finally died down.

Just then, Ted popped back into the shop, carrying two red T-shirts the same shade as Mario's brand. "While you ladies were chatting, I whipped up a quick sample of my work to show you. I know you make the purchasing decisions for Mario's, and I think you're really gonna like these."

Samantha suppressed a sigh. Ted was just trying to get his T-shirt business off the ground, and while his interruption wasn't helping matters, he was allowing them to use his shop for their conversation.

Ted hovered with the two shirts, one clutched in each hand. "May I show them to you?"

"Why not," Samantha said, bracing for an amateurish job. "But the budget is really tight this month and I can't make any promises."

Grinning proudly, Ted spread the shirts out on the table.

The job was not amateurish. In fact, it was quite professional. What bothered Samantha, was what Ted had printed on the T-shirts. One said: TEAM NICK. The other: TEAM LUCA.

And there, written on T-shirts, was her dilemma. Samantha shot Ted a look.

He shrugged and had the good grace to look embarrassed. "Okay, so I eavesdropped on your conversation."

"Oh my," one of the tourists said. "I'd love to have one of those."

Samantha glanced over to see the two women had approached the table.

Ted picked up the shirts. "Which one do you want? Team Nick or Team Luca?"

"Which one came back from the dead?" asked the second tourist.

"Nick," Ted said.

"I'll take that one." The first tourist snatched it out of his hand. "This'll make a great souvenir for my daughter. She's been glued to YouTube since the story broke."

"I want a Team Nick shirt too," said the other woman. "But in an XL."

"I can make that happen." Ted took out his phone. "What color?"

"Blue."

"Got it. Come back in an hour and I'll have it ready for you."

"Well, if you're taking special orders, I also want a Team Nick in a black size medium," the first woman said.

Feeling bushwhacked, Samantha watched Ted make a profit off her drama.

The shopkeeper caught her staring at him. "Which shirt would you like, Samantha? Yours is on the house."

Samantha realized everyone was studying her, waiting to hear her answer, but they'd just have to be disappointed. "Me? I don't want a shirt. I'm off to claim my Destiny."

CHAPTER 25

In the end we discover that to love and let go can be the same thing.

—Jack Kornfield

It was Friday, almost three weeks since Nick's return, and he had one goal.

Get his old life back.

And on the road to that goal, he met Piper at the gym for his first training session. People were staring at them, but he was getting used to being gawked at and whispered about wherever he went. He was *that* guy. The one who'd come back from the dead. His story was irresistible fodder for gossip.

Several major media networks had approached Nick for interviews, and he'd turned them all down. He just wasn't ready to talk about his ordeal publicly. They'd been contacted by filmmakers and publishers vying for the rights to his story. Unfortunately, the brouhaha made it almost impossible to go out in public without a cadre, and more than once, his mother had called the police on trespassers digging through their trash and peering in their windows.

The gym was about the only safe place outside his parents' home, mainly because Piper had such influence here. Gym members respected her and kept their distance, while the manager kicked out idle curious onlookers.

Piper had him at the bench press machine, and she'd started him out with ridiculously light weights that were still much too heavy for him.

"Anything new?" Piper asked.

"Luca and Samantha started the process for their annulment."

"Yeah, Sammie told me." Piper stood beside him, hands on her hips, looking large and in charge. "Keep your back straight."

Damn but he adored her bossiness, such a contrast to Samantha's easy compliance. Nick straightened his back and executed the perfect lift.

Piper applauded and he felt absurdly pleased with himself. "What's Luca gonna do?"

"He's selling his house."

"No kidding."

"He listed it yesterday."

"Hmm," Piper said. "Maybe I'll buy it."

The thought of having Piper living across the street from Sammie had his pulse thumping in an unexpected way, and he didn't know why. He wasn't even living in his house. Samantha had banished him to his parents' home indefinitely. He was a little put out about that, but he understood why it was necessary.

"Again," Piper prodded. "Do three sets of three reps each."

Once upon a time, he could have bench-pressed three times the weight at five times the reps, but for now, he was grateful that Piper was starting him out at ground zero. Already, his arms felt like overcooked noodles.

Chuffing out his breath, Nick closed his eyes and concentrated on the lift.

"Good job, Ginelli. We'll have you back in fighting shape in no time. Now, c'mon, let's hit the pull-up station."

He followed her to the next challenge, already exhausted, and they'd only been in the gym for fifteen minutes. He settled onto the pull-up machine, and Piper went over to adjust the weights, starting him at the lowest possible pounds.

"Keep your abs engaged."

Gritting his teeth, Nick put all his effort into the maneuver . . . and he couldn't lift himself up. No way, no how.

Piper met his gaze, and he hated the look of pity in her eyes.

"Told you," he said. "I'm starting at scratch."

She took off that paltry weight. The last ounce of challenge gone. "Try it now."

Even without any weight at all, he still couldn't pull himself up. Nick felt his last shred of positive self-image dissolve. Had he actually thought he could waltz in here and do a serious workout? What a fool.

All the times he'd dreamed of rescue, he'd had this fantasy of recapturing his strong-man days. Of picking up right where he'd left off as if he hadn't spent a huge chunk of his twenties stranded on a desert island.

How naïve.

He had no idea who he was anymore and, worse, his homecoming had ruined Luca's and Samantha's lives too. He should have stayed on that island. It would have been better for everyone involved.

"Nick?" Piper came around to the front of the machine, where he sat forward on bended knees, his head down and his hands still clinging to the overhead bars. "Are you all right?"

True concern laced her voice, but he heard something else there too.

He raised his head and met her steady gaze. "I feel like I'm the Monkey's Paw. You remember that story from high school English?"

"You're not the Monkey's Paw."

"The hell I'm not. Everyone wished to have me back, but when I returned, they're not so thrilled with the shape I'm in."

"Wait a minute. This isn't the Nick Ginelli I know. That Nick Ginelli didn't wallow in self-pity."

"See, told ya. Monkey's Paw."

"I'm not going to listen to this," Piper said. "So stop it. If the weights aren't working for you today, let's hit cardio. Come on, get up."

"I don't see the point. I chased my brother off the block. My wife relegated me to my parents' garage apartment, and my own daughter is leery of me. Even my body has betrayed me. Everyone would be better off if I wasn't here."

"Well, I for one would not be better off. I'm thrilled you're home, and I'll take you any way I can get you. Strong, weak, pouty, resolute. I'm here for the long haul."

"You say that now—"

"Nicholas Anthony Ginelli, get on your feet." Piper snapped her fingers. "Now. I will not allow you to quit."

"Why? Why are you so invested in me, Piper?"

"Are you really that dumb, Ginelli?"

"Yeah. I'm clueless."

"C'mon, up, up, up." She motioned with two fingers.

"I just don't see the point, and before you jump on me again, I'm not wallowing—I'm being honest with myself. Maybe for the first time since I came home."

Behind them, a machine clanged loudly as someone didn't control their release and let the weights plummet.

"You're really in an existential crisis?" Piper asked.

"Yeah, I am."

"Then you need to go talk to Samantha. The meaning of life is something she enjoys gnawing on like an old bone. Me? I prefer to work that shit out of my body and free my mind."

"And when your body isn't up for the challenge?"

Piper chewed her bottom lip. "Then I do something else to take my mind off my troubles."

"Like what?"

She lowered her lashes and sent him a suggestive glance. "Like have sex."

"Oh."

Then Piper leaned down and kissed him right there on the pull-up machine.

* * *

STILL CAUGHT UP in her mental turmoil, Samantha worked from home for the next two days, telling everyone she needed time alone with her daughter. She got no pushback from her family, and she appreciated that they gave her space to sort through her issues.

The Ginellis were good people. That was never in doubt. What had come into question was her dependence on them. Were her loose boundaries unhealthy?

To distract herself, she took Destiny to the beach, and they built sandcastles and people-watched and ate Italian ices. Just mother-daughter time with no one else around, and it was truly nice. She could manage motherhood alone without her in-laws' help, even if she didn't want to.

She thought about scheduling an appointment with her therapist, to ask her which man she should choose, but she knew the therapist wouldn't offer easy answers. It was up to Samantha to find the path that was best for her and her daughter.

Introspection and self-examination took a lot of work. There was no shortcut. No magic wand. Samantha had already spent too much of her life looking for fairy-tale solutions to her problems.

On Friday afternoon while Destiny was watching *Frozen* in the den, Samantha took out a pen and paper in her home office and made a pros-and-cons list for each husband. It looked like this.

Nick	Luca
PROS	
The Lightning Strike	Mature love
Destiny's dad	Family oriented
Exciting	Stable
Opposites attract	Two peas in a pod
Needs me	
CONS	
PTSD	Lets go too easily

Samantha paused in her list making. One of the biggest cons for both men was that they were brothers, and no matter what choice she made, she would destroy the family. The bottom line was this: Her grown-up love for Luca was much deeper than her teenage lust for Nick, and while she mourned what she and Nick had lost, she couldn't ever really see how they could repair their marriage. Too much had happened. Too many years had passed.

But she and Nick were forever entangled. They had a daughter together, and nothing would ever change that.

And most importantly, Luca had basically told her she needed to get her act together before she could be with him, and in her heart, she knew he was right.

She wadded up the notebook paper, threw it in the trash, and started another pros-and-cons list.

<u>Staying</u>	<u>Going</u>
PROS	
Comfort zone	Independence
Family support	Personal growth
Financial security	Role model for Destiny
CONS	
Stunts me	Fear
	Financial struggle
	Loss of family

She studied the cons list for breaking out on her own, and nausea climbed into her throat. She had very strong reasons to stay, but staying meant choosing one man over the other, and she was right back where she started.

* * *

SATURDAY MORNING, DESTINY had her first soccer game, and the entire family planned on attending. As she packed snacks, sunscreen, and other supplies, Samantha braced herself for seeing everyone again after two days in contemplative isolation.

Hopefully, everything would be just fine. A normal family gathering. Nothing unusual. That's the way she was determined to approach it.

When she and Destiny arrived at the soccer field, Ruth and Heath had already staked out seats on the top bleachers underneath the shade of a large oak tree. They waved to her.

Samantha exhaled when she saw her foster parents and relaxed. She had support and a simple goal. Watch her child's first soccer match.

Today she was no different from any of the other moms, and it felt so good. That is until she took Destiny over to where her daughter's team was huddled, turned to head for the bleachers, and was immediately accosted by paparazzi.

Three people surrounded her, two men and a woman, all with cameras and microphones. She'd seen this same trio camped out on her in-laws' front lawn in the days following Nick's return.

Squaring her shoulders, she raised her chin and sailed past them.

"Mrs. Ginelli, Mrs. Ginelli!" The greyhound-thin woman trotted beside her with a microphone thrust toward Samantha. She was tanned a nutty brown, but her skin was more wrinkled than most her age. She wore lash extensions, dip nails, and expensive gold jewelry. "Which team are you on?"

"My daughter is playing for the Wild Cats, but I'd appreciate it if you don't report on my child."

"I'm not talking about soccer," the woman said.

Don't engage, don't engage.

But one of the male paparazzi, whose rumpled clothing and beard stubble suggested he'd been living out of his car, ran around in front of her, blocking Samantha's path. "You can't run from this. Like it or not, you've got your fifteen minutes of fame. Might as well enjoy it."

Irritated, she stopped. "Please get out of my way. I don't have to say anything to you."

"We just want to know which team you're on," the woman said.

"What are you talking about?" Samantha glowered.

"You haven't seen it?"

"Seen what?"

The woman gestured toward the concession stand beside the bleachers. Samantha's gaze followed the woman's motions.

A banner above the concession stand read: T-SHIRTS $20 OR THREE FOR $50. Inside the booth sat Ted from the Yarn Nest selling T-shirts to a long line of people. As folks made their purchases, they were pulling the shirts on over their clothing, wearing their choices on their chest. TEAM NICK OR TEAM LUCA.

Samantha felt the blood drain from her face, and despite the summer heat, her body went as cold as if someone had doused her with ice water.

Oh no, he didn't. Clenching her jaw, Samantha started for the concession stand. The paparazzi scurried after her. Livid, Samantha halted, and her shadows almost smacked into her. She spun around, shook a finger in their faces.

"Back off, if you don't want to get slapped with a restraining order."

Wide-eyed, all three of them backed up.

Fueled by her anger, Samantha charged toward Ted. People noticed and moved out of her way. She knew most of them, wearing shirts that mocked her life. Having fun with the situation, clueless as to how it was upsetting her family.

"Seriously?" she said to Ted. "You're making money off our suffering?"

"C'mon, Samantha, don't view it that way," Ted said. "It's all in good fun."

"And to line your pockets." She gritted her teeth, surprised by just how hurt and angry she was.

Ted shrugged unabashedly and made shooing motions at her. "Your story doesn't belong to just you anymore. Face it, life presents us with a lot of hard choices. Now if you could scooch out of line, I've got customers waiting."

Samantha spun away from the concession stand, barely about to keep herself in check. Everywhere she looked someone was wearing one of those wretched T-shirts.

Pull it together. Let this go. Today is about Destiny.

People were watching her. The paparazzi were filming. She felt trapped.

She wanted to flee. To run away from it all. But she could not. Destiny's life was in enough turmoil without her mom losing her marbles on top of everything. Forcing a smile, she moved toward the bleachers, anxious for the sanctuary of her family.

Ruth scooted over and patted the spot beside her. "Don't pay those nosy folks any mind, sweetheart."

Heath reached over Ruth's lap to briefly squeeze Samantha's hand. "We've got your back."

"Thanks." She scanned the crowd, overwhelmed by the number of people wearing the ridiculous T-shirts. She supposed people just wanted to show their support for what the Ginellis were going through and hadn't really considered how it would feel if they were in her shoes, because if they did, they wouldn't have bought the divisive tees.

She caught herself counting the number of shirts sporting each guy's name, polling the crowd for their vote as if the opinion of others mattered. They didn't know her or the depth of the situation. She counted anyway and it was pretty much even Stephen.

No help at all.

Piper came tromping up the bleachers carrying a large soda, a bag of popcorn, and wearing a TEAM LUCA shirt. Seriously?

"Et tu?" Samantha asked as her foster sister plunked down beside her.

"What?" Piper blinked.

"You actually bought one of those T-shirts?"

"Ted gave me half off because he knew you were mad at him."

"What's Nick gonna think?"

"He knows I think Luca is a better mate for you."

"You two have talked about it?"

"Well, yeah." Piper eyeballed her. "Why are you so upset? I'm on your side."

"It doesn't feel like it."

"Sweetie," Ruth said. "Samantha is going through a lot right now. Cut her some slack."

What was this? Didn't anyone seem to think it was inappropriate to pit brother against brother? Were they all just caught up in the story? Was she being overly sensitive? Maybe, but this just felt *wrong*.

"Could you please take it off?"

Finally, Piper looked embarrassed. "Yeah, yeah, sure, sure."

"Thank you."

"Here hold this." Piper shoved her drink and popcorn at Samantha and wrestled out of the T-shirt.

Samantha sat holding Piper's refreshments at the same time the Mario's delivery van pulled into the parking lot, Marcella at the wheel. Thank heavens they hadn't seen Piper wearing the shirt, but a lot of other people were wearing them. What did Nick and her in-laws think about that?

Down on the field, the game was about to start.

Samantha ping-ponged her attention from her daughter to the van. The hairs on her arms stood up, and she had the oddest feeling like she could spot a car crash on the freeway just before it happened. A sensation that something untoward was about to happen. Something that she couldn't stop or control.

Marcella got out of the van, followed by Tino from the passenger seat and Nick from the back.

Samantha held her breath and watched their faces as they registered the crowd. Marcella looked startled, Tino confused, and Nick?

Well, Nick stood stock-still with his arms plastered against his sides. His skin was too pale, and it was hard to tell from this distance, but he seemed to be sweating profusely. He lifted an arm, swiped it over his forehead, and swayed on his feet.

Her heart sprung into her throat. She darted a quick glance

back to the field. The game had started, and she searched for Destiny in the group of second graders and didn't immediately see her. By the time she located her daughter and shifted her attention back to Nick, the paparazzi, reporters, and busybodies had descended upon him and his parents.

Dozens of people were encircling him, many of them wearing those damned T-shirts. TEAM NICK. TEAM LUCA.

Samantha's stomach soured, and she jumped up from her seat.

"What is it?" Piper asked.

"What's wrong?" Ruth's voice went higher.

"Nick." Samantha didn't wait to explain, just charged down the bleachers and raced to where her mother-in-law had parked. The therapist had said crowds could be a stressor for Nick's complex PTSD symptoms.

By the time Samantha reached him, Nick was already screaming . . .

* * *

LUCA LEFT MARIO's and headed to the soccer field to support Destiny in her first game. He hadn't seen or talked to Samantha since their heart-to-heart on Wednesday, not even a text had passed between them, even though he lived right across the street.

It was the longest they'd gone without communicating since they'd started dating, and it was killing him not to make contact. Why had he told her she should go off on her own? Neither of them wanted that.

But whether he liked it or not, distance from the situation was what she needed, and he couldn't put his own self-interest above what was best for Samantha and her daughter. A bitter pill to swallow, for sure, but if he kept holding on, he'd end up stunting her growth as a person.

For the time being, he had to let her go.

And if she chooses Nick?

Well, he'd be happy for them, but he'd do it from Alaska.

An ambulance siren wailed from behind him, and Luca pulled over to let the vehicle zoom past, lights flashing. The ambulance turned the corner ahead of him, headed in the same direction he was going, and suddenly the siren went silent as if they'd arrived at their destination.

Had something happened at the municipal park where Destiny's soccer game was being held?

Luca wasn't an alarmist. Normally, he waited to weigh the evidence before making a conclusion, but a sick feeling hit him in the pit of his stomach, and when he rounded the corner, he wasn't surprised to see the ambulance parked near the soccer field.

Doesn't mean it has anything to do with your family.

He found a parking spot some distance from the crowd that was gathering around the ambulance, trying to tamp down the fear nibbling at his mind. He killed the engine, got out, and walked toward the soccer field.

It took a minute before he noticed the T-shirts so many people were wearing. TEAM NICK. TEAM LUCA.

What the living hell?

Then he saw the Mario's van parked right where the ambulance had come to a stop, and he started running.

A throng encircled the paramedics. Luca spied his mom and dad standing off to one side of the thickening group. Ma was wringing her hands, and Pop was patting her shoulder. He swung his gaze, scanning the area, searching for Samantha, and saw Destiny huddled with the soccer team, the coach keeping the kids out of the way.

That was good, but where were Nick and Sammie?

He approached the crowd ringing the paramedics. People saw him and got out of his way. Uh-oh.

Through the parted path, he saw the paramedics kneeling on either side of his brother, who was shaking so violently, it looked as if he was having a seizure. Samantha was on the ground as well, cradling Nick's head in her lap and murmuring soothing words.

"Shh, shh, it's okay, it's all right. You're safe. I'm here," she said to Nick.

"What happened?"

Samantha shook her head, but someone in the audience said, "He went berserk. Screaming and throwing things for no apparent reason, and then he just collapsed and started seizing."

Luca's heart wrenched as Samantha nodded, confirming the account. Their gazes met over the body of his trembling sibling, and in her eyes, Luca saw an unrelenting anguish that mirrored his own.

CHAPTER 26

When you love someone, you love the person as they are, and not as you'd like them to be.

—Leo Tolstoy

The ER doctor who examined Nick after his episode at the park recommended a seventy-two-hour stay at a psychiatric facility. The seizure he'd experienced was diagnosed as psychogenic nonepileptic and stemmed from the trauma he'd suffered surviving in isolation on the island.

Nick readily agreed to go, and they transferred him to a place in Houston. Samantha asked if she could go with him—he looked so lost and alone lying on the gurney—but the doctor told her this was part of Nick's journey and he had to travel alone.

The counselor they'd been seeing held an emergency session for the family. Afterward, Heath and Ruth took Destiny home with them for a sleepover, to give Samantha time to process what had happened.

She and Luca stood in the corridor of the therapist's office. He had his car keys in his hand and a look of yearning on his face that took her breath away.

"I'm going to spend the night at Ma and Pop's," he said. "Ma's pretty shook up, and I noticed Pop was mangling his words more than usual."

"That's a good idea." She held Luca's gaze, wanting so badly to ask him for a hug, but this wasn't the time or the place. Plus, she couldn't bear it if she asked and he said no.

"I guess we all deluded ourselves about Nick's condition. How stupid of us to think he could just pick up right where he'd left off."

"Yes."

For sure. She'd even made out a pros-and-cons list, as if reuniting with Nick was a rational possibility. Her husband was broken by his trauma, and he wouldn't heal without a lot of intensive inner work. And that was his burden to carry. She couldn't shoulder it for him, although every cell in her body ached to do so. That was *her* burden to carry. The knowledge that she couldn't fix other people, no matter how much she loved them and longed to take away their pain. Nick had to tread his path alone.

"Will you be okay?" Luca asked.

She nodded because how could she tell him she had no idea? Her world had turned upside down, and she was the only one who could repair it. Luca had been right all along. She had to find out who she was before the two of them could ever be in a relationship again.

He leaned in and softly kissed her cheek. "Be safe."

"You too," she said, lifting a hand to touch her skin where his lips had just been.

He turned to his parents, put his arms across their shoulders, and guided them to the elevator.

Samantha stood watching them go, feeling lonelier than she'd felt since her postpartum depression, as a wistful thought echoed through her mind.

This is me, trying to let you all go.

* * *

THE FOLLOWING WEEK was busy for everyone. Tourist season was in full bloom, and Mario's had a line out the door for every meal. The food was great, yes, but Luca had a sneaking suspicion people packed in because of the publicity over Nick's return as much as for the calamari and linguini.

Luca didn't ask Samantha if she'd given any more thought to finding a job elsewhere. One, because he needed the help and, two, because he was beginning to think he'd been too hasty in telling her that she should strike out on her own. It was clear to everyone that Nick wasn't in any condition to be a husband and father. That it would take months—hell, years even—of therapy, and he still might never be able to fulfill those roles.

Samantha, however, seemed to have taken Luca's advice to heart and did whatever she could to stay out of his way. Not in a passive-aggressive manner, but simply honoring his request. Now, he regretted making it.

He'd put his house on the market, not knowing where he'd live if it sold. He could get an apartment somewhere until he and Samantha figured out if their relationship stood a chance. But that was something else he regretted. By leaving the block, had he made it easier for her to stay in her house? She'd never learn what she was capable of if she continued to shelter beneath Ginelli and Dellaney wings.

On Tuesday, trying his best not to stew, he picked Nick up in Houston and drove him home to their parents' house. The conversation was stilted and awkward. Nick's eyes were dull and his responses slow.

"What's up with you, man?" Luca asked at last. "Doesn't seem like you're tracking."

"Thorazine."

"You can't focus?"

"Opposite. I can't stop focusing, but on the wrong things. For instance, I can't stop staring at your jaw. You missed a patch of hair when you shaved."

Luca lifted his palm to his face and felt the scratch of stubble and Nick's stare burning his skin. Goose bumps spread up his arm. "Could you focus on something out the window?"

"Yeah, yeah, sure, sure." Nick turned his head away.

Luca let out a long, slow breath, and they didn't say anything else for the rest of the trip.

* * *

IN ALL THE things that had happened since the day Samantha rescued Allie Montgomery from the bell tower, she'd forgotten she'd scheduled a playdate for the girls.

That Saturday morning, three days before the Fourth of July, Samantha tore off the top page of the magnetic calendar posted on the door of her fridge and found herself face-to-face with the appointment she'd penned there.

Playdate with Allie. Paradise Pier @ Noon. Horseback riding @ five.

Oh, ugh! Not that she didn't want to take the girls. It was just that she didn't wish to run the gauntlet of reporters, gossipmongers, and curiosity seekers that inevitably cropped up whenever she went out in public.

Since Nick's breakdown at the soccer game, the attention on the family had only gotten more intense. Luca had insisted on hiring a bodyguard for Nick. Not just to ward off the people who couldn't seem to leave him alone, but to keep Nick in check as well.

Nick protested the expense, but Marcello and Tino were grateful to have the security.

Samantha felt sad about the whole thing and had to keep telling herself this wasn't her problem to solve, but it sure as heck felt like it was. She wanted Nick healthy and whole. She wanted a man she could trust around her child. Destiny was still a little weird about what had happened at the soccer game, but the therapist told Samantha not to push Destiny to talk if she wasn't ready.

It had been five weeks since Nick had returned, and honestly things were just as confusing as ever. Each time she considered leaving Mario's or Moonglow Cove, something else would happen to distract her from it.

And so, she lingered in limbo, although this time her choice wasn't between Nick and Luca. Now, she understood that any beliefs she might have entertained about her responsibility to honor her first marriage had been idealistic and shortsighted. She simply hadn't understood what she was getting into.

And so, she gave herself grace to learn from her mistakes.

Now, her choice had come down to staying or leaving.

Leaving Moonglow Cove had never crossed her mind from the moment the Dellaneys had brought her here and she had gotten a good look at that beach and thought, *I'm home.*

And three generations of Ginellis were woven into the fabric of this town. She couldn't separate the people from the place. Luca's point was underscored. She had to leave Moonglow Cove, at least for a little while, to root out her values and beliefs without undue influence from family and community, or forever live in the shadows of others, never opening up to her full potential.

But the thought of actually leaving, the complicated process of change, overwhelmed her, and her feet seemed welded to the floor.

Her cell phone buzzed. She pulled it from her pocket and checked the caller ID.

It was Allie's mom, Jane Montgomery.

"Hello?"

"Hi! Just wanted to touch base on the playdate. I'm not going to be able to make it to Paradise Pier with you guys. Something came up at work and I have to go in, but I'll be done in plenty of time for the horseback riding. Are you okay to handle the girls by yourself? We could reschedule, but Allie has been so looking forward to today and I didn't want to disappoint her."

"Sure," Samantha said without even thinking about it. "Destiny's excited about it too. I'm sorry you'll be stuck at work and we'll miss you, but I agree about not rescheduling. Our lives have been in such turmoil lately, I'm looking forward to doing something normal."

"You're absolutely sure that you're good with going it alone?"

"It'll be fine and, as you said, you'll be there for the challenging part. Horseback riding gives me pause. I'm so not a horsewoman."

Jane chuckled. "You'll love it. I promise. Meet you at the pier entrance at four thirty."

"That sounds great." Samantha ended the call. Marshaling her reserves, she went upstairs to wake Destiny.

* * *

PARADISE PIER WAS so packed with holiday revelers that Samantha almost suggested they do something else. But the girls were so excited and chattering about the rides they planned to go on that she didn't have the heart to burst their bubble.

Suck it up.

They passed by Madame D'Veaux's tent, and Samantha fingered the pendant, recalling the tarot card reading.

A new opportunity will present itself. Your challenge is not to retreat as you have done in the past, but to accept the opportunity life is offering you and move forward.

Yeah, whatever that meant. She was a little weary of challenges at the moment.

"Can we go on the Ferris wheel, Mom?"

Samantha looked at the long line for the ride and stifled a groan. "Sure. Let's go."

They waited for twenty minutes, the girls wiggling like puppies and playing I Spy. Samantha took joy in their excitement. The kids grounded her and got her out of her head. Finally, their turn came. The cages of the Ferris wheel were small, accommodating only two riders at a time.

"You're coming with us, right, Mom?" Destiny asked.

"There's not enough room, honey."

"But you could ride behind us in another car."

"I'll wait right here for you."

"Please, Mommy, come with us." Destiny pressed her palms together.

"Please, Mrs. Ginelli," Allie begged.

She almost said no, but it felt nice that they wanted her to come with them, and she knew that in fewer years than she cared to think about, Destiny wouldn't want to hang out with her mother.

"All right. I'll catch the next car."

"Yay!" The girls bounced on their toes and clapped their hands as the attendant ushered them into the cage and buckled them up. When he finished, he pressed the button to call the next car for Samantha. She had her attention on the girls and didn't notice the person who had come up behind her.

"Sorry, it's too busy to let anyone ride solo," the attendant said. "You'll have to ride with the next person in line."

Okay. That was fine. She was only going on the ride to please the girls.

The attendant swung open the cage and Samantha crawled inside, and the next thing Samantha knew Victor Jorge was climbing into the car and settling himself on the seat facing her.

"Oh, hell no," she said, and tried to stand up, but the seat belt she'd just buckled yanked her back down at the same moment the attendant locked the door and sent the cage upward.

* * *

"Now this is what I call a captive audience." Victor Jorge looked at her through half-lidded eyes and rubbed his palms together like a cartoon villain.

"You were following me, you weasel," Samantha said through gritted teeth.

"We got off on the wrong foot, Mrs. Ginelli. I'd like a chance to start over."

"I'm not giving you an interview."

"Did I ask for one?"

"No, but you hijacked my carnival ride while I'm with my kid and her friend."

"Guilty as charged." He grinned impishly.

"Why?"

"Because I like you."

She rolled her eyes. "Well, I don't like you."

He bobbed his head. "I'm aware."

"How did you jump the line?"

"Got a fast pass." He held up the expensive ticket that allowed him to skip lines. "That and I slipped the attendant a dead president."

"What if I hadn't gotten on the ride?"

"But you did."

"What was your plan B?"

"Not giving away my secrets."

The Ferris wheel moved up another notch, letting more people get off and loading others in their place. "Why have you made persecuting my family your mission in life?"

"Honey," he said. "There's only one thing that gets me out of bed in the morning and that's a wedding scandal and, right now, you're the only game in town. You've got two husbands and you're not hanging out with either one of them. I want to know why."

Samantha called him a dirty name.

"Ouch. What a paper cut!"

"You're despicable."

"And you are absolutely adorable. So sweet and innocent."

She folded her arms over her chest and glowered at the odious human being as the Ferris wheel edged upward.

"You girls okay?" Samantha called to the children in the car ahead of them.

"Fine!" Destiny and Allie called back in unison.

"Kids are all good, Mom, now let's get down to brass tacks." Victor Jorge stretched his legs out to her side of the car, invading her personal space. "Hope you don't mind the manspreading. I've got long legs."

"I'm not talking to you."

"That's okay. I'll do all the talking."

"Let me just put this out there. I'm filing a restraining order against you."

"Hold on to that thought. Once you hear what I have to say, you might just thank me for overstepping my bounds."

"Do not hold your breath. Wait, on second thought *do* hold it."

He laughed. "You're funny."

Finally, the Ferris wheel finished loading new passengers and started its rotation. They were at the top, and Samantha could see the chapel and the beach where she and Luca had gotten married. Had it really just been a little over a month ago? It felt like a lifetime.

"Your honeymoon didn't turn out the way you planned, did it, pet?"

She gave him a disdainful stare and didn't bother to answer. She was serious about the restraining order.

"Shame." Victor Jorge clicked his tongue. "If you'd just understood what was going on, you wouldn't have hooked up with the wrong brother in the first place, and you and Luca could be happily-ever-after-ing as we speak."

She blinked.

"Still not talking, huh? That's your prerogative." He shrugged. "Hope you don't mind if I hog the convo. Do you know what I discovered when I started looking into your romance with Nick?"

Samantha just stared at him.

"Of course, you do." The YouTube influencer waved a hand. "You bought it hook, line, and sinker. The infamous Ginelli Lightning Strike. You and Nick were destined from the first time you laid eyes on each other way back in high school. Although, in your defense, the poor little Orphan Annie thing did put you at serious risk for limerence."

"What?"

His grin broke wide. "Gotcha."

The Ferris wheel went on its third rotation, the pier traveling past their view and the smell of funnel cakes riding with them. One more rotation and the ride was over. Thank heavens.

She didn't want to encourage the creep, but her curiosity got the better of her and she couldn't help asking, "What's limerence?"

"Well, I'm glad you asked. I'm gonna go out on a limb here and say when you and the first Mr. Ginelli met, it was like a lightning strike. A bolt from the blue. Am I right?"

She nodded.

"The chemistry was undeniable. Whenever you were near Nick, your stomach did cartwheels and your pulse sped up. He was everything you ever dreamed love could be. He was perfection, and you just knew you'd found your one and only."

Yes.

The Ferris wheel didn't stop on the fourth rotation, instead it shot skyward for a fifth turn. "Hey," she said. "The ride is supposed to be over."

"A hundred-dollar bill did buy us a few more times around." Victor Jorge winked.

He had essentially taken her hostage to reel off a monologue? Why?

"Speaking of limerence," he said. "It's the thing that movies and fantasies have taught us to believe is love. That white-hot infatuation. An obsession with the Other."

That's exactly what had happened with Nick, and she'd labeled the dramatic emotions as *love*. Stunned, Samantha sank back against the seat. She felt as if all the air had left her lungs.

"Don't feel bad about yourself. It happens to people who've had childhood trauma or inattentive parents who couldn't meet their needs for whatever reason." Victor Jorge peered at her, but he wasn't seeing her, his gaze glazed over. He was in the past, she realized. Remembering something that had happened to him.

"You experienced limerence," she said. "That's why you love wedding scandals. Someone's made you bitter about love."

"You're not listening. Love and limerence are two different things, although they can feel similar."

"What's the difference?"

"Let's get our checklist, shall we?" He took out a laminated card from his pocket as the Ferris wheel started on the sixth rotation.

"You carry a limerence list around with you?"

"How do you think I identify a wedding scandal in the making? Where limerence is involved, drama follows. When you met Nick, did you feel like he completed you?"

"Oh, yes. We were inseparable."

Victor Jorge nodded. "Did you want him even when you knew he might not be all that good for you?"

Samantha sucked in her breath, and she was hit with a memory of when they were first dating and Nick had shoplifted beer. She'd been alarmed, but he'd sweet-talked her into letting it go. "Uh-huh."

"Did you ignore his flaws?"

"I don't think focusing on a person's flaws is helpful."

"That's not what I asked. Were there red-flag behaviors?"

Silently, she nodded. At times, Nick had been possessive, selfish, and arrogant. She'd thought that was just the way guys were until Luca showed her differently.

"You neglected your own needs in favor of his."

She had. That's what they'd fought about the day he'd left.

"And last but not least . . ." He handed her the card. "You were afraid of an honest connection. You were an orphan who bounced around foster homes, and you learned to keep your distance to keep your heart safe. Idolizing Nick kept you from having a real bond with someone. A bond that terrified you."

Samantha was physically sick to her stomach. Every single word coming out of the man's mouth was on the nose. She tried to give the card back to him, but he held up a hand.

"Keep it. You need the reminder more than I do."

"I can't trust my own judgment in romantic relationships." She stared at the card in her palm.

"For what it's worth—and I've seen a lot of limerence in action, so I do know what I'm talking about here—I've been there. I, too, had a shitty childhood. I, too, loved the wrong person. I, too, sacrificed myself for someone who didn't have my best interests at heart, and I just want you to understand what's really going on."

"Why are you doing this to me?" Samantha wailed. "Why are you trying to destroy my life? What have I done to you?"

"My dear," he said. "I'm not trying to destroy you. I'm trying to free you."

"Free me? Free me from what? Love? A family? Security? Everything I ever wanted?"

"I'm trying to free you from yourself. You got wrapped up in fantasy and superstition, just like I did, and you can't find your way out of it. The worse things get, the more you cling to the fantastical. You gotta break free from the idea that there is only one special person for you. It's simply not true."

Stunned, Samantha's jaw loosened, and she felt hot and cold at the same time.

"I'm afraid I've got a bit more bad news, though."

The man wasn't finished demolishing her? She put a hand over her mouth. "Please, don't . . ."

"Your dear friend Piper? You might not want to trust her."

"What?"

He took out his cell phone, shuffled through his photos, and then turned the screen so she could see the picture. It was a photograph of Piper kissing Nick at the gym. This was the real reason Jorge had hopped into the car with her. He wanted her reaction to an incendiary photograph.

"Give me your phone number and I'll text it to you."

"Eep." Samantha felt all the blood drain from her face as her belly roiled. That's when the ride stopped . . .

And Samantha threw up on Victor Jorge's shoes.

CHAPTER 27

If two people love each other, there can be no happy end to it.

—Ernest Hemingway

Samantha," Jane Montgomery said when she met them on the boardwalk at four thirty. "Are you all right?"

"I'm feeling queasy." Samantha put a hand to her stomach. "Do you mind if I beg off from horseback riding?"

"Not at all. I'll take good care of Destiny."

"I do appreciate you inviting her. She's excited about horseback riding."

"Hey, it's the least I can do after you saved Allie's life. No way I can ever repay you."

"No repayment necessary. Just have a great time."

Samantha sent Destiny off with a hug and a wave goodbye as Allie's mom herded the girls toward her car.

Leaving Samantha standing lost, lonely, and directionless amid the thickening crowd. The way she saw it, she had three choices.

One, she could jump to conclusions about the photograph Victor Jorge had shown her, play right into his conniving hands, and assume Piper's intentions in kissing Nick had been nefarious as he seemed to suggest. Two, she could make up a pleasant story for why Piper had behaved the way she had and give her foster sister the benefit of doubt. Or three, make no value judgments at all and simply ask Piper why she'd kissed her husband.

If she took the first option—the choice that was screaming at her to confront her friend—she risked giving into her temper and blowing up her entire life. If she took the second, she'd be sliding back into the self-deception that had kept her locked in limerence mythology for fourteen years. As for the third option, she didn't know if she had the mental fortitude to stay calm and nonreactive.

Number two was out. It was way past time to stop believing in fairy tales. Options one and three required the same action, just completely different states of mind.

She wished Luca was here to calm her racing thoughts, but that was over. She had no one to depend on but herself. And then a fourth option occurred to her. One she'd never considered before but made the most sense.

Go speak to her in-laws.

But before she went over to see Marcella and Tino, she had one more thing to do. Turning, Samantha left the Paradise Pier and headed for the stone jetty where the Coast Guard had come ashore with Nick.

It was a mile to the end of that pier, and as she walked, she passed by people fishing. Some turned to stare and point, others whispered and gossiped. She heard snippets of conversations as she strolled by.

That's Samantha Ginelli.

She has two husbands.

Which one will she choose?

Her first love or her last?

Neither, Samantha thought. She chose Destiny. She chose herself.

Brightly colored boats bobbed on the water. Gulls circled overhead. Clouds thickened. She hadn't checked the weather that morning, but it looked as if rain might be in the forecast.

What had been real between her and Nick, she wondered as she studied the sky. Had any of it been real?

The end of the pier was quite crowded, and it took her a minute to find a spot that wasn't elbow to elbow with tourists. She navigated an outcropping and sat on a rock, knees drawn to her chest as she stared at the turbulent sea.

After a moment, she fingered the necklace she'd gotten from Madame D'Veaux. The pendant featuring two lovers clasped in an embrace. The pendant the psychic had told her would protect her in love.

The pendant had no power, and nothing could protect her from love.

She took off the necklace and dropped it into the water, watching it slowly sink from sight.

As it disappeared, along with her unrealistic idea of romantic love, she felt a sweet relief that she hadn't expected.

* * *

WHEN SHE GOT to her in-laws' house, she waved at the reporters hanging out on the street in front of the house. At least they weren't trespassing. They called to her, asking for an interview, but she didn't stop.

The bodyguard Luca had hired answered the door at her knock. He was one of the security guards who'd worked the wedding.

"Are Marcella and Tino home?" she asked. She should have texted before showing up here, but she feared if she didn't just come on over, she'd lose her courage. What she was about to do would cut her in-laws to the quick. It's why she'd avoided this conversation for too long.

"They're in the backyard."

"Thanks." She paused, peering up at the burly man. "And Nick?"

"He's napping."

Oh good, her in-laws were alone. That would make this a little easier. Samantha headed for the backyard, bracing herself for the emotional fallout.

Marcella and Tino were sitting at the patio table underneath a colored umbrella, with a pitcher of fresh-squeezed lemonade in front of them. Marcella's garden gloves rested beside the pitcher along with Tino's sun hat. A basket on the ground was filled with fresh colorful produce picked from the garden on the far side of the big backyard.

A kidney-shaped pool took up the other half of the yard, and the flowers planted along the fencerow drew butterflies and bees, while hummingbirds drank at the numerous feeders hanging below the eaves. Wind chimes clanged softly in the breeze that stirred the wind spinners.

It was so peaceful in this sweet backyard oasis.

"Sammie!" Her mother-in-law's face was wreathed with a beatific smile.

Misery crawled through her. She was about to erase that smile.

"What are you doing here?" Marcella asked.

"Come, sit." Tino motioned for Samantha to join them.

"Would you like some lemonade? I can go get another glass." Marcella started for the back sliding-glass door.

"I'm good. I don't need anything to drink." Samantha paused and took a deep breath. "I'd like to talk to you both."

Something in her voice must have put Marcella on alert. She splayed her hand to her throat and sank back down. "Is there a problem?"

Oh, this was going to be so hard.

Exhaling, Samantha pulled out the patio chair situated between Marcella and Tino and sat down. Marcella placed a hand over Samantha's. Her skin was soft and warm, and she smelled of lavender-scented lotion.

"You've made a decision, haven't you," Marcella said.

"Shh, let her tell us in her own time." Tino touched his wife's shoulder.

The two older people looked so vulnerable, it drove a spike through Samantha's chest, but it was better to just say what she had to say than try to blunt the blow. Watering down the truth wouldn't serve any of them. For far too long, she'd taken the safe path and kept herself stunted.

"Yes," she said as straightforwardly and calmly as she could. "I've made my decision."

"It's Luca, isn't it?" Marcella fingered her bottom lip, her chocolate-brown eyes filling with worry.

Samantha shook her head. "No."

"I knew it!" Tino said. "Nick is your Lightning Strike. Your one and only."

"It's not Nick."

Marcella and Tino exchanged startled glances, and then they both focused on Samantha with deep concern in their eyes.

"There's someone else?" Marcella whispered.

"Yes," Samantha said. "Destiny."

"I don't understand." Marcella blinked rapidly.

"This is a very difficult decision for me. I hope you can support me. You both mean the world to me. So do Luca and Nick. But what's happened to our family is unique and strange. I can't pick one brother over the other. I can't quantify my love."

"What does this mean?" Marcella wrung her hands.

"It means I love you all so very much, and that very love has kept me blinded to a few things about myself." In detail, Samantha went on to tell them what she'd learned about herself over the course of the past few weeks and how limerence had played a big role in her relationship with Nick.

"That makes sense." Marcella nodded. "I've never heard that term 'limerence' before."

"But what about Luca?" Tino asked. "You don't have that limerence thing with him. Why not just choose him?"

"Luca was the one who told me I needed to learn to stand on my own two feet before I could find out who I really was deep inside," Samantha explained. "And he's right. I spent so many years trying to be what everyone else wanted me to be that I lost sight of myself."

"So, it's over? You're divorcing them both?" Marcella said.

"According to the lawyer, my marriage to Luca was never legitimate, but to be on the safe side legally, we've filed for an annulment. I can't divorce Nick until the courts restore his identity, which could take years. It's a big mess."

"I know Nick has many challenges ahead, but are you sure you want to give up on him?" Marcella's eyes beseeched her.

"I have to consider Destiny's needs first."

Marcella plastered a palm over her chest, and she was breathing too quickly. "You—you're not going to take her away from her dad, are you? Away from us?"

"Oh, no, no." Samantha's heart ached for what her in-laws

were going through. She couldn't begin to imagine how difficult this must be for them. If she was in their shoes and Destiny was in Nick's place, she wouldn't be handling the situation with nearly as much grace and acceptance as Marcella and Tino. "You are wonderful grandparents, and Nick will always be Destiny's father, no matter what."

"How will things change?" Tino asked.

"I'm going to leave Moonglow Cove."

Marcella gasped and clutched the edge of the table with both hands as if to keep herself from toppling over. "B-but Moonglow Cove has been your home for almost fifteen years."

"Where will you go?" Tino wrapped an arm around Marcella's waist. A hummingbird zipped gaily over their heads on its way to the feeders.

"Not far. I'm not cutting you out of my life. I just need space to be me. I'll probably find a rental in a neighboring community."

"What will you do about the house?"

"Nick can move in when he's ready."

"You're giving him the house?"

Samantha nodded. "He's lost so much. It's only fair. I got his life insurance money, and my lawyer says I won't have to return it."

"That's good," Tino said.

"I also need to stop working at Mario's. I can still keep your books for you, but I can't strike out on my own if my financials are entangled with the family."

"You've worked for us since you were sixteen." Angst laced Marcella's voice.

"That's the problem. I got too comfortable. I've never worked anywhere else. It's time for me to find my own way."

"Oh, sweetheart . . ." Marcella reached for Samantha's hand. "This has got to be so difficult for you."

"No more than for you."

They smiled softly at each other, tears in their eyes. Marcella swiped away the tears that dusted her lashes. "It's going to be okay. We'll still be here, cheering you on, no matter what path you take."

"Thank you."

"We're so blessed to have you in our lives in whatever capacity that turns out to be."

"I feel the same about you too. This is a rough time for us all."

"But we've got each other. We'll get through it," Tino said.

The sliding-glass door opened, and the three of them turned to see Nick standing there.

He was shirtless and wore navy-blue swim trunks. Over his heart, she saw the simple blue tattoo he'd gotten that matched the one on her right hip.

Destiny

Samantha touched her hip, remembering that day at Indy's Ink when they'd gotten the tats as a declaration of their "special" love, and it had only been later they'd given their daughter the same name.

"You're here," he said.

"I came to talk to your parents."

"About me?"

She nodded.

"C'mon, Ma." Tino got up and extended his arm to Marcella. "Let's leave the kids to sort things out."

Marcella linked her arm through her husband's and let him

lead her inside. When the door shut behind them, Nick moved toward the pool, with an air of desolation about him. How lonely he must be. No one could understand what he'd gone through.

If only she had a magic wand and could wave away their mistakes but, alas, she could not. All she could do was make the best of a rotten situation.

She stood for a moment, watching him. He was so thin even after five weeks of Marcella's delicious cooking. It hurt her soul to compare how he used to look, buff and bulky. His physical suffering was evident in his weight loss.

He took a kitschy red strawberry-shaped float from the edge of the pool, tossed it into the water, and climbed on it. Was he going to ignore her?

She padded over, kicked off her sandals, and sat down on the edge to dangle her feet in the water. This pool held so many memories of parties and family get-togethers. The tears that she'd shed with Marcella returned and pressed against her throat.

Cocking her head, she kept studying him, this man she'd once loved with a blind obsession.

Except it hadn't been love, had it? Not really. She'd thought it was love, believed it with all her heart, but now she knew differently. She'd been addicted to the fantasy and so had he.

"How are you feeling?"

"Okay. Still getting used to the medication they put me on. It makes me dull-headed."

"Maybe you need a different prescription."

"They said I have to give it time before switching."

"I see."

They fell silent. Nick spun lazily on the strawberry float.

"Have you ever heard the term 'limerence'?" she asked after a few minutes. She glanced at the house, saw Marcella peeking out the window at them.

"No."

She pulled out the card the YouTube influencer had given her and passed it to him. "Victor Jorge jumped on the Ferris wheel with me when I took Destiny and her friend to the pier today, and he handed me this."

"The guy is just trying to stir up trouble." Nick gave the card a cursory glance and handed it back to her.

"Granted, but I also think he has a point. I googled it and he's spot-on."

Nick looked as if he was five years old and she'd just told him Santa Claus wasn't real. "You think this limerence thing was what we had?"

"We were obsessed with each other."

"You're calling our love into question now?" His face slackened. "How can you suggest that? I never felt anything as intense as my feelings when I first saw you."

"That's the point. That hot, fast intensity is based on a fantasy. When real life hit us, when we got married and had a baby, that's when our 'love' started to fall apart, and no amount of pushing the Lightning Strike mythology could change it."

An uncomfortable look came into his eyes, and he pressed his palm to his nape. "It doesn't really matter now, does it? I'm not that young punk anymore, and you're certainly not the helpless damsel you once were."

"No," she said, "I'm not. We've grown up a lot and that's a good thing. Although I am sorry for what we both had to go through to get here."

"Are you saying you don't love me?"

She offered him a soft half smile. "Nick, I will always love you. You're the father of my child. You're the love of my childhood. I'm just not *in* love with you."

"Sammie . . . I'm not fully human right now. Please give me some time. Give *us* time. We can recapture what we had. I know it."

"That's the thing. I don't *want* to recapture it, Nick. Love-obsessed is no way to live."

"We wouldn't be that way now." He let go of the pool edge and drifted away from her.

"Do you honestly think we'd still be together if you hadn't gone off in your sailboat?" she asked.

"I don't know."

"Or would we still be sticking it out and telling ourselves lies just to keep the myth of the Lightning Strike alive?"

"Probably that." His float twirled in a circle.

Samantha stuck out her toe and stopped the raft from floating off. "Maybe there's another relationship you'd really rather be pursuing?"

"Huh?" He blinked up at her.

She took out her phone and called up the picture that Jorge had texted her of Piper kissing Nick and turned her phone so he could see it.

Nick leaned forward for a better look and his face paled. "Th-that's not what it looks like."

"Care to explain?"

"Piper kissed me. It was out of nowhere."

"Seriously, for no reason at all?"

"You kissed Luca," he said. "I saw you that night I came home when he took Destiny up to her bedroom."

"I had just married him, Nick. It was our wedding night."

"What can I say? Piper kissed me. It happened."

"Why?"

"I don't know." He was stonewalling her.

"You can tell me the truth. I won't judge you. I get it. Seven years on a desert island and you're starved for any kind of attention. I don't blame you. Just tell me what's going on."

Nick didn't answer her. Instead, he just rolled off the float and sank to the bottom of the deep end.

CHAPTER 28

True love is like ghosts, which everyone talks about and few have seen.

—François de La Rochefoucauld

He wasn't going to win Samantha back.

Nick knew that now. He'd had high hopes, lofty goals, and big dreams, lingering vestiges of the old privileged Nick who'd gotten everything he'd ever wanted.

But she was the new Samantha, no longer accepting of people crossing her boundaries with blatant disregard. She was steadfast, and he admired her for it.

Even knowing that she'd married his brother, stubbornly Nick had just assumed he and Samantha would eventually find their way back to each other, given enough time and therapy. She had been his destiny after all.

Nick put a hand over his heart, over the tattoo. Water bubbles escaped from his mouth, and he buoyed to the surface, treading water and wishing he could just disappear.

He didn't belong here anymore. The world had passed him by.

Samantha moved from the side of the pool to the patio table. She perched on the edge of a chair, legs crossed at the ankles, waiting for him to stop being an idiot and come talk to her.

He peered at her through the water droplets on his lashes, shiny and distant, like the mirages of ships he'd seen on the island. He considered going underwater again and waiting her out, but he knew Samantha and she wouldn't let him off the hook so easily. While she was an understanding woman, she had learned how to set her limits. She was done tolerating immature behavior, and he couldn't blame her. He'd put her through hell and back.

She picked up his towel and walked to the edge of the pool, unfolded it, and held the beach towel up the way she would have done for Destiny, sending a silent message.

Get out of the pool.

Resigned, Nick pushed the bobbing strawberry float aside and treaded water to the spot where his toes could touch the bottom and started walking toward her.

As he emerged from the water, Nick watched his wife's face. Her gaze flicked over his body, but instead of the awe that had once lit her eyes whenever she'd looked at his bare chest, all he saw was pity.

That didn't do much for a guy's ego.

She stoked your ego long enough, joker.

And then Nick was deeply ashamed of the way he'd treated her in the name of love. She and that kook Victor Jorge were right. Their relationship had been one of her adoration of him and him basking in the glory of her admiration.

Her young heart had been a wide-open door, and he'd taken one look at her, walked right in, and made himself at home without ever asking himself if that was fair to her. He'd taken advantage of her neediness and she'd let him.

Their dynamic, fueled by his family and the Lightning Strike

legend, had been unhealthy. It bred codependency and compla-
cency. They'd believed their love to be epically grand, but it had
been a delusion. Real love had nothing to do with fireworks and
butterflies in the stomach and galloping pulses.

That was lust, chemistry.

He saw that now, and he also knew they'd be better apart. It
hurt. The death of an illusion.

Yet, reality freed him as he dropped the self-deception and
climbed the steps of the pool and let her wrap the beach towel
around him. He was shivering in the sunlight, and it was as if he'd
been born anew and she was midwife to this process.

"There's something I should tell you," he said.

"I suspected."

"Let's go on the swings," he said, drawing the towel more
tightly around him. "And sit in the sun."

She nodded and he led the way out of the gated area around
the pool to the sturdy swing set his parents had erected in the
backyard for Destiny. The structure was of high quality and made
from cedar timbers, the swings solid enough to hold lightweight
adults. Once upon a time, it wouldn't have held his 210-pound
frame, but now at 150 pounds, it was no sweat Chet.

Nick plunked down on the seat, and Samantha took the swing
next to him. Without saying anything, he began to swing, pushing
his feet back to get started, then lifting them to sway forward.

Samantha joined him.

The chains creaked.

And then they were swinging in opposite directions. Him going forward, her back. Her forward, him back. His beach towel
fluttering in the breeze behind him.

He wished they could keep swinging like this forever. He wished he didn't have to ruin everything. Wished he didn't have to break her heart one more time.

But he did.

If he ever hoped to leave the past behind him and step into the future a changed man, he had to tell her the truth. Had to reveal the secret he'd kept from her for a decade.

"I slept with Piper." His voice seemed to boom, far louder than he'd intended.

"Wh-what?" Samantha jumped from her swing, firmly planting both feet on the St. Augustine grass.

Nick kept swinging. He had too much momentum to stop now.

"What did you say?" Her face had gone slack, and she looked as if he'd gut-punched her.

He closed his eyes, felt his body hurtling through the air as he pumped his legs and swung faster.

"Nick, stop swinging. You don't get to drop a bomb like that and not explain."

He opened his eyes and jumped as she had, but he didn't land as gracefully and staggered into her, the beach towel dropping off his shoulders and sliding to the grass.

She put out a hand to keep him from toppling over.

He stood before her, naked except for his swim trunks. He'd just confessed his greatest sin against her, and still she was helping him. He didn't deserve her. Never had.

"You slept with Piper?"

"I did." Goose bumps spread over his body. He could see her jaw muscles clenching beneath her skin.

"When?" Her voice came out hoarse and hurt.

"The night before our wedding." He watched her process the information, her gaze fixing on the center of his forehead as if unable to look him squarely in the eyes.

She pressed a palm to her mouth and made a sound like a wounded animal.

"When you went to bed after the rehearsal dinner party, we got drunk together and it just sort of happened."

Tears were in her eyes now, her palm still covering her mouth. He closed his eyes again, unable to bear the pain he'd caused.

"You slept with her the day before our wedding?"

"We didn't mean for it to happen. We both love you and we knew it was wrong."

"But you did it anyway."

"She told me I was *her* Lightning Strike. That she'd loved me from the minute she'd seen *me* in the high school hallway."

"No, no." Samantha shook her head, her eyes dark and filled with sorrow. "No."

"I thought maybe I'd gotten it wrong. That since the two of you were walking together, I'd mixed up which one of you was my Lightning Strike."

"No. This is . . . I can't hear this." She pressed her palms over her ears.

He reached out a hand to comfort her, but she batted him away.

"Don't touch me."

"Afterward, we knew it was wrong, we knew we messed up."

"How many times did this happen?"

"Just the once, I swear to you."

Tears were streaming down her cheeks. "I'm gutted."

"Oh, baby, I'm so, so sorry."

"No, no. You don't get to be sorry. You willfully slept with my foster sister, my best friend, my maid of honor on the night before our wedding. There's no excuse for that. None."

"I know." He hung his head.

"All this time . . . all this time I loved you so slavishly. I put you on a pedestal." Her voice cracked. "I thought what we had was special."

"We did! It was!"

"I was so stupid. So desperate for love that I mistook infatuation for something remarkable." She trembled from head to toe, tears streaming down her cheeks.

"Sammie, I—"

"I can't be here." Samantha turned and fled, running away as fast as her legs would carry her.

"Please wait," he called. "You can't drive in the state you're in."

She spun around. "You don't get to tell me what to do ever again, Nick Ginelli. I survived just fine those seven years you were gone. Not just survived, I *thrived* and came into my own."

"With the help of my family," he said, instantly regretting it. The last thing he wanted was to compound her pain.

"This is over, Nick."

He understood. He knew that when he confessed he'd slept with Piper that things were over between them.

The guilt he felt was crushing. All along he'd thought getting stranded on the desert island had been God's punishment for his stupidity. He'd thought his penitence had been paid. He'd been wrong.

The misery and pain surpassed any suffering he'd experienced on that island, but in the end, he was at fault. It was time to own his part in everything.

Because this time, it wasn't just his own skin he was worried about. This time, he could see with his own eyes what his selfishness had done.

He'd destroyed the woman who'd once loved him like no other and he'd thrown it all away.

CHAPTER 29

Love is that condition in which the happiness of another person is essential to your own.

—Robert A. Heinlein

By the time Samantha collected herself enough to drive to the gym, it was early evening and rain clouds puffed along the horizon. She'd texted Jane Montgomery to check in on Destiny, and once she knew her daughter was safe, she was ready to confront Piper.

Hard-driving workout music piped through the speakers as gymgoers pumped iron and ran on treadmills.

When she found her, Piper was coaching a middle-aged woman at the bench press. She glanced up, saw Samantha, and broke into a grin, but with each step she took closer, Piper's smile faded.

"Hey," Piper said. She was dressed in snug-fitting Lululemon, her muscular body on full display. Beside her, Samantha felt like a dull little brown wren. "What are you doing here?"

"We need to talk."

"Um . . ." Piper glanced at the woman who grunted as she pushed the weights. "I'm kinda busy. We could grab a drink when I finish in half an hour?"

"Now." Samantha injected steel into her voice.

Piper's eyes rounded. "Sure, sure, okay." To the woman, she said, "Take a break, Lucy. This workout is on me."

"Wow, thanks." Lucy looked relieved. "I'll just hit the elliptical while you and your friend have a talk."

"Sounds like a plan. BRB," Piper said to her client. To Samantha, she said, "Let's go to the yoga room. There are no classes now."

Piper led the way, as she always did. Inside the yoga room, Piper closed the door and turned to face Samantha, muffling the sound of the hot-body anthem throbbing throughout the main room.

Samantha cataloged her foster sister's features, embedding this moment in her memory so that she wouldn't forget what betrayal looked like. The wide hazel eyes, the thick long lashes. The short auburn hair with just the right amount of curl. The shapely body. The high-end sneakers and double-knotted laces. The neon-pink sports bra screaming, *Look at me.*

Treachery felt like home.

Smelled like familiarity.

Looked like the last person you would ever suspect.

A hundred questions charged through Samantha's brain. *Why? Where? What position? How did it unfold? Who kissed who first? Did you think about me even once?*

Her knees wobbled and she had to put her hand against the rack holding the yoga equipment—mats, blankets, blocks, straps, bolsters—to stabilize herself. A plaque on the wall in front of her read: *Namaste.*

It was hot in the room, the thermostat set to an uncomfortable temperature. Stuffy and airless. Outside, there came a flash of lightning and a rumble of thunder. The wind gusted, sending a tree branch scratching against the window screen.

The calf of Samantha's right leg spasmed, as if she'd just run a marathon. She winced and bit her lip.

Piper studied Samantha's face and her skin turned ashen. A secret spilled. A burden lifted and shifted onto Samantha. "You know."

Samantha nodded. Did Piper look relieved?

"How?"

"Nick told me."

"Why?"

"Because Victor Jorge took a picture of you kissing him in the gym and he showed it to me."

"That snake."

"He's not the snake in the garden." Sweat trickled down Samantha's neck, pooled at the hollow of her throat. She wiped her neck with the back of her hand.

"I wondered when you would find out. It took longer than I expected."

The fury she'd felt with Nick flared, and she wanted to knock the yoga shelving to the floor, kick the colored yoga balls, scream at the top of her lungs.

But she did none of those things.

"How could you? We were like sisters. Closer than most sisters. We were best friends."

"Were?" Piper's bottom lip quivered, and fear sparked in her brown-green eyes.

"You really don't think we can just go back to the way things were, do you?"

There were tiny lines at the corners of Piper's eyes that Samantha hadn't noticed before, the faint beginnings of the crow's-feet that would one day settle on her face. Piper stood between her and the door, a beseeching expression pulling her mouth taut.

Samantha's knees completely gave out then, and she plunked down on the hardwood floor sitting cross-legged, yoga style. She came here to do yoga every Monday morning on the one day of the week that Mario's was closed. If Piper had the day off, she'd come with her and they would lay their mats out side by side, giggling together like the schoolgirls they'd once been. She was going to miss that.

Outside, another lightning flash, another rumble of thunder. The storm was moving closer.

Piper sank down on the floor in front of her, making the whole thing infinitely more intimate. Samantha closed her eyes, understanding now why Nick had sunk to the bottom of the pool. She was trying not to look as vulnerable as she felt, to hide just how flattened she felt.

Blowing out her breath, she surveyed the room, looking everywhere except at Piper. The bamboo blinds raised above the windowpanes splattered with raindrops. The fat-bellied Buddha fountain gurgling softly in the corner. The ceiling fans circling overhead on lazy speed, stirring the warm air. She wondered where her rage had gone, replaced by a veneer of numbness, worn thin by the shock of her discovery.

Piper must have known this day would eventually come. Had anticipated it. Imagined the scenarios how it would play out. Samantha had no preparation. Nothing to give her traction.

"You want to know how it happened?" Piper asked.

Nick had said they were both drunk, but Samantha wanted to hear her foster sister's side of the story. Samantha had an unexpected memory. The night of their wedding rehearsal dinner. Unlike her rehearsal dinner with Luca, it had been held at the yacht club, and a band comprised of Coast Guard members had played a short set after the meal and numerous rounds of toasting. There'd been dancing and Samantha had gone to the restroom to reapply her makeup, and when she'd returned, Nick and Piper had been dancing to a cover of Katy Perry's "The One That Got Away."

She remembered standing there watching them together and losing her breath. She hadn't recognized the omen for what it had been. Then Nick had seen her from across the room, dropped Piper's hand, and moved toward her like a magnet, smiling to see her, and her little hiccup of fear had vanished.

Her mind flashed another picture, this one a created image instead of a memory. A flash of a younger Piper and Nick naked in bed together, their bodies entangled.

The nausea that consumed her on the Ferris wheel returned with a vengeance. She closed her eyes again, shook her head, desperate to knock loose the vision of her husband in her best friend's arms.

"It was after the rehearsal dinner and you'd already gone home," Piper said.

Samantha recalled it now, how she'd been anxious to get some rest before her big day while Nick and Piper had wanted to hang out with the band. She'd gone home with Ruth and Heath, and Piper hadn't come in until dawn. She told Samantha that Nick had gone home right after she left, while Piper partied with the band, and Samantha, having no reason not to, had believed her.

Right now, Piper's face was flushed—her creamy complexion colored easily with her moods—and the muscle at her temple jerked in a perceptible spasm.

"All these years." Samantha shook her head. Her voice came

out weird, like it belonged to a stranger. It was dreamy and languid, as if someone had slipped her a drug.

"I felt so guilty. I wanted to tell you. So many times, but Nick said I couldn't."

Secrets. Her husband and her foster sister had not only cheated on her, but they'd also kept it a secret for a decade.

"So why didn't you tell me after we thought Nick was dead?"

"I couldn't hurt you any more than you already were, Sammie. And what would have been the point? Nick was gone."

"The point would have been honesty."

"I couldn't lose you, Samantha." Piper reached for her the same way Nick had at the pool.

Samantha put up both palms, holding her at bay. "You're losing me now, Piper."

"I know." A fat tear rolled down Piper's cheek and plopped to the floor, but Samantha was unmoved.

The storm gathered strength, the lightning and thunder intensifying. Rain pelted the window. Clouds cloaked the sun, giving the impression of early nightfall. From outside the yoga room, Perturbator was punishing his instruments in the careening beat of "Humans Are Such Easy Prey."

Sweating profusely, Samantha hopped up from the floor and started to pace the same way Luca had paced the day he'd told her he was leaving. The walls felt as if they were closing in, the room growing smaller and smaller. Samantha had the mad urge to strip off her clothes and run screaming into the slashing rain.

One of the yoga balls had rolled a little farther away from the wall than the rest. Samantha booted it as hard as she could. It smacked into the opposite wall, bouncing, and then sailed over to thump against Piper, who'd also gotten to her feet.

"Go ahead. Kick yoga balls at me. I deserve it," Piper said.

"You *wish* I'd let you off that easy," Samantha roared at her, the anger that had bubbled up unstoppable now.

"I've suffered too!" Piper howled. "It wasn't just you."

Startled, Samantha jumped back.

"I love him too! And *I* saw him first."

"So, you sleep with him the night before our wedding to get back at me?"

"We were *drunk*."

"That's no excuse. No one poured alcohol down your throat." Samantha squared off with her.

"It never happened again."

"Not once?"

"No."

"You two were so close. As close as you and I."

"Nick was my friend, Sammie. He *is* my friend. Do you have any idea how hard it was for me to work with him, be near him, and not be able to act on my feelings? Pure torture."

"And yet you stayed my friend. Knowing you slept with my husband, knowing you loved him, you still showed up after you'd stabbed me in the back. And you stayed working with him. You could have quit. You could have left town. You could have found a man of your own. Why did you do that? Why did you stay?"

"I loved you. I loved you both. I made a mistake. A huge one. Why should I cut myself off from the two people I care about most because I screwed up? Nick got it. He understood. Why can't you?"

"Because I just found out about it!" Samantha gestured broadly, swinging her hands around in expression of her anger and frustration. "You two have been covering up your secret for ten years. Laughing at me behind my back—"

"We didn't laugh at you, and we both felt wretched about it."

"I don't believe you."

"It's true."

Samantha closed her eyes. The pain was intolerable. The betrayal flayed her to her bones. Nick and Piper might not have had a sexual affair after that one night, but they'd had an emotional one. Their closeness at work was legendary and, stupid woman that she was, Samantha had loved that her husband and her best friend got along so well. She'd never dreamed, not for one second, that Nick had strayed with Piper.

He was supposed to have been her Lightning Strike, and she'd believed they were meant to be, hook, line and sinker. She felt like such an utter fool.

Suddenly, something ugly occurred to Samantha. "You knew who Victor Jorge was when you brought him to the rehearsal dinner. You knew who he was all along."

Piper looked as if she might deny it, but finally notched up her chin and said, "Yeah, I did. When I saw him on Brushfire, I couldn't resist contacting him."

"Why? Why would you do that to Luca and me?"

"Why? Because you got *two* great guys. Two men and I didn't have one. Day in and day out, I had to be there and be happy for you and all the joy you'd found after you lost your Lightning Strike. I had to listen to you carry on about losing Nick as if I hadn't lost him, too, and then when you hooked up with Luca, I had to hear about how lucky you were. I thought why not invite Victor Jorge? Bring a few rain clouds into your oh-so-perfect life."

Stunned at the expression on Piper's face and the vitriol in her voice, Samantha staggered backward. "You've been jealous of *me?*"

"My parents get a wild idea to foster a kid and they drag you in and you're prettier than I am and everyone adores you."

"I was an orphan, Piper. I had no one. Your family was so good to me, and I fell in love with you all and then I met Nick and, yes, I lived a charmed Cinderella life for a while, or so I thought. But behind my back, you plotted against me. Why? You're smart and gorgeous and strong and—"

"I don't know," Piper wailed, and dropped her face into her hands. "I don't know why I did any of it. I'm a terrible, rotten person. I'm petty and underhanded and passive-aggressive."

Was this a pity play or was she truly contrite? Samantha couldn't tell. "I guess you are all those things. I didn't think so until today, but here we are."

Piper was the one pacing now, agitated, worked up. She brought a fist to her mouth, pressed her knuckles against her lips. "My jealousy ruined everything."

"Yes," Samantha said, trying to remember if she'd ever had a hint of Piper's dark qualities, her shadow side. If she'd ever suspected for a second the things Piper was capable of, but she simply hadn't. She'd taken her at face value.

Piper winced as if Samantha had slapped her across the face.

"Just as my naïveté and my desperate need for love and validation led me to trust people I shouldn't have trusted."

Piper wrung her hands. "I hate myself."

"Right now, Piper, I kind of hate you too."

"You think it was easy for me? Carrying that guilt and shame around with me all these years?" Piper said, and behind her words came a fresh crack of thunder as the rain poured down ever harder.

"No, I suppose it wasn't, but you brought it on yourself."

"When Nick came home and you were so in love with Luca, I thought maybe now was my chance." Piper's voice caught. She paused. Gulped. "But when I kissed Nick, he didn't kiss me back. He doesn't want me, Samantha. He wants you."

"No, Piper. He wants the idea of me. It's a big difference."

"Well, Samantha, what in the hell *do* you want?"

Luca.

But that's not what she said because she no longer trusted her feelings. They'd led her astray one time too often. She no longer trusted her own judgment.

"Me? I need to find out who I am without a Ginelli in my life, and now I get to do it without you too."

"You're not going back with Nick?" Piper asked, unable to hide the hope in her voice.

"I am not."

"What *are* you going to do?"

Samantha met Piper's gaze. "I'm going to raise my daughter with so much love and compassion that she won't ever doubt her own worth and turn herself into a pretzel to please other people."

CHAPTER 30

Love never dies a natural death. It dies because we don't know how to replenish its source. It dies of blindness and errors and betrayals.

—Anaïs Nin

At least the rain camouflaged her tears.

Samantha intended to make good her escape, jump in her car, and drive away, but she'd locked her keys in her car. Rather than go back inside and call for a locksmith, forcing her to see Piper again, she decided to walk home. It was only five blocks to her house, and since she was in the same sensible Birkenstocks she'd worn to Paradise Pier that afternoon, Samantha took off on foot.

Unfortunately, the rain picked up speed, and it was coming down in sheets. The five blocks felt like five miles. Her hair was plastered to her face, and she had to keep pushing it back to see where she was walking. Most of the cars had disappeared from the road, the smart people taking cover. Water flowed down her back, drenching her through and through. Nature's commentary on her life.

You're washed up.

She trudged through torrents flowing over the sidewalks and

rushing to the gutters. Cold and shivering, she huddled in on herself, drawing her arms around her and keeping her head down. Just four more blocks.

Her mind peppered her with images of her past. The day she came to live with the Dellaneys, how happy Piper had seemed to have a sister. She'd taken her new friend at face value, not imagining that Piper felt differently on the inside than how she acted on the outside. Her mind drifted to that morning in the hallways of Moonglow Cove High when Nick Ginelli had zeroed in on her and made her feel so special.

"Stupid, stupid girl," she muttered, dragging herself off the curb and over the crosswalk. She was needy. That's all there was to it. No one had ever taught her how to be discerning. She was learning those hard lessons now.

The memories kept rising and converging as she saw things through a different lens. The way Nick and Piper had finished each other's sentences. The way Piper had hung out at their house several times a week, and Nick didn't seem to mind. How Samantha would come into a room with the two of them in it, and they'd suddenly stop their conversation.

Right under my nose.

They'd both claimed they'd only had sex that one time, before Nick and Samantha were married, but, honestly, could she believe anything they said?

A car horn honked at her and she startled, glancing up to realize she'd almost walked into oncoming traffic.

Her pulsed jumped in alarm.

She was trashed. Wasted as surely as if she'd downed a fifth of whiskey. Her brain stuck in second gear, revving high and hot on anxiety and adrenaline. Hand to her chest, she got back on the sidewalk and moved away from Moonglow Boulevard toward home.

Except now even home felt like an alien place. So many happy times spent there, so she'd thought. Now she understood that Nick hadn't been happy. He'd felt trapped by marriage and parenthood.

And her? She hadn't been happy either. She'd been trapped in a fantasy of her own making, an illusion of the perfect grand love. It hadn't been love at all, but limerence.

She thought of what Victor Jorge had said. That she'd been afraid of an honest connection. That she'd bounced around foster homes and used fantasies and stories to keep her heart safe. That idolizing Nick had kept her from forming a real bond.

But then along had come Luca, and she'd had no fantastical myth or legend with him and, paradoxically, she'd worried about that at times because they hadn't had that secret sauce, that special something that set them apart from ordinary lovers.

All along, that had been the right way to love, not the crazy, obsessed, one-and-only thing she and Nick had cooked up, trying to shoehorn real life into a fairy tale.

Samantha trudged into the gathering gloom, the weather matching her mood. A car passed by and hit a puddle, sending a sluice of water splashing over her. Sending a message. *You're hosed.*

Rock bottom.

She turned on her block. Her house was just up ahead. Taking a deep breath, she began to run, pushed by rain and grief. She rushed up the sidewalk, panting and breathless. The pumping of her heart pulsated hot blood throughout her body, heating her up on the inside while her outside was coldly wet.

At last, she arrived at the front door and automatically reached for her purse to pull out her key, remembering it was locked in her car.

Groaning, she sank to the welcome mat on her knees, too drenched and discouraged to fight back. The symbolism too ironic to bear. Home and family were the only values that meant anything to her, and here she was locked out of them both.

Dazed, Samantha shifted onto her butt and drew her knees to her chest, shivering so hard, her teeth chattered. Despair was her cloak. She pulled it over her like a blanket and buried herself deep within the folds. She had no hope left. All her optimism was gone, and she had no emotional energy left to formulate a plan.

She stared across the street at Luca's house, and her heart dropped to the pit of her stomach. The only thing she'd ever wanted from childhood, the dream that had kept her going through foster home after foster home, the fervent wish that had drawn her to loving families like the Dellaneys and Ginellis, the fantasy that made her believe in signs and superstitions, had slipped through her fingers no matter how tightly she'd grasped on to it.

She'd lost her family.

Luca had told her she needed to find herself, Nick was forever changed, and Piper had betrayed her in the most fundamental way.

You could always surrender, whispered the voice in the back of her mind. The voice that feared conflict and longed for peace and safety. The part of her that had no boundaries in love and accepted the authority of others over her own wants and needs in order to hang on to that love.

She must stop clinging to her outdated ideas and accept that life was messy and complicated and there was no safety net, nothing to catch her if she fell, or else she would stay stuck at the mercy of others' whims and desires, forever placing the needs of those she loved above her own. Did she really want to teach her daughter that others mattered more than she did just so she could hold on to her skewed model of love?

She hadn't loved Nick for who he was. She'd loved an ideal. No wonder he had bristled under the weight of her expectations. She'd demanded too much of him. He couldn't give what he didn't have.

Her brain kicked out a startling thought. *Every decision you've ever made was based on fear.* Every. Single. One.

Reality might feel stark, but she preferred it to the self-delusion of living in denial. No one was going to save her. She had to save herself.

Pushing her wet hair out of her face, she dragged herself up off the mat. Time for action. She sorted through her options, searching for the one that would solve her dilemma the quickest without involving her family.

She remembered the night Nick came home and had opened the kitchen windows to let the fresh air in. She'd shut them but couldn't recall if she'd locked them. It was worth a shot.

Bogging down in the muddy flower bed underneath the kitchen window, she strained at the window and, miraculously, it pushed up. Thank heavens that she'd been so exhausted and dazed that night, otherwise, she would have locked the windows.

Shimmying in the window, she landed on the kitchen floor, covered in mud, but at least she was home.

Finally, she took a deep breath just as she heard a vehicle pull into the driveway. Sitting up, she peered out the window.

It was Allie's mom, bringing Destiny home.

She watched her daughter get out of the car, her face alight with joy as she popped open a pink Hello Kitty umbrella, waved goodbye to her new friend, and danced up the sidewalk.

This was what was important. This little girl. Nothing else mattered.

It was up to Samantha and her alone to rebuild her life for her daughter. She had to set an example. Had to show Destiny how to be a strong, loving woman without selling herself short in the process. This was her mission now. She would stop searching for a family and *be* the family she'd always craved. She didn't need others to make her whole. She was whole all on her own.

From her position at the open window, Samantha waved at Allie and her mother, who waved back and drove away in the rain.

Samantha closed the window, kicked off her muddy shoes, and grabbed a kitchen towel to rub her wet hair as she headed to the front door to greet her daughter.

Destiny burst in, excitement oozing from her every pore. "Mom, Mom! Guess what, guess what?"

"What is it, sweetheart?" Samantha asked, so happy her daughter had had a great time.

"I met *my* Lightning Strike!"

Oh, hells to the no, Samantha wanted to say to her daughter, but she wouldn't do anything to wipe the bliss off her child's face.

And yet, the emotional jolt of realizing Destiny was falling into Samantha's starry-eyed footsteps was almost too much to bear. She'd have to find a subtle, gentle way of teaching her daughter the difference between a fairy tale and real love.

Hold your tongue. You've had a bad day. Don't let it bleed into your relationship with your daughter.

"Mom?" Destiny blinked, fully noticing Samantha for the first time as she closed her pink umbrella and scattered water droplets over the foyer tile. "Why are you all muddy?"

"I got caught in the rain without an umbrella. Silly me. Come on upstairs while I change into dry clothes, and you can tell me about the rest of your day." Samantha headed up the stairs toward her bedroom.

"It was the *best!*" Destiny bounced up the steps after her.

"You get in some horseback riding before the rain started?"

"Oh yes!" Behind her, Destiny's voice vibrated with delight.

Because she'd met her Lightning Strike? Samantha wondered, wincing. Dear Lord, the child was only seven years old. The Ginelli fable had saturated her daughter's subconscious as surely as rain had soaked through Samantha's clothes.

Samantha entered her bedroom, stripping off her clothes as she went, until she was in just her underwear. She went into the en suite bathroom to drape her wet shirt and pants over the edge of the bathtub to dry, then returned to go through her drawers for dry clothing.

Her daughter flopped onto Samantha's mattress, sank into the pillow, and sighed dreamily. "I wish you could have been with us when I met him."

Samantha padded back to the bathroom, leaving the door open so they could keep conversing. As she took off her wet undergarments to put on dry ones, she caught sight of the tattoo on her hip.

Destiny

Whatever had happened between her and Nick, whether it was a Lightning Strike or limerence, one thing remained. They had done something right. They had made that beautiful little girl in there.

Quickly, Samantha got dressed and wrapped her hair in a bath towel. "Honey, you do know that the Lightning Strike isn't really real. It's just a fairy tale, like *Cinderella* and *Snow White*. A fun story, but that's all it is."

"Oh, no, Mom, the Lightning Strike is *real*."

Sighing, Samantha sank down on the edge of the bed and put a palm on her daughter's knee. "Tell me about this boy who's captured your heart."

Destiny sat up and stared at her. "No, no, Mommy. My Lightning Strike isn't a boy."

"It isn't?"

"No way. *Blech.* Boys have cooties. My Lightning Strike is a *horse!*"

* * *

ALTHOUGH SHE WAS thankful to learn Destiny's insta-crush was a gelding named Sir Lancelot, Samantha wouldn't waver from her mission. It was time for her to stand on her own two feet and stop depending on others to chart her course.

"You hungry?" she asked Destiny.

"Starving."

"Would you like to go to Mario's for dinner? You can tell MawMaw and Poppy all about Sir Lancelot."

"Yes. That's a splendid idea." Destiny pronounced "splendid" with an abundance of flare that put a smile on Samantha's face.

She called a locksmith and then got an Uber to drive them to the gym, where it only took a few minutes for the locksmith to get inside. Samantha noticed that Piper's SUV was no longer parked there, and a fresh wave of regret and disappointment tasted like burnt beans in her mouth.

It was eight thirty by the time they got to Mario's, and the rain had finally let up. The place was hopping as usual on a Saturday. Yolanda greeted them as they came in.

"Hi, Sammie, here for dinner or just to see the folks?"

"Both. Could you ask Tino and Marcella to join us if they can spare the time?"

"Sure thing." Yolanda buzzed off to the kitchen and in a few minutes, her in-laws came out to sit with them. Samantha had passed Destiny her phone so she could play *Animal Crossing* and to keep her distracted while she checked on Nick's parents.

"How are you guys doing?" Samantha asked them. "Since I dropped my decision on you?"

"We could ask you the same question." Marcella's expression was filled with sad acceptance.

"Hanging on by a thread."

Marcella reached over to pat her hand. "It's okay. It's all right. We understand and we don't blame you for anything. Life has thrown us all curve balls."

"We love you and Destiny, no matter what. You are our family and have been since the moment you walked through that door." Tino pointed in the direction of Mario's front door.

"What about the Lightning Strike?" Samantha asked, still a little awed that the Ginellis were so calm about the end of her marriage to Nick.

"What about it?" Marcella asked, interlacing her fingers and dropping her hands into her lap.

"Nick and I no longer live up to the family legend."

Tino's gaze was sad, but optimism laced his voice. "Legends are just love affairs that outgrew their britches."

"What are you saying?" Samantha asked. "That the Lightning Strike isn't real?"

"We're saying life is complicated." Tears misted Marcella's eyes, but she blinked them back. "And no tidy fable can encompass the majesty and complexity of real love."

"Life is messy." Tino pressed a knuckle at his own eyes. "It took our son away but gave him back. He's different now, but we still love him. We still love you."

How much she appreciated their love and support and how she wanted them to remain a big part of her and Destiny's lives.

"Thank you. Thank you both for being shining examples of love in action."

"And maybe one day, you and Luca . . . ?" Tino lifted his eyebrows hopefully.

Samantha let out a long exhale. She didn't want to hope too hard that she and Luca could repair things in case it didn't work out. Didn't want to put expectations on him. "I can't think about that right now. I have too much else to sort out."

"We understand. We want you to fly free and find your happiness," Tino said as the food arrived. "Now let's dig in."

The four of them sat eating stromboli and Caesar salad just like normal. They laughed and joked and listened to Destiny describe her love of Sir Lancelot.

Samantha spied a smear of tomato sauce on Destiny's cheek and reached over for a napkin to hand to her daughter but knocked over the saltshaker in the process. She scooped the loose grains into her palm and was about to toss them over her shoulder but caught herself. No more superstitions. No more magical thinking. No more irrational beliefs.

Getting up, she tossed the salt into the trash, and when she returned to the table, Marcella gave her a knowing wink and raised her glass of wine. "To logic and reason."

Samantha clinked her glass with her mother-in-law and said, "To mature love."

* * *

IT WAS ALMOST eleven by the time she and Destiny got back home. She tucked her daughter into bed and read a few pages from *Amelia Bedelia*. She'd just turned out the lights and started downstairs to lock up when the doorbell chimed.

Who was it at this time of night?

She looked through the peephole.

It was Piper. She held up a bottle of limoncello. The first alcoholic beverage they'd gotten drunk on as teenagers. Blast from the past.

"Peace offering."

Samantha hesitated. Did she really want to let her in? The evening with Tino and Marcella had gone much better than expected, and she really didn't want to mess with her mellow mood by having another conversation with Piper.

"Please," Piper said.

Samantha rested her forehead on the door, struggling with her warring emotions. Rage, hurt, and fear on one side. Love, compassion, and hope on the other. She had two options. Choose righteousness or forgiveness.

"Please, Sammie. I'll do whatever it takes to make amends. You're my sister and I can't bear to lose you."

She clenched her hand into a fist. Gulped. Closed her eyes.

"I'm so sorry," Piper called. "Please, give me another chance."

Swallowing the silence that stretched between the door, Samantha debated. Who did she want to be? A woman who held grudges, or one who accepted that people screwed up?

"Okay, I'm gonna go, but I want you to know that you don't have to forgive me," Piper said. "It doesn't matter. I love you now and forever, no matter what."

Sighing, Samantha opened the door and let her in.

CHAPTER 31

You found parts of me I didn't know existed and in you I found a love I no longer believed was real.

—Unknown

Three months later . . .

Destiny stretched long against the top of the stepladder, positioned beside the Moonglow pear tree in the backyard of their new beachside cottage in Edenville, just twelve miles south of Moonglow Cove. Her daughter reached for the plump, ripened pear.

"Mom, did you see this one?"

"It's huge."

"And the birds haven't pecked on it yet."

"Be careful on that ladder, the ground is uneven."

Samantha could see the green and red flesh of the fruits Destiny had already plucked and stacked in the woven bushel basket. She was perched on her own ladder, with another basket below her. For half an hour, they'd been having a pear-picking competition, and Destiny was in the lead. She'd picked several pears and hoarded them, using her Cinderella T-shirt as a carry sling.

Destiny scampered down to lay her pears in the basket, then

shimmied up the ladder again. Her daughter looked like a sun-bronzed monkey, all elbows and knees.

Nick and Piper would be coming over later to help peel pears and make tartlets for the annual Moonglow Pear Cook-Off. Whichever recipe won the competition would have their dessert featured in *Texas Monthly*, and Destiny was determined to take first place. She'd inherited her father's competitive streak.

Samantha and Nick had sold their house and split the proceeds. He'd bought a condo in the town center where Piper lived, and he thrived being around people, while Samantha had rented this two-bedroom beach bungalow for her and Destiny until she was ready to purchase a property.

Bit by bit, the fun-loving extroverted Nick was returning, but this time without the arrogant hubris that had plagued his younger self. Nick had grown and changed, and she was so very proud of the way he'd been able to admit his flaws, do his best to make amends, and lean into his healing. She was a little sorry that it had happened too late to save their marriage, and she had to admit that Piper was good for him in a way that she hadn't been.

"Seven more," Destiny announced proudly as she climbed down the ladder with her T-shirt full. "Mom, you're falling way behind."

"You beat me again," Samantha said, descending her ladder as well, two pears clutched in each hand.

"The shirt's the secret." Destiny giggled and dumped her latest haul on top of the others.

Samantha added her pears to the pile. "You're such a problem solver."

She wrapped her arm around her daughter, hugged her close, and kissed the top of her sunshine-scented head. Destiny's hair had lightened into a lovely beachy honey-brown over the summer, and it twisted with lively corkscrew curls. She wore cut-off blue jeans, and her feet were bare.

"I think we have enough to start making the tarts," Samantha said.

"But there are more pears to pick."

"We'll get those tomorrow. Your dad and Piper will be here soon, so grab hold of the handle and let's carry the baskets inside."

Piper took hold of one side of the basket handle, and Samantha picked up the other. Together, they made their way up the stepstones to the back porch.

They climbed the steps, and as Samantha reached for the door with her free hand, Destiny said, "Thank you for bringing me to live here."

That surprised and pleased her after the fuss Destiny had made about moving out of Moonglow Cove. "I'm so happy you like it."

"I love it," Destiny said, beaming. "But I love you most of all."

* * *

That Saturday, Samantha sat on the front porch of her beachside cottage. Tipping back her head, she eyed the fluffy clouds and listened to the seagulls caw as they floated on the gentle currents.

It was another halcyon early fall coastal day, and she was enjoying a glass of iced tea and one of the pear tartlets they'd baked the night before. Destiny, Piper, and Nick had taken the rest of the baked goods to the competition. Samantha stayed behind, wanting to give Nick time to shine with his daughter. It was his recipe they'd made after all.

This morning, she'd seen the three of them off at dawn and

witnessed all by herself a spectacular sunrise. The darker morning clouds had parted, letting in a slip of lavender-orange light that slowly ripened into cotton-candy pink as a sleepy pelican skimmed the water.

As she watched, she stood barefoot on the wooden deck, a cup of coffee in her hand. The vibrant sun popped like a firecracker over the sea, and for a few magnificent minutes, in the whisper of her breathing, the water glimmered seafoam green, and she'd pulled out her phone to snap a picture, but it was already fading. The breathtaking beauty, only there for a very short time. She learned to appreciate fleeting moments like this and put them in the treasure box of her memory.

It was in these brief moments that she missed Luca the most, when she caught herself turning to say something to him and he wasn't there. He'd asked her not to contact him unless it was about the family, and so they rarely saw each other these days.

She was proud of herself that she was able to honor Luca's boundaries and develop some of her own. Starting her own business had been a good thing for her. It had gotten her out from under the shadow of the Ginellis. But she still saw them, of course. Still kept their books. She loved Marcella and Tino with all her heart, but now she understood that she hadn't fully formed an identity of her own, and the distance had been a positive thing. She knew her own mind better now, and she wasn't always looking for validation and affirmation as she once had.

Not that it had been easy.

In fact, striking out on her own had been one of the hardest things she'd ever done, carving out her own space away from the people who loved her most in the world. Because of Victor Jorge, she'd started therapy again and learned more about limerence and how her childhood beliefs and superstitions had kept her small. As inconsiderate as the man's revelation was, it had been the thing she needed to light a fire under her, and for that she was grateful to him. The media circus had finally died down, and she and Destiny were settling into their new life with hope and optimism.

She thought of all this as she listened to the wind chimes tinkling softly in the breeze and savored a tasty bite of pear tart. It was good. Really good. They stood a decent chance of winning.

After she scarfed up the flaky pastry and washed it down with tea, Samantha kicked off her sandals and padded down to the beach. The steady rhythm of the tide called to her. It was something she could rely on. No matter what, the water would come in and go out. She might not always be able to depend on others to be there for her, and that was okay. She was there for herself, and she could depend on the tides.

She picked up seashells and put them in her pocket. She and Destiny were making a collage for Destiny's bedroom wall.

And then she saw it.

The pendant she'd dropped off the pier. Two lovers locked in an embrace. The amulet designated to protect her in love.

She bent to pick it up. It was worse for the wear and slimy with seaweed, but she pocketed it along with the seashells and smiled. She was in a much better place than she'd been that day she chucked it into the sea. She could accept it now for what it was. A talisman for the mystery of life and love.

Samantha straightened up and there *he* was, standing several yards away from her down the beach. Looking at her with such tenderness, it took her breath away. She blinked, wondering if he was a mirage. She put a hand to her chest and felt the restless pounding of her heart.

As if in a trance, she moved forward, scarcely daring to believe he was here.

He walked toward her, his hair blowing in the wind, his blue T-shirt rippling over his muscular chest. He wore tan cargo shorts and a welcoming smile. His hair was shorter and sun burnished.

She started running then, her pounding feet kicking up sand. He was running too, flying to her with outstretched arms.

They reached each other, and she flung herself into his embrace. He clutched her to him and spun her around until they were both dizzy, and they collapsed on the beach laughing. They lay in the sand, holding hands and staring up at the clear blue sky.

"How are you?" he asked.

"I'm good."

"I can see that." He turned on his side and stuck his palm under his sand-dusted cheek. "You've got a new house far from the madding crowd."

"I do. It's much smaller but it's right on the beach. We love it here." She turned to face him too.

"I made the wrong choice. I should never have broken up with you. Can you forgive me?"

She'd had a lot of practice in forgiving people, herself most of all. "It was the only way for me to grow."

"You've bloomed," he said. "I can see it in your eyes."

"I have." She smiled at his gentle gaze.

"Beautiful." He reached over to brush a strand of hair from her face. "You're so beautiful."

"Sweet talker."

"May I kiss you?"

"I don't know."

"When will you know?"

In answer, she got to her feet and held her hand out to him. Led him up the path past the sea oats to the front porch and into the house, the screen door snapping closed behind them.

"Where is Destiny?" he asked.

"With Nick and Piper at the Moonglow Pear Festival. They'll be gone for hours."

"You don't say."

"Shall I give you a tour of the house?"

"Sure."

"Let's start with the bedroom."

"I like the way you think."

Still holding his hand, she guided him toward her bedroom. The windows were wide open, the white sheer curtains billowing lightly in the breeze. On the queen-size bed was a purple-and-green handmade quilt in the Jinny Beyer's Moon Glow pattern and a white lace eyelet bed skirt. The walls were painted a soft lavender. She could feel the giddy smile etched on her face, could see the same smile on his.

"I love this room," he said. "It's all you."

"Not too girlie?"

"It's perfect."

She sat on the edge of the bed, the box springs squeaking softly on the black metal frame. His eyes widened and she laughed.

He cupped her cheek and gazed down at her, eyes enrapt.

They undressed, the morning sunlight spilling through the windows. She watched as he pulled the T-shirt over his head and dropped it to the floor. Noticed how his fingers unbuckled his woven belt and slipped it from the loops. He slid down the zipper, let his pants fall to his ankles. He was not, she observed, wearing underwear.

And she was quite impressed with what she saw.

She stood up and he untied the laces at the front of her dress, his hands gently caressing her bare skin as he helped her out of it. He paused, staring at her with hungry eyes.

"I love you," he whispered.

"I love you too."

"For now and forever, Samantha. Until the end of time. It's always been you."

There was no need to say anything else. Forgiveness was understood. Together, they folded back the quilt and slipped under the covers. They rolled on their sides facing each other as they'd done on the beach, both with sand in their hair.

"Do we need a condom?" she whispered.

"I haven't been with anyone, and I got a clean bill of health on my last physical."

"Ditto."

Slowly, they began to touch each other. Taking their time, learning each other's bodies in a way they hadn't done before. Fully immersing themselves in the experience and in the softness of the hour that followed, they touched each other's souls in a profound and primal way, and when at last he entered her, Samantha smiled into his face, knowing, that at long last, she'd finally found her true home.

EPILOGUE

The greatest happiness of life is the conviction that we are loved; loved for ourselves, or rather, loved in spite of ourselves.

—Victor Hugo

Two years later . . .

The third time Samantha married into the Ginelli family, everyone whispered that it was charmed. But Samantha had learned that there wasn't one special love that could sustain you through an entire lifetime. Like diamonds, love was multifaceted.

Luca and Samantha married on the private beach in front of her bungalow with just their families and Victor Jorge, whom they'd invited to keep him from crashing the party. He served as their wedding videographer. Ruth, once again, officiated.

The reception was on the porch deck, the music a handpicked playlist. The weather was perfect. The sea breeze gentle.

For their first dance, they only had eyes for each other. But then they shared their love and joy. Luca danced with Marcella. Tino waltzed with Ruth. Heath and Piper did the two-step.

And then Samantha danced with Nick.

"I'm so happy to see you happy," he said. "So glad you found your way back to Luca."

"And I'm thrilled you and Piper are together at last." She peered over Nick's shoulder and caught her new husband's eye.

Luca winked and she shivered, knowing what was in store for her later. A lifetime of love.

She and Nick would always be in each other's lives, and Luca willingly accepted that. Their unusual family dynamics were too intertwined to ignore, and besides there were different types of love. Her love for Nick had begun one way and ended up another, but they both wanted the best for each other, and they always would.

As Samantha looked out on the people in her life, her heart overflowed. She saw love in the gentle smiles and heard it in the soft laughter. Felt it in the kind kisses and tender hugs of their families. Tasted it in the food so carefully prepared. Smelled it in the flower blossoms. Heard it in the love songs and the feet waltzing across the dance floor.

In every mistake absolved, in every prodigal welcomed home, she saw evidence of love.

And so, the fabled Lightning Strike had grown and matured, adding flavor and depth to the story as it came to include more people. Healthy love was not diminished by the sharing, nor watered down, but enhanced and strengthened.

Love was messy and filled with uncertainty, but that didn't mean she should run from it. She'd learned love shows up in many forms and in many faces. That didn't mean love conquered all problems. In fact, it could cause as many as it solved.

But love, whether it was fleeting or permanent, was worth giving a try, and Samantha gave herself to Luca, the man who'd always provided a firm foundation under the shifting sands of time.

He wasn't special and neither was she. They were just two people, loving each other to the best of their abilities. They didn't need a myth or a legend. All they needed was each other, open and honest communication, and the ability to admit when they were wrong, make amends for their mistakes, and forgive.

Because that was love in action.